D0960205

INHERIT MIDNIGHT

ALSO BY KATE KAE MYERS

The Vanishing Game

INHERIT MIDNIGHT

Kate Kae Myers

BLOOMSBURY

NEW YORK   LONDON   NEW DELHI   SYDNEY

First published in the United States of America in February 2015
by Bloomsbury Children's Books
www.bloomsbury.com

Bloomsbury is a registered trademark of Bloomsbury Publishing Plc

For information about permission to reproduce selections from this book, write to
Permissions, Bloomsbury Children's Books, 1385 Broadway, New York, New York 10018
Bloomsbury books may be purchased for business or promotional use. For information on bulk purchases please contact
Macmillan Corporate and Premium Sales Department at specialmarkets@macmillan.com

Library of Congress Cataloging-in-Publication Data
Myers, Kate Kae.
Inherit midnight / by Kate Kae Myers.
pages   cm
Summary: Avery is the black sheep of the wealthy VanDemere clan—the ostracized illegitimate daughter. So she's
less than excited when her grandmother ropes her into a competition to determine the VanDemere most worthy of
inheriting the family fortune, until a chance to gain information about her long-lost mother motivates Avery to try
to win the game.
ISBN 978-1-61963-219-6 (hardcover) • ISBN 978-1-61963-220-2 (e-book)
[1. Inheritance and succession—Fiction. 2. Families—Fiction. 3. Contests—Fiction.] I. Title.
PZ7.M9872In 2015   [Fic]—dc23   2014009652

Book design by Nicole Gastonguay
Typeset by Westchester Book Composition
Printed and bound in the U.S.A. by Thomson-Shore Inc., Dexter, Michigan
2 4 6 8 10 9 7 5 3 1

To Kelly

INHERIT MIDNIGHT

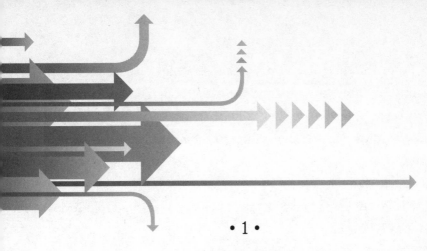

• 1 •

ESCAPE

They say, "Don't look down."

But *down* lets you know how high up you are. How far you'll fall. How serious it will be. Black and white: you'll die. Grayscale: you'll be hurt but survive.

I stood at the open window. The gentle night air was draped in summer, beckoning. It came to me on the kind of breeze that made filmy curtains billow. Except, of course, there were no curtains around this window. Until thirty seconds ago, there were bars.

Only a few stars winked through the cloudy sky. The view made me feel safe, if somewhat disoriented, but when my eyes shifted down to the cement far below, dread tightened my stomach.

"It's okay, Avery," I whispered to myself. "You can do this."

Escaping was my best skill. After all, I'd lived my entire life in prisons. One looked like a mansion, the others like schools. But they were still prisons.

From this height and dim view, the night was a charcoal etching, and freedom called to me even though anxiety pressed down on my chest. A weight similar to the one when I was twelve, and my cousin Chase shoved me to the ground and sat on top of me.

"Eat it, Avery."

His voice echoed back across time, along with a rapid series of sensory images:

The taste of dirt mingled with blood from my lip.

Ugly stains on my white party dress.

Laughter as the others watched.

Humiliation that wouldn't go away, no matter how much time passed.

"Maybe that's enough," someone said. "What if your grandmother finds out?"

Chase loomed over me, smirking. "Do you think she'd really care? Not even she can stand having this little brat around."

I squeezed my eyes shut so tight they hurt—as if the pain could push away the memory. Finally I opened them and blinked away the blur. I didn't have time to waste.

The low creak of footsteps sounded in the hallway, and I turned to stare at the door. Had someone figured out the acetylene torch was missing from the welding classroom? Or did one of the staff on a late-night stroll happen to look up and see the wrought-iron bars gone from this third-story window? My heartbeat ticked out the time like the jerky second hand of a classroom clock until the steps passed.

I folded my pillowcase in half, draped it over the raw ends of the cut bars, and climbed onto the windowsill. As I crouched there and looked down, the ground seemed to rush up.

"It's just like rock climbing," I whispered. "You've been on the wall dozens of times. This isn't any different."

Except that now I didn't have a harness, and the concrete was a whole lot harder than a safety mat. I flipped onto my stomach. Even with the pillowcase, the bars stabbed me. I pushed away and lowered myself over the side. The toes of my shoes brushed the stone wall, and I scrambled for a hold. Finally I found it. I'd spent the majority of outdoor time secretly studying the building, memorizing ledges and the flat, wide spaces that would be the most difficult to cross. The arched windows were covered with wrought-iron that I could use as an escape ladder. Even the ancient ivy might help, except it didn't grow past the second story. I had a long way to go before I could grab it.

I started to move lower. My fingertips throbbed from the full weight of my body, and I stretched my foot down to touch the decorative stonework that made a shelf above the window beneath mine. Nothing but air. I had misjudged the distance. In my head I'd climbed down this building dozens of times, even visualized it when I was on the rock wall. But now I was hanging three stories up and wondering where the stupid ledge was.

Breathing through clenched teeth, I released my left hand and touched the pitted stones until I found the crack I'd memorized, then dug in with my fingertips. Stretching with every muscle and pointing my left toe, I finally made contact and let go.

The ledge was about eight inches wide, which should have been enough, but I wobbled. I tried not to envision falling backward and smacking the cement below, yet the mental image was there: me lying in an ugly fatal pose. A couple of seconds later my body centered itself and my balance held. I clung to the building with giddy relief before starting to climb down.

When my feet touched the bars on the second-story window, a flame of hope sparked. What would Grandmother think when I escaped? I remembered the long, winding drive here through the California Redwoods and the frantic thrum I felt the farther away we got from home.

"But why is she sending me away?" I asked for the third time.

Ms. Brown slid one hand higher on the steering wheel. "I'm sure you know the answer to that, Avery."

She was an associate of my grandmother's lawyer and about as kind as a cactus. She pulled an envelope from her case and handed it to me. Inside were photos. Three showed me sneaking off the VanDemere Estate through the delivery entrance. Seeing them, my courage withered. Who'd been spying on me? Two more photos of me and my best friend, Megan, at the mall as we talked to a couple of cute guys. Last of all was an enlarged glossy that made my breath stick in my throat: Megan's brother, Kyle, alone with me on their deck at night.

My hands rested on Kyle's chest, one of his low on my back; the window behind us gave a glimpse of the party inside. The picture looked passionate and intense, when instead it had been sweet, a little awkward, and my first real kiss—with the guy I'd secretly been crushing on for months.

I shoved the photos back in the envelope and threw it on the car floor. "It's not a crime, you know."

But to my overprotective grandmother, who spent her life guarding the VanDemere family name, it was. "How'd she get them?"

Ms. Brown guided the car around a wide curve. "They were mailed last week from an anonymous source."

I knew what happened. One of my cousins wanted to get me in trouble. And it didn't take much, since I already carried the stigma of being the grandchild born under a cloud of scandal.

Something tickled my foot and I flinched before looking down and seeing the first tendrils of ivy. The thick stems I could grab onto weren't far below. As I inched lower, I thought about Kyle. Shy and a little geeky, he had the same thick black hair as his sister, plus gorgeous brown eyes and a small dimple in his chin—completely cute but not aware of it. After all these months, that night on his deck still lingered in my mind. Megan, oblivious that I'd ever had a thing for her brother, sent me regular chatty e-mails full of news—including the fact that Kyle was now seeing someone.

That kiss hadn't meant anything to him, but it ruined my life. Pulled out of Greenleaf, my private all-girls academy in Santa Rosa, I was dumped at St. Frederick's in the northernmost part of California, where I'd spent more than four months. And the worst part of the whole thing? Grandmother wouldn't talk to me. My calls to her kept getting routed to Henry, her secretary, who always said the same thing: she was away on a trip. The last time I phoned, he'd sighed like I was the most annoying person he knew.

"Avery, your grandmother wants you to use this time to think about what you've done. Make the best of it." Then he hung up.

I'd never liked Henry, but this made me practically hate him. Both he and Grandmother ignored the fact that I was almost eighteen. They treated me like I was still a little kid, with rules that made my life not all that different from being locked in a tower.

I kept climbing down and finally slid between the wall and a large bush. As my feet touched the ground I let out a quiet laugh—until my knees started to buckle. My arms and legs were trembling, and I steadied myself against the wall.

Thirty seconds to catch my breath before I headed across the lawn, following my planned route and loving the feel of the breeze on my face. I moved from bush to tree, trying to blend with the shadows. When I glanced back at the school, just to check, my steps faltered. On the top floor of the darkened building, one rectangle glowed like a yellow beacon. It was my window. My room! And someone stood there looking out.

I expected an alarm to sound. A shrill whistle or maybe some shouts. But the only thing I heard was my own jagged breathing as I took off running. *Why?*

Why did someone go inside my room? Ten o'clock was lights-out. There wasn't a reason for anyone to check in! I felt sick knowing the staff and student monitors would now start searching for me. Going faster, I told myself to forget using the shadows for cover.

I ran past a long row of bushes ringed with marigolds, the flowers' unpleasant scent staining the air. Raspy breaths dried out my throat, and I paused behind a bush to scan the area. It seemed clear, but there were so many shadows it was hard to tell. I was ready to take off again when a ringtone pierced the quiet night. A dim light appeared a few feet ahead and I crouched down as someone answered the cell phone. I could barely see the outline of a boy's face as he stood under a towering oak. He gave a quick reply and I recognized his voice. No. Not him. *Please, not him!*

Gavin Waylenz disconnected and the faint light from his

phone vanished; he disappeared into the darkness beneath the tree. I closed my lips to silence my breathing.

Gavin and I had an unpleasant history; I couldn't stand him, and he didn't get that. He was a guy who embraced everything the staff of St. Frederick's said. The school's director was Mr. Hatlierre, a glorified coach whose speeches reminded me of pep talks before a game. Gavin always cheered the loudest. He even waved his fist in the air like a total idiot. How could I ever respect that? Plus, the school had four times as many boys as girls, and he'd shown a lot of interest in me when I first got here—with all the charm of a caveman.

Holding still for so long, my legs started to cramp; but I didn't dare get up from my crouch. In the distance I saw a couple of flashlight beams focused on the bushes below my window. I turned back to the shadowy scene in front of me. Why didn't Gavin use his flashlight and join the others?

"Come out, come out, wherever you are," he said.

An electric jolt went through me, and my heart pounded faster.

"Avery VanDemere, you're out here somewhere. I heard you running. Give it up!"

I held my breath.

His phone rang again. He answered, and in the faint light I saw his back was to me. He started down the path that ran beside the enormous fence, limping slightly because of the knee injury that had ruined his hopes of becoming a pro football player. I'd heard a rumor that his anger over his destroyed dreams was what landed him here, where Mr. Hatlierre helped him become a new person—but not a better one.

I hurried in the opposite direction, to a large pine tree, and by some miracle made it from there across an open piece of lawn. Just before heading around the side of the school, I saw more flashlights fanning out from the building. I sprinted across the lawn until the view of those beams was cut off.

A minute more and I finally saw my goal. From my first day here I'd known the fence would be impossible to climb. It was made of straight bars eight feet high and had decorative spikes. More subtle than a chain-link fence with barbed wire curling across the top, it still made this place a prison. But in the same way that I'd figured out how to sneak off the VanDemere Estate, I'd discovered the flaw in St. Frederick's security.

I reached the shallow stream that was part of the elegant landscaping. Man-made and lined with smooth stones, the little brook meandered across the lawn and beneath a bridge. Best of all, it passed under the fence and into a cement canal that surrounded the property like a moat.

The decorative bridge was about three feet from the fence. A week ago, I noticed there was just enough room where the stream passed through for me to squeeze under the fence. It would be a tight fit, too low for any of the larger boys to get through, but I was small-boned.

Once I crossed the canal and road, I planned to hide in the woods and head south. Traveling through the trees, I could make my way back to the nearest town and find a phone. Then I could call Megan, who would be eager to drive up from Santa Rosa and help me.

I stepped in the water where it ran between the bridge and fence. It was cold and quickly soaked through my thin shoes, but

I felt excited at being so close to getting out. Moving fast, I sat down in the stream and shoved my feet under the fence rail as water surged around me. I grabbed the bars and worked my legs through up to my hips. It was a tighter fit than I'd thought, partly because the bars went down a couple of inches into the water.

I lay back in the stream. The water flowed over me in a shock of cold but I scooted under. Soon the back of my head was submerged and then my ears. My stomach slid below the fence as I strained to keep my mouth and nose above water. I gulped in three deep breaths, sinking beneath.

I pulled on the bars, but just after my chest went under the railing I got stuck. My bulky St. Frederick's T-shirt had snagged and trapped me below the fence. In a panic I twisted but the bars pinned me down. I lifted my head to get a gulp of air, but the surface of the stream was just above my face and no matter how I strained I couldn't reach it. Why had I been stupid enough to leave on the shirt?

There was a strange roaring in my ears. Through the glassy blur I saw a smudge of dirty yellow that was the moon, and just then my thoughts became calm. I'd heard it said a person could drown in six inches of water. This was a foot, at least. I could definitely drown. *Would drown,* if I didn't keep trying.

My arms were weak as rubber bands, but I held on to the bottom of the fence and pulled with all my strength. There was a jerk, a sensation of tearing, and a sharp pain on my collarbone. And then I was sliding forward with an easy glide. I passed under the fence, lifted up, and whacked my head on the bar. For a few seconds I gulped in air like it was the sweetest thing I'd ever tasted.

I was on the other side of the fence! The free side. And I was alive. Breathing. An image came to mind of my body trapped under the fence, my long dark hair floating around me like some modern-day Ophelia. That would make my grandmother regret abandoning me here.

I let out a choked laugh that sounded like a sob. At last I was out of the prison school! It didn't matter that my arms and hands were so weak I couldn't make a fist, or that something warm trickled down my face. Every bit of it was worth the price of freedom.

I slid down into the canal, the water even colder than the stream. It was deep and murky. I let the current lead me on for a minute, then tried to climb out. The sides were slick with algae. I lost my handhold and fell back but kept trying. Finally I reached the place where water went under a round metal culvert below the main driveway that led to the front of the school.

Using all my willpower, I grabbed the cement edge where the driveway and canal made an angled corner. I pushed with my feet and was able to pull myself up onto a grassy strip of land. Exhausted and overcome with relief, I crawled forward. That's when I saw the pair of black shoes.

Someone grabbed a handful of my wet hair and jerked my head back. I looked up into the furious face of Gavin Waylenz.

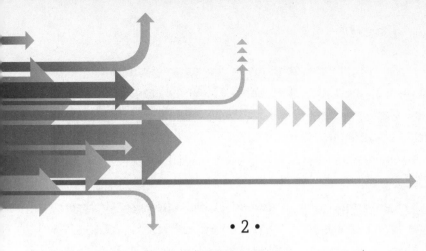

2

CAPTURE

"We've got her," Gavin said into his cell phone as two of the student monitors dragged me up the driveway and through the open gates.

I didn't struggle. In fact, it was all I could do to walk; no way to shake off the tight grip they had on my upper arms. One of them was a tall, scrawny guy who hung out with Gavin; the other, a girl with a ponytail and an athletic build. If I had my normal strength, I could probably get away from the boy, but no chance with the girl. Her favorite pastime was arm wrestling the guys, and she usually won. As it was, her fingers cut into me like pincers.

Gavin led the way, slowing us a bit because of his limp, and again spoke into his phone. "You heard how she cut through the bars on her window?" He paused, listening. "She must've climbed down the building. I've watched her on the rock wall and she could do it." Another pause. "No, I don't know how she got over the fence, but she'll tell us."

He shoved the phone in his pocket as we went up the steps and through the double front doors. I squinted at the bright lights. There was the sound of locks turning behind us, and a sinking sensation settled inside me.

Gavin held up a hand. "Stop there. She's dripping on the floor. Sheena, get a towel."

The girl let go of my arm, and he called after her, "Grab some paper towels so she doesn't bleed on the carpet."

I glanced up at the tall guy. "You can let go. I'm not going anywhere."

Gavin turned on me with a savage snarl. "Shut it! You don't say a word until I tell you to, understand?"

I just looked at him.

He folded his arms and glared at me. "All this time you've been playing hard to get, not willing to hang out with any of us. But that shy crap is just an act, isn't it?"

Gavin was a whole lot more of a mental case than I'd realized.

"Answer me!"

First he told me to shut up, then he screamed at me to answer. I worked at keeping my gaze steady. "This is the right school for you, Gavin."

"But what, not for you? Haven't you learned anything from being here?"

I'd learned a lot, mostly that this was a place where even neglectful parents wouldn't want to leave their kids if they knew the truth.

The tall boy let go of my arm and wiped his damp hand on his shirt. Gavin shook his head. "Avery, you've caused a lot of trouble tonight. Mr. Hatlierre is in Medford, where he's setting up an important recruiting seminar. Now he has to come back just to deal with you."

He turned to the tall guy. "Go see what's keeping Sheena."

The boy left and I was alone with Gavin. He came closer. "You know, your behavior tonight is really disappointing. But if you're willing to cooperate, it'll go easier for you."

"Cooperate?"

He reached out and took hold of my arm, squeezing. "You can start by telling me who helped you. It's obvious you couldn't have gotten over the fence by yourself."

"Let go."

"You're going to tell me. That's a promise."

The squeeze got tighter, and he smiled in a way that gave me the creeps. Months of pent-up anger surged through me. I dropped to the floor and jerked hard on my arm to break his hold. Then with all the energy I could summon, I elbowed him in his bad knee. He toppled backward and started yowling like a basset hound.

I scrambled to my feet and raced down the hallway that led to the empty schoolrooms. Shouts followed, but I skidded around a corner and zigzagged down every turn I came to. The school was large, the ground floor a maze of classrooms and offices. I passed doors with darkened windows and tried to think where to go. I turned another corner and rushed down a long hallway. That's when I saw the graphic-design classroom.

The room was left open so students could work on computer projects or check e-mail. I entered and scrunched behind a row of monitors. Sheena and the tall boy ran past. Panting, my head pounding and my wet clothes clinging to me, I crawled forward until I was behind the teacher's desk. I grabbed the handle to the darkroom—the place where I'd first hid the acetylene torch. I slipped inside and closed the door except for a crack.

About ten seconds later someone barged into the room and flipped on the lights. I blinked at the glare. Gavin was limping even more than before, Sheena close behind him. He glanced down at the floor and stopped as his eyes seemed to follow a trail. Had my wet clothes left a line of drips?

My heart hammered against my ribs as he came closer. And then he was there, jerking the door open. His hands shoved me hard enough to knock me backward, and I hit a box. It toppled over and I landed on the floor beside it. Gavin slammed the door, cutting off all light.

"You can stay in there and rot!" he screamed.

Gasping for breath, I struggled to my feet.

"Hey, VanDemere," Sheena called. "How'd you like to spend some alone time with Trigger?"

Were they going to put Trigger in here with me? He was the scariest kid at our school, even worse than Gavin. He was huge, lumbering, and hardly ever talked. At first I thought he was harmless, until a kid accidentally stepped on his foot. I didn't know someone that big could move so fast or be so violent. Later, I asked a few other students if Trigger was his real name, or if he was called that because any little thing could trigger a fit of rage. No one seemed to know. One girl told me his father was a senator who didn't want people to see his strange son.

I felt around for the handle and pulled up. It didn't move. I leaned against the door and listened but couldn't hear anything from the other side. Turning back around, I blinked and stared into the total blackness. It was then I heard something, a small movement. Was there a rat in here?

It sounded like someone was shuffling. Someone much bigger than a rat.

I held my breath, but then the shuffling stopped. I almost convinced myself it was just nerves when I noticed the sound of breathing. A clear picture of Trigger came to mind: the droopy lids and fingers fat as hot dogs. Worst of all, the weird little licking motion he made with his tongue across his teeth. Was that what Sheena meant about spending time with Trigger? That he was already in here? A chill went through me that had nothing to do with wet clothes.

I decided to say something that might calm him and moved my lips, but no sound came out. My back pressed against the door. If only I could see something, even the gray outline of him to know where he was!

Normally, a darkroom has a red bulb. But the one in here was burned out, and after the photography class went digital, no one bothered to replace it. I couldn't even see my hand when I wiped a damp trickle from my face.

The shuffling sound again . . . Something brushed against me and I choked back a scream, scooted sideways, and hit a stack of cardboard boxes. "Stay away from me!"

He made a strangled sigh and tried to talk. Only it didn't come out in words and I wondered if Trigger was stoned. He came closer. I shoved myself in a corner. Seconds later I sensed him so near I could feel his warmth. I waited for him to grab me with his meaty fists.

Time ticked off with awful slowness until there was another

sound. Muffled words. I also caught an unusual scent. Sort of a clean linen aroma coupled with something spicy. Cologne? Trigger definitely didn't use aftershave.

I inched my fingers forward into the inky blackness. It was all I could do not to jerk my hand back, but I couldn't continue standing there with no idea as to who cornered me. My hand touched someone on what felt like an arm.

He tried to talk again but I couldn't understand him. Suddenly it hit me. "Oh. Are you tied up and gagged?"

"Mm-hmm."

My hand moved higher, brushing against a throat and a jaw roughened with stubble. There was something plastic across his mouth. Duct tape. I found the outside edge. "This might hurt."

I yanked it off and heard a few gasps for air. "Thanks," a masculine voice said.

"You're not Trigger."

"No. I'm Riley."

The name wasn't familiar. A new student, maybe? "Hi, Riley."

He said, "Are you Avery VanDemere?"

"How do you know that?"

"The girl on the other side of the door said your last name. I figured there's only one VanDemere in this place."

He chuckled—a low sound with a lot of humor in it, which seemed out of place. "Wow, this is one freaky, crazy night! I drive all the way from Santa Rosa to find you, get locked in this room for trespassing, and then you end up in here with me."

My head started to buzz. "You came to find me?"

"Your grandmother sent me. Well, actually she told her law firm to send someone. I'm the lucky guy who got the job."

"So you're a lawyer?" That seemed strange; his voice didn't sound very old.

"Not exactly. I intern for Tate, Bingham, and Brown."

I nodded but realized he couldn't see me. "Right. Your firm takes care of VanDemere Enterprises and my grandmother's estate. I know Mr. Tate. And Ms. Brown was the one who drove me up here and dumped me off." My voice turned sour. "She wasn't exactly helpful. Kind of like talking to a wall."

"Yeah, that's Matilda Brown. Friendly as a praying mantis in a business suit."

Now it was my turn to laugh. Riley said, "But you like Mr. Tate all right, don't you?"

"Sure. He's nice. Sometimes I see him when he brings papers to the house. He always takes time to talk to me, even back when I was a little girl."

"Good, because he's my dad."

"Oh. And that's why you intern at his firm?"

"Yep."

I tried to imagine what Riley looked like. His father was ordinary, with flat brown hair and glasses. He had a slender build and friendly smile I'd always liked. I came up with a mental version of Mr. Tate but thirty years younger.

"Speaking of my dad, if you can help me get untied, I can call him on my cell phone."

"Sure. What should I do?"

"They used a plastic strap to bind my wrists behind my back. On my keychain there's a penknife you can use to cut me loose. It's in my jeans pocket."

"Which one?"

"My right."

I reached out and my fingers touched his chest. When I slid my hand over and across his ribs, he snickered.

"Sorry," he said. "Ticklish."

A couple of seconds more and I found his pocket, hooked the key ring with my finger, and pulled it out.

The sleeve of my shirt brushed against him. "Avery, are your clothes wet?"

"Soaking."

"Why?"

I hesitated. The silence between us became a little awkward and he said, "You don't have to explain if you don't want to."

For more than four months now I'd been in a place where demands for immediate responses were the norm, so I appreciated that. "I was in the canal."

"The canal that goes around the outside of the grounds?"

"That's the one." I found the penknife and opened the blade. "Turn around."

He did, and I felt for his hands. They were crossed at the wrists. "Riley, this band is tight. Is it hurting you?"

"Yeah, kind of pins and needles right now."

"Why did they tie you up and throw you in here?"

"For trying to break in."

I froze. "You're joking."

"Nope."

"But why would you do that?"

"You cut and I'll explain. Just don't nick me with the blade if you can help it."

I worked carefully as he talked. "The drive up here took

longer than I thought it would, so I didn't get to the main door until after ten. I pressed the intercom and some kid answered. I explained about being sent from your law firm to see you. He told me to come back tomorrow, but I said I needed to see you tonight. It didn't faze him, and even though I leaned on the buzzer, he blew me off. I tried calling the school's number and got a recording. I decided if the little snot running the intercom wasn't going to cooperate, I'd find a way in myself."

The knife finally cut through the plastic and freed his hands. "Thanks, Avery."

I could hear him rubbing his wrists.

"How are your hands?"

"Not great. It'll take a minute for the feeling to come back."

"How'd you get onto the property? This place is like a prison, if you haven't noticed."

"Oh yeah, I noticed, especially once I started to look around. I walked along the fence until I came to this giant oak near the back."

I knew the exact tree he meant. If it was inside the fence, escape would be easy. "You dropped from the branches? That's a long way down."

"The limb I was hanging on bent with my weight, so it wasn't bad. Once I was inside the fence, I went around to the front door and knocked. That's when these kids tackled me. I tried to fight them off, but three against one aren't great odds. So instead I started shouting every legal threat I could think of."

Riley was the reason the student monitors discovered I climbed out the window. After he showed up, someone must have come for me. The irony of it was cruel. If Riley hadn't come here tonight, I would have gotten away. However, now didn't seem the best time to point that out.

My eyes ached from the strain of trying to see through the pitch-black darkness. "I'm guessing your threats didn't work."

"No. That's when they used the duct tape."

"Oh wow, I'm sorry." I really did feel sorry for him. "I think they learned that trick from Mr. Hatlierre, the director. I heard a rumor he tapes the mouths of kids who talk back, though I don't know for sure."

"How could he get away with that? Parents would throw a fit."

"The sad truth is that kids get dropped here by parents who don't want to be bothered. Or, in my case, by a grandmother who's really upset. Why'd she send you? Did she finally decide to talk to me?"

"I'll explain in a second, but since there's feeling in my hands again, let me call my dad."

I felt an inward drop as my hopes deflated. Was Grandmother still angry? The light from Riley's cell phone came on, and I caught my first glimpse of him. He didn't look like his father at all. In fact, Riley was as handsome as his father was plain. He had a strong jaw and blond hair that in this lighting was a mellow gold. The shadows caused by his cell phone made him look a bit eerie but in a striking way.

I learned a lot from the one-sided conversation, including the fact that Mr. Tate was furious with how his son had been treated. What would it be like to have a parent concerned about what happened to me?

Riley disconnected. "My dad's going back to his office. He's got Mr. Hatlierre's cell number in a file there."

He turned the light from his phone in my direction, and I realized that while I'd been studying him, he hadn't been able to see me. He stepped closer. "There's blood on your face."

I reached up and touched the sore spot where I'd hit my head on the fence. My hair felt like a wet snarl from when Gavin grabbed it.

"What did they do to you, Avery?"

"I did that myself when I tried to escape."

He studied me for a couple of seconds. "This I've got to hear. But first, maybe you should sit down."

Using the light from his phone, we looked around the room and found a space between stacks of plastic crates. I sank to the floor.

He knelt beside me. "Let me take a look at your cut." He focused the cell phone light on my head and gently moved my hair aside. "I don't think it needs stitches, so that's good. I was kind of worried because there's a lot of blood on your face, but it's stopped flowing."

"Maybe I should use the hem of my shirt to wipe it off."

He looked thoughtful for a few seconds. "No. Once Mr. Hatlierre gets here, it's probably to our advantage if you look beat up. That way I can go on the attack if I need to. In fact, let me get some pictures."

He used his cell phone to click a few and I blinked. "You really are a lawyer."

"No, just an intern who has an attorney for a dad. Besides, I only work at the firm during summers. Last fall was my first year at CalPoly."

"Where?"

"California Polytechnic State. I'm going into architecture." Riley closed his phone, plunging us into darkness. "I don't want the battery to run down."

I missed the little light but knew he was right. He said, "So, your turn. Tell me about your escape."

Again I hesitated but then reminded myself that Riley had been open with me. And maybe he and his dad would help me get out of St. Frederick's. "I've been here four months, though it feels like a year. They're super strict and have rules for everything. It's not a military school, but almost like one. And there aren't any breaks or a chance to go home. Not even for holidays. Summer vacation doesn't exist."

"That's rough."

"So when I was in my welding class next door, I stole an acetylene torch."

"How'd you pull that off?"

"I pretended to barf in the wastebasket where I'd stashed it a few minutes before. The teacher let me take the basket out to the hall. I sneaked inside here to hide the torch, since they don't use this darkroom except for storage. Later, when everyone was in the dining hall and I was still faking being sick, I picked it up and took it to my room. Once the bars were off the window, I climbed down the outside of the building."

"You're joking."

"Nope."

I told him the rest though I skimmed the part about almost drowning. That still shook me up more than I wanted to admit. I did explain about hitting my head when I passed under the fence.

The room was so dark, and he was so quiet, that it felt like I'd just been talking to myself. I shivered and rested my arms on bent knees. "That's the story."

When he didn't say anything, I added, "Did it put you to sleep?"

A couple more seconds passed, and I wondered if it really had. Finally he said, "No, I'm just speechless. Can't believe you did all that."

"Don't forget, I also got caught."

"Yeah, because they saw you were gone. Sorry. That's my fault."

I shifted my position on the hard floor. "None of it matters if my grandmother will just let me out of this place."

"I guess you'll get your wish, since tomorrow morning there's a meeting for your entire family. It's at our law office and starts at nine. I can't really say more. I mean, I'm not supposed to. Her orders, and that's for everyone in your family. It'll all be explained once you get there."

Though I was excited to leave the school, I wondered what she was up to now. I detested the VanDemere gatherings. "What about my dad? Is he coming?" I hadn't seen him in over a year.

Riley paused for a couple of seconds. "He's the only one who won't be there. The last address for him was a rehab center that he left six months ago. Your grandmother lost touch with him, so she's not even sure where he is."

"Yep. That's my dad." I tried to keep my voice light. "He's an expert at disappearing."

"I met him once. He seemed nice."

"He is nice. In fact, I'd say he's the nicest stranger I know." I meant it as a joke, but it didn't sound funny.

"After you escaped, where were you planning to go?"

His question sounded casual and I was going to answer, but then I thought about how he worked for my grandmother's law firm. In the last few months I'd learned to be cautious.

Before I could decide what to say, there were voices on the other side of the door. A man said, "Honestly, Gavin! What were you thinking?"

Riley helped me to my feet as the door was unlocked. Light from the other room made us blink like prisoners let out of isolation. Through my squinting I saw Mr. Donovan, assistant to the director, motion to us. Gavin and Sheena stood behind him, looking subdued.

"You must be Mr. Tate's son," Mr. Donovan said in a considerate voice.

"Yes."

Now that we were in the light, I got a better look at Riley. He was tall, with an athlete's build. Beneath his blond hair, dark eyebrows slanted up and then made a sharp downward curve at the outside edge. He had deep blue eyes and an expressive mouth pulled into a frown. I had no idea where I'd seen him before, but he was definitely familiar.

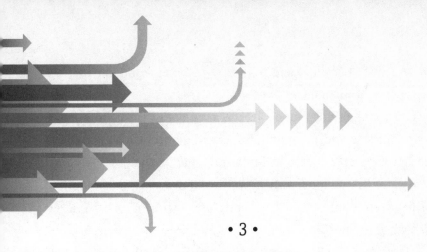

3

RELEASE

In the nurse's office, Mrs. Lambert examined the cut on my head. She said it wasn't serious and followed up with her first-aid thing. Then she gave me a towel and clean uniform and sent me into the small bathroom.

The first thing I did after changing was grab a paper cup and drink water. I also took a comb from one of the hygiene kits and smoothed out tangles until a loud knock startled me. Sheena was waiting, arms folded. "Mr. Hatlierre wants to see you."

I didn't want to see him but knew I had to. I went with her. She scowled at me. "You don't deserve to be here."

"No, I don't. I've never done anything bad enough to get me sent to a school like this."

Sheena called me a dirty name but at that point I didn't care. When we got to Hatlierre's office, she stopped outside the door that had a large pane of frosted glass in the center. The sound of voices reached us and I heard Riley say, "Don't talk to me like I'm one of your students."

She rapped lightly, and Mr. Hatlierre called for us to enter. I stepped inside and, without a backward glance, shut the door in her face. The office was elegantly furnished to the point of being overdone. Riley stood in front of a mahogany desk, while Mr. Hatlierre sat behind it in a leather chair. I walked over to Riley. "What's going on?"

He wore a small, mocking smile. "St. Frederick's has decided not to file trespassing charges against me. And my father and I have agreed not to sue for assault."

Mr. Hatlierre's control didn't waver. "As I've explained, the students involved will be disciplined." He turned to me. "Avery, sit down. We need to talk."

How I hated the sound of his condescending voice! In a room like this, with Riley watching, he could act so sincere. And in a crowded auditorium, he could boom with persuasive power that was nearly magnetic. But always, just beneath, there was something that warned me not to trust him. In the last few months, I'd wondered if I was the only kid in this miserable locked-down school who could see he was nothing but a smarmy creep.

I ignored the chair he pointed to. "I'd rather stand."

He reached in a drawer and took out the acetylene torch and window bars and set them on his desk. "Surprisingly resourceful. If only you'd put that same effort into your studies."

"My grandmother sent for me. When can I leave?"

"If you were so unhappy here, why didn't you say something? Our counselors would've met with you. None of us had any idea you weren't adjusting, except for the drop in your grades. We thought it's because our curriculum is more demanding."

I just looked at him. One of the other girls told me he got up every morning at five and spent two hours in the workout facility. Muscles bulged beneath his tight black T-shirt, but I always thought he looked top heavy since he wasn't very tall.

He stood. "We'll be billing your grandmother for the damage to the window. And you're being suspended for a week. You can collect your personal items from Mrs. Lambert."

Hope soared. A week! Anything could happen in a week.

Riley motioned to me. "Let's get out of here."

We turned to leave. Behind us, Mr. Hatlierre cleared his throat. "Avery, just some advice before you go. This week, put real effort into changing the direction of your life. When you come back, I'm expecting improvement in both attitude and grades."

It took all my self-control not to blurt out what I really thought of him and his school. Riley opened the door and we walked through. Once we were partway down the hall, he said, "That guy is a complete wacko."

"Oh yeah." Then I grinned at him and scrunched up my shoulders. "I'm suspended!"

He chuckled and I added, "Just so you know? I'd have appreciated your getting here before I climbed down the building and under the fence."

We stopped at the nurse's office. Mrs. Lambert handed me a white cardboard box, my name written on the lid. "Sign this."

I scribbled my name on a paper. It reminded me of the way prisoners paroled from jail got back their personal property. I picked up the box and we headed down the main hall. Sheena and another student waited by the front door. She unlocked it and hissed something when I went through, but I acted like she wasn't even there.

I glanced up at the sky. Clouds were moving in, and they looked like folds of gray velvet against the black sky. I took a deep breath that smelled like freedom.

The doors closed behind us, and we headed down the steps. An elated smile sprang to my lips but disappeared when a voice spoke from the dark. "I'll be waiting."

Gavin rose from the steps where he sat in the shadows of a tall bush. He limped closer, his features elongated by strange shadows. "I heard the news, Avery. About your getting suspended."

Right then, I disliked him even more than I disliked Hatlierre. "What's it to you?"

He acted like he didn't hear me. "Only for a week, though. You'll be back before you know it."

"Not if I can help it."

He moved closer, his face getting that nasty look I'd seen before, until Riley stepped in front of me. "Back off."

Even though it was only two words, they came with a silent warning. It caught Gavin off guard and he didn't say anything else.

Riley guided me down the steps. We hurried along the winding driveway, and I felt Gavin's stare drilling into my spine. "Let's get out of here before anyone else stops us."

"Definitely."

Tall lampposts cast pools of light on the ground and made the pines on either side of the drive look like gigantic arrowheads. We reached the main gates, where Mr. Donovan waited. He didn't say anything as we passed through, and I followed Riley to his car, an impressive silver Jaguar.

As St. Frederick's disappeared behind the trees, I slumped in the seat. "Thanks for getting me out of there."

Riley smiled and sent a small wink in my direction. "You're welcome. Bet you're happy to be going home."

I thought about the mansion where I lived with my grandmother, Justine VanDemere, because my real mother died when I was a baby. There were other members of the VanDemere family: the father I rarely saw, an older half brother named Warren who ignored me, unkind cousins and uncles who came to visit.

Home. The word so important to most people had a very different meaning for me.

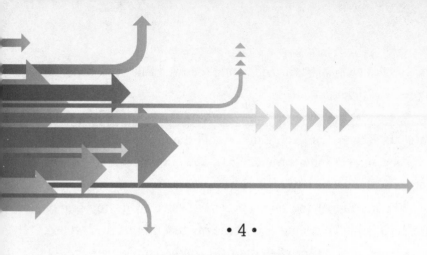

HEADING HOME

Riley let his Jaguar tear up the road, and at four in the morning there was little traffic to slow us down. Leaving Crescent City, in the northern part of the state, we traveled down California's Highway 101 as it followed the coast. In the darkness, the ocean looked like colorless glass far below the cliffs.

He slid his hands down the steering wheel. "You're quiet."

"Just thinking."

I didn't add that my head was achy and the painkiller the nurse gave me wasn't working.

"You can put the seat back and sleep if you want. We've got more than five hours until we get to Santa Rosa."

I decided to accept his offer and closed my eyes. I breathed in the leathery scent of the Jaguar. It was hard to imagine how great it would be to drive a car like this. Any car, in fact. Grandmother kept putting off my pleas to take driver's ed, since our chauffeur, Mateo, took me everywhere. A few months ago I finally got her to agree, but then she left on a trip without signing the paperwork or paying the fees. After that, I ended up at St. Frederick's, where learning to drive was the least of my worries.

Now, though, I was free.

Escaping had become a hidden infatuation that kept growing. Sneaking off the VanDemere Estate for the first time more than a year ago gave me an excited buzz. After that, I had to do it again. And the more I did it, the more I wanted to. Eventually it expanded to cutting school without getting caught. I hadn't done that a lot, and not enough to affect my grades. Especially since the older I got, the more stifling it felt to live under my grandmother's strict rules. Thinking of her, I felt an anxious hitch. How would she react to my suspension?

Even to someone like me, who grew up with Justine VanDemere as a guardian, she seemed an odd woman. She always dressed fancy; I never saw her without jewelry and makeup, though there was nothing soft about my grandmother. She loved to read. Her interest was historical biographies, and she had a ton of knowledge about the past, but her biggest obsession was the history of our own family.

Our ancestors, she kept telling us, were incredible men and women who did everything from arriving on the *Mayflower* to fighting in the Civil War. In her mind, they were courageous heroes we should look up to. The rest of the family didn't exactly agree.

Grandmother never went to movies, plays, or parties, not even the overpriced fundraisers she was always invited to. Instead, when Justine VanDemere wasn't attending company board meetings, she collected antique heirlooms and traveled to historical sites. In her spare time she watched reality TV shows.

As the miles passed, worry about facing her dimmed. There'd

be time to deal with her freaked-out reactions about my suspension once she agreed to see me.

A couple of hours later I woke to the low hum of the car's engine, surprised I'd fallen asleep after all. I stretched and looked out the window. The sky was just starting to lighten in the east. To the west the ocean was still dark, with colorless clouds hovering on the horizon.

I looked over at Riley as he guided the car around a sharp curve. "Where are we?"

"About ready to leave the coast. We'll be going through the Redwoods, one of my favorite places. Just ahead is Fortuna, a little town. I want to stop and buy gas."

Soon we pulled into the parking lot of a mini-mart. While he refueled, I grabbed my cardboard box and headed for the ladies' room. I took off the khaki pants and the shirt with the St. Frederick's logo and stuffed them in the trash.

Inside the box was my purse. I set it aside and pulled out the clothes I'd worn the day I'd gotten dumped at the boarding school. Maybe it was a small thing, but putting on my own clothes was sweet. My jeans were like an old friend, though looser at the waist and hips now. It felt so good to wear something other than the baggy school uniform!

In the bottom of the box were my favorite flip-flops. I slipped them on. I picked up my cell phone, the thing I'd missed most, but of course it was dead. I pulled a small makeup bag out of my purse and put on eye shadow, mascara, bronzer, and lip gloss. I smiled at my reflection. It was me again.

There was a light rap at the door, and I heard Riley's voice. "Avery?"

I put the strap of my purse over my shoulder and stepped outside. His eyes scanned me with appreciation. "Look at you."

Smiling, I followed him back to the car. He handed me a sack. As he started the car, I pulled out a box. "Doughnuts!"

I grabbed one, took a bite, and closed my eyes for a second to savor the taste. When I looked up, Riley was studying me. "Didn't they feed you?"

"No sugar. Not a lot of carbs, either. Mr. Hatlierre's philosophy includes strict nutritional guidelines."

The car sped along the road. I remembered this same forest from my ride with Ms. Brown. Back then I felt too stressed to appreciate its beauty.

I turned in my seat to study him. "It's kind of weird. I have this feeling that I know you from somewhere. But I don't see how we could've met, because . . ." My voice trailed off. I almost told him I would have remembered running into a guy like him.

"Because?"

"Before I got stuck at St. Frederick's, I went to Greenleaf Girls' Academy. If you can't tell from the name, it's an all-girls school."

"Thing is, we have met. Several times, in fact. Except it was years ago. Every so often your grandmother invited the kids of her employees to her parties. Ronnie and I loved coming to them."

"Ronnie?"

"Veronica, my sister. She's four years older than me and just graduated from UC Davis. Anyway, those parties were loads of fun. We especially liked the ones on the Fourth of July and the birthday parties at the end of January."

"Hmm."

"Meaning?"

"Nothing."

He glanced at me. "No, not nothing. You didn't like them?"

"Not really. It's fine you did. I'm sure most kids thought they were great, with all the fireworks and food."

"And gifts. Ronnie and I thought it was cool that on your grandmother's birthday she threw a big party for all her grand-kids and invited us, too. We couldn't believe we actually got to open gifts at someone else's party."

I stared at the massive tree trunks that lined the road, and the way the car headlights bounced off them. "Put that way, I can see why you liked the parties."

"So tell me your perspective."

A pinched half smile lifted one corner of my mouth. "This'll probably make me sound like a grinch, but I always secretly wanted my own birthday gifts."

He raised an eyebrow. "You never got any?"

"Grandmother doesn't do individual celebrations. She has one big party every year on her own birthday, January thirtieth, and gives us all the same gifts—usually nonfiction books. When my birthday comes around on September fifth, it's just another day. Well, that's not really true. Connie and Peter, our cook and gar-dener who are married and my two favorite people in the world, always do something for me. I get this terrific feast and can choose whatever dessert I want."

Riley said, "What about Christmas?"

"Kind of the same thing. I have to wait to open gifts until the rest of the family gets there, and then Grandmother gives us grandkids identical presents. She's very exact in her fairness."

He looked at me with a sympathetic expression that made me

self-conscious. "Actually, my real celebration has always been on Christmas Eve."

"With the staff?"

I adjusted the seat belt strap so it didn't dig into my shoulder. "Connie and Peter aren't just staff. And our Christmas Eves together are great. I help Connie cook her traditional handmade tamales and it takes most of the day, but they're so delicious. I bet you've never had anything like them."

"Probably not."

"And usually their grown son, Dean, is home from the navy. The four of us play board games and make caramel corn. Then we stay up until midnight watching old Christmas movies. After that, we open the gifts we've made for each other. It's like . . . well, I don't know . . ."

"Like a real family," he said in a quiet voice.

I didn't answer, wishing I hadn't tried to explain.

"And," he said, "the rest of your family, the VanDemeres, don't treat you well."

"How do you know that?"

"I was at your grandmother's summer garden party. The one a few years ago, when your cousin was picking on you."

I studied his features in the growing light and it hit me. When I spoke, my words came out as a gravelly whisper. "You. You're the boy."

"The kid who got in a fistfight with Chase?" He nodded. "That was me."

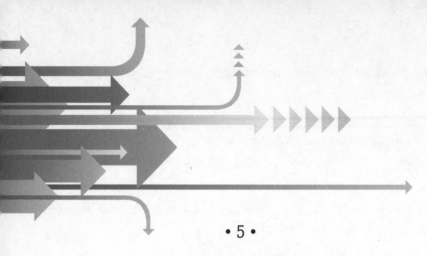

5

HUMILIATION

"Get off!" I whispered, hardly able to breathe because Chase was sitting on me. At twelve, I was a year younger than my cousin and a lot smaller.

Far away, the orchestra played in the gazebo and the music wafted through the flowering trees; it combined with the distant murmur of party guests.

His knees were on my upper arms, pushing down on them until they throbbed. The pain was almost more than I could stand, but I didn't cry. Crying would give him what he wanted. With his knuckle he rapped a steady beat on the bony part of my chest. It hurt, but worst of all was the sense of being helpless as his two friends stood watching. Chase leaned over me with a smirk on his face. The knuckle tapping moved from my chest to my forehead.

"Hey, Chase," Devin said. "Look at this."

I couldn't see what it was, but a second later he handed something to my cousin. The tapping stopped and Chase smiled. He held up a wriggling worm and swung it in front of my face. "Look, Avery. Lunch. Open up."

Devin gave a snort. "It's like that book. Isn't there a book about a kid who eats worms?"

Chase laughed. "If there is, Avery should know. All she does is read."

He brought it down and slid it across my mouth. I clamped my lips together and tried to turn my head. He grabbed my nose and pinched hard. I held my breath as long as I could, then finally took in a gulp of air but kept my teeth clenched. He used the heel of his hand to grind the worm against my teeth. It smashed my lip. There was the taste of dirt and blood, but I still kept my teeth together.

"Maybe that's enough." Topher glanced over his shoulder. "What if your grandmother finds out?"

A sneer twisted Chase's mouth. "Do you think she'd really care? Not even she can stand having this little brat around."

I closed my eyes at his words and scrunched them tight to cut off the view of him. A lump of misery made my throat ache, but I wouldn't let it out. I wouldn't cry.

There was a grunt from Chase and suddenly he was off me. I sat up and saw him rolling on the ground with another boy. They were slugging each other.

"Stop it!" a girl's voice said. "Don't you dare hit my brother!"

Chase froze with his fist still in the air, aimed at the face of a blond boy. He looked up at the girl who stood near a yew tree. I stared at her too. She was older than us, maybe sixteen, and had perfect features. Wavy blond hair fell halfway to her waist, and in a filmy aqua dress, she looked like a princess.

She walked over to Chase. "Picking on your little cousin? What will your parents say if I tell them?"

Chase stood, brushed grass from his slacks, and mumbled something none of us could hear.

She turned to the other boy. "Riley, get up."

As Riley pushed to his feet, I studied them both. They looked alike, though he was younger, around Chase's age. He was a handsome, blue-eyed boy who now had smudges of dirt on his shirt and a red mark on his face.

I stood as he turned and glared at Chase. "What were you doing that for, when you're so much bigger than her?"

My cousin looked down his nose at Riley like he was a speck of dust. He was ready to say something but the girl stepped in again. She put a hand on her brother's shoulder. "Why don't you go see if she's all right? In the meantime, I'll walk Chase and his friends back to the party."

Her voice turned steely as she faced the three boys. "Let's go."

They marched off, though a few seconds later they ditched her and took off running. I straightened the skirt of my white satin dress, upset that there were grass stains on it. Near the hem was the toe print of a shoe. I adjusted my pink sash so the bow helped hide one of the dirty spots.

I rubbed the inside of my upper arms and looked at the boy. "Thanks."

He walked over to me. "There's blood on your lip."

Touching my mouth with my fingers, I wiped it away. "It's not bad."

"How come he did that to you?"

I shrugged. Riley just kept looking at me until I finally said, "Chase doesn't like me, that's all. No reason."

We heard snickering and turned in that direction. My cousin Thisby stepped around a large bush. "Oh, there's a reason all right."

Behind her came Chase's little sister, Daisy. Both girl cousins were my age; Daisy four months older, Thisby a month younger. But they pretended to be more grown up and treated me like a little kid because I was small for my age. I stared at them. Had they been there the whole time, watching?

It was hard to decide who I disliked the most. Thisby was the only child of my Uncle Logan. Tall and pretty, she had the pale gold hair of a true VanDemere, which she liked to flip back in the most annoying way. My other girl cousin, Daisy, was just the opposite, and the only other VanDemere besides me who had dark hair. Her pale, pinched face beneath too-short bangs never looked happy. Whenever they came to visit, Grandmother expected the three of us to play together, but it was clear they didn't want to be around me.

Thisby smiled at Riley in an odd cat's-got-the-bird way. "Want to know why everyone hates Avery?"

His expression seemed unsure, but Thisby didn't wait for an answer. She looked at me as if I were a moth pinned on a board. "Because Avery's mother was a servant. She was a nanny to Avery's older brother, Warren. That's why he's only her half brother."

For a few seconds I just stared at my cousin and tried to make sense of her words. Thisby said, "It's true. When Avery's daddy was still married to Warren's mom, they hired this nanny who came here from Russia. She took care of Warren from the time he was born until he was almost five. But then she got pregnant by Warren's dad. It was a huge scandal that almost destroyed our family."

She moved her hands to show how big the scandal really was. "It made our grandparents very upset. Then the nanny died when Avery was born. Warren's parents got divorced, and her daddy's drinking got worse. That's why Grandmother is stuck raising her."

I felt my cheeks get hot as Daisy sent Thisby an uncertain glance.

Thisby studied my face and a tight little smile danced on her lips. "See, Avery? You're the reason Warren's parents got divorced. And it's why no one in the family can stand you."

I couldn't answer. It felt like Chase was sitting on my stomach again, and my breaths came in shallow little gasps. Unable to look at Thisby's smug face, I stared down at the stains on my white dress.

Riley said to her, "You're not very nice."

I turned and ran. I passed Peter's sculpted yews and kept going until I couldn't hear the music from the party. Yet no matter how fast I ran, Thisby's words followed. The story about my mother and father cut deep into my mind.

Finally, when my side ached so badly I could barely breathe, I stopped running. I sank down to the ground behind a bush covered in pink blooms. The tears I'd been so determined to hold back started, falling in wet drops onto my dress.

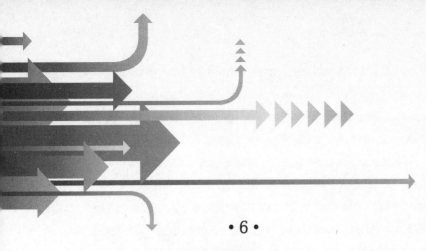

6

HEADS-UP

The morning sun inched skyward, sending rays of light between the branches. I studied the shadows as we sped along the winding road, but I couldn't look at Riley. To realize he had witnessed the most humiliating experience of my life—and was actually a part of it—left me without words. I should thank him, but bringing it up might start a discussion about that day. And right now, I just couldn't handle it.

Riley seemed to sense this. "Mind if I turn on some music?"

A second later a pulsing beat filled the silence.

Though Grandmother didn't know the full story, she did learn that Chase had been picking on me and demanded he be punished. I never found out what came of it, except he was forced to write a letter saying he was sorry. It was short and messy; I crumpled it up. He still bullied me but was a lot sneakier.

I began dreading seeing my relatives at the family meeting. Uncle Marshall was the father of Chase, Daisy, and young Jordan.

He had a way of looking through me like I wasn't there—kind of how he treated the servants. When he did happen to notice me, it was with snobbish dismissal, as if his eyes were saying, *Get out of the way, Avery. You're blocking the view.*

My Uncle Logan would be there too, with his phony smile and fading good looks. For some reason, I liked him even less. Maybe because at least Uncle Marshall made it clear how he felt about me, while Uncle Logan put on a fake act of being friendly when Grandmother was around. And, of course, his daughter was Thisby.

If only my dad, Preston, was going to be there, it wouldn't be so hard to face them. Of course, even if the law firm had been able to find him, why would he show up? That meant he'd have to deal with crap from his older brothers and get snubbed by my half brother, Warren, who hadn't talked to him in years.

Riley turned down the volume. "Can I ask you something?"

"Sure."

"How'd you manage to sneak off your grandmother's estate?" He glanced over at me and smiled. "Dumb question, I guess, after what you did at St. Frederick's. But my dad says your mansion has really good security. He was kind of surprised you managed it."

"Compared to St. Frederick's, it was nothing. Security at the estate is meant to keep people out, not trapped inside. Cameras watch the outer walls, and they're run by an off-site firm. But I know where all of them are. And at the back of the property there's the delivery entrance. The gate is controlled by an electronic button the kitchen staff and master gardener can use. And there's an outside entrance key card. Grandmother's secretary, Henry, has that."

I grabbed my wallet and pulled out a plastic rectangle. "The backup card is kept in the security company's file inside Henry's office." I thought about the weird little man. When I was a child and tried to talk to him, he acted like I was an annoying pest. And as I got older, he had to keep tabs on where I went—something else he didn't like.

I gave an evil smile and waved the card in the air. "Or so he thinks."

Riley grinned. "That's smart. You just let yourself in or out at the delivery gate but made sure to avoid the cameras along the way. And that was all?"

"Well, there's also Max and Caesar, our guard dogs. They're released at night and are happy to tear the legs off anybody who trespasses. But I've roughhoused with them since they were puppies. My biggest problem is they won't let me in or out until I scratch their ears."

He laughed and I put my wallet away. "Timing was important, too. I had to be careful when I went out. Before going to bed, I was supposed to check in with Henry. I don't see my grandmother a lot these days, except for Sunday brunch, but once in a while she asks me up to her rooms for a chat at bedtime. So it was best to wait until she'd gone on a trip. Or be sure she was busy, like when one of my uncles came over. I always knew if she found out, she'd freak. That's actually what happened, I guess."

"But if you knew she'd go ballistic, why risk it?"

"Why wouldn't I? Until I started sneaking off, I wasn't allowed to go to my friends' houses. And friends couldn't come over to the estate either, since my grandmother has major privacy issues."

I tugged a thread on the worn knee of my jeans. "She's so

overprotective. Always afraid I'll get kidnapped and held for ransom. I can't even go to the mall without a chaperone. I got driven to Greenleaf by our chauffeur, and once a week he also took me to the drugstore to buy stuff I needed. That was it. It wasn't so bad during the school year. But summers were long, boring stretches. If it wasn't for helping Connie in the kitchen and Peter in the garden, I would've gone nuts."

My voice sounded too angry. I felt a flush of embarrassment and stared out the passenger window. I heard him say, "I had no idea."

"Disneyland. That's what started it. One of my friends invited me to go with her family over spring break. I mean, it's not even that far from Santa Rosa. A seven-hour drive, maybe less. I knew Grandmother wouldn't want me to, but I still got my hopes up."

I made my voice light, as if this had now become a humorous story. "So while Megan and her family were having fun, I spent last year's spring break making an escape plan. That's when I remembered Henry's electronic key and decided to risk sneaking into his office at night. After that, everything fell into place."

"Good for you, Avery. What you did was genius."

I glanced over at Riley, surprised by how serious he looked. It gave me a glimpse of the same boy who'd been so furious with Chase. I couldn't help but smile. "Thanks."

"What are you going to do next? I mean, it won't be easy to sneak out again since Henry and your grandmother must know how you did it."

"I've been kind of worrying about that. I'm hoping when we get back to Santa Rosa, I can explain how bad that boarding school is. Grandmother's always been big on sincere apologies.

Maybe if I act really sorry and promise to never do it again, she won't send me back."

"Actually, she's not staying at the estate right now. And she isn't taking calls, either."

"Oh great." I rubbed the sore spot on my collarbone. "All I know is I'm not going back to that prison. If I have to, I'll run away."

"Can't say I blame you, but where would you go?"

I shrugged. Why was I telling Riley about running away when he worked for my grandmother's law firm? Maybe that wasn't smart.

He said, "If she does let you stay, would you keep your word and not sneak off the estate again?"

"Sure. Compared to the boarding school, the VanDemere Mansion is a resort. I can just hang out with Connie and Peter until the end of summer. Then, on September fifth, I turn eighteen."

"You plan to move out?"

This part I didn't care if Grandmother knew. "My bags will be packed and ready. After I eat my birthday breakfast with Connie and Peter, I'll hug them good-bye and leave the mansion for good."

"Hmm."

"What does that mean?"

"Just wondering. Do you have money to live on?"

I scanned the lines of his profile as he kept his eyes on the road. Being the son of Mr. Tate, no doubt he knew a lot about how tight my grandmother's fist could be. "Know something, Riley? You're starting to sound like a parent, when you're only, what . . . a year older than me?"

One corner of his mouth dipped down. "Can I help it if I'm a realist?"

I didn't tell him the rest, how I'd been saving money ever since I was fourteen. That was when Grandmother started giving me what she called a "sundries fund" of forty dollars a week for stuff like shampoo and makeup. She said she wanted to teach me the value of money, but she had no idea how careful I'd been. I managed to save almost two thousand dollars. And though I wouldn't be able to finish my senior year at Greenleaf, public school would probably be more fun anyway. I'd have to get a job, but that might be fun too.

"Enough about me," I said. "Can we talk about you for a while?"

He chuckled. "Compared to you, I'm boring."

"That's hard to believe. What kind of stuff do you like?"

"Swimming. I was on the swim and dive team in high school. Music. Listening, not playing. And architecture, like I told you before. I got hooked after taking a CAD course in high school. Using different computer programs for designing is sort of a passion. Anyway, that's about it."

"Friends?"

"My two best friends went to different universities. And this school year I didn't have much time for socializing at CalPoly, since classes were demanding."

I asked the question that had been lurking in the back of my mind for a while, keeping my voice casual. "Girlfriend?"

When he answered, his voice was also casual. "Not since high school."

We left the Redwoods and the highway straightened out. I

glanced at the speedometer. "Riley, you can stop breaking the speed limit. I've been thinking about it, and I'm not going to the family meeting."

He turned his head to stare at me so long it made me nervous. I pointed to the windshield. "Would you watch the road?"

"Trust me. You're going."

I gaped at him a few seconds. "No, I'm not. Look, I appreciate all you did in helping me get out of St. Frederick's, but I don't want to hear the boring family business. One of my cousins sent those pictures to Grandmother of me sneaking off the estate. If I never see any of my relatives again, then life is good."

"Sorry, Avery, but this meeting is not optional."

I watched the way Riley's face grew tense. The hand that had been dangling across the top of the steering wheel moved down and gripped it. "Whatever childish issues you have against your relatives, you need to put them aside."

"Childish!"

"Not that I blame you for wanting to avoid them. I'm not exactly crazy about the VanDemere snobs, either. But this is necessary."

I folded my arms. "For who, exactly?"

"You. And us."

"Us?"

"Tate, Bingham, and Brown."

I blew out a breath in an effort to hide my frustration. How could I have been so stupid as to think Riley was some knight in a shining Jaguar come to rescue me from the tower?

"Right," I said. "Got it. Pull over."

"What?"

"I'm getting out."

He smiled and shook his head, motioning to the rolling land-scape. "Now that really would be childish."

My irritation flared to anger. "I'm not going, and you can't make me!"

The set of his jaw turned stubborn. "Actually, if I have to throw you over my shoulder and carry you up in the elevator, I'll do it."

Fuming, I scrunched down in the seat and turned my head to stare out the passenger window. The longer I sat there, the more betrayed I felt.

Neither of us said anything for several miles. I refused to look at him, just pretended the car was driving itself—getting closer to Santa Rosa and farther from St. Frederick's. I didn't really know anything about Riley Tate, and I'd told him too much about myself.

I half listened to the music coming from the Jaguar's speak-ers. Riley liked intense songs with painful, passionate lyrics. What was wrong with me in the first place, that I'd been willing to trust a guy who was a stranger? Once outside the school gates, I should've made a run for it.

"You know," he said, "it's not often that my dad needs some-thing. I don't think there's been more than two or three times in his whole life he's asked for my help. And none of them were like this. I'm not willing to let him down, even if it means making you mad."

His cell phone rang and he answered using the Bluetooth device in his car's speakers. A woman's voice came on and asked where we were. I recognized Ms. Brown. He glanced at the navigation. "We're just outside Healdsburg, but it's the morning rush. We've got maybe another twenty minutes."

"But it's already nine."

"I know that, Matilda. Tell my dad he'll just have to stall."

He disconnected and from my peripheral vision I saw him study me. "Just so you know, missing this meeting would be the worst mistake of your life. That's the other reason you've got to go."

I didn't answer.

"Avery. Look at me."

When I refused, he reached over and gently touched my chin, giving it a slight tug. It wasn't forceful, so I allowed it. Our eyes met and he said, "I know I've handled this wrong. Especially after the night you've had. I'm sorry."

I swallowed but didn't say anything. He let his fingers drop but smiled at me in a pleading way. "How about I make it up to you? Have you ever eaten at Tobello's?"

I shook my head.

"Then you haven't lived. Their food is the best. How about I take you there Saturday night?"

He was right about one thing. I'd never lived. I'd been locked away in a mansion. In an all-girls school. And then at St. Frederick's. It wasn't like I'd had many chances to date.

Riley dipped his head to look at me with persuading eyes. "For dessert, they have the best strawberry cheesecake in town."

"Okay," I said at last.

We neared the outskirts of Santa Rosa and our car slowed in the heavy morning traffic. Riley seemed preoccupied. "Avery," he finally said. "I think there's something else about this meeting you need to know. I have some information involving you, but I'm not supposed to say anything. If your grandmother finds out, she'll have me fired for giving you a heads-up."

"What's going on?"

He didn't answer right away, and when he spoke I could hear caution in his voice. "Look, if I tell you, will you promise not to ask for a bunch of details?"

This, I knew, would be a challenge. "Sure."

"Remember when you said if your grandmother tries to send you back to St. Frederick's, you'll run away?"

I gazed at the curve of his mouth as if a clue were hidden there. "Yes."

"Well, you won't have to go back if you just do what she asks."

"Huh?"

Keeping his tone vague, he added, "You'll learn more during the meeting. Our law firm, on behalf of Mrs. VanDemere, is going to tell you to do something."

"Me?" Now I was really confused.

"Not just you. Everyone. As in all of her kids and grandkids." He studied my face for a couple of seconds. "But for you, it's extra important. It'll give you a way to stay out of that boarding school."

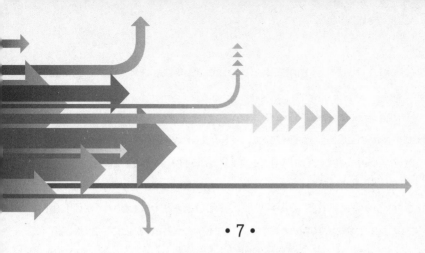

7

THE MEETING

Riley and I hurried from the elevator and into the twelfth-floor lobby of Tate, Bingham, and Brown. Actually, he hurried and shoved me along. I dragged my feet like a doomed prisoner going to the guillotine.

On the way to the conference room, we passed two women sitting in a fancy waiting area. One of them was a gorgeous blonde in a tight-fitting tan dress with matching heels. The other had shoulder-length red hair and was much younger. She was even prettier, with huge brown eyes and cheekbones sharp enough to slice through plastic wrap. More than their striking looks, what caught my attention was how they stopped talking and stared at me as we passed.

"Wow," I mouthed to Riley after we rounded a corner.

"You don't recognize them?"

I shook my head.

"That's Warren's mother, Beatrice. And the redhead is Stasia, his wife."

My steps slowed. "Oh . . . wow again. I heard he got married last Christmas. By some oversight I wasn't invited to the wedding."

Riley chuckled. "Did you get a good look at his mom?"

"Yes. She doesn't seem old enough to have a kid his age." I tried to envision her with my dad before I was born, all that vibrant beauty overshadowing his mild temperament—like staring at the sun all day. Maybe that's why he'd gotten involved with my mother. I doubted a nanny from Russia would be intimidating.

"Did you notice Beatrice was glaring at me?"

He grinned in a conspiratorial way. "Glaring as much as she can, considering all the Botox."

"Why are they waiting out there?"

"Because extended family members aren't allow in the meeting. My guess is they're here to support Warren."

When we were a few feet from the conference room door, I stopped walking. The only thing that kept me from turning around was the idea of walking past Warren's mom and wife again. Riley studied me. "Deep breath."

I brushed my bangs to the side, and his hands grasped my upper arms and gave an encouraging squeeze. "Look at me."

I did.

"You're fearless about climbing down from a third-story window, but you can't go in a room with some of your pathetic relatives?"

In this light his eyes were a shade of blue that had all the depths of a mountain lake. "You're better than any of them, Avery. Don't you think it's time you started standing up for yourself?"

I let my mouth quirk into a smile. "Probably. But I still don't want to be around them."

"Except you do want to see the PowerPoint I made for your grandma. I put in hours of work getting it just how she wanted. And no one in your family is going to appreciate that except for maybe you."

Without giving me time to answer, he opened the door and ushered me inside. The VanDemeres were sitting around a long conference table. I prepared myself for more unfriendly glares, but everyone's attention was focused on Uncle Marshall. He pounded the table and pointed an accusing finger at Mr. Tate. "Tell us where our mother is right now, or so help me . . ."

His words faltered as he seemed to search for a threat serious enough to intimidate Grandmother's lawyer. When he couldn't think of one, his tone turned even more superior. "I demand you tell us where she is!"

Uncle Logan placed a calming hand on his brother's arm but looked fiercely at Mr. Tate. "We have a right to know."

The attorney straightened his shoulders. "I assure you nobody at this firm knows where Mrs. VanDemere is. She communicates with us through the same cell phone number and e-mail address that the rest of you have."

Uncle Logan straightened his tie. "But she won't answer."

"Everything will be explained soon." Mr. Tate looked in our direction, and I caught a glimpse of relief on his face. "Come in, Avery. Have a seat."

Now all the eyes in the room did turn to me, and I wished I were still out in the hall. Or better yet, that I had never come into the building. I took the closest empty chair next to my cousin

Daisy, who sat beside her little brother, Jordan. She was dressed all in black, the only color she'd worn since she turned fourteen and first dyed her hair. She also played drums in a band, but I'd never heard her perform. These days, we weren't around each other enough for me to know what kind of music she liked. And the few times she did come to the estate, I avoided her.

Thisby was farther down the conference table. Her light blond hair was much shorter now. It fell in messy layers around her face and complemented her features. She looked like she could do a fashion spread with Warren's mother and wife.

I glanced at Warren and saw him staring at me, though it was hard to know what he was thinking. He didn't nod or smile; didn't even frown. Beside him was Chase, lounging back in his chair in a posture of total boredom.

He tipped his head in my direction. "She the reason we had to wait?"

Mr. Tate didn't reply but instead said, "Mrs. VanDemere called this meeting because she has some new information for you."

As if on cue, Riley pressed a remote. The lights dimmed and the wall near the far end of the table divided to show a SMART Board. A PowerPoint presentation appeared. Black letters on a blue background read:

HERITAGE
and
INHERITANCE

Then, to everyone's surprise, we heard Grandmother's voice. It took a couple of seconds to realize the message was recorded.

"Hello, my family: my sons Marshall and Logan, and my six grandchildren. I have asked you here today for very specific reasons, so please pay attention. Heritage and inheritance. You might ask yourselves what these two words have in common."

The slide faded and a picture came up. It was an old sepia photo of a man with a handlebar mustache who wore a wool suit and a bowler hat. He stood very stiff and without a smile. The caption read: *Otis Lawrence VanDemere–1889*.

I overheard Chase say, "Not more of the boring family crap."

His father shushed him, but my cousin had a point. At every family party, Grandmother insisted she teach us about our ancestors. Before we could eat Thanksgiving dinner, we had to hear about the *Mayflower*. On July Fourth, there was always some story about the Founding Fathers.

Most mind-numbing of all was when we sat around the Christmas tree and waited to open presents. We were forced to hear about the struggles of our early ancestors. Grandmother would read journal entries from some poor little immigrant girl who was thrilled because her single Christmas gift was an orange. Or there was the story about the family that almost froze to death on the prairie when an ice storm hit on Christmas Eve, and the best gift of all was that they were still alive the next morning.

That's why it didn't surprise me when Grandmother's recorded voice said, "We all owe a great deal to Otis VanDemere, my husband's grandfather, who grew up in Holland. Seeking his fortune, he spent eight years in the diamond mines of South America. In Venezuela, he finally found success in the diamond trade. Once he immigrated to the United States, he and his heirs lived in immense wealth."

The picture of Otis faded, replaced by a rapid series of other family photos, all ancestors who died years ago. Then the screen went black and we heard her say, "Unfortunately, Otis VanDemere's children squandered their inheritances. Very little of the family assets were left by the time my husband received his portion."

Another photograph popped up, this one of a man I recognized even though I'd never met him. My grandfather.

Her voice said, "I'm not sure if you can even appreciate what a remarkable man William VanDemere, your father and grandfather, truly was. At the age of twenty-four he began working as a diamond courier for the family company, but less than a decade later he became the executive director. Twice he brought the VanDemere Company back from the brink of bankruptcy."

The picture changed. It showed him standing beside large machinery with workmen in the background. "Using profits from a newly discovered diamond mine, he branched into production of parts for everything from dams to airplanes. Eight months before his death, he set up a research laboratory focused on the creation of man-made diamonds. That was the beginning of one of our most successful ventures, which evolved into Industrial Diamond Producers. These are only a few accomplishments of William VanDemere and the empire he created. Despite his being gone eighteen years, I am still very proud to have been part of his life."

A new photograph phased into view. This one showed our grandfather several years older. He wore a yellow hard hat and held a shovel at a groundbreaking ceremony. Beneath were the words:

The Birth of VanDemere Enterprises

More pictures followed, including him shaking hands with one of California's past governors. Then the screen went blank until new words appeared:

You can't know where you're going
if you don't know where you're from.

Her voice came on again. "For most of my life I've tried to impress upon you the importance of your heritage, but I've seen your lack of interest. During my lessons you even roll your eyes when you think I'm not looking. Recently, I have more fully come to realize my failures as a mother and grandmother, and I've given a great deal of thought to the future of you, as my heirs, and your inheritances."

I could hear some uncomfortable squirming and glanced around the room. It seemed a little funny to see my relatives look nervous. In the last couple of years I'd been dying to get out of the VanDemere Mansion, while the rest of them were dying to move in and take it over.

The PowerPoint brought up a different picture. This one was of Grandmother, maybe ten years ago. In spite of her age, she looked pretty with her short blond hair. There wasn't a wrinkle or even a freckle on her face. I wondered how much digital work Riley had done to it.

She said, "As I've examined each of your lives, it's clear you've become like the spoiled and disrespectful children of Otis Van-Demere. Especially you, my grandchildren. The lifestyles you've been allowed to live, and the way you are wasting your future, is very distressing. Marshall, since you're the oldest, let's start by looking at your three children.

"Chase barely graduated high school last year and hasn't applied to even one university yet. No doubt he thinks an education isn't necessary for someone who's supposed to inherit millions. He doesn't know how to work, and all he's interested in is sports."

Chase stuck his chin in the air. Grandmother continued. "Daisy and Jordan have equally foolish pursuits, with their obsessions for rock music and computer games, though at least Daisy gets decent grades."

Uncle Marshall glared at Grandmother's picture. Her recorded message kept going. "As for Logan, you've spoiled Thisby. Your daughter only thinks about shopping, dating, and trying to be a model, of all things."

Thisby folded her arms with an annoyed huff.

"Worst of all was the DUI she got last spring. I told you to take away her car, but you wouldn't listen."

Someone snickered. I didn't. Instead I braced myself for what was coming. She said, "Moving on to Preston's two offspring. My oldest grandchild, Warren, is far too young to be married, although at least he's doing well in college. But he's also made the disappointing decision to change his major from business to psychology, in spite of my advice." She took an impatient-sounding breath. "And then there's Avery."

Several heads turned in my direction. "She's the one child I'd hoped to raise without a sense of entitlement. Yet you, my granddaughter, deceitfully went behind my back and disobeyed my house rules. I can't even express to you the disappointment I feel in your rebellious actions."

Although I'd prepared myself, her words stung. A groveling apology wouldn't be enough to stop her from sending me back to St. Frederick's. She said, "Yet it is not my grandchildren, alone, who cause me concern. Logan, your series of failed relationships and lack of ambition have set a terrible example for Thisby."

Her middle son muttered a few swearwords under his breath as she added, "Of course, there is also your younger brother, Preston, whose whereabouts we don't even know at this time. His life has been a wretched failure. It's no wonder Warren and Avery have problems."

I glanced over at my half brother, who tried to hide his embarrassment with an uncaring shrug.

"As for you, my oldest son, Marshall, I am very aware how at every turn you try to take control of VanDemere Enterprises. And how you despise my interference."

The picture changed to a family photo taken at her birthday party in late January. All of us grandkids stood in front of the huge fireplace in the library, posed in rows behind Grandmother, who was seated between her two sons. My father was missing. We looked stiff, the lack of family love obvious. I was in the back, hiding behind my bangs and leaning away from the others as much as I could. At that time, I thought my life was full of unhappy challenges, but I was clueless. Three weeks later, I was shipped off to St. Frederick's.

Grandmother's recorded voice continued. "However, it's not just the behavior of you as my heirs that has prompted my decision for a needed change. The turning point happened the evening of my last birthday party, when I became very ill and almost died."

Comments erupted throughout the conference room as a picture came on the screen showing the Santa Rosa Memorial Hospital. Grandmother started speaking again and everyone quieted down. "If it weren't for the quick actions of several physicians, I would not have survived my episode of heart failure. After leaving the hospital, I removed myself to a private clinic in order to recuperate."

The next slide showed the same portrait of her as before. "During my recovery I spent a lot of time thinking about the future of you as my heirs. Facing my own mortality made me see it's time to prepare for what happens when I do pass away. Especially since I recently found out that my death will make some of you happy. Does this sound familiar? 'I wish the old bag would just die so we could get what we deserve.'"

Shocked, I glanced around the room. Everyone wore masks that seemed to say, *It wasn't me.*

"You know who you are," Grandmother said. "And while it made me angry, I've since wondered if that's how everyone else feels, too. Except I'm not willing to let you squander your inheritances and ruin your lives. That's why I've decided to give each of you a chance to prove yourself as a potential heir. I've created an excellent plan to discover who is the most worthy of receiving the family legacy. As you'll soon see, my competition will weed out the undeserving and find the single heir best suited to take over my responsibilities and, therefore, the family fortune."

There were a couple of gasps that faded to silence when a new slide appeared.

LAST STANDING HEIR
Challenge Guidelines

1. This competition will consist of seven tests and/or challenges.

2. Any heir may drop out of the competition at any time. Said heir, if of legal age, will then be given $100,000 as his or her complete inheritance. Any heir under the age of eighteen will have the allotted funds placed in a trust until his or her eighteenth birthday.

3. Any heir who fails to complete a challenge will be eliminated and given $100,000 as his or her inheritance. A bonus of $25,000 per challenge will be added as each is completed.

4. At the end of each challenge—unless outlined by the rules of a particular challenge—the person who either scores the lowest, or fails to finish the required task, will be eliminated from further competition. Said heir will then be given $100,000 plus the total of his or her earned bonuses.

5. All parts of the competition will be monitored by an impartial security team whose names will remain anonymous in order to deflect efforts at coercion and/or financial enticement.

6. Very few specific rules govern this competition, and these will be explained at the onset of each challenge.

7. There is a fine line between ingenuity and what might be deemed cheating. Therefore, the security

team has been instructed not to interfere should you choose to form partnerships with other family members or use paid assistance, unless it goes against the specific rules of an individual challenge. However, there is one very important condition. All individual heirs must complete the challenge themselves. (This means you can't pay someone to take your test or cross the finish line for you.)

8. The last standing heir will immediately be assigned control of VanDemere Enterprises and all that goes with it.

Uncle Marshall began to protest, and this time Uncle Logan joined him. Warren snapped a picture of the slide with his cell phone. Chase complained about how ridiculous $100,000 was as an inheritance, which Thisby referred to as spending money. To me, though, it sounded like an amazing windfall. I'd saved for months just to get my little collection of twenties and tens kept in a small chocolate box hidden on my closet shelf. One hundred thousand dollars would change my life. If only I could get it now instead of waiting until my eighteenth birthday!

This was what Riley meant about how I could avoid getting sent back to St. Frederick's after my suspension was up. As long as I passed the challenges, and stayed in the competition, Grandmother wouldn't send me back to boarding school.

"No pressure," I whispered.

The slide changed to the same picture of her as before, and everyone quieted down. In a calm voice she said, "A few final words. Only eight of you are given the option to compete. Since my youngest son, Preston, seems to have moved on with no forwarding address, he's already been eliminated. When he does show up, he'll be given his one hundred thousand-dollar inheritance.

"Please also note that I have paid a great deal of money not only to set this up but to make sure everything is legal and binding. This is a current inheritance resolution and not a will. So instead of wasting time trying to find a legal way around it, I suggest you prepare yourselves for the challenges that lie ahead. Now is the time to show exactly what you are worth, and which one of you deserves to inherit the VanDemere Empire."

The slide changed to a shot of the mansion and:

Monday, 9:00 a.m.

She said, "If you choose to compete, arrive at the estate this coming Monday at nine o'clock in the morning. If you decide to opt out, then those of you who are of legal age may tell Mr. Tate and receive your inheritance now."

A new picture appeared showing our grandfather. It was a duplicate of the portrait that hung above the hearth in the downstairs library. The slide said:

"An honorable name is the best inheritance
you can offer your family."
(Author Unknown)

A final slide rolled into view. It was the same as the first one at the beginning of the PowerPoint:

HERITAGE
and
INHERITANCE

Everyone stared at it as if some strange clue were written there.

"By the way," Grandmother's voice said, cutting into the silence, "the first challenge starts now."

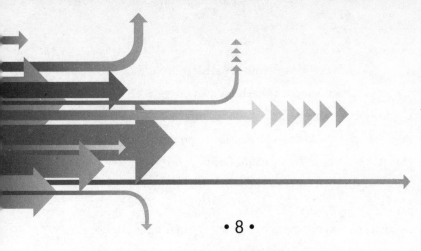

8

THE TEST

The door opened and Ms. Brown entered. She wore the same type of business suit as she had on the day she drove me to St. Frederick's. She began passing out papers.

Uncle Marshall folded his arms in a huffy way that made him look silly. "This is unbelievable."

Mr. Tate looked at him with a steady gaze. "You're free to leave at any time."

No one said anything after that, not even Uncle Marshall. Riley gave us each a pencil, and I took the test from Ms. Brown.

Mr. Tate checked his watch. "You may begin."

There were three pages stapled together and I flipped through to the end. Forty-four questions plus a final one labeled *Bonus*. Back at the top of the first page, I read:

HERITAGE and INHERITANCE
VanDemere Inheritance Challenge #1

<u>Directions</u>: You have 60 minutes to complete this test. All questions are either multiple-choice (2 points) or fill-in-the-blank (5 points). When you are finished, turn your test facedown in the center of the table and wait quietly while others continue to work.

Any person choosing to exit the room for any reason during the 60-minute examination period will leave their test facedown in the center of the table and not be allowed to return. Any person attempting to use a cell phone during this time will have their test taken and be asked to leave.

At the end of the 60 minutes, all tests will be graded, regardless of completion.

Scoring of the exams will be done by an impartial third-party security team, and results will be immediate. A specific required percentage point, not revealed at this time, must be achieved to stay in the competition. Any score falling below that point will be cause for elimination. In the case that all heirs exceed the required percentage point, the heir with the lowest score will be eliminated from the competition.

Reading the directions brought home how serious Grandmother felt about this. Daisy, I noticed, was already circling answers. She'd turned eighteen last month and would get her inheritance money if she failed. I picked up my pencil, wrote my name in the blank at the top, and read the first question.

1. What terrible tragedy did your ancestor Jedediah Taylor endure?

    A) His wife drowned while crossing the Missouri River when a ferry sank.

    B) He lost a foot in a bear trap.

    C) He buried an infant son along the Oregon Trail.

    D) While panning for gold, he was shot by a claim jumper.

I wished there was a fifth option: E) No clue.

At first I circled A. Then I erased that and circled C. A couple of seconds later, I erased that answer too and decided to skip the question until later. Unfortunately, the next three were just as hard. Some of the names sounded familiar, but I really had no idea what the right answers were. I looked around the table. Almost everyone was either reading or circling answers. Uncle Logan flipped to the second page, already finished with the first twelve questions while I hadn't answered even one.

Jordan, thirteen and the youngest, glanced up. He was the only other family member who seemed as unsure as I was. A pathetic-looking kid with straw-colored hair, he had a round face that made him look chubby even though he wasn't. I'd always felt a little sorry for him. When our eyes met I smiled, but he glared at me with all the dislike he'd learned from his father and siblings. It was hard to believe even that pitiful little lump figured he had a right to look down on me.

I read the next question and felt a spark of encouragement. It was a fill-in-the-blank, worth five points, and I knew the answer.

5. What important contribution to history did your
    ancestor John Avery make?

Grandmother picked her sons' first names from our ancestor's surnames, and mine, too. John *Avery* was someone I remembered. On the line I wrote: Deputy Secretary, Continental Congress, 1776.

More confident, I moved on. I knew a few of the answers; for the rest, I tried hard to remember some of the stories Grandmother told me and went with my best guess.

I was only halfway through the second page when Thisby flipped her test facedown in the center of the table with a theatrical flourish. I glanced up and saw her father smile at her.

I'd just started on the top of the third page when my uncles turned in their tests. A little bit later, so did Daisy. I tried not to let it fluster me and read faster. In the following fifteen minutes, just about everyone finished—including Jordan, who had never seemed smarter than a Pekingese.

Finally I reached the bonus question:

The Battle of Little Big Horn was also known as Custer's
Last _____.

Easier than any of the others, it had to be a giveaway. On the blank, I scribbled in the word *Stand* and turned to the first page. I started going over the skipped questions and was half through when Mr. Tate said, "Ten minutes."

Warren turned in his test, and I felt all their eyes on me as I wrote my best guess for another fill-in-the-blank. Daisy gave an annoyed snort. "Hurry up, stupid, so we can get out of here."

Not looking up from the test, I said, "Just a suggestion, Daisy. Stop cutting your own bangs."

The comment shocked me. I may have thought it every time I saw her, but I never planned to say it. Someone snickered and Uncle Marshall's voice turned cross. "Avery, that was uncalled-for."

I circled another answer, then glanced up. "But it's fine for her to say I'm stupid?"

Even though he looked at me in a snooty way, I knew he was surprised that I actually talked back to him. I flipped my test face-down on the pile just as Mr. Tate tapped his watch. "Time's up."

Ms. Brown walked over to the door and ushered in two people. One was a slender man in his late thirties who had lean and somewhat homely features. The other was an attractive African American woman with short hair. Both wore black suits and crisp white shirts.

Mr. Tate picked up the tests and handed them to the woman. She said, "Good morning. I am Ms. Franklin. This is Mr. Benjamin. We are agents of the security firm hired by Justine VanDemere to act as challenge moderators. There will now be a short break while Mr. Benjamin and I correct the exams."

Uncle Logan made a joke about their fake names. Benjamin Franklin was one of Grandmother's favorite people. Ignoring him, they turned and left. I followed them through the door and made my way to the ladies' room. On the way back, I noticed Daisy standing in front of a decorative mirror and fiddling with her bangs. Until now, nothing I'd ever said made a dent in her tough attitude, though most of my conversations with her and Thisby centered on defending my parents.

In the hallway outside the conference room, Thisby was talking to Riley. I slowed and studied them. They were both attractive and golden haired. Her slim fingers were tucked in the back pockets of her white jeans, and the open neck of her gauzy lavender blouse had slipped off one shoulder. With her perfect makeup, she couldn't have looked more glam if a photographer posed her.

Riley saw me and excused himself. Thisby's mouth formed a sour pout that killed the whole fashion-model image, but since he was walking away he missed it.

"How'd it go with the test?"

I shrugged and tried to hide how nervous I felt. "Hard to know. There were all these questions about ancestors whose names I've maybe heard but can't remember. Add in almost no sleep and everything that happened last night . . ."

Looking around, I made sure no one stood close enough to hear. "It's what you meant about Grandmother asking us to do something. If I pass the test, I'll stay in the competition and won't get sent back to boarding school."

Riley nodded.

"Thanks for telling me. It definitely made me try my hardest." My shoulders sagged. "But what if it's not good enough?"

"Maybe the fact that you really were trying, and it showed, will help."

"What do you mean?"

He leaned near and I could feel his breath against my jaw. "Your grandma may not be here, but she's watching everything."

My eyes widened and he added, "There's a camera in the conference room. A live streaming feed is being sent to her."

"Oh . . . of course."

Grandmother would want to see what was going on. I remembered what I said to Daisy about her bangs but also knew I wasn't the only one acting out. Uncle Marshall had carried on like a tyrant, and there were bored and annoyed looks on the faces of all my cousins during the first part of the PowerPoint.

Ms. Brown called out, "Please return to the conference room."

We began filing back in and sat in our same chairs. I looked around for the camera and found it, wishing Riley had told me about it when we were in the car.

Warren hurried in, the last to join us. The Benjamin–Franklin team stepped inside, and Ms. Franklin shut the door. "We've graded your exams and will now pass them back."

The tests were folded in half, and as they were handed out, everyone kept them hidden. Mr. Benjamin gave me mine, and I eagerly took a peek: *63 percent.*

Not good. At Greenleaf Academy, anything below a seventy-four was failing. If this were a school test, I'd have to retake it. I doubted Grandmother was letting us do that.

Folding the paper in half again, my mind began to race. If I was eliminated, then I'd need to start making plans. Before my St. Frederick's suspension ended, I'd have to think of a way to hide out until my birthday. It wouldn't be easy, because Grandmother would send both the police and her personal security company to look for me. I'd been flippant with Riley when I talked about running away, because the reality of it scared me. But, it wouldn't take long to eat through my small savings if I was living on the run. And what if Grandmother was so angry that she took back the $100,000 inheritance once I did turn eighteen? That was a lot to forfeit for two months' freedom.

Ms. Franklin stood at the head of the table. "This completes the first challenge. All of you, except one, scored above the required percentage on your tests to stay in the competition. Mr. Tate has an envelope for the first eliminated heir."

He entered the room and all eyes went to him as he walked around the table. Panicked, I saw he was heading straight for me! My eyes focused on the white envelope, and I couldn't look away as my heart started thumping. I braced myself for snide laughter from my cousins and for Uncle Marshall's smirk.

Mr. Tate's eyes met mine. I went on autopilot and almost reached up for the envelope, but he kept walking. I could hardly believe it and let out the breath I'd been holding. He stopped in front of Jordan and handed him the envelope.

"Jordan," Ms. Franklin said, "we're sorry to inform you that you've been eliminated from the competition."

Uncle Marshall erupted from his chair and yelled that the whole thing was unfair to Jordan, who was so much younger. He shouted it was unscrupulous, and that Grandmother was obviously mentally unbalanced. I glanced at the camera.

Jordan opened the flap of the envelope, thumbed through the papers, and whined loudly that he should get the money now and not in five years when he turned eighteen. Ms. Franklin and Mr. Benjamin didn't answer either of them.

Ms. Franklin looked across the room at the rest of us. "For those who wish to continue in the competition, remember to meet us at the VanDemere Estate at nine o'clock Monday morning.

Bring your passport, photo ID, and a bag with several changes of clothing and whatever necessities you need. Also, have comfortable footwear."

Warren leaned forward to peer around Chase. "Passport? Where are we going?"

Thisby frowned. "I've got a portfolio session that day."

"You can't just expect us to put our lives on hold," Uncle Logan said.

Neither Ms. Franklin nor Mr. Benjamin answered as they left. Uncle Marshall's face grew even redder. He turned on Mr. Tate, who was several inches shorter. "You can't do this to my son. This foolishness will never stand up in a court of law."

Mr. Tate stared coolly back. "I assure you, it will. In agreement with Mrs. VanDemere's instructions, we've done a very thorough job regarding our legal responsibilities."

My uncle shoved a finger against Mr. Tate's chest. "Know this, Jimmy Tate. Once I take control of VanDemere Enterprises, the first thing I'm going to do is fire you. More than that, I'll use everything in my power to destroy this outdated company of yours!"

Riley stepped forward and in a calm but firm manner pushed Uncle Marshall's hand away from his father. "That's enough, Mr. VanDemere."

I couldn't help but be impressed, though for a couple of seconds I was afraid Uncle Marshall would punch Riley. But then he straightened up and turned to his kids. "Let's go."

He marched from the room and Daisy followed. Riley walked behind them, a silent escort from the law office. Chase put his arm across Jordan's shoulders, talking to his little brother encouragingly as they left.

Once the show was over, the rest of the family filed out of the conference room, most of them looking a little deflated. They headed off in their own directions. I folded my test even smaller and shoved it in my purse, the last VanDemere to step through the door. The whole meeting was just as stupid as I knew it would be. All I wanted to do was go see Connie, let her hug me and feed me, and then crash on my bed.

"Avery?" Mr. Tate said.

I glanced over my shoulder as he caught up with me. "Yes, Mr. Tate?"

"Just a few words with you. Would you mind coming into my office?"

The last of my relatives headed to the elevators, and I tried to think of a way to put him off. But he stood there looking at me with the same gentle expression I'd often seen when he came to the mansion to meet with my grandmother. Along with the memory of my uncle poking him in the chest, I felt too sorry to refuse.

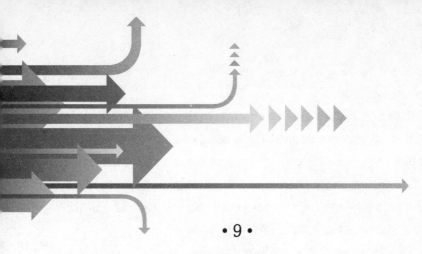

THE DEAL

Mr. Tate's office was impressive, with a large oak desk near one wall. I expected him to sit behind it. Instead he led me over to a couple of leather chairs cornering a coffee table.

"I won't keep you long, Avery. First of all, is there anything from the meeting you want to ask about?"

This morning, as I looked at him, it was with a new perspective. There was little resemblance to Riley except in the eyes. They both had a sharp edge of intelligence lurking behind good humor. As for the rest, I figured Mr. Tate had married a tall, beautiful blonde.

I said, "How sick is my grandmother?"

"I'm not sure. All I can tell you is that during her family birthday party back in January, she had your chauffeur drive her to the hospital."

"But she called later that night and told me it was nothing. She never said a thing about going to a clinic, just that she was taking a short vacation."

Not that I'd bothered to check on her, as I was busy sneaking off to be with my friends. I felt a pang of guilt. It was only three weeks after her birthday party that my grandmother gave the orders for me to be shipped off to St. Frederick's. I thought her refusal to take my calls was because she was furious. But what if being sick was the reason she'd withdrawn?

Mr. Tate said, "The vacation story is just what she told everyone. Since then, she hasn't come home even once."

I studied the handblown glass vase sitting on his inlaid coffee table. It was obvious that working as the sole legal counsel for VanDemere Enterprises had been profitable for him. "There's something else I want to ask."

"Go ahead."

"Grandmother brought me home so I can compete in this contest. If I'm eliminated, I'll be sent back to St. Frederick's?" I wanted to make sure Riley knew what he was talking about.

"Yes."

"How long is she going to punish me? Has she even asked about me?"

Mr. Tate's face showed a mixture of sympathy and something else I couldn't quite decipher. I sank against the chair back. "And how am I supposed to do this competition with constant fear hanging over my head?"

"Think of it as motivation to do well." He gave me a rueful smile. "Freedom from boarding school and a massive inheritance is quite a prize."

"But I don't want to inherit the stupid family business!"

"You don't?"

"I'd hate running VanDemere Enterprises." Maybe there was a little of my father in me, since he'd also rebelled against the family name his whole life. "Besides, there's nothing in Grandmother's big empty house that I want."

"Empty?"

I didn't answer for a few seconds. "It might be packed with expensive stuff, but it's always felt empty to me. If it became mine, I'd probably run through the halls and knock the paintings off center. Break a few priceless statues. Does that surprise you, Mr. Tate?"

He shook his head. "I tried to tell Justine that her mansion would be a lonely place to raise an only child."

For some reason I felt touched by this. "I'm not the right VanDemere to inherit that stone museum, especially with both my uncles so desperate to own it."

"But winning the competition would provide for your every financial need for the rest of your life. The thing is, Avery, you should try your best. You might be able to win."

"You're wrong about that. My uncles have every advantage, and they'll support their kids because it gives their families more chances to get the big money. Besides, you heard what Grandmother said. They'll do anything for an edge, including hiring someone to help them cheat. The other VanDemeres have their own fat wallets to back them."

Mr. Tate stood and went to his desk. He brought over a tan envelope and sat down again. "Justine left you a credit card, your passport, and other papers you'll need."

"Grandmother wants me to compete?"

He held it out. "She didn't want you to be excluded. It was important to her that each of the heirs have a chance."

"That sounds like her." I didn't take the envelope.

He set it on the coffee table. "I understand your concerns, because your cousins have their fathers to help them. They'll work as teams."

"Not Warren."

"No, but your brother has his wife to go with him. And I'm sure his mother will help him financially. You, though, would compete by yourself."

I thought about my father and felt a pang of loss for the relationship I never had with him. What would it be like to team with him, to spend more than an hour talking about something besides the weather? I'd known the lack of him in a hundred different ways. Now, imagining my two uncles working eagerly with their kids, and seeing how furious Uncle Marshall was about Jordan's elimination, it hurt to admit what I didn't have.

Mr. Tate said, "Your grandmother knows it will be nearly impossible for you to compete without help. For one thing, because you're not yet eighteen, you'll need an adult to assist you. For this reason she's given our law firm the responsibility of providing a chaperone. My associate, Ms. Brown, has agreed to take on that role."

It was all I could do to keep from rolling my eyes. As if I'd ever go anywhere with her again.

"One other thing," he said. "You'd also have an additional advantage. Our firm is willing to back you. We'll give you extra funds for whatever your credit card doesn't cover. And provide anything you need, including a research team accessible at any hour. Just ask, and it's yours."

Puzzled, I folded my arms. "Why would you do that?"

"Because it's our hope that should you become the sole inheritor, you would continue to retain the services of Tate, Bingham, and Brown."

"Oh." I remembered Uncle Marshall's threat to fire the law firm. "I'd consider it, sure. But don't you get it, Mr. Tate? You're gambling on the wrong VanDemere."

Tired of the conversation, I scooted forward and glanced at the door.

"Avery, I meant it when I said you have a good chance to win this." He leaned forward in a confiding way. "You got the highest score on the test."

I gazed at him for a couple of surprised seconds. "But I got a sixty-three. That's failing."

Mr. Tate smiled. "Not if it's graded on the curve."

"Oh."

"The test was difficult because your grandmother spent most of her recuperation working on it. In fact, I was surprised how well you did."

"Everyone scored less than me." My mind buzzed with satisfaction.

He nodded. "And it's probably unethical to tell you that your Uncle Marshall got the next highest score. But as he has plans to dismiss our firm, I'm not feeling particularly loyal." There was an amused glint in his eyes. "Tell me something, Avery, will you? How did you know so many of the answers?"

I thought about it. "Sunday brunches, I guess. Grandmother told me stories from the research she was doing about our ancestors. Whether or not I got dessert depended on my answering her questions right."

He chuckled and I stood, which pretty much killed his good humor.

"I'm sorry, Mr. Tate. I just don't think my grandmother would like it if I made an agreement with you. Let's wait and see what happens. If I somehow manage to win this thing, then I'll seriously consider retaining your firm. Right now, though, I need to do whatever I can to stay on her good side."

Mr. Tate stood too, his eyes thoughtful. "Over the years I've secretly felt you have more worth than any of your family. And your refusal to accept our help only supports that. But what if there was something in it for you? Something outside of the Van-Demere inheritance?"

He walked over to his desk and brought back a folder. "You might not know this, but our firm handled the paperwork that set up your grandmother as your legal guardian."

Mr. Tate opened the file. There was a packet labeled *photographs* and more than a dozen handwritten letters folded in thirds and bound together with a rubber band. The top one was stamped *Received* and dated September of the previous year.

Before I could see more, he closed the cover and returned it to his desk. "Despite my counsel to your grandmother, Justine has always insisted that any information about your birth remain undisclosed."

"My mother," I managed as he walked back to me. "Was she Russian?"

"No, she is Croatian."

Is.

Air left me the same way it had when Chase once slugged me in the stomach. It took a few seconds to find my voice. "She's still alive?"

"Yes."

"And those letters?"

"She sends one to our office each year, for your birthday."

I couldn't have been more surprised, or furious, if he'd slapped me. I turned away, fists clenched so hard my knuckles hurt. It was all I could do to keep from grabbing the fancy vase on his coffee table and throwing it against the wall.

I stomped away from him to the window. I wanted to storm through the door, but that meant running away from the file on his desk. Instead I stared through the glass, my posture stiff. My lips were clamped together because if I opened my mouth I knew I'd yell every dirty word I'd ever heard.

I gazed through the window where the sun made the sky too bright. Far below, the street was full of what looked like toy cars inching their way between stoplights. Then suddenly it was all blurry and I didn't realize why until Mr. Tate gave me his hand-kerchief.

"I'm sorry, Avery."

I could hear that he really was. It didn't help. When I spoke, my voice sounded hoarse. "And every year you just stick those letters in a file? Do you read them?"

"No." He paused. "My secretary takes care of them. I've kept them in the hope that your grandmother might one day explain what happened. If so, they'd be waiting for you."

I turned to him, struggling to understand. "But why did she tell me my mother's dead?"

"I'm sure she believed it was easier that way."

Then I did swear, the words coming out on their own. I headed for the file on his desk, surprised when he got there before me. I didn't know he could move that fast.

"Please calm down."

He looked so anxious that I laughed. It wasn't a pleasant sound.

There was a knock and the door opened. Riley came in and shut it behind him. He walked over to me. "Are you all right?"

I appreciated that he didn't ask, "What's going on?" or "Why are you yelling at my dad?"

Mr. Tate glanced at his son but didn't say anything. He looked uneasy.

I folded my arms, self-conscious but still seriously upset. "Do you have my birth certificate? And the legal papers about my guardianship?"

"No, your grandmother insisted she keep those."

The vault in her office. I'd only seen it open a few times, when she took out pieces of jewelry. To think that something way more important than diamonds was locked inside it all this time!

My eyes fell on the file. "How soon can I get those letters? When I turn eighteen? Or twenty-one?"

He shook his head. "They're the property of VanDemere Enterprises. If you become the last standing heir, then I'll be taking orders from you. As with all of the company documents, you'll have access to this file."

That's when I understood he held the grandmaster of bargaining chips. "You're playing me, Mr. Tate."

Embarrassment touched his face. "Yes, I guess I am. Though only because I'm desperate. Please understand, Avery. Your uncle's threat wasn't a surprise. I've faced that kind of intimidation before and not just from him. But the thing is, I've worked for VanDemere Enterprises nearly half my life, and I'm not willing to let one of your relatives discard us. At least not without a fight."

"So you're picking on me?"

Riley shifted his stance. How much did he know about this forced deal his father was trying to negotiate? "Fine, Mr. Tate," I said, except my tone sounded anything but fine. "What do you want?"

"You sign a notarized statement that if you win the competition, you'll retain Tate, Bingham, and Brown."

"What happens if I lose?"

He didn't answer, and I felt a little sick knowing I might never get a chance to read the letters in my file or see the pictures.

"Beating out the others in this competition is going to be nearly impossible," I said to myself as much as him. "And if I do somehow manage to win, you promise you'll give me the letters?"

"Absolutely."

"Well, that's not good enough."

He raised his hands in a helpless gesture. "I'm not sure what else I can do."

"Every time I pass a test and move on, you give me something from the file. A letter or the pictures."

He took a quick look at the folder on his desk. I could see his hesitation and said, "Ten seconds to agree Mr. Tate, or I'm gone."

"It's not that easy."

Riley came a few steps closer. "Yes it is, Dad. If she's willing to help our company survive, then you owe her something."

That surprised me. Riley knew exactly what was going on.

"Time's up." I headed for the door.

"All right," Mr. Tate called, then chuckled and shook his head. "I guess such determination should give me confidence in your ability to succeed."

I walked back to him. "You agree, then?"

He nodded and I held out my hand. "Something from my file, please."

"What?"

"I passed the first test, remember? Got a sixty-three."

Riley laughed and turned to his father. "What did I tell you during the break? Anyone who'd climb down three stories just to get out of a boarding school is a player you want to sponsor."

Riley smiled at me. Mr. Tate went to his desk, took the top letter from under the rubber band, and slid it inside a white envelope. "Here. This is the most recent letter. It came last September."

I snatched it from him like a starving person might grab a piece of bread.

He said, "Monday morning then, at the estate? Your family will be there at nine, but Ms. Brown and I will meet you at eight thirty. We'll have the contract for you to sign."

I shook my head. "Don't bring Ms. Brown. I'm not going to try to pass these tests with her hanging around. No offense, Mr. Tate, but I really don't like her."

He looked more uncertain than he had since I entered his office. "There's nothing else we can do. I'm afraid my agenda is extremely full, and Mr. Bingham is away on international business."

I pointed at Riley. "Your son will do just fine."

Riley looked as surprised as his father. His eyes met mine. I held a steady gaze and hoped no blush betrayed me. He seemed to be thinking it over, working through what it would involve. Finally he gave a slight nod. "I'm in."

"Wait a minute, both of you! Riley, you're only nineteen. You're not old enough to be a chaperone for Avery."

"I drove her all the way here from Crescent City."

I started walking to the door. "Take it or leave it, Mr. Tate. If you two don't show up Monday morning, I'll assume our deal is off."

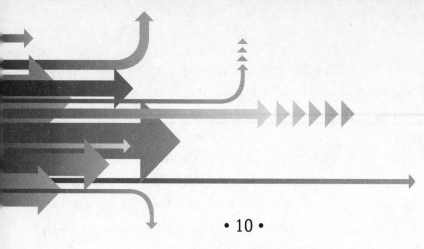

THE LETTER

I slipped the letter out of the envelope and studied the date stamp. The law firm got the letter ten days after my last birthday—around nine months ago. All these years of believing my mother was dead! And yet she was writing letters to me each year on my birthday. Who was she? Croatian instead of Russian, for one thing.

I got an A in geography at Greenleaf. Even if I didn't remember much about Croatia, I knew it was a lot closer to Italy than Russia. So why did my cousins call my mother Russian? Probably because people like their parents never bothered to find out anything about the hired help.

The elevator doors opened and I hurried through the lobby. A little ways down the block, a tree walled in by a cement circle made a shaded bench. I sat down and opened the letter. There were two pages covered with delicate writing.

To my daughter on her seventeenth birthday,

It is nearly nine at night. I am sitting at my favorite outdoor café on Ilica Street and sipping a glass of *bijelo*. As happens every year, the time is now to write you a letter.

Today should have been a regular workday for me, but I have learned from the past that I cannot clearly think when it is the anniversary of your birth: the first and last day I saw you. And so I arranged with my superiors for a replacement and have spent the day walking through Zagreb.

This afternoon I wished so much you could be with me, that I played a foolish game of pretend. Wherever I went, I imagined you beside me. We shopped for painted silk scarves, and I bought you one that is teal and pink, though I don't know your favorite colors. We looked at paintings, books, and jewelry, and I saw earrings of hammered silver I felt sure you would like. I dreamed of treating you to delicious *kifles* and also *breskue*. That last is my favorite, a cookie with apricot filling.

Though I don't know your real name, in my mind I always call you Tatjana. From my language, it means "father's daughter," which I think fits. I often wonder about you. Do you have your father's blond hair, or is yours dark like mine? Do you have a second mother, what you would say in the US is a stepmom? I hope you do, and that she and he have raised you with goodness. Perhaps you have younger brothers or sisters, and maybe Warren brings you a birthday gift. He was always such a sweet boy.

I stopped reading, a strange pressure inside my chest.

She had no idea I grew up inside the VanDemere Mansion instead of living with my dad! She didn't even know my name.

"Tatjana," I said out loud.

In time the shopping lost pleasure and so I walked through a very historical part of Zagreb and thought to show it to you. Most of the city has changed very much since I was a girl. Now it is modern, busy, and filled with tourists. But in the Gornji Grad, on the upper end of town, it is not so. The old architecture is quite beautiful.

I saw two buildings next to each other. One of them had been restored with new fresco and molding, painted in shades of yellow and cream. Next to it stood a building that has not yet been updated. It was still covered in many bullet holes from the street fighting, and although the windows were long ago replaced, some of the sculpted stone angels are still missing pieces of their faces and wings from when they were shot away.

Those bullet holes reminded me of the gunfire that still haunts my dreams from when my family and I lived in constant fear. I was just four years older than you when I left, escaping danger and grief by coming to the US. I started out with many hopes, only to end up returning home a few days after you were born. In some ways life has been a circle, and today I compared myself to that pretty yellow building. It looks untouched. You can't see the scars from the bullets beneath the new plaster and paint. And yet the strangeness of it is that they are still buried there.

Well then, enough of that. In so many ways my life is

prosperous. I have my work and friends, my music and learning. And today there is peace in our thriving Zagreb.

I hope that my daughter, who is now seventeen, is happy and well in her own life. I wish you a very good year!

All my love to you,

Your mother, Marija

I stared at the words until they blurred. For years I'd trained myself not to cry, yet today it happened twice in one hour. How could I help it? Grief and joy were knotted together at knowing my mother was not only alive, but that she loved me and wanted to be with me—and all this time, we'd been kept apart!

Pushing down my anger, I felt a deep longing to know more about her, as if I'd been given only a sip of water that made my thirst even more desperate. What kind of work did my mother do? What kind of music did she enjoy? And most of all, what was her last name? Without that key piece of information, how would I be able to find her?

The envelopes had each been removed and the letters date-stamped like everyday correspondence, when they were so much more. And without the envelope this letter came in, I didn't have a return address, either. I felt a surge of resentment for Mr. Tate.

The VanDemere limousine pulled up to the curb. I stood and waved at Mateo as he hurried around the front to open my door. A wide smile split his face. "Welcome back, Ms. VanDemere."

No matter how many times I'd told him to call me Avery, he always insisted on the more formal name. "Hey, Mateo. It's great to be back."

And it was! Despite my plans to leave when I turned eighteen, it still felt good to be heading home to Connie and Peter. I asked Mateo how he'd been.

"Bored. Since you and Mrs. VanDemere have been gone, there's no driving. And I can only wash and wax the cars so many times."

"How're Connie and Peter?"

"Missing you."

Mateo was Connie's cousin and had been our driver for four years. He was also the reason I did so well in Spanish class, since during the drive to and from school he helped me practice.

As he guided the car through dense noon traffic, I reopened the letter and read it again. I memorized the unusual Croatian words and envisioned myself walking with my mother and shopping in Zagreb. She'd tell me all the sad things from her childhood, and I'd share mine.

I slowly folded the letter and studied the date stamp. Beneath, in smaller print, was the law firm's info. I picked up the car phone, punched in their number, and asked to speak to Mr. Tate. It didn't take him long to answer.

"Hello, Avery."

"What happened to the envelopes my letters came in?"

He paused for a couple of seconds. "I told you, all of that's handled by my secretary. She date-stamps items and discards the envelopes."

I took in a slow breath and told myself not to shout. "But you've got to have my mother's address written down some-where. I want it."

"Try and understand. I always assumed that if your

grandmother decided to tell you about your mother, she'd give you the personal file that she keeps in her safe. Or, if she passed away and you became an inheritor, it was my plan to hand over the letters to you."

"Until today, when you needed leverage."

Mr. Tate didn't answer.

"At least tell me my mother's last name."

Another brief pause. "Your grandmother has no idea I've kept these. If you win the challenge, you'll get them. But until then, I can't risk doing more."

I shoved the car phone back in its cradle. Sixteen unread letters. Each was the special birthday gift I'd never received, and now Mr. Tate held them for ransom.

The car turned onto our private road, and at the end of the long drive I saw the VanDemere Estate. Grandmother wanted us to learn about our heritage, and that was exactly what I'd do. Not that I cared even a little about the VanDemere ancestors. It was my own personal heritage I was determined to secretly discover. Suddenly, it was all about the game. I needed to win.

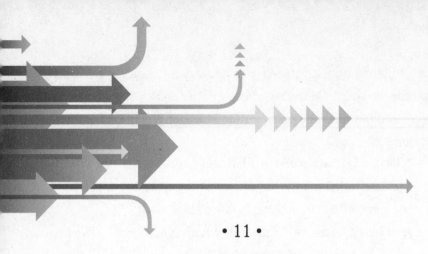

• 11 •

THE WARNING

Connie hugged me and exclaimed at how much weight I'd lost. Worrying that I was now too thin, she whipped up a truly delicious turkey and bacon sandwich with potato chips, and cut a big piece of chocolate cream pie for me.

It felt great to sit in the kitchen with her and Peter, eating and talking about everything. When I gave them an update on the family meeting, including Grandmother's claim of nearly dying, they were both shocked.

Connie said, "I knew Mrs. VanDemere was ill, but she left the hospital the next day. Then she went on a trip, or at least that's what she told us."

I took another bite of pie. "There's more."

Connie clamped her hands together when I finished explaining the competition. "Oh no. I think she's going too far with this whole contest thing." That was as close as she would ever come to criticizing my grandmother.

I didn't discuss my agreement with Mr. Tate about the letters from my mother. For now, it was all too raw.

Connie started cleaning off the table. "It's been strange having Mrs. VanDemere away this long."

"What's Henry got to say about it?" I asked.

"Nothing. The clod's gone, too," Peter answered in his blunt way. "She sent for him a few days after she left."

That was an interesting bit of news. Henry almost never traveled with Grandmother, but maybe this time she needed his help with setting up the challenges. It was great news, because now he wouldn't be checking on me. The three of us were alone in the house.

Unlike other large mansions that had full on-site staffs, the VanDemere Estate hired very few live-in employees. Grandmother preferred privacy. There were no butlers, valets, or maids. Instead, a cleaning crew came in twice a week. Additional part-time gardeners from a landscaping company worked under Peter's direction. And Connie had a catering service for special events, but that was it.

Of course years ago, there was my nanny. In fact, I had two but didn't remember the first one. The second was named Jean, and she had been with me from the age of two until I was almost six and ready to start all-day kindergarten. Then Grandmother said I no longer needed Jean and sent her away. I cried for days, though now my old nanny was a faded memory. I felt a flush of sudden anger. There was a mother out there who wanted me.

Once I finished eating, I went upstairs. It felt strange to be home, and I looked around my bedroom with a new perspective. Professionally decorated in ivory and shades of green, the furniture was expensive. Yet for the first time I realized it had always looked more like a guest room than a girl's bedroom.

I walked over to my computer desk, the single area that had my touch. Above it was a shelf with pictures. I scanned them all but focused on my favorite. It was of me with my dad when I was six. I wore a red velvet dress and sat on his lap. We were in front of the Christmas tree and looked happy. I think I really was, since there were so few Christmases when he came to see me. He looked down with affection on his handsome face, and for once there wasn't his usual trace of sadness. It was a single moment frozen forever in a photograph that pretended to be something more than it really was.

I thought about Marija's letter and wondered if my dad knew where she was. Maybe he didn't care about her any more than he cared about me. My mother must have been as disposable as my nanny.

I researched Croatia on the Internet, and its largest city, Zagreb. I also searched my mother's name and soon saw Marija was very common there. Without her last name, it was hopeless. That made me angry at Mr. Tate all over again. I spent a long time reading about the country and its culture; this included the Croatian War of Independence. I started to understand why my mother wrote of the fighting in the streets and bullet holes in walls. But what I really longed to know about was Marija herself. Did she lose family members during the war? And how did she manage to escape a country tearing itself apart? My biggest question was why she decided to go back to Croatia.

"And why didn't you take me with you?" I whispered.

Needing someone to talk to, I called my friend Megan. She

squealed with joy when I told her I was home again. At one point she said, "It's all so crazy! I can't believe everyone lied to you about your mother. It's cruel! And then you've been locked away for months. To think I've been upset because this new guy hasn't called me."

Since I'd let my problems dominate our conversation, I insisted she tell me what was going on in her life. She talked a lot about a boy she liked but was also excited that her family was taking a trip to Europe next week. I casually asked about Kyle and learned he was still dating the girl he'd met over spring break. Slugging my pillow, I flopped back on it. Had he even asked Megan about me when I was sent away?

Eventually her mother made her get off the phone, and after promising she'd call me tomorrow, we said good-bye.

That evening, I went to bed earlier than usual. The next morning, as I woke and lay beneath the covers, an odd sadness settled in. My mind drifted between thoughts until a memory surfaced from half a lifetime ago, when I was nine and at brunch.

"Well done, Avery." Grandmother adjusted her pearl necklace. "You've remembered everything I taught you last week about the Revolutionary War. Now you may have dessert."

I glanced at the cream puffs. This morning Connie had prepared my grandmother's favorite foods in the hopes that it might help put her in a good mood. She'd also told me to wait until dessert before asking.

When I spoke, my words came out in a rush. "My friend Page from school invited me to her house for a playdate."

Grandmother put down her fork and studied me. "I can't have you going off to some stranger's house."

My voice turned a little squeaky. "Then can Page ride home from school with me? We could play for just an hour."

"Avery, you know we don't allow people who are not family to randomly come here. You have plenty of children to play with. Your cousins visit several times a month."

"They don't like me," I mumbled.

"Nonsense! Don't slump like that, child." Her expression softened but not enough to let me hope she might give in. *"We're not the same as others. There are certain responsibilities about being part of this family that you won't understand until you're older."*

I picked up the letter from my nightstand and read it again. The words my mother wrote filled a secret emptiness that I'd spent my entire life trying to ignore. I couldn't stop thinking about her. After breakfast I did more Internet research about Croatia. I learned that Zagreb recovered from the war and was now a thriving city with more than half a million people. I also looked through tons of images of the Gornji Grad section of the city that she wrote about.

By lunchtime I felt emotionally drained and went for a swim in our indoor pool. When I came back to my room, I decided to focus on something else for a while. I answered a ton of e-mails, then opened my blog, *About Avery.* In my graphic-design class at Greenleaf, our teacher gave us several options for projects and I'd decided to make a blog. In the beginning I wrote a few posts; not that anyone but a handful of friends ever read them. And I hadn't added anything for a long time. Now, thanks to Megan's suggestion that I blog about my experience at the boarding school, I had the perfect topic.

I started typing up my story of being in St. Frederick's. The words poured out and once I finished, I saw that place was even worse than I first thought. If only I'd been expelled instead of suspended! I added pictures to my blog from the St. Frederick's Web site, then published my post and linked it to my social media profiles. Now my friends would finally know everything I went through in the last four months, including why I hadn't come back to Greenleaf.

I dozed off at my desk and when my eyes finally opened again, everything looked blurry. My computer screen showed it was after ten. Pushing away from the desk, I stood and stretched.

After brushing my teeth and washing my face, I came back to the bedroom and changed into pajamas. Ready to sleep, I glanced at my desk and sensed something was out of place. I walked over to my computer. The mouse still sat on its pad and the desk phone rested behind it. My notebook was on top of a couple of books, open to a blank page. Three pens in different colors lay next to it, along with a tin of breath mints. It all seemed exactly normal—until I looked up at the shelf.

The framed Christmas picture of me with my dad had vanished. In its place was a folded piece of paper torn from the notebook on my desk. I grabbed it and stared at the blocky printing in blue ink.

Avery, drop out now or you'll get hurt.

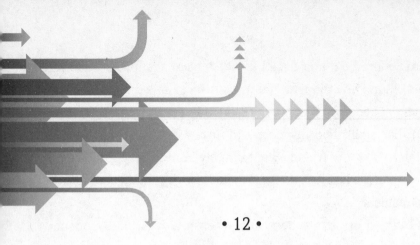

12

RILEY'S GIFT

"It's the first threat of the competition," I said to Riley. "Guess it's obvious this sort of thing is going to happen."

He didn't seem so sure. We were sitting in Tobello's on the date he'd promised. The food was really good, and I could see why he liked it. But I'd been spoiled by Connie's fabulous cooking, and even expensive restaurants couldn't compare.

"So who left the note?" he asked.

"Well, that's the confusing part, isn't it? A little too low-key for Chase. His version would be shoving me against a wall."

"Daisy or Warren? Or one of your uncles?"

"Maybe, but how would they get in?"

He looked a little puzzled. "It's where your uncles grew up. It's their home."

"Right. But even they can't just come through the gates without someone pressing the button to let them in. Either Connie, Peter, or Henry, who isn't here right now—or someone from the off-site security company—has to release the gate. They didn't. I called and checked."

"Maybe whoever it was climbed the wall. I mean, it's high and there are lots of security cameras, but it could be done. Especially if they were inside the property often enough to know where all the cameras are hidden."

"What about the guard dogs? Max and Caesar won't let anyone in. They don't like my uncles. And Max once got off his daytime leash and pinned Chase to the ground."

Riley laughed. "Bet you loved that."

I grinned and scooped up a forkful of fettuccini. "If only I'd gotten video of it on my phone. Anyway, my point is that if someone wants to come on the property after dark, Peter has to blow a whistle and kennel the dogs."

"Why did the intruder steal a photograph of you? That's creepy."

I shrugged, bothered by it, too.

As we ate dessert, Riley picked up a slim leather bag and handed it to me. "This is from my dad. He thought you'd like your stuff now, instead of waiting until Monday."

I opened it and pulled out an expensive tablet. There was also cash in an envelope and the items from my grandmother, which included a credit card. I looked at my passport's outdated photo. "It's so weird how she always insists I have a current passport. Not like I ever travel outside the US."

A slight frown touched his lips. "It must've sucked growing up under so much control."

"Yeah, but she does care about me. In her own way, at least." I didn't say the rest, of how I'd longed for her approval. A brief mental image came to mind: the two of us reading a book together when I was little. Her simple praise for how I could sound out big words, which made me determined to try even harder.

Riley looked doubtful. "Sure. She cared about you so much she dumped you at that boot camp boarding school."

I wondered why I felt the need to defend her when I had my own list of criticisms two pages long. "Some of that's my fault, I guess. I knew Grandmother would flip if she found out I was sneaking off the estate. Especially because of my dad."

"What do you mean?"

"He started drinking when he was in high school. He was a senior the first time she sent him to rehab." I felt a little surprised to be confessing this to Riley. "Guess she tried to make up for his problems by smothering me."

"But you weren't drinking, were you?"

"No. I was super careful not to do anything illegal." Wanting to change the topic, and wishing I hadn't told about my father, I turned on the tablet. "This is great."

"My dad got me one, too. He thinks we'll need them for the competition. I'll tell him you like it."

"What I really want is my mother's last name. Why won't he tell me?"

Riley didn't answer right away. "Know something, Avery? He's not much of a gambler, but he's willing to gamble on you."

"He's using me."

Riley pulled back and stared at me for a few angry seconds. He looked away and I studied his profile, which included a tense jaw.

I said, "I'm just being honest."

When he turned back, his eyebrows were drawn together, making a slight crease between them. It gave him a stormy look more intriguing than intimidating. "If you had your mother's last name, you'd want to go looking for her. But trust me, Avery. I've played enough sports to figure out that your head can't be in two places at once."

I stared at him in a way that showed I was annoyed.

He handed me a manila envelope. "How about a peace offering?"

"What's this?"

"Something from me. It's not the real thing, since I snuck the originals from the file and copied them. Just don't let my dad know."

Surprised at this contrast to his earlier loyalty, I took the envelope and slid out a single sheet of paper. It was color copies of four photographs, and I stared at them, hardly able to believe what I saw. "This is my mother?"

"It is."

A jumble of emotions fluttered inside me as I finally got to see what she looked like. I studied her and mouthed the words, "She's beautiful."

Riley must have read my lips. "And you look like her."

I examined every detail. The young woman in the middle picture was a few years older than me. I guessed that it was Marija when she first came to the US. She looked into the camera with confidence, her smile mysterious as Mona Lisa's. She had large eyes, and her dark hair was parted in the center and long enough to brush her shoulders. It was the kind of glossy hair that would swing when she moved.

Two other photos showed her standing in different poses. In the background were red roses; I felt sure the garden was on our estate. She wore black slacks and a white blouse with three-quarter-length sleeves—probably her uniform as a nanny. We had similar builds, too. In very many ways we looked alike, with our almond-shaped eyes and the same brown hair that caught bronze glints. The curve of my top lip was like hers, too, as was the straight line of my nose. Her skin was ivory, her lips a deep rose color; all of that mirrored in me. Her genetic makeup had managed to dominate my VanDemere DNA.

The fourth picture was the least posed and in some ways the most likable. It was taken in a child's room, the details in the background blurred and the lighting subdued. Marija smiled at a blond-haired toddler on her lap. The little boy laughed and reached up to pat her face. There was deep kindness in her gaze. Love, even.

I squeezed my own eyes shut for a few seconds. Riley's fingers touched my hand. I slowly looked up at him as a tear slid free. I brushed it off. Maybe I'd judged him unfairly for being too supportive of his father, since he took a risk by giving me these.

"Thank you," I said in a throaty voice.

"I didn't think you should have to wait to see them."

"Want to know something ugly about me?" I pointed to the nursery photo. "I'm jealous of that little boy."

"Warren."

"Yes. I wish it were me in the picture. That it was me she loved."

We were quiet for a while until Riley took out his wallet. "That's only natural. Kids need a mother they can trust."

I detected an unhappy note in his voice, and his face showed an ache that he tried to hide. I respected his privacy and started telling him about the letter from Marija and how she longed to meet me. He was a good listener. I slid the paper back inside the envelope as Riley accepted the tab from the waiter.

Seeing the pictures, I felt even more determined to win the competition. "Riley, if I'm going to beat out my other relatives, I need some information."

"What kind?"

"Stuff from Grandmother's library. Want to help me break into her office?"

He took several long seconds to think this over. "Okay."

We drove back to the estate and I led him to the second floor. "We have to stop here first."

I opened a door and peeked inside. It didn't matter that Grandmother's secretary was gone, old habits made me cautious. "Come on."

"Where are we?"

"Henry's office. But he's not here."

"Right. He's with your grandmother."

I walked to an antique display case and dumped out the key hidden inside an oriental vase. "Henry doesn't know I saw him put this in here, and until now I never needed it."

We went upstairs and headed down the hall until reaching the large carved cherrywood doors. I paused for a couple of seconds and looked at the key. "If she finds out I sneaked into her office, she won't be happy."

"Probably not, but she's the one who set the rules. According to her, rule bending will happen."

We unlocked the door and Riley grabbed the handle. I took a deep breath, as if preparing to jump off a diving board. "This is kind of like entering the dragon's lair, you know."

He chuckled. "Well, at least the dragon is away."

We went inside and he locked the door behind us. There was a little bit of light from two lamps on timer switches that came on in the evening. He said, "Wow, your grandma's office is huge."

"Along with her suite, it takes up almost the whole third floor."

"Where do we start?"

I walked across the thick carpet that swallowed my footsteps. Behind her large desk, an antique bookshelf held very old volumes and bound manuscripts.

"Here, I think. This is where she keeps most of her research. For the last four or five years, she's been writing our family history. She's planning to publish it in a fancy leather book. And nearly every one of these old journals is from an ancestor. It's where she gets the stories."

Riley grinned. "Which means she's probably going to use some of this information in the challenges."

"Exactly. Heritage and inheritance, just like the PowerPoint."

"But we'll never be able to read them all, or even photocopy them. Not by Monday, anyway."

"We don't need to." I reached up to the corner of the top shelf and brought down a thin notebook that had a maroon leather cover. Flipping it open, I pointed at the neat rows of my grandmother's writing.

"See? She listed the names of most of the journal writers, when they lived, and a few sentences about them. And she put a star by the most important ones. Look at this column."

"'Significant historical accomplishments,'" he read.

I closed the cover. "I can't tell you how many times I watched her get this down to figure out what journal story she wanted to read to me during brunch."

He smiled. "So it's the master list."

Pointing to the photocopier, I said, "Let's get going."

"I have a better idea." He put the binder on the desk and opened it. Taking his cell phone from his pocket, he snapped a picture of the first page and then looked at it. "A digital copy will be more useful."

"Can you get a clear enough picture with your phone?"

"I bought it for the high quality of the camera."

I got my camera out of my purse. "Then while you do that, I'm going to get pictures of other stuff that might help."

For the next half hour we worked without saying much. I took snapshots of all the framed family trees on the wall and anything Grandmother cherished. That included heirlooms in seven display cases; they ranged from tattered pioneer dolls to porcelain figurines. She'd shown me her collections so many times.

"Look at this Noah's Ark," Grandmother once said, pointing to a *very old carved wooden toy in the third display case. "When my great-great-grandfather Gregory Farlay was a little boy, this was the only toy he was allowed to play with on the Sabbath. His parents were very strict Methodists."*

I raised my camera. *Click.*

A memory surfaced of Grandmother showing me a framed sampler. *"See this cross-stitch, Avery? Genoa Stuart's family lived in Ohio during the Civil War. As a girl, she put in each one of these stitches.*

Both her brothers fought for the Union and died at the Battle of Chicka-
mauga. It's very valuable."

To me it looked brown, faded, and not pretty at all, especially
with odd leaves at the bottom circling a Bible verse in tiny letters.
I studied the sampler with critical eyes and remembered it was
one of my grandmother's favorite heirlooms. I clicked the camera
and moved on. The painting of a Yankee clipper. *Click.* An antique
sword from the French and Indian War. *Click.* Framed pedigree
charts, an original teddy bear from the Roosevelt collection, wedding slippers worn by a long-dead ancestor. *Click, click, click.*

I worked my way around the room and came to a large painting of George Washington and his horse. Reaching behind the
edge of the mahogany frame, I pushed a lever and stepped back.
An entire portion of the wall slowly opened on hydraulic mounts
to reveal a safe nearly as big as me. On the other side of its thick
door were Grandmother's most valuable items, including important family documents. Somewhere in there was information
about me, including my birth certificate, which would have my
mother's last name. There might even be other personal information on Marija to help me find her.

I studied the electronic touch pad and guessed at several
combinations of dates. The door stayed locked. Finally I stepped
back and gave the wall a slight push; the hydraulics did the rest. I
heard the latch click.

After taking a few more pictures, I stuck the camera in my
purse. Riley put the notebook back on the shelf and started to
say something but stopped; he turned to glance at the door.
There was the sound of a key in the lock and the handle moved.
Grabbing his arm, I pulled him after me. We hurried around a

bookshelf to the far end of the room. The large west-facing window got the heaviest sun in the afternoon and was covered by thick draperies of midnight blue. As I had a couple of times when I was a little girl, I slid behind them. Riley stood close to me.

The door opened and we heard muffled steps. There was a rustling noise and Riley peeked around the drapery. I gave him a warning tug but he ignored it.

A few seconds later the door slammed and he pulled me back into the room. "Guess who that was?"

"Who?"

"Your uncle Marshall." He pointed to the now-empty top corner of the shelf. "Looks like you aren't the only one who knew about that notebook."

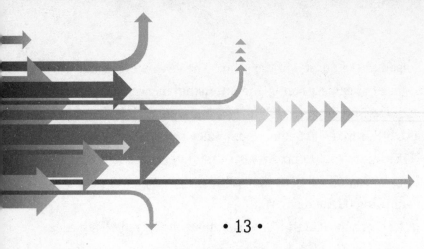

13

READY OR NOT

Riley and Mr. Tate showed up at eight thirty Monday morning, just as I was finishing one of Connie's cranberry muffins. We headed to the first-floor library.

Riley seemed alert and ready for the day; probably a morning person—the total opposite of me. He also looked handsome in jeans and a navy cotton shirt with sunglasses sticking out of the pocket. His blond hair fell attractively messed, his chin clean shaven. I caught a whiff of that same spicy linen scent I first noticed in the darkroom. He came over to me, thumbs shoved in his pockets. There was something playful in his posture that I couldn't help but like. "Ready for all this?"

I smiled up at him. "Hope so."

Mr. Tate studied us with one of those concerned-parent expressions. I wondered if he was rethinking his agreement to let Riley be my chaperone. He opened his briefcase. "Avery, here are the papers for you to sign."

He handed me the contract, which I skimmed. I took the pen he offered, hoping this wasn't a mistake. "If I make it through the next competition without getting eliminated, I want the first letter my mother wrote me."

He didn't hesitate. "That's fine."

I signed everything in triplicate and ran my copy upstairs. As I came back, I heard Thisby on her phone. "No, I'm not grounded. I just have to do a stupid family thing. . . . I'll text you."

Chase was talking to his dad, while Daisy's back was to them, her earbuds in.

Mr. Benjamin and Ms. Franklin ushered us into the formal dining room. We sat around the table—the same group as in the law firm's conference room, except for Jordan. And this time Warren's wife, Stasia, sat beside him the way Riley sat next to me. Stasia's red hair fell in a smooth veil, and she wore expert makeup that made her skin flawless. She looked around the room and her gaze turned on me; our eyes held. I didn't smile or nod; neither did she. It seemed that my new sister-in-law fit right in with the rest of the VanDemeres.

Mr. Benjamin walked over to the end of the table, a remote in his hand. "Welcome everyone. To start, there's a message for you."

He pressed a button and Grandmother's voice came out of the house speakers. "Good morning, family. You are now at the beginning of the second challenge, and after the first elimination, that leaves seven of you. Before we begin, I want to explain something. There are two reasons for this competition. The first you already know from the meeting. The second one I'll tell you now.

"Have any of you ever asked why I've been so persistent in trying to teach you about your heritage? It's because there are qualities many of your ancestors had that are far more important than money."

She paused and no one said anything, though Thisby rolled her eyes and Chase made a face. I thought about the camera hidden at the law office and looked around. Was there another one here?

Grandmother said, "For this reason I have based each challenge on a different character trait that I wish to instill in you."

Mr. Benjamin used the remote to pause, while Ms. Franklin handed a paper to each of us. He pressed the button again, and I silently read along as Grandmother's voice went down each item on the list.

CHARACTER TRAITS
1. Intellect
2. Fortitude
3. Resourcefulness
4. Unity
5. Commitment
6. Courage
7. Integrity

Grandmother's voice sounded a little theatrical. "I have a favorite quote from Abraham Lincoln: 'Character is like a tree and reputation like a shadow. The shadow is what we think of it; the tree is the real thing.' Much the same as with the early heirs of Otis VanDemere, your trees are truly weak. You may have been given strong roots, but you've been overwatered with too much money and a sense of entitlement."

Uncle Marshall leaned forward, fists on the table. It looked like he wanted to crumple up the paper.

"In an effort to help you overcome these weaknesses, I'm giving you an opportunity to show who can build a stronger character. However, I do have concerns. The results of the first challenge, based on the trait of *intellect*, were dreadful. I was shocked at how poorly each of you did. Jordan, at least, had some excuse as he's the youngest. But the rest of you? Every question was based on a historical story I told at family gatherings at least once. Let's hope you can do better on the next challenge. Now, turn your papers over."

We did. There was a black-and-white photo of a man with blond hair parted in the middle and combed in a wave on either side. He had a mustache and pale eyebrows. Beneath was written: *Otis Lawrence VanDemere–1889*

"Oh yeah, him," I whispered to Riley.

He started to say something but Grandmother's voice went on. "This is where your financial heritage began. Otis VanDemere helped create everything you have today. He also possessed many of the character traits on my list, though I would say his greatest strength was fortitude. He worked for eight long years in the diamond mines of South America. Perhaps really learning about him, and what he went through, will help you gain some of his determination and perseverance—traits you will need to be successful in life.

"Number two on your list, *fortitude,* is the next challenge. It begins immediately. Grab what you brought and head out to the vehicles waiting to drive you to the airport."

There was some confused discussion. Warren whispered to

his wife, and Daisy tried to get her father's attention, but he was busy talking to Chase. Riley leaned over to me and said, "Here we go."

Grandmother's voice sliced across the noise. "Just so you know, you're traveling to Venezuela."

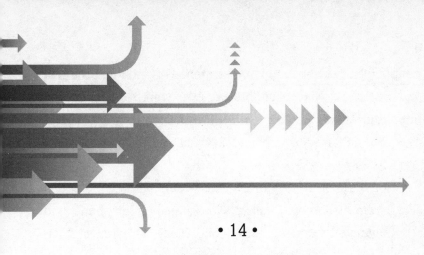

14

AN AMAZING TRIP

The flight in the VanDemere private jet lasted nearly eight hours, and during the first half, Riley and I did a lot of reading. On our way to the Santa Rosa Airport, he sent a text to the research team his father set up. Before we took off, they e-mailed a bunch of attachments that I opened with my tablet. A couple of the articles were about Otis VanDemere, but the rest covered diamond mining in South America.

We sat in the back, away from my relatives, and read everything. I turned to Riley. "Want to bet we're going to mine for diamonds?"

Near the end of the trip we flew over dense jungles. Most of the time I stared out the window as Riley looked over my shoulder and made comments. Far below we saw miles of emerald green split apart by rushing rivers, all unbelievably exotic.

Most of my family members didn't even care about the view. Warren and Stasia had their heads together, whispering.

A couple of times she stood and stretched, glancing at the rest of us; the action was casual, but her eyes weren't. Beneath the pretty exterior was a sharper edge. Stasia seemed to be analyzing us, but most especially me. I wasn't sure what to make of her.

As for the rest of the family, Uncle Marshall never stopped reading from his laptop; Chase played games on his phone, and Uncle Logan softly snored. Thisby and Daisy sat by each other, chatting.

I turned back to the window. "Look how high that waterfall is. It's amazing!"

I glanced at Riley and saw he was looking at me, not the waterfall. He was also smiling.

"So? I don't get out much, if you haven't heard." I turned back to the window.

He chuckled and leaned near; his breath brushed my cheek. "I think it's great."

The sun began to set, light glistening like gold dust on the water. It didn't take long for night to settle in, and soon the plane began to land. It got a little scary, and Uncle Logan woke up with a funny snort. The rough runway was a narrow strip between dense trees, and it didn't look nearly long enough. After a couple of bumps, we came to a jerky stop.

When we stepped off the plane, the humidity was like getting hit with a hot, wet towel. Riley slid his pack to one shoulder. "Wow. It's a sauna here."

In seconds my clothes clung to me. We had to go through customs, the airport stuffy and nearly as uncomfortable as outside. It was a relief to finally climb in one of the air-conditioned cars that drove us to a hotel.

Santa Elena de Uairén, in La Gran Sabana, was a charming little town that looked centuries old. Ms. Franklin, who rode in our car, explained we were just outside Venezuela's Canaima National Park and near the Brazilian border. Also, there was a two-and-a-half-hour time difference from home, so it was nine o'clock.

After dinner at the elegant old-world hotel, Mr. Benjamin told us to meet in the conference room tomorrow morning at eight. Instead of going to our rooms, Riley and I went for a walk. It was still humid, but the heat was starting to ease up. We passed a row of closed shops and I glanced at the darkened windows. "It's so different. I love being someplace new."

"I've noticed. It's fun seeing the world through your eyes. Like you're an explorer from another planet."

I laughed. "The most exotic place I've been to is San Francisco with Grandmother. We go to the bookstores and museums. Then we have clam chowder in bread bowls on the pier."

"That's your most exciting adventure?"

"Unless you include escaping the estate."

His smile faded. "Wow, Avery. I mean, it's like you were raised in a box. If you win the competition, you can travel anywhere you want."

I thought about Croatia and Marija's descriptions in her letter. I hoped he was right. "Have you traveled much?"

"Let's see . . . Europe, Mexico, Venice, and Greece. And Hawaii several times."

"I can't imagine. That must be great."

"It was. Our family used to go lots of places." Riley paused, then added, "Until my parents got divorced." He said this last part like it was no big deal, but I sensed his unhappiness.

"Oh. I'm sorry. When did they split up?"

"Two years ago."

We heard music and wandered down a narrow street until reaching an outdoor restaurant. Couples danced beneath colored lights hung in a lopsided square. Riley smiled at me. "Want to dance?"

I nodded and he guided me to the edge. At first my steps were awkward because I hadn't done much dancing, but soon I was distracted by the feel of his hands on my waist, my fingers resting on his chest. The pulse of the music. I began to relax and enjoy the way we swayed together. Being in a place like this, and pressed so close to him, was intoxicating. Riley looked down into my eyes, his casual gaze changing to become more serious. Suddenly he stepped back, and his hands slid away from me.

"Let's get out of here."

I trailed after him, hurrying to match his stride and trying to figure out what was wrong. The friendly, talkative guy I'd been with had disappeared. Now he walked like he couldn't wait to get back to the hotel. Shadow and light edged the planes of his face and masked whatever he was thinking. Behind us the music faded, but the memory of his touch, and the feel of my fingers on his chest, still lingered. I wished he'd say something.

In the lit hallway of the hotel, so close together that our hands could touch but didn't, I glanced up at him. He didn't meet my gaze, just focused on finding my room. I unlocked my door and he said, "Tomorrow at eight, then."

He left and I sat on the bed. I kicked off my shoes, trying to make sense of what happened. For a few minutes we had danced and I slipped into an exotic dream that had nothing to do with why either of us was here. Maybe that's what he'd realized, too. When it came to the competition, Riley agreed to help me because—on an impulse—I'd asked him to. But to him, it was only about saving his dad's law firm. I needed to remember that.

The next morning everyone met in the conference room. Ms. Franklin had changed from her black suit into hiking clothes. "As you may have guessed, we'll be going to a diamond mine today. The drive takes about a half hour followed by a hike to the site. Mr. Benjamin will meet us there."

Riley came over and stood beside me, a half-eaten bagel in his hand. He smiled with his usual open expression, as if last night's awkwardness hadn't happened. "Ready for this?"

I met his gaze and tried not to notice how blue his eyes looked. "Definitely."

We headed for the cars, where a couple of local men joined Uncle Marshall. He must have paid them to work in the mine, and this worried me. If he and his kids had extra help, it might be harder for me to stay in the game.

On the drive there, Riley and I ended up in the same vehicle as Uncle Logan and Thisby. We sat in the back, behind her, and my uncle took the seat by the driver. After we'd been driving for a while, Thisby turned around and studied us. I noticed she'd put a lot of effort into her makeup and clothes. She was wearing gold nail polish.

She focused on Riley. "Whose idea was it for you to tag along?"

He gave her a light smile. "Mine. And Avery's."

"Cute."

She asked what university he was going to and about his major. Riley answered with ease, and I watched the two of them. A memory suddenly came to me from Grandmother's rendezvous party nearly two years ago. Across the grounds filled with mountain men and Native American dancers, I'd glimpsed Thisby. She wore a short, swishy skirt and cowboy boots and was busy flirting with a handsome blond boy. Had that been Riley? The memory was too pale for me to know for sure, but it still caused a twinge of uncertainty.

The car turned onto a rough dirt road. I wasn't sure how the driver could even see, since the vehicle ahead threw up huge plumes of dust. A few miles later we jerked to a stop and got out to join the others. Ms. Franklin passed around bottles of water. She also gave us bug repellent, and after we sprayed ourselves, we followed her along a foot trail that wound upward.

The dense brush made thick walls on either side of the path, and the overhead limbs formed a leafy ceiling. All the colors around us gleamed bright, the plants the most vivid shades of green I'd ever seen. I wondered what Peter would think and pulled out my camera to snap a few pictures.

Uncle Logan started wheezing as we climbed. We passed through swarms of gnats and tried to bat them away. Distracted, I tripped on a tree root, but Riley caught my arm.

"Still think it's fun?"

Since Thisby was already complaining, I smiled. "Hey, I'm in Venezuela. What's not to enjoy?" I took a gulp of water.

By the time we stepped out of the tunnel of greenery to an open area, everyone was drenched and breathing hard. Uncle Marshall's face glowed red, and Thisby's makeup ran and made her skin looked blotchy.

Ms. Franklin led us forward and I suddenly saw why there weren't any trees. Before us the earth dropped away into the most gigantic, gaping hole I'd ever seen.

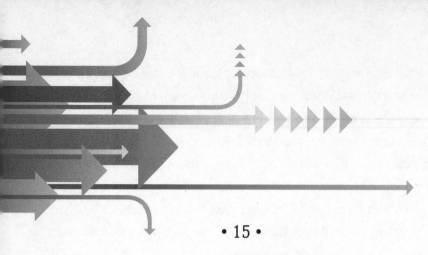

15

THE DEEP ABYSS

We'd been following Ms. Franklin around the vast circular chasm for nearly twenty minutes. I kept staring at the rim covered with dangling moss and ferns. A stream dropped off the edge and made a tiny waterfall that fell in a cascade of white mist. I studied the way it disappeared into the hole and felt my stomach drop.

Thisby ran her fingers through her short hair. "Do you think we're going down inside there?"

"Probably," her father answered.

"But I thought a diamond mine would be in a cave or something," Chase said.

"This is something." Daisy playfully slapped her brother on his arm as she passed. "Didn't you read about the volcanic pipes?"

He waved his hand at the chasm. "This is crazy!"

"For once," I whispered to Riley, "I actually agree with him."

Overhead, bright rays pierced through the clouds and made the heat intense. I wouldn't have thought we could be hotter than before, but as the sun hammered our heads, several people groaned. At least the trail had leveled out and we weren't climbing.

Farther ahead of us a group of men worked together; some of them hooked up ropes. As we got closer, I saw a small, natural clearing formed near the rim. Ropes were anchored to trees that grew a ways back from the opening. Mr. Benjamin, dressed in a khaki shirt and shorts, handed out more water bottles.

Uncle Marshall plopped onto a moss-covered log in a shady spot. I overheard him say to his kids, "I guessed it might be something like this. I just didn't think she'd actually send us to Diamante Abismo."

"What's that?" Chase asked.

"The original mine where Otis VanDemere made his greatest strike. This was formed thousands of years ago by a collapsed volcano." He looked at Ms. Franklin, who took a sip of her water. "I heard the government reclaimed this site years ago and closed it when they established the Canaima National Park."

"They did, mainly because during the rainy season it floods. But it's not dangerous this time of year. And Mrs. VanDemere came to a special arrangement with Venezuela's Industries and Mining Ministry to allow a one-day excursion for her family."

Stasia said to Warren, "Does that mean your grandmother bribed them?"

He pulled off his baseball cap and wiped his forehead. "Yes."

Two of the men brought over boxes, and Mr. Benjamin stood in front of us. "There's a lot of information to go over and time is limited, so listen without interrupting. First, this challenge has several rules, most of them for safety reasons. By now it's obvious that to pass this test, you must mine a diamond from Diamante

Abismo, or as it's formally known, El Abismo de Diamante. Out of the eight years Otis VanDemere spent in South America, six of them were here. It's your grandmother's wish that you come to understand what he went through in seeking his fortune."

Ms. Franklin held up a plastic folder. "In a few minutes you'll each be given a map of the mine. There are eight main volcanic pipes or mine caverns. Once your pipe is assigned, that's where you need to go and mine until you find a diamond. Don't leave your pipe or wander off. Mr. Benjamin and I will not be down there but will try to contact you with one of these." She pulled a small walkie-talkie from her pocket. "However, there might be times when you're too deep inside to receive a transmission. That means if you want to contact us, you need to head back to the main cavern."

Mr. Benjamin checked his watch. "It's now nearly nine o'clock. Once we start, you'll have nine hours to work. You'll each be given the same supplies and relative amount of time. Also, as a special condition of this challenge, only the VanDemere heirs will be allowed to enter the caverns. This means that Riley, Stasia, and the two men Marshall hired must all wait here."

Stasia put her hands on her hips. "So I hiked all this way for nothing? Why didn't you tell us back at the hotel?"

She brushed away a trickle of sweat from her temple as Warren protested that she was a VanDemere by marriage and had far more rights to go with him than the others. Uncle Marshall got even more upset. He shouted in anger as Daisy turned to him. "Dad, I tried to tell you they wouldn't let us bring paid workers. Why don't you ever listen to me?"

Ms. Franklin spoke in a loud, clear voice. "You are free to leave the competition at any time."

My brother and uncle stopped talking. I turned to Riley, who looked as unhappy as me about this new rule. Suddenly the adventure of it deflated. The idea of going down into that deep cavern scared me. Plus after the threatening note, I knew it wouldn't be safe to be alone. Riley reached over and squeezed my fingers.

Ms. Franklin started taking out the pieces of folded parchment from the file. "It's important to go over some safety information. We've hired professionals who will show you how to rappel into the cavern. They'll handle your ropes and help guide you both down and back up again. Most important of all, you have to get out of the cavern and up here by six o'clock, before sunset. That's when the bats leave the cave."

Uncle Marshall stood up from the log. "Bats?"

Mr. Benjamin nodded. "This is one of the largest natural bat preserves in the world, but you don't need to worry about them. They're nocturnal and won't bother you, so long as you get out before sundown. However, just a warning—sometimes they fall. If you see one, do not touch it."

"Don't bats carry rabies?" Uncle Logan asked. "What kind of rotten mother would risk her kids and grandkids by sending us in there?"

Ms. Franklin handed out the papers. I opened mine and examined the details. It was a copy of an old hand-drawn map. Otis VanDemere must have made it, and Grandmother probably owned the original. There were eight pipes, each labeled with a precise handwritten number in a small box. The first one was closest to the main cavern, the eighth farthest away.

Mr. Benjamin opened a box and brought out coveralls made

of thin white fabric. "You'll be given one of these to wear. Make sure to zip it all the way closed and tighten the Velcro straps at your ankles and wrists." He held up a yellow spelunking helmet with an LED light on the front, then a work belt equipped with several tools, including a collapsible shovel and pick. There was a small backpack filled with water bottles, energy bars, and a first-aid kit. Last of all, he held up a breathing mask. "When you pass through the main cavern, wear one of these. Its carbon filter will last for several hours."

"Why?" Uncle Logan asked.

"The decomposing bat droppings release ammonia and methane. It might not be safe to breathe."

Thisby brushed a piece of dirt from her shorts. "Lovely."

Mr. Benjamin opened another box that had duplicate supplies. "Also, each of you will be able to choose five extra items to go in your sack."

"How do we know what pipe we'll be in?" Warren asked.

"The winner of the last challenge gets first choice, but the rest of you will draw numbers. This brings us to one more thing. Your grandmother decided that the heir who does best in each challenge will be given an additional reward. That means Avery gets to pick which pipe she mines. Also, she can choose one extra item to take down into the cavern."

Suddenly all eyes were on me and the variety of shocked expressions made me want to laugh.

Thisby blurted out what they were all thinking. "Avery got the highest score on the test?"

"She did."

"What'd you do, Avery, cheat?" Chase scoffed.

I wondered how someone could be that dense. "Sure. Before the test, I wrote all the answers on my arm."

"Einstein," Daisy said with a laugh. He shoved her; she shoved back.

Uncle Marshall put out a hand. "Stop it, you two." Then he studied me with a new and suspicious interest, and I realized that until now no one thought of me as serious competition. I wished Mr. Benjamin hadn't told them.

Ms. Franklin came over. "Avery, look at the map and choose the pipe you want to mine."

I scanned it for several seconds. "Number eight."

She removed that number and held the pouch out to my relatives. "You're down to eight hours, thirty-five minutes. If I were you, I'd start moving."

They crowded around to draw their numbers, then hurried to meet with the men who would help us rappel down. Mr. Benjamin walked up to me. "What extra item do you want to take into the cavern?"

"Does it have to be from your supplies, or can it be anything?"

"Anything."

"Such as?"

"Whatever you've got, so long as it's not a weapon."

"I can take something I brought?"

"Yes."

"Even if the others can't have one?"

He nodded.

I glanced around, thinking. "So I could take something from out here."

"Yes, Avery. Take a rock, if you want. A coconut. Just decide."

"Okay," I slowly said. "Then I pick Riley."

Mr. Benjamin wrinkled his brow in surprise. A couple of seconds later he grabbed another coverall set from the box and tossed it to Riley, who grinned. Warren was passing by, and he stopped to confront Mr. Benjamin. "But you just said . . ."

"I know, except Avery won the last challenge and this is her reward. If you bring in the biggest diamond, you get the next prize."

Stasia took hold of Warren's arm. "It's not fair! I'm a VanDemere and should be able to go with my husband."

"That's right," Warren said. "She has a stake in this, a lot more than the lawyer's kid."

Mr. Benjamin studied him with a tolerant expression. "Do you really want to take your bride down there? It's not a good place."

His last words wiped away my happiness at having Riley come with me. Stasia and Warren seemed startled by it, too. They hurried off.

I pulled on my white coveralls, which were suffocating in the heat, and buckled on the tool belt. Riley plopped a yellow helmet on my head and laughed. He was already wearing his. "Brilliant, Avery. How'd you think of asking for me as your extra item?"

"You were the one thing I most wanted to take. But I didn't think about how asking you is selfish. I mean, you're not a VanDemere. You don't need to risk your life."

"Seriously? I'd rather go with you than sit up here in the heat all day."

We listened to the instructor who explained about the ATC belay device and static rope we'd be using. The man had a strong Spanish accent. "It's simple. You don't need to do anything because we'll belay you down. It's climbing back up that will be hard."

He showed me how to use the two ascension devices and foot loops. "To come up, you must first clip these slide ascenders to your harness with the slings. The foot loops attach here. Once you're ready, stick your feet in these aiders. Slide the ascenders up one at a time, like this, and you'll rise up the rope."

"Got it."

He gave me a pair of fingerless gloves. "Don't lose these."

I put on my harness, similar to those I'd used on the rock-climbing wall at St. Frederick's. Riley was already wearing his.

"You've done this before?"

There was an excited glint in his eyes. "Lots. It's one of my favorite sports."

I couldn't help but be impressed.

Ready, with my harness attached to the ropes, I got on my hands and knees and inched over to the edge of the cavern. Looking down, my breath seemed to get stuck in my throat. It was such an incredibly long way to the bottom, where sunlight hit a sandy spot far below. All around that was darkness.

Warren was the first to go over the side. Thisby and Uncle Logan followed, and Mr. Benjamin filmed them with a small video recorder. The more I looked down, the more that deep well seemed to rush up at me in a dreadful, dizzying way. I sat back on my heels and gulped air. I could feel the blood draining from my face.

Riley knelt beside me. "Avery, what's wrong?"

I closed my eyes and hoped it would go away. His hand touched my arm. "Are you sick?"

I shook my head and opened my eyes. He was near, studying my face. "What is it?"

"Did I mention I have a fear of falling?"

He laughed. Then, when he saw I wasn't teasing, his playful manner faded. "You're really afraid of heights?"

"No. Being up high, like in a plane, is fine. It's the possibility of falling that scares me." I was panting a little and felt embarrassed by the breathy sound.

"I don't get it, Avery. You climbed down a three-story building. Without a harness."

"I know."

Riley just stared at me.

I pulled my hair back and twisted it behind my neck. "All right, so I did do that. But it wasn't easy. And I didn't say I'm not doing this drop, either. I just need a minute."

"You were this scared, but you still climbed down St. Frederick's?"

I blew out a slow breath. "It's all relative."

"Meaning?"

"My hatred of being locked up outweighed my fear of falling."

Thisby and Uncle Logan were already down and unhooking their harnesses. Warren, ahead of them, took off into the cavern. Daisy went over the edge, but Uncle Marshall seemed anxious. I watched as Chase helped him, and then he went over, too.

I pulled on the gloves. "Let's do this."

"Just so you know, with this harness on, it's a lot less dangerous than what you did at the school."

"Fear isn't always logical, is it?"

"Guess not."

The man anchoring my rope helped guide me over the edge, and my feet dangled in the air. I gripped the ledge with one of my gloved hands; the other squeezed the bright orange cord. I began to sink into the cavern.

My heart started running its own marathon, my breath coming fast. The man called to me, "Señorita, don't look down."

"That's what they say." My voice was so shallow I doubt he heard me.

Like spiders sliding along a thread, Riley and I rappelled into Diamante Abismo. Mossy tendrils hung over the edge as if eager to crawl inside the chasm. The small stream I'd noticed fell in a misty veil, and I felt its cool spray. Far below it hit the ground and trickled under a rock wall.

Below us, the others had landed. Chase was helping his dad get out of the harness.

"You're doing great!" Riley called to me.

He really did love this. We started going faster and whizzed past the rock walls. The hole above grew smaller, showing only a circular picture of clouds and blue sky. Mr. Benjamin peered over the rim, filming me with his small video recorder.

A minute later my feet hit the ground, which was littered with pebbly debris, and I experienced the same shaky euphoria as when I made it down the outside of St. Frederick's.

Riley unhooked his harness from the carabiner and came over to me, a wide grin on his handsome face. He was ready to say something when we were startled by a scream—the most high-pitched, terrified scream I had ever heard.

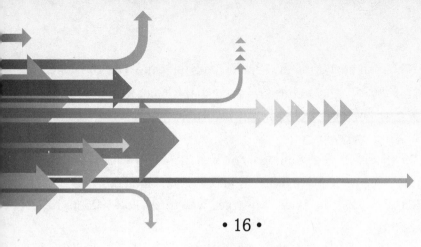

16

FORTITUDE

Thisby ran back out of the shadows and into the light. A scream continued to pour from her gaping mouth. Her face mask hung around her neck, flopping as she ran, her helmet off center. She hit the far wall, and for a couple of seconds, I thought she was literally going to start climbing up it. Without a rope.

Uncle Logan ran after her and grabbed her arms. She turned around and started sobbing, hysterical and clinging to him like a petrified child.

"I can't," she wailed. "Daddy, please don't make me go in there!"

Daisy, who had her mask ready to put on, stopped and turned around. "What's wrong?"

Uncle Logan gave Thisby a little shake. "Get control of yourself!"

"But did you see?" she sobbed. "Did you *see*!"

Daisy started walking over to them. "What is it, Thisby?"

Uncle Logan scowled at her. "Stay away from us."

Her face screwed up. "Fine! Be that way." She stalked off after her father and Chase, who had just passed through the large archway.

Riley and I unfolded the parchment as my uncle dragged Thisby off. Though he lowered his voice, the sound echoed, and we heard him say, "Are you going to throw away a fortune just because you're scared? If you leave without a diamond, you'll forfeit everything."

I showed Riley the map. "Let's study this out here in the sunlight, just to get our bearings."

We examined the drawings of the tunnels and where they branched from the main cavern. He traced the eighth pipe with his finger. "To get there, we have to go into the seventh tunnel. It'll be a far hike."

A high-pitched yelp echoed back to us from the dark cavern, and then voices shouted. Thisby began weeping again.

"She must really be afraid of the dark." Riley looked at me and gave a small, conspiratorial wink. "Ready to go?"

"Let's do it."

We pulled on our face masks and started walking. I glanced over my shoulder and heard Uncle Logan say to Thisby, "Stay here, then. I'll do what I can."

Her back against the shaft wall, she slid down and sat on the ground in a dejected heap. Her eyes met mine for just a second, and then she looked away.

Riley and I passed under the high stone arch and stepped across a threshold from daylight into darkness. We followed the curved bend where it looked as if an ancient river had once eroded a wide path, only a little light seeping in from the opening behind us. The cavern was huge, even wider than the drop hole we'd rappelled into, and the ground sloped up sharply. I heard a strange shushing sound like the wind blowing leaves.

"Look!" I pointed over our heads.

The ceiling trembled with small black bodies, as did the top rim of the cavern walls. Thousands of bats hung upside down, packed in next to each other, leathery wings wrapped tight. I'd never seen anything like it, and a shiver went through me. It was amazing and eerie all at the same time.

"Uh, Avery?" Riley said in a voice muffled by his mask as he tapped my arm.

I turned my head to look at him. "Yes?"

He pointed in front of us at the sloping hill. "Why is the ground moving?"

We clicked on our helmet lights and the twin beams revealed something that made us both take startled steps back. "Oh no. That's not . . ."

"Yeah," Riley said in an unnerved voice. "Bugs."

Suddenly I understood Thisby's screaming terror. The floor of the cavern was alive. It squirmed with fat cockroaches, wriggling centipedes, and beetles of every size. Our lights picked up the shine of brown, black, and reddish carapaces and the waving of long antennae. The creatures swarmed over each other in a rippling undulation that made me feel ill. This was what caused the rustling sound: the movement of gazillions of bug bodies.

"Why are they here?" I asked in a choked voice.

"Bat droppings. Remember what Mr. Benjamin said? It's why we need the masks."

"The bugs are eating bat poop?"

"Yup."

"Gross!"

"It's a life cycle."

I shuddered. "I wonder if they were here when Otis VanDemere first came, clear back in the eighteen hundreds."

"Probably. Too bad your grandmother isn't with us to share the excitement."

I laughed; it sounded strange inside the mask. "All right, let's not put it off any longer."

I told myself I could do it. The writhing bug carpet was hideous and creepy, but it wasn't as frightening as going over the lip of the shaft. "This way?"

He nodded, the light on his helmet bouncing. "Let's hurry."

There was no way to avoid the insects. Some of them scuttled out of our path, but there were too many. They crunched beneath our soles and I grimaced.

"Thisby's been terrified of bugs ever since Chase put a grasshopper down her shirt."

"Well, I'm sure that if the modeling thing doesn't work out, she could star in one of those slasher movies. I've never heard anyone scream that loud."

Even with the face mask on, I still caught whiffs of the decomposing droppings from the mound that seemed to grow continually larger. Scrambling over the top became really difficult. "This is a nightmare," I said, wheezing beneath the mask.

Eventually we reached the top of the mound and made our way down the other side. Then, as if we'd come to a finish line at the end of a grisly race, the cavern narrowed, and we left the bats and bugs behind. We both struggled for breath and stopped a minute. I bent over, hands resting on my knees. "It's good we're finally past that."

"Yeah, but don't forget, we have to come back through."

I groaned and dug out the map. Riley grabbed my shoulder. "Hold still."

He started brushing my back, knocking off cockroaches. I cringed at the idea that they'd been crawling on me. Then I checked him, found a few—including one hiding under his collar—and knocked them off.

He took a flashlight from his utility belt, and we looked at the map, then started walking. No trail led the way, and we had to climb over rocks and around holes. In time we passed the entrances to other pipes and heard voices echoing. Maybe, despite each person having his or her own tunnel, some family members worked together. I felt so relieved to have Riley with me, I couldn't blame them. This was not a place I would ever want to be alone, and I wondered about my ancestor, Otis VanDemere. Grandmother said he had fortitude. Instead, maybe he was just a crazy hermit who liked caves.

The deeper we moved, the blacker it got. The place reminded me of the darkroom at St. Frederick's, and I knew without our flashlights, we wouldn't be able to see a thing. It also grew colder, especially now that we were away from the hill of bat droppings that generated warmth as it decomposed.

Riley adjusted his helmet. "Avery, can I ask why you chose the eighth tunnel, when you could have picked any? Especially since it's so far?"

"It's probably stupid, but I kind of followed my instincts. I figured the closer pipes might've been mined out."

"That makes sense."

"And it seemed there were clues. You know; eight heirs starting out in the competition, eight tunnels? Plus Grandmother kept saying how Otis worked eight years in the diamond mines. She used to say we should always investigate coincidences. So I thought, maybe the best diamonds are in the eighth pipe. I just didn't see it would take us this long to get there."

"If you find the biggest diamond, it'll be worth it."

Lifting his mask, he sniffed the air, then took it off and stuffed it in his knapsack. "We don't need these now."

Riley started to climb boulders that formed giant steps. He reached down and offered his hand. My fingers in his, we steadied each other. As we struggled through a grueling upward climb, I tried not to focus on how strong his hand felt, the way he touched my back, how close we were to each other.

The lights from our helmets flashed over the walls until I felt disoriented. I finally bent my head as much as I could so the beam pointed down at the rocks. With each step my utility belt and knapsack weighed more. We stopped to rest a minute and take a drink of water. When we looked up, the cavern ceiling was so high it disappeared into blackness; I had the strangest feeling that it was night. Both of us were out of breath by the time we reached the wide ledge that stuck out from the cliff wall. We stopped and studied the map again. I pointed. "It's that way."

"Yeah, but we'll have to go single file."

I followed Riley along the ledge that steadily rose. In places it narrowed, and we had to press our backs against the rough stone wall.

He kicked a couple of small rocks out of the way. "You know, it's kind of impressive Otis found this place. It's one thing to have a map, but it would be totally different climbing around here just exploring."

"He must've been good at it. He worked in those other mines and then stayed here for six more years. I can't imagine that."

"One day in this place is enough to last me a lifetime."

I laughed and the sound echoed through the cavern. We were quiet after that, shuffling along the ledge until Riley slowed. "Hear that?"

Straining to listen, a sloshing whisper reached my ears. He pointed his light down and far below we saw a narrow river. It was inky black and glided like a snake along the cliff.

"I think it's probably deep."

A shiver passed through me. "I must've been nuts to pick the far tunnel."

"Don't worry about it. We're here."

Riley moved to a narrow slit in the wall; he turned sideways to squeeze through. I followed him and it soon opened up. We went around a curve and climbed over jagged stones. The pipe wall was an odd bluish black and pockmarked with holes from old excavations. Farther down the tunnel, there was the movement of light and a chipping sound. We froze in our steps as Chase spun around. The light from his helmet was blinding, and I could only see his dark outline.

"What're you doing here?" he demanded.

I squinted and held up the map. "We're going to the eighth pipe."

"Get out."

Riley stepped forward. "Just passing through. Our tunnel leads off yours."

"That's unlucky for you."

Chase walked forward, holding his pick like a weapon. I'd seen that arrogant self-confidence many times; it made me furious.

"Look," I said, "Grandmother expects us to each mine a pipe. All we're trying to do is get to ours."

He stopped in front of us, the sneer on his face distorted by shadows. "Always her spoiled brat. Well this time you can't go running . . ."

Riley's hand shot out, and he jerked the pick from Chase's fist. He raised it high and Chase ducked with an angry shout. Riley didn't hit him; instead, he threw the pick back along the narrow pipe, where it clattered to the cave floor. Chase stood, swearing at Riley, who said, "You really want to waste time fighting?"

There was a flicker of uncertainty in my cousin's face as if realizing he was outmatched, especially considering how quickly Riley snatched away his pick. Flipping us off with both hands, Chase hurried away. "You're not getting past me!" he shouted over his shoulder.

I turned to Riley, but he only smiled and pointed to a low hole on the wall next to the ground. "We don't have to. This is our entrance."

"We're going in there?" My voice made an embarrassing squeak.

Riley crouched down and shone his flashlight inside. The next thing I knew, he disappeared headfirst. It was like the cave opening swallowed him. For a few seconds I panicked but then bit my lip; the last thing I wanted was to let Chase see how frightened I felt. Then I saw light flashing around inside the hole. Half a minute later, Riley stuck his head through. "Come on. You're not going to believe this."

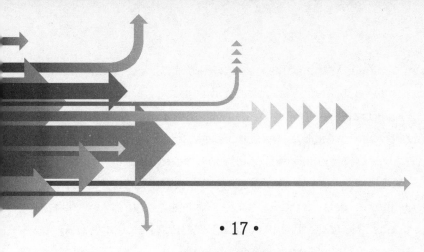

17

THE EIGHTH PIPE

"Avery," Riley called. "Come down feetfirst. It'll be easier."

I handed him our knapsacks and watched them disappear. Then I sat down and slid my hiking boots into the opening. I started to squirm through until my utility belt snagged on a rock; Riley's hands moved to my hips and guided me lower. A few seconds later I was all the way inside, and he helped me stand.

"Watch your step."

I avoided some sharp rocks, then looked up and gasped. "Wow!"

Delicate white stalactites twisted and spiraled down from the ceiling like melted candle wax. Water slid down some of them and dripped into milky puddles. I couldn't help but wonder what my ancestor thought the first time he found this place.

"Wow is right." Riley studied the ceiling, which was much lower in this tiny cavern. "This is a lot different. There's a limestone deposit here, and groundwater must be seeping through from overhead. I think this is really rare, since everything we've seen so far is formed from volcanic magma."

"Like that over there?" I pointed to a rough wall of bluish rock. It was marred by several mining holes from a long time ago but wasn't as pockmarked as those in Chase's pipe.

"Yes. I guess that's kimberlite, the rock we read about. It forms in the volcanic pipes, and all the heat and pressure makes diamonds." He glanced at his watch. "We better get started. Some of the others have almost an hour on us."

We took the collapsible shovels and picks from our belts and began working. The cave was humid, a wet and clammy cold different from any since we entered. And the leftover sweat from our hike added to the chill. I couldn't believe that just a while ago I sweltered in a muggy jungle.

In several places the wall was hard when I chipped away at it with my pick. Other spots were more like patches of packed mud. Riley dug out some of those with his shovel. He threw clumps on the ground, broke them apart, but found nothing. I didn't have any luck, either.

We'd been doing that for about a half hour when I felt something strange against my skin. Startled, I straightened up and held still. Maybe it was my imagination. I felt it again, a soft but quick movement on my side, and I panicked. Slapping my hand there, I touched a long lump. It moved, and then there was a sharp pinch.

I screamed, grabbed the zipper of my coveralls, and yanked it down. I jerked my arm out of the sleeve as Riley ran over. Without saying anything, he pulled hard on the white suit and peeled it off. I raised the hem of my shirt. The thing scurried around my back and I started screaming again.

I felt Riley grab it. He threw a fat centipede against the wall. I tore the coveralls off and yanked the ankle part over my boots until I was out of it. Then I whipped off my shirt and shook it out as his hands brushed my skin. "There's nothing, Avery! You're all right."

Heavy shudders passed through me, and I held my shirt to my chest, only partly aware that I was in just my bra. He knelt and checked my shorts and bare legs. Next he put his hands in one pocket and then grabbed something. Jerking his fist, he threw a large cockroach against the wall.

I let out a shocked squeal. "What was it doing in there?" My eyes widened in complete horror. "Not eggs!"

He shoved his hands in my pockets and turned them both inside out. A five-dollar bill fell to the ground along with a button.

"No eggs, Avery, see? And the bugs are gone. It's okay now." His hands stroked my upper arms.

Choking breaths caught in my throat. "They've been on me all this time!"

"But they're gone now."

We stood together—me trying to slow my panicked breathing, him too close and looking down at my face. His hand was still on my arm, just below the shoulder, and his thumb lightly brushed across my skin. "You okay?"

I squeezed the shirt I was holding, my thoughts getting tangled as a crazy mental image of us kissing darted through my head. I tried to think of something to say; nothing logical made it to my lips. He didn't say anything, either. Instead, he bent his head, though not to kiss me, only to look deeper into my eyes.

"Avery?"

I took a step back, and he let his fingers slide away from me. Was I as transparent to him as I felt? I glanced down at my side and saw red marks. "The centipede bit me."

Riley looked closer. "Doesn't seem like it broke the skin."

He guided me over to a boulder crusted with white limestone. "Sit down."

I sat, and so did he. After digging through his knapsack, Riley pulled out a small first-aid kit. He found a tube of antibacterial salve and uncapped it. I didn't move as he applied the ointment. After topping it with an adhesive bandage, he shook out my shirt and checked it for bugs. I took it back and quickly pulled it on.

He yanked off his own coveralls and shook them. "All clear."

Then he grabbed mine and held up the leg where the Velcro strap was loose. "Maybe this is how they got in."

"Thanks for helping me." I wanted to say more but felt a bit stuck.

Riley handed me a water bottle and I drank, deciding I had to get my mind back in the game and find a diamond. I stood, grabbed the pick, and started chipping again. An hour passed. Then another.

We took a break, sat next to each other on the boulder, and ate energy bars. It made us thirsty, but we were hesitant to drink the last of our water.

"Sorry about falling apart like that," I said.

He smiled and gave me a friendly bump with his shoulder. "Hey, your scream wasn't nearly as loud as Thisby's. And she only looked at the bugs."

"Yeah, but I still freaked."

"No big deal, especially since I was secretly freaking out with you. And thinking what idiots we were not to check our coveralls once we got past the bat poop."

Even if he was probably just being nice, I felt better. "What time is it?"

He glanced at his watch. "Almost two thirty."

I pushed off the boulder and stepped around a milky puddle to a new section. Wherever there was a bulge, I tapped it with the pick. The rock would sometimes crumble away like pieces of a stale chocolate bar. Other times the shards were sharp as glass. Every so often I dug out a stone, hopeful when it fell into my palm. But then I'd study it and see a small chunk of granite or weird and shiny bits of minerals.

For at least another hour we worked our way around the cave, moving in opposite directions. My arms began to ache but I kept at it. Was this what Grandmother meant by fortitude?

And then I heard Riley say, "Over here!"

I lowered my pick and hurried around several stalagmites. He was kneeling on the ground and when he stood, he opened his palm. There were muddy clumps in his hand, but as he rubbed them I saw a glint.

"Diamonds?"

Riley nodded, an excited look on his face. "But they're small. We need to find bigger ones if you're going to beat out the others."

"Still, this is a start."

"Hold out your hand." He dropped them into my palm. "Put them in your pocket."

"But you dug them."

"There'll be more."

I started working with him in the same spot, breaking up clumps of clay and chiseling the blue-black stone. Something clear and yellow reflected the light from my helmet. I tugged on a small diamond until it came out. "There's some here!"

He helped me get them out and we studied the little stones. I said, "They're yellow and really tiny. And not very pretty. How do we know they're diamonds?"

"Uncut stones aren't the same as you see in a jewelry store, and that article from the research team said diamonds come in different colors."

I put them in my pocket and we kept working. He found three more, all small. I told him to hang onto them.

Riley looked at his watch. "It's about four thirty. Think we should head back?"

I nodded. "At least we got a few. Together, they might all make a decent gem. But I bet they'll only let us turn in one."

"That's my guess, too. But maybe someone else didn't find any, and one of these will be enough to keep you in the game."

I got my camera out of the satchel. "This place is unreal."

Riley kept on working as I snapped several photos of the cave, including close-ups of the limestone sculptures. The flash seemed blindingly bright compared to the gloom we worked in. I took a couple of him using his pick on the wall. He held out his hand. "Let me get some of you."

I stood beside the largest stalagmite. He took a picture and I blinked against the glare of the flash. Riley kept clicking. "Good enough," I said, reaching for my camera.

He ignored me, taking more pictures but walking past me. He clicked again and again. "Look!"

I watched him take a picture of a spot low on the wall and saw a bright glint. "Is that a diamond?"

We knelt together and Riley shone his flashlight on the spot that had glowed for a fraction of a second. There it was again, a bright reflection. He rubbed it with his fingers, and a large diamond fell to the ground. I picked it up, holding it in the light. It was huge, dazzling and bluish-white.

I squealed and stared at it. Riley let out a wild hoot. "The thing's gigantic! You were right about the eighth pipe!"

We shouted and laughed; our voices bounced across the chamber. I threw my arms around him in a big hug, and he squeezed back.

"Hurry, Avery. Put it in your pocket."

Riley knelt down to study the hole. "There's another!"

He used his fingers to get a second diamond free. "This one is a lot smaller, but it's still better than the tiny stones."

"You hang on to that one," I said. "We better go."

He glanced at his watch and nodded. Hurrying over to our coveralls, we pulled them on. I cinched the Velcro straps extra tight around my ankles and wrists. Riley did the same.

He grabbed his satchel. "Leave the utility belts. If someone else wants to mine diamonds, they'll be glad to get them. For now, it weighs us down."

He shoved our knapsacks through the opening and crawled up. It was harder getting out than it had been sliding in, and I was grateful for his help.

"Chase has already gone." He glanced at his watch. "It's past five."

We left the seventh pipe through the narrow crevice and once again stood on the ledge. Far beneath us the black river rushed on its way to another underground chamber. I followed him along the downward slope and around the cavern wall. Ahead of us we heard a noise of clanking, like metal striking stone, and when Riley stopped I bumped into him. The sound started again and he said, "Chase, what are you doing?"

Chase hit the ledge between us with his shovel. It was a narrow part, and some of the rock had already crumbled away. He slammed it again and another big stone tumbled into the river with a loud plunk. If much more of it dropped away, we'd be trapped.

"Stop!" I shouted.

He straightened up and looked at me. "Sure. First give me the diamond you found."

Riley glared at him across the breach. "I'm warning you, get out of our way."

"Or what?" Chase slammed the shovel down in a loud strike and the ledge cracked.

Riley made a threatening move, but I grabbed his arm. "No. You try to jump across, he'll hit you and you'll fall."

I could feel his tense muscles beneath my fingers. With his other hand he threw the flashlight. One end struck the narrow brim of Chase's helmet but the other smacked him on the cheek. Chase yelped and took a step back as the flashlight hit the ledge and then plummeted over the side. The ricocheting beam of light was swallowed by the river.

Chase swung out with his shovel and the point grazed Riley's side. He staggered back. I grabbed him but we almost fell, barely able to brace ourselves against the cliff wall.

"Stop it, both of you!" I shouted. With the flashlight gone, the only light cutting through the gloom came from our helmets. Chase touched his cheek and swore.

"Riley," I said, "let me past right now."

"No. It's too dangerous."

Again Chase brought his shovel down. This time the crack gave way and another chunk dropped into the river. I held up my hand, fingers splayed. "If I give you my diamonds, will you stop doing that?"

He straightened and stared at me. In the murky shadows I could barely see the glint of his eyes beneath his helmet. "Sure."

Riley was fuming. "You can't trust him."

"He knows if he knocks us in the river, the diamonds go with us. Isn't that right?"

Chase nodded. "Looks like she's finally figured it out."

Riley still hesitated until I said, "I want to get out of here in one piece, okay?"

After a few seconds he let me inch my way around him. The light from Chase's helmet blinded me. I leaned to the side to see his face under the beam. It was dark with grime, though his eyes gloated. I'd spent enough time near him to know words were useless with someone so spiteful. He held out his hand.

I unzipped my coveralls, dug in the left pocket of my shorts, and pulled out the small diamonds. Reaching across the chasm, I opened my palm. "Here. Take them."

Chase leaned forward and shone a flashlight on them. Then he slapped my hand hard. They went flying and disappeared into the darkness.

"Why'd you do that?"

"I want the real diamond, brat! I heard you two shouting. I know you found a huge one."

Riley began to unzip his coveralls. "Fine, I'll give it to you."

Chase slammed his shovel against the shelf again. "I'm not stupid!" His voice echoed through the cavern. "I heard everything. Avery, I know it's in your pocket, not his."

He hit the ledge until more stone broke free. We shouted at him to stop. If any more fell, we definitely couldn't cross. I slid my fingers into the other pocket.

"Don't," Riley said.

Bringing out the large diamond, holding it tight for just a couple of seconds, I offered it to Chase. His eyes grew wide, and he reached out, but I closed my fingers and snatched it back. "First, toss the shovel."

He glared at me and lifted it, ready to slam another piece out of the ledge. I held my fist over the river. "Do that, and it's gone." He paused and I added, "Don't forget, Chase. I know what you're like. I'm not going to give you my diamond and then let you destroy the ledge to trap us here."

Thinking it over, he finally tossed the shovel out into the air and it splashed in the river. "Fine, but if you don't give it to me, I can still block you if you try to cross."

I didn't say anything else, just shoved my hand across the gap. I gave the diamond one last squeeze and let it drop into his palm.

"Whoa!" He grinned, his teeth white against his dirty face. "Who's the smart one now, huh, Avery?"

He grasped it and headed away from us along the ledge. We waited until he went around a bend. Riley inched past me. "You had no choice." I could hear the anger and disappointment in his voice. I felt it, too.

He focused the helmet light on the ledge. "We've still got the second diamond in my pocket. You're not out of the game yet."

He leaped across the break and teetered until he caught hold of a rock that jutted from the wall. Turning to face me, he held out his hand. I jumped and he grabbed my arm. When rock from the shelf crumbled away beneath my heels, he pulled me forward. I looked over my shoulder at the jagged cliff and the river far below.

"That was close," he said, sounding unnerved.

Moving as fast as we dared, we hurried along the downward slant of the shelf. The lower it got, the faster we went, especially when the river veered away and we weren't afraid of falling in. We reached the boulders that looked like giant, tumbled blocks and struggled to see without the beam from Riley's flashlight. Then the light on my helmet began to wink. If both the lights on our helmets died, we'd have no chance of getting out. The thought filled me with sick fear.

We continued climbing down the huge stones that slowed our pace, and I kept scanning everything, trying to memorize our surroundings if our lights gave out. When mine dimmed and then faded away, Riley said, "Hurry!"

Once we hit the ground we started running, leaping over rocks and cracks in the earth. I was vaguely aware of passing the different pipes, where all was quiet.

Riley tripped over a jutting piece of rock and sprawled, his hands taking a painful hit on the rough stone floor. He jumped up and we ran until, in the distance, we saw a very faint glow of light.

In front of it was the vast mound of bat droppings. I couldn't believe how eagerly we sprinted for it.

The sound of a crackling voice startled us; Mr. Benjamin on one of the walkie-talkies. "Are you there? Do you need help?"

"Masks!" Riley shouted at me, sliding to a halt.

We both panted hard. My throat was terribly dry, and my entire body nagged for water. Digging my mask out of the knapsack, I pulled it on, then slapped the helmet back in place. A few seconds later Riley led the way across the squirming mound of insects. I tried not to hear their clicking and skittering sounds. When they crunched beneath my shoes, I told myself not to look down.

Soon we emerged from the dark, gasping for breath beneath our masks. Riley grabbed the walkie-talkie. "We're back!"

We reached the open shaft filled with muted gray-blue light. The sky was beautiful, a rich pewter color full of fiery clouds. Shoving our helmets and masks in our packs, we leaped for the harnesses and buckled the straps. Two of the men were leaning over the rim, calling to us. Riley helped me clip on the slings that hooked the ascenders to my harness. I slipped the strap of the knapsack across my chest and pulled on the gloves.

"Like this." Riley showed me how to put my feet in the aider loops. "You alternate by pushing down with your feet. Do one first, then the other. And you've got to hold your own weight on the rope. Don't let go."

I tried it, immediately worried by how hard it was. *Just climb.* I set up a rhythm of pushing down with one foot as the slide ascender went up, and then the other. I inched skyward. Halfway up my arms trembled with exhaustion.

"You're doing great! Keep going," Riley called.

He reached out and grabbed my rope with one fist to help hold my weight. I didn't know how he could bear his own weight and some of mine, too. I wanted to tell him I was impressed but was breathing too hard to talk.

My hands ached from the strain. Looking down, I felt dizzy. I was high enough that if I dropped now, I'd be badly hurt.

The light softened and when I looked up, I saw that the clouds had faded to gray. Sweat dripped into my eyes, stinging. I blinked hard and closed them for a few seconds. I wasn't going to make it.

"Señorita," called a voice from far above. I looked up. A man's face peered over the edge. "Hold tight. We pull you up."

I squeezed the ascension devices with both hands, braced my feet in the loops, and suddenly rose through the air. I looked back at Riley, who worked his way up faster now that he didn't have to help me. Still, he was a lot farther down the shaft. A couple of minutes more and strong hands grabbed my wrists, pulling me up and over the edge. I lay on top of crushed ferns and gasped for breath. Mr. Benjamin and two other men moved away and worked on Riley's rope to pull him up. I felt a huge sense of relief.

Above my own jagged gasps, I heard a strange sound like a wild wind skittering dry leaves across sand. It grew to a shriek—the beating of a million wings.

The men dropped to the ground and covered their heads. Riley's rope still hung over the edge of the shaft.

As bats poured from the mouth of Diamante Abismo, I screamed his name.

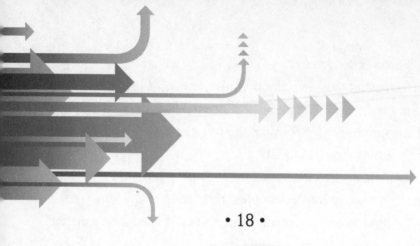

FLAWED

The dead volcano came to life and spewed a black cloud up to the sky. Except that instead of drifting off like ash, this one separated into twisting spirals as the bats took off in the evening sky. The air was so thick with them that they blocked the light, dark as midnight.

I curled into a protective ball and peeked between my arms, which were wrapped across my head. The flapping of leathery wings was like nothing I'd ever heard. Finally the last of them left the mouth of the abyss and joined the others overhead. They darted in crazy acrobatics through the evening sky.

I sat up, crawled to the edge of the rim, and looked over. No Riley. A few terrifying seconds passed as I peered straight down into the gloomy shadows. Finally I saw him clinging to the face of the cliff.

"Are you all right?" My voice held a sob.

He didn't answer right away, but then said, "Yes."

The men jumped to their feet and grabbed hold of his rope. They reeled him in with surprising speed until he was up over the edge and kneeling on the ground. I tried to go to him, but my harness stopped me. With trembling fingers I undid the buckles. I ran to Riley just as he slid out of his, and I threw my arms around him.

"I'm so sorry!" There was a weepy sound in my voice, but I felt too shaken to be embarrassed. I leaned back and looked up at him. "Are you hurt? Did they bite you?"

He shook his head. His face was covered with dirt, and sweat left tracks along his temples and jaw. There was an imprint across his forehead from where the helmet band sat—the only clean place on his skin. Truthfully, Riley Tate never looked more wonderful to me.

Mr. Benjamin came over. "You're sure you didn't get bitten? Because if you did, we need to get you to a hospital in Caracas for rabies shots."

"They never touched me. Just flew over my head. It was like being under a freight train, and I don't ever want to do that again." Riley laughed unsteadily.

"You're the bravest guy I know," I told him.

Mr. Benjamin frowned at us. "Or the stupidest! You were both told to be back here before six."

I folded my arms and studied him. "Have you been down inside there?"

"No."

"Then don't lecture us." I explained the horrors of the cave. "And on the way back . . ." I paused, not sure what to say about Chase.

Riley picked up the story. "Chase destroyed part of the ledge to stop us from leaving, and then the jerk demanded Avery's diamond."

Mr. Benjamin's stern expression slipped a little. "Did you give it to him?"

I nodded, angry all over again. "We didn't have a choice if we were going to get out of there. As it was, we almost didn't make it across. If Riley hadn't grabbed me, I would've fallen in the river and been swept underground."

"What about the diamond?" Riley asked. "Chase didn't mine it, and he shouldn't get credit for it."

Mr. Benjamin studied us in the deepening twilight. "There's nothing you can do since you've got no proof. It'll be his word against yours."

"That stinks!"

"Especially since without a diamond, you'll be eliminated."

We looked at each other. Riley unzipped his coveralls and pulled the last diamond from his pocket.

"All right, then." Mr. Benjamin slid it inside a small plastic bag with my name on it and tossed us each a bottle of water. "Let's go before it gets darker."

He guided us along the path, and I took one last look at the huge volcanic crater before we went into the jungle. It was barely light enough to see, but the downhill trek was easier in the cool air. After we walked for a while, I fell back a bit and motioned to Riley. In a low voice I said, "I've been thinking. Since we can't prove Chase stole our diamond, let's not say anything to the rest of the family."

"Why not? He shouldn't get away with it."

"You can't expect fairness out of this. No one will take my side against Chase."

"So you're going to keep quiet, like nothing happened?"

I ducked under a vine. "Yes, but only because it wouldn't be smart to do anything that might make them think I'm a threat. It's bad enough that Mr. Benjamin announced I won the first challenge."

"I guess you're right." Riley pushed aside a branch that had huge, waxy leaves. "They looked like they couldn't believe it. Your Uncle Logan was so surprised he about gave himself whiplash turning to stare at you."

I smiled. "That's why I'm thinking if the diamond we gave Mr. Benjamin is good enough to keep me in the competition, let's play it low-key."

"Agreed. But if you get eliminated, I'm going after Chase. My side still hurts from where he hit me with his shovel. Not to mention, he risked our lives."

Mr. Benjamin called over his shoulder, "Keep up."

A little while later we reached the dirt road and the SUV waiting for us. Uncle Logan and Thisby sat where they had before.

"It's about time," my uncle said as we climbed in. "You know how long we've been sitting here? The others are probably already back at the hotel."

Riley clicked his seat belt. "Must've been rough on you."

The car pulled onto the dirt road, and we drove through the dark, hitting bumps. After a while I noticed the way Thisby sat scrunched down. The self-confident girl with the glittery nail polish had disappeared, replaced by someone in shock. As the miles slipped past, I thought about her terrified scream. She might be one of my most stuck-up cousins, but I couldn't help feeling sorry for her. Had she sat at the bottom of the shaft all day, shuddering in fear of the squirming insects just around the bend?

Finally I leaned forward on the side nearest the window and said quietly, "Thisby?"

I wondered if she was dozing until she finally answered. "What, Avery?"

"You made a smart choice. It was really bad in there." She didn't say anything, and I added, "A couple of bugs got inside my coveralls. A cockroach. And a centipede that bit me. I freaked out."

Thisby stirred a little, and it looked like she shivered. "I've always been afraid of bugs. Spiders. Stuff like that."

"Yeah. I feel the same way about being up high. I was so scared to rappel down into the crater. I didn't think I could do it."

"But you did do it." She sounded even more miserable.

I watched the headlights bounce off shadowy trees and bushes. Then I heard Thisby's whisper as she spoke against the window. "Thanks, Avery."

Once we got back to the hotel, I glanced at the bottom of my hiking shoes and shuddered. The tread was full of goo and squished bug parts. No way was I going to dig that disgusting mush out of the soles. I threw them away. I also tossed the filthy shorts. With Grandmother's credit card, I could afford a few new things. Maybe when the stores opened, I'd get to go shopping.

I spent a long time in the shower and shampooed my hair three times to get rid of the grime. I let the water pour over my head and face until I was waterlogged. By the time I did my makeup, I looked like a much different girl than the one who climbed out of the crater.

There was a knock at the door; I slid my feet into flip-flops and opened it. Riley stood there dressed in a blue-and-gray plaid shirt and dark denim shorts. His hair was still damp and there was a scraped spot on his jaw that must have happened when he fell. He looked me over, a smile on his lips. "Nice."

Downstairs, the family gathered at a huge buffet. Chase stood in line with Warren and Stasia; they were whispering. Their socializing seemed strange, since my brother had never interacted much with his younger cousins. I wondered if they were agreeing to work together. But then Stasia shook her head, and the two of them moved away from Chase.

Riley and I filled our plates and sat next to each other, not saying much. Finally I turned to him. "I just want you to know I couldn't have done that without you. Not any of it. If I had to go down those ropes by myself, I would've quit. Just making it to the eighth pipe and having the nerve to climb in that hole?" I shook my head.

"You're braver than you know."

"Anyway, thanks for everything." It sounded lame. I wanted to say more but sitting this close to him, my thoughts became jumbled.

He studied me with a solemn expression. "The one who should thank me is Ms. Brown. If it weren't for me, she'd have to be here."

Imagining Mr. Tate's associate rappelling down into the crater in a business suit struck me as really funny. Riley must've pictured the same thing because he laughed, too.

After everyone finished eating, Ms. Franklin asked us to join her in a room next door. We filed in and found Mr. Benjamin waiting for us. Nearby, seated at a table, was an elderly man. He was small and his shoulders hunched forward. Spread out in front of him, on top of dark green felt, were diamonds beside name tags. There were also several pieces of equipment, including a scale and an odd-looking microscope.

Ms. Franklin introduced him. "This is Alberto deLeone Juarez, an expert jeweler and diamond exporter from Caracas. He's been invited here to evaluate your finds."

"We've asked him to tell us about their value," Mr. Benjamin said. "Mr. Juarez?"

Riley nudged me and glanced up at a corner of the room where the wall and ceiling met. I saw a small black box mounted there and questioned him with my eyes, as if to say, *Another camera?*

He made a slight nod.

"There is much variety here," Mr. Juarez said in clear English. "Most of these diamonds are small or poor in quality, but that is to be expected. At the time your ancestor began to mine el Abismo de Diamante, it lay untouched. Originally, the indigenous people of this area called it el Diablo Volcán, or the Devil's Volcano. They considered it a cursed place."

I could see from several expressions that many of us agreed with this idea. He continued, "Within less than a decade, the best diamond veins had been tapped."

Using a pair of tweezers, he picked up a small gem. "For instance, let's look at this stone belonging to . . ." He leaned over and checked the name tag on the green felt. "Thisby Van-Demere."

I glanced at her, surprised she had a diamond to turn in. Mr.

Juarez bent over it. "This stone is of a fairly good size but has a number of fractures. In the cutting process, a master jeweler first finds the point cut that lets him follow the natural shape of the raw crystal. However, this diamond simply has too many flaws to create a valuable faceted gem. So despite the size, it's nearly worthless."

He pointed to the two largest. "These are the biggest and best diamonds. In fact, one has almost no flaws. The other, however, is by far the most valuable." Picking up both a name tag and diamond, he said, "Chase VanDemere mined the winning diamond. It's blue-white and weighs nearly four carats."

Chase let out a triumphant shout while several others in the family murmured to one another.

Uncle Marshall pounded his son's shoulder. "Your cousins and sister could learn a few things from you!"

Daisy glared at both of them; so did Riley and I. Chase grinned like he'd won the state championship. In his mind, stealing my diamond was probably a bigger accomplishment than mining it. I wanted to slap him on his bruised cheek.

Ms. Franklin said, "Go on, Mr. Juarez."

I studied the row of diamonds on the table, especially the one by my name tag. It looked small compared to most of the others, and I wondered if I was in trouble. The jeweler reached into a fat carrying case and lifted out a black wand. He clicked a button and it lit up. Running it back and forth across the diamonds, he asked Ms. Franklin to turn off the lights.

We crowded in for a closer look. In the dark, the big diamond Chase stole from us shone with a vivid blue fluorescence. A couple of the others, including the stone I turned in, did the same but weren't as bright. Some gave off no reflected light. The other large diamond was a strange greenish yellow, much different from the others, and I heard some whispers. The lights came on again, and Mr. Juarez picked up the gem that glowed green.

"This four-carat stone, belonging to Logan VanDemere, is a perfect diamond. It has no flaws."

I glanced at my uncle, who stood to the side. He watched with a stance that seemed practiced but couldn't hide the nervous look in his eyes.

The old man opened a black plastic case and took out an electronic reader. "This is the most advanced diamond tester on the market and completely reliable."

He ran it across Uncle Logan's diamond, peered at the digital readout, and nodded. "And it proves what I already guessed after looking under the microscope. The reason this gemstone is so perfect is because it's man-made—what's called moissanite. Still an excellent diamond, to be sure, but it came from a laboratory. It's not possible that it was mined in Diamante Abismo."

"That's a lie," Uncle Logan said.

Ms. Franklin turned to him. "One of your executive responsibilities for VanDemere Enterprises is to oversee IDP, where your labs make industrial diamonds."

A red flush began to inch up his neck. "So what?"

"Just before the plane left Santa Rosa, you had your secretary make a delivery. You said it was documents you needed to work on during the flight. But we must also assume she brought you that four-carat moissanite."

Mr. Benjamin nodded at the elderly gentleman. "Thank you for your services, Mr. Juarez." Then he looked across our little group. "The single main condition of this challenge was that each of you must bring back a diamond mined from Diamante Abismo. Therefore, all of you will compete in the next challenge, except for Logan VanDemere."

He turned to my uncle. "You are the second heir to be eliminated. When we return to the States, you can contact Tate, Bingham, and Brown for your check."

Thisby lifted her hands. "No! This is my fault . . ."

Suddenly I understood. Her father had probably only been able to mine one diamond, and he gave it to Thisby. Then he turned in the man-made stone he'd brought as backup. We were all staring at Uncle Logan, but before anyone could say anything, he leaped through the air at Mr. Benjamin. They slammed into the small table, and Mr. Juarez scooted back with a startled cry.

Mr. Benjamin moved surprisingly fast, like one of those martial arts actors in a movie. He pinned my uncle to the floor. Thisby and Uncle Marshall hurried forward and shouted at him to stop. Mr. Benjamin stood and helped Uncle Logan to his feet, but my uncle lurched away as Ms. Franklin came forward. She quietly spoke to her counterpart, who looked upset. He nodded and stepped back.

She said, "Before something like this happens again, I should warn you that Mr. Benjamin is a fourth-degree black belt."

Uncle Marshall strode forward. There was more than anger in his eyes; there was relief that such a strong competitor was eliminated. He covered it by threatening Mr. Benjamin with legal action. But then Uncle Logan's bitter laugh interrupted him. He pointed to Warren and then me. "You two should be proud of your dad."

The room grew very quiet. Thisby took hold of her father's arm and gave a little tug. She tried to talk to him, but he didn't notice. Uncle Logan said, "Everybody thinks our youngest brother is just an alcoholic loser. But really, is he?" He shook his head, and the wave in his dark blond hair flopped a bit.

"It took a while, but Preston learned how to stop being one of our mother's puppets. Poor old Marshall and me? We're far worse losers than your father. We've gone on for years letting her pull our strings. She tells us what to do and how to live our lives. And even when we do what she wants, it's never good enough. Neither one of us had the nerve to tell her to go hang herself. Maybe now I can."

I studied this middle son, the golden boy with so much promise who never accomplished anything on his own. Thisby gave another tug on his arm, leading him away. His back was to us and I couldn't see his face, but she looked devastated.

Ms. Franklin broke into the silence. "You may each collect your diamond from Mr. Juarez. Then go get your things. We're heading back to the US tonight."

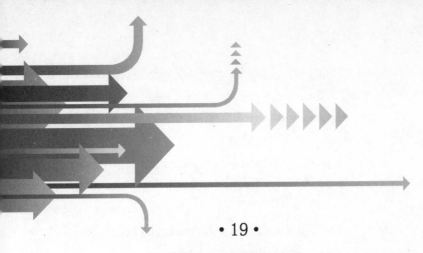

19

RILEY'S STORY

"What city is that?" Uncle Marshall was crabby. "I thought we were going back to California."

I stretched and squinted up at Riley, who was already awake and reading something on his tablet. Morning light from outside the window edged his lashes and the curve of his mouth. Even after a long night of trying to rest on the airplane, he looked great.

"Good morning," he said.

"What time is it?"

"Nearly seven." Riley dropped his voice to a whisper. "I overheard something, though it's not a surprise. Your Uncle Logan is staying in the game as Thisby's guardian, since she isn't eighteen yet."

"So now his whole focus will be helping her win, and he knows more about our family history than she does."

"Plus he's good at cheating."

Mr. Benjamin came over to us, holding his cell phone. "I'm

collecting everyone's numbers in case we need to contact you. You might want mine, too."

After we swapped numbers, Riley asked, "How long have you studied martial arts?"

He looked a little surprised by the question, and it seemed clear no one else bothered to make small talk. "About fifteen years."

"That's a long time. I always wanted to take classes. But with swimming, track, and school, I couldn't squeeze it in."

I pointed to his wedding ring. "You're married. Do you have kids?"

"Yes, a son who's almost two. Why are you both so chatty? I'm not going to give anything away."

His attitude irked me. "We're just being nice. There's not a lot of that going around in this group, if you haven't noticed."

He held back a smile. "You're right about that."

Ms. Franklin stepped to the front of the plane, and he went to join her. She motioned for our attention. "We need to go over a few things before we land in Boston."

"I thought we were going home," Chase complained. "I've got a softball game."

Uncle Marshall shushed him as Ms. Franklin opened a thin binder. "This third challenge is different from the last two. The first measured your actual knowledge, and the second was a physical test. This one will judge your investigative abilities."

"So we don't have to climb down inside a bat cave again?" Daisy asked.

There was an amused glint in Ms. Franklin's dark eyes. "No. If you remember from your list, the third character trait is *resourcefulness*. To start, here's another recorded message."

She pressed a remote, and our grandmother's voice filled the plane's cabin. "When it comes to your heritage, you have many ancestors to be proud of. Especially those who helped create our nation. The very birth of our country began with the *Mayflower*. In November 1620, the ship landed at Plymouth, and it's through my side of the family, the Harringtons, that we trace our lineage back to that important event."

Murmuring broke out, and I leaned over to Riley. "No surprise she'd test us on this."

My grandmother had always believed the crowning event of her pedigree was the *Mayflower*.

"It's rare for a person to be descended from one of the Pilgrims who helped establish the first settlement in the New World. However, through the Harrington line, we are descended from two separate settlers who were not related to each other. You should be very proud of this."

No one looked proud, though Uncle Marshall was already typing notes.

Grandmother's voice picked up a thread of emotion. "We have no idea how difficult it was for the passengers of the *Mayflower*. Nearly half of them died during the first winter. Yet the survivors used their *resourcefulness* to stay alive, and that's the character trait of your third challenge."

Ms. Franklin clicked the remote, and all was silent except for the low hum of the jet's engines. Mr. Benjamin handed out papers, and we looked over the information as he read aloud.

VanDemere Inheritance Challenge #3: *Resourcefulness*

1. You have until tomorrow morning to complete this next challenge. Unlike the last two, there will be no winner and no elimination if all requirements are met. This is a pass/fail test.

2. First, choose one of your two ancestors who came across on the *Mayflower* and research him or her.

3. Mr. Benjamin will contact you at 9:00 tomorrow morning with an address. Arrive there by 11:00 a.m. You must bring with you these five items:

   a. A printed pedigree chart that shows your line of heritage back to the ancestor you choose to research.

   b. Proof you have seen <u>four</u> pieces of physical evidence that confirm your ancestor was on the *Mayflower*. This will be most easily accomplished by taking a picture of yourself with each artifact. For this reason, any image or text from books or the Internet won't qualify. All submissions must be printed.

<u>Note</u>: Once you turn in your challenge items, you will be given a unique and special opportunity. Also, at that time, the last challenge winner will receive an additional reward.

I wondered what prize should have been mine and glared at Chase. He was busy ignoring me. Ms. Franklin said, "We'll be landing soon. Please put on your seat belts."

Daisy waved her hand in the air. "Hang on. This doesn't tell us the names of our *Mayflower* ancestors."

A small smile touched Ms. Franklin's lips. "No, it doesn't."

Riley and I locked eyes. We were lucky to have a copy of the notes in Grandmother's binder.

After the plane landed, Riley took a picture of the challenge info with his phone and sent it to both his dad and the research team. I sent Mr. Tate a text, too, and reminded him I wanted the first letter written by my mother.

When our shuttle stopped in downtown Boston, Mr. Benjamin said, "Everything you need to find in this challenge is within a fifty-mile radius. Good luck, and we'll see you tomorrow morning."

Riley and I started walking in the opposite direction from my relatives, and I gazed at the many shops and buildings. "Just look at this place! I could spend a month exploring."

I glanced up and saw him studying me with the same amused smile as when we were in Venezuela. It made me feel a little shy.

After another block we turned a corner crowded with people. When Riley's steps slowed, I followed his gaze and saw Thisby and Uncle Logan headed in our direction. They were talking and didn't notice us.

"Ugh! Why can't we get away from them?"

Riley reached out and took my hand. "This way."

A stoplight changed and we hurried to join a group of pedestrians at a crosswalk. It was hard to ignore the feel of my fingers in his; different than in the cave, when he helped me climb.

After a couple more blocks, he said, "Let's hope we don't run into any more of your family. Now, I think the first thing we need to do is find a quiet place and start researching."

We passed a really awesome-looking store and I stopped. "Hang on a minute." Riley came back as I dug out my wallet. I flipped it open, and with a playful smile I pointed to Grandmother's credit card. "The first thing we need to do is shop. And she's paying."

"You want to buy clothes now?"

"A half hour isn't going to make us lose. And I need shoes."

He looked down at my flip-flops. "What happened to your hiking boots?"

"Uh . . . well, they had bug guts squished in the bottom, so I threw them away."

He laughed and opened the shop door. I tried on shorts, jeans, a few cute shirts, and shoes. Riley bought a couple of items but refused to use my credit card. Finally he tapped his watch. "Thirty minutes."

I grabbed a pile of clothes and hurried to the counter. When I learned the shocking total, I just smiled and handed over the card. As I shoved them in my backpack, for the first time I really thought about what it would be like to win the competition—to have money for whatever I wanted.

I decided to wear my new shoes, and after we left the shop, I stopped to tie the laces. Riley's cell phone rang and he answered, but after just a couple of sentences, his face turned angry. "Sorry. Can't make it. No, Mom, I'm fine . . . What does it matter where I am?" He stared across the street, tense and preoccupied. "Whatever. Why don't you call Ronnie instead?"

I moved a few steps away to give him privacy, but his voice still carried, and his sharp tone surprised me. Through the many emotions that made up Riley Tate's personality, this was one I'd

168

never seen. "Well that's too bad, because I'm nineteen now, remember?"

He shoved the phone in his pocket and stormed away. I hurried to catch up with him. We were silent for a couple of blocks, and then I did something I'd never done before. I reached out and took his hand. Until now, Riley had been the one doing the reaching.

His steps slowed a little. "Sorry you had to hear that. I'm just so mad at her."

"Because your parents got divorced?"

He raised questioning eyebrows. "How'd you know?"

"In Venezuela. During our walk you mentioned it."

"Oh. I forgot."

We came to a tiny park with a fountain and paved path. I pointed to a bench. "Can we sit for a minute?"

He nodded. "We need to check e-mail and see if the research team sent anything."

We took off our backpacks and sat. I studied the way shade dappled the ground and made leaf-shaped patterns on my bare knees. "Why'd your parents get divorced? Was it complicated?"

"No. Simple, actually. My mother had an affair."

"That's rough."

Riley looked across the park as if hardly aware of his surroundings. "I know it's stupid to act this way. Kids' parents get divorced all the time, right? It's the American way. I mean, some of my friends have been through their parents' breakups two or three times and have layers of stepparents. They don't get why I'm upset. And you don't even live with your mom and dad. Why should I complain?"

"You can't compare what hurts. Maybe losing something great feels worse than never having it."

He thought this over. "It *was* great. When some of the guys at school used to complain about their families, I never did. Most of that was because of my dad. He's only had two things in his life, his law firm and his family. He never went golfing or fishing, unless it was with me. Not for an evening with the guys or a drink after work. If he had free time, he spent it with us. He planned these amazing trips and activities. It seemed his main goal was to do fun stuff as a family. And he really talked to us. He wanted to know everything going on in our lives. This'll sound weird, but I can tell him almost anything."

"That's awesome." It was hard for me to even imagine how that would be. "What about your mother?"

"She cared, too. At least, I thought she did." His voice took on a harsher edge. "That's the toughest part, feeling I never really knew her. I thought she was happy with my dad. Especially since he treated her like she was an angel who fell to earth."

Riley leaned forward and rested his forearms on his knees. He gazed down at the paved path, and I sensed the awkwardness he felt.

"I think your mother was really lucky. Too bad she didn't know it."

"Yeah." He turned his head to look up at me, and from that angle a small leaf shadow rested on his jaw like a trembling kiss. He'd never looked more handsome. "Do you remember seeing my sister, Ronnie? Sometimes she came to your grandmother's parties."

I nodded. "She's hard to forget. More beautiful than even Thisby."

"Thisby's beauty is debatable, but yes, Ronnie is a knockout. She looks a lot like our mother."

"You must, too."

He sat up and leaned back against the bench. "I don't know. Maybe. I'm blond like her. The thing is, my dad's just an average guy. Not bad looking, but not really handsome, either. And he lived his whole married life acting like a commoner who was lucky enough to win over the princess."

"Did she love your dad? In the beginning, at least?"

Riley shrugged. "You would've thought so, especially how she acted when he gave her gifts. And trust me; my mom got anything she ever asked for. On their twenty-fifth wedding anniversary, he gave her an emerald bracelet. Then a week later, she took off to Cancun with her personal trainer. How cliché is that?"

"Pretty bad."

"After she filed for divorce, my dad just kept on giving. Gave her our house and furniture. Her cars, half his savings, and anything else she wanted. He moved into a condo, and a week later I moved in with him. It was the beginning of my senior year, but I refused to stay at the house. I only went back a couple of times to get my things."

I reached over, my hands circling his upper arm. I could feel his physical strength beneath my fingers, but it was his vulnerability that drew me to him. "I'm sorry, Riley." I gave his arm a squeeze. "That's a totally dumb thing to say, but really I am."

He studied me with those deep blue eyes. "Guess that's why I'm trying hard to support my dad. I hated the way your uncle Marshall threatened him, because the last thing he needs is to have his law firm crash. Ever since your grandpa met him when he was a young man, he's worked to make the company successful."

"Doesn't he have other clients?"

"A few. But his partner, Mr. Bingham, takes care of those. During the last few years, VanDemere Enterprises has taken more and more of his time. And your uncle Marshall's threats are real. It makes me nervous to think what he'll do if he wins."

"That's why you're doing everything you can to make sure I succeed." My fingers slid away from his arm. "Why you were so determined I show up at the family meeting in the first place."

He was quiet and I looked down at my hands. Finally I said, "We should go over the stuff the Benjamin–Franklin team gave us and figure out what to do."

Riley surprised me by reaching up and brushing away a strand of hair from my eyes. "Thanks for being such a good listener, Avery."

My concern softened. "Anytime."

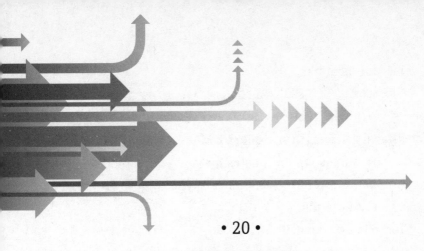

20

HEARTACHE

Riley and I spent more than an hour on our tablets, without success. Finally, he rubbed the back of his neck and stretched. "I hoped this would be easy."

"Me too."

We'd just finished cross-referencing the *Mayflower*'s passenger list the research team sent us against my grandmother's notes. No matches.

"I don't get it," he said. "If those two *Mayflower* ancestors of yours are Mrs. VanDemere's biggest bragging points, why aren't they here?"

I started to shrug, then glanced down at the names. "Uh . . . maybe she didn't need to write them in her notebook? The list lets her keep track of the ones she doesn't have memorized. But the *Mayflower* ancestors she knows all about, right?"

He let out a long-suffering moan. "Could you've thought of that before?"

I just stared at him.

"Okay, okay," he said, "though we've got to figure this out. The research team sent me a text a few minutes ago. They have a professional genealogist standing by. My dad already gave her the VanDemere names and birthdates for you, your father, and your grandmother. But until we tell her who your *Mayflower* ancestor is, she can't do anything."

"So, where do we go from here?"

Riley reached out and gently drummed his fingers on my temple. "Inside here."

I scoffed. "But I don't know who they are!"

"Not true. If the *Mayflower* ancestors were important to your grandmother, she must've talked about them. That's how you got the highest score on the test."

"I got a sixty-three, which means I missed a little less than half."

Riley pointed to the passenger list. "Let's try going over these names again. Something might jump out at you."

He started to scroll down the screen, and I soon got distracted by looking at him. After spending the night on a plane, there was now stubble on his jaw. I never really cared for that, even on guy actors, but on him it was golden, prickly-looking stuff that made my fingers long to touch it. As the sun rose higher, morning light rested on his handsome features and turned his eyes their purest shade of cold-water blue. And when he concentrated, one corner of his mouth pulled in a little. His lips looked so soft and tempting.

"Hmm, what do you think?" He turned his head to look at me.

I widened my eyes and tried for an expression of: *This*

whole research thing is riveting, and I'm not drooling over you even a little bit.

Riley scrolled down the list on his tablet. "What about this name: Moses Fletcher? He was from Canterbury."

I shook my head.

"Thomas Tinker?"

"Nope."

"John Crackstone?"

I snickered.

"Constance Hopkins? Solomon Prower?"

"No and no. This isn't working. My guess is that dessert never depended on answering questions about the *Mayflower* ancestors."

Riley set his tablet down and his hands reached for me. "I've got an idea. Come here."

He guided me to rest my head against his shoulder and slid his arm around my back. "Close your eyes and relax."

"Whatever you say."

I started to giggle, then felt embarrassed. I peeked through my lashes and saw he was smiling down at me.

"I'm serious, Avery."

"You don't look serious."

"Cooperate. Close your eyes. Relax. Now, think about brunch with your grandmother."

The smile left my lips. "Way to kill a good time."

"Focus on the *Mayflower*. What did she say about those ancestors?"

I closed my eyes. How could he smell so good after being stuck on a plane all night? His arm was in a relaxed half hug around me, his shoulder comfortable beneath the side of my face. For just a minute I stopped worrying about the competition and let my thoughts drift to a drowsy place.

Several minutes passed and he quietly said, "You're not sleeping, are you?"

"Children." Slowly opening my eyes, I sat up. "The stories were about a girl and boy. At least, I think that's right."

A hazy memory came to mind of sitting on the gold brocade chaise in Grandmother's library while she searched through a stack of very old books. For some reason I couldn't now remember, I'd felt a little teary but was trying not to show it. She took off her reading glasses to look at me. "Avery, you really must learn not to be so sensitive. Think about brave Mary facing her life in the New World. She had no idea what her future would be, but she couldn't wait to meet it."

The scene faded and I turned to Riley. "Also, the name Mary might be important."

"Great!" He pulled up the passenger list. "Here's Mary Allerton. She had a daughter named Mary. Is it one of them?"

I studied the list, too. "Uh-oh. Look, there's also Mary Brewster, Mary Chilton, and Mary Prower Martin."

"Five Marys? That's a lot." He scrolled to the next page. "Can you remember anything else?"

I started to shake my head, but then a little more of the story popped into my mind. "The girl jumped off the boat!"

"Into the sea?"

"No. As the rowboat from the *Mayflower* got near land, she was so excited that she jumped out and waded to shore. She was the first person to step on Plymouth Rock."

Riley smiled at me and started scanning the info the research team sent. "Got it! The boat story is right here. It says that according to legend, twelve-year-old Mary Chilton was the first female passenger to step ashore at Plymouth. Daughter of James and Susanna Chilton, she was one of eleven girls on board. Her parents died during the winter, and she became the ward of either Myles Standish or John Alden."

I grabbed my cell phone, called the research team, and gave them the name Mary Chilton. While we were talking, I e-mailed them copies of five pictures I took in Grandmother's office that showed family trees. After disconnecting I set the phone down. "They'll call as soon as the genealogist gets the line traced."

Riley again touched my temple with his fingers and smiled in a teasing way. "I told you it was all in there."

My cell phone hummed with a text from Mr. Tate. "Your dad says he sent me an e-mail. I hope it's the letter."

I grabbed my tablet and opened the message. Mr. Tate wrote:

Avery, congratulations on making it through the second challenge.

The attachment line showed:

Letter 1

I saved it and closed out my e-mail. I scanned the first page and saw it wasn't written in English.

"Oh no. Look at this." I showed Riley.

"It's in a foreign language?"

"Croatian, I guess. But how can I get it translated?"

"Scroll down."

I did, relieved there was a second page written in English. Riley busied himself with his own tablet to give me privacy as I started to read.

To my daughter,

It is with a heart broken I write these words to you. I wrote them first in the Croatian before trying in the English, as my thoughts are too scattered. I do not know if I will ever see you again. I am forced to leave you in America, but it is to save your life that I do this.

Only now can I see how foolish I am. I believed your father would come for me at the hospital, but instead, his mother came. She brought with her an agent from the Immigration Department of the US. This man said because I no longer work I have lost my work visa and very soon am deported. I begged Mrs. VanDemere to stop him and tried very much to tell her about the danger to a tiny baby.

Then the man explained that because you were born in America, the Croatian Department of Immigration may not let you enter the border when I am sent back. Even with my tears he would not tell me what would happen if they take you from me.

Mrs. VanDemere finally said she would offer help. If I leave you with her, she will let your father raise you and you will be safe.

I do not know what waits for me when I am sent back. There is no family left. My father was a soldier who died in the first uprising. My mother and sister, and my sister's husband, all killed when a bomb destroyed the building where we lived. I have no one except perhaps some cousins, if I can find them.

How can I take you with me, to a place where there was so much shooting and explosions when I left? And what if the government of Croatia will not let me bring you across the border? Will they leave you in a different country, in an orphanage there? Or send you back here? No one will answer my questions.

You are so tiny. So beautiful with your sweet face and dark hair. I will remember you always. If I leave you with your father, at least I know you will live. And yet two days ago, when I let them take you from my arms, it was the most anguish of my life.

There is one more thing I must write. Mrs. VanDemere also offered me money. She said it will help me move on. As if I can simply go and forget all this! Forget my sorrowful heart for a love that was a lie. Forget my child. I am afraid of returning to a destroyed place of poverty with no means to survive. But to take her money also seems a terrible thing, as if I am selling my daughter.

At first I refused. Now the man who is her lawyer says many things. He reminds me that I am going back to a dangerous place where there is no family left. He says I must take what she gives and start a new life. But what life can there be without my baby?

Right now I sit in the lawyer's office to write this letter. Soon the man from Immigration will be here and take me to the airport. I am being rejected by my new country, the place where I had so many dreams of an education and freedom from fear.

I will pray for you. I will tell myself you are happy and have a good life with your father. You will never know me. But I will never forget you, my baby girl. And my love for you will always be.

Your Mother

I looked up. The fountain sprayed water in a delicate arch and I watched the drops. It felt like they were falling on my face.

"Avery?" Riley murmured.

And then I was up and running across the park. Rage and misery pounded inside me. I didn't want to believe it. Almost couldn't, but I knew every bit of it was true. Images flashed through my mind: Grandmother not wanting to answer my questions. The secret dream I held on to of a mother who wanted me but died when I was born. My dad being absent from my life. Uncle Marshall looking down on me—the nanny's child—like I was nothing. My cousins' nasty words about my mother... *No one loves Avery.*

Knowing the truth made me want to scream. I reached a sidewalk and my feet slapped the concrete, beating out a rhythm of hateful anger. My heart pounded and it felt like a fist slugged the inside of my head. I raced around a corner and nearly ran into a truck as it pulled from an alley.

Hands grabbed me. Riley spoke to me but his voice only filtered through a haze. Looking up at his concerned face, it was as if the flood of my grief broke through a wall. I started crying. He held me. His arms were tight around me as I sobbed against his shirt.

An older woman stopped. "Is she all right?"

I felt his hesitant nod.

"Do you need help?" she asked.

"No, I've got her."

I heard her heels on the sidewalk as she left. Heard car engines and tires on the road, distant voices and Riley's winded breathing. He stroked my hair; we stood that way for a while. A few minutes later he guided me to a quieter area inside the alley. He used the hem of his shirt to dry my eyes.

"Will you tell me, Avery?"

I pulled in a gulp of air. "She took me from my mother! Forced her to give me up."

The story began to pour out, my breath shuddery from crying. Speaking the words made the misery of it more real. Yet beneath it ran shocked disbelief, as if I couldn't put the pieces together of what I'd once believed and the truth of what I now knew. My grandmother had done something monstrous, but I'd never seen her as a monster. Old-fashioned, strict, eccentric. Not cruel.

My voice fell silent as bits of random memories rioted inside my head. I remembered Grandmother's pleased smile as she reviewed my report cards. How in awe of her I felt, always eager for her attention. Going with her to a fancy luncheon, her pride in how I presented myself to the other ladies. The times she said, "Well done, Avery," and I'd felt happy.

Suddenly all of that was replaced with a new mental image: Grandmother with a heart of stone, standing in a hospital room and looking down on weeping Marija with not even a little pity.

Riley said, "I'm really sorry, Avery."

"Will you call your dad for me?"

Riley got out his cell phone and after his father answered, he explained I wanted to talk. He handed me the phone and I said, "Why did you let her do that to my mother?"

He was quiet for so long I wasn't sure he was even there until he cleared his throat. "What is it you think I could've done, Avery? Fight the government and your grandmother? Me, a nothing lawyer, who had no power?"

"You should have tried to do something!"

Riley shook his head, but I turned away.

Mr. Tate let out a troubled sigh. "Yes, but what exactly? For a long time now I've wondered what I could've done differently. Even now, I'm not sure. The Department of Immigration is a tough one to fight. If your grandfather was still alive, maybe it would've been possible to persuade him to step in. But he'd died three months earlier, and at that time I hadn't worked much with your grandmother. She wouldn't listen to anything I had to say."

"Did you even try?"

A few more seconds ticked by. "No. And just so you know, I regret it. There aren't very many things in my life I'm ashamed of. But sitting there and watching your mother sign those surrender papers is something I've never been able to forget. That's the reason I kept the letters she sent."

He sounded so sincere that a little of my anger began to seep away, though my heartache didn't. "My mother wanted me," I whispered, and felt the tears start again.

"Yes, she did. She wanted you very much."

"You should've given me her letters."

He paused for a few seconds. "I'm giving them to you now. And it's a risk, Avery. If Mrs. VanDemere finds out, I won't have to wait for your uncle to fire me."

I handed the phone back to Riley, who talked a little to his dad before disconnecting. He reached out, took my hand, and gave a slight tug. "Come on. We left our stuff in the park."

He interlaced his fingers with mine and gave a comforting squeeze. I glanced down at his long, tan fingers threaded through my more tapered ones.

We walked for a couple of blocks and I asked, "Are you mad about what I said to your father?"

"No. Dad told me he read the letter right before sending it to you. He knew you'd be upset when you saw it. He thinks that blaming him is a safe thing for you to do."

We crossed the street to the park and headed along the path to the bench.

"Oh no." Riley let go of my hand and ran over to it.

Our backpacks were still there. So was my cell phone, right where I left it. "What's wrong?"

"Our tablets," Riley answered. "They're gone!"

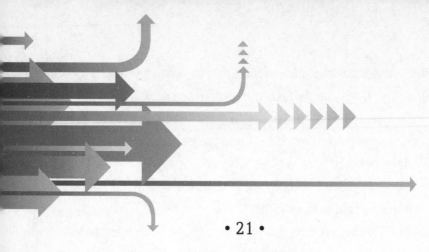

21

THE SEARCH

I sat on a bench outside a bookshop while Riley talked to his dad. After our tablets were stolen, we left the park to search the streets for any sign of them. Right away I knew it was useless, but Riley was so upset I went with him anyway. We looked until we both got tired of walking.

Riley switched the phone to his other ear. "No, Dad, just the tablets. Even Avery's wallet was still inside her backpack." He stopped to listen and added, "Yeah. It's got to be one of the VanDemeres. A regular thief would've taken everything."

He listened some more and gave a slight nod. "Sure, that's fine. I'll buy a replacement tablet we can share. Lucky for us, I still have the pictures of those notebook pages on my cell phone." Another pause and his brows drew together. "I know, but the biggest problem is that now somebody else has a copy of those notes. Not only that, but my tablet had a bunch of info about Mary Chilton."

I wondered how he could be so focused on the competition right now, when my whole world was unraveling. My mother's story kept circling through my head, and I wanted to read her letter again. I hated that someone had my tablet and with it, the letter.

I thought about Grandmother's list of character traits she wanted us to develop; now it seemed a ridiculous joke, because Justine VanDemere was the most flawed of us all. I could envision my mother in the hospital, holding a newborn baby in her arms and weeping—begging for mercy. And yet the best thing my grandmother could come up with was to offer Marija money. Mercy, I noticed, was not on her list of character traits. Neither was kindness, compassion, or sympathy.

Riley ended his call, came over, and stood in front of me. He didn't say anything, just held out his hand. I hesitated, then slipped mine into his, and he pulled me to my feet. We started walking and after several blocks he said, "It's almost one thirty. Let's get something to eat."

He guided me inside a deli and went to get food. A few minutes later he came back with a tray. On it were drinks, sandwiches, and chips. I appreciated the fact that he didn't ask what I wanted to eat. My eyes drifted around the room, my mind still churning.

"Avery," he said in a gentle tone, "you need to eat something."

That's when I noticed he was halfway through his sandwich. I picked mine up and took a bite. He pushed my cup closer. "Drink."

I did that, too.

After a couple of bites, I put down the sandwich. "I can't eat more."

His phone rang and he answered, listening for a few seconds. "Thanks, that's great. I'll get back to you."

After Riley disconnected and finished his sandwich, we grabbed our backpacks and left the deli. Outside, the early afternoon air was warm. We walked for a couple of blocks until he guided me into an alcove between two shops. I felt his hands on my waist and looked up at him. His face was serious; the compelling look in his eyes drew me in.

"Avery, I know you're hurting. This whole thing's got to be killing you. What your grandmother did . . ."

I blinked hard, demanding my body hold back tears even though the sound of them filled my voice. "Everything's different now. It's like I've been looking at my life but never seeing it. Never seeing my grandmother for the woman she really is. She acted like she cared, and I groveled for any crumbs she'd toss me. I desperately wanted her to like me. To love me. As if she even has a heart!"

My voice broke. "And then there's my gutless father. I can imagine exactly how it was. Marija waiting in the hospital room, thinking he was going to come see his newborn daughter. Hoping he'd keep his promises, but of course he'd never do that because he's a shallow, worthless coward. So instead he let my grandmother handle his problem with the nanny. No wonder he hardly ever visits. And when he does, he can't stand to be around me for more than five minutes. I'm so stupid! Why didn't I figure it out before now?"

"Because even when we grow up, there's this little kid in us still wanting to believe what we had was real." His hands moved to my back, trying to comfort me. "It's why I kept making excuses for the way my mom treated my dad, clear up until the day she dumped him."

The sound of his anger helped me, as if somehow his own pain validated mine. "Yeah," I said with a shaky exhale. "That's exactly what it is. Being a little kid and holding on to the lies you tell yourself, desperate to believe in them."

I lifted my eyes and saw our reflection against the dark glass of a shop window: a boy and girl standing together. I watched him pull me closer. Felt it. He was just tall enough to rest his chin on the top of my head. When he spoke, I felt his chin move slightly. "What do you want to do?"

I blew out an angry breath. "I'd love to walk away from this idiotic competition and throw it back in Grandmother's face. But I can't do that, can I? Not if I'm going to stay out of St. Frederick's. Except it'll be harder now. It's not just us and my Uncle Marshall who have her notes."

His hands slid away from me and he looked down at my face. "Maybe we don't need them. That phone call was from the research team. The genealogist finished your pedigree chart from you all the way back to Mary Chilton."

"Oh. Then she is one of the ancestors."

Riley had said the information we needed was inside my head, and it must be true. Maybe we had a stronger edge over my relatives than I'd realized. "So now all we have to do is find the stuff that proves Mary lived. How do we do that?"

"The research team is working on it. Until they get back to us, I've kind of got this one idea."

"Tell me."

"What single thing always proves a person lived?"

"I don't know. A birth certificate, maybe? But Mary wouldn't have one of those here in Boston, since she came from England."

"We are born," he said with dramatic flair, "and then we die."

It took a couple of seconds to register. "You mean a cemetery? Think she's buried around here somewhere?"

"Maybe. It's worth a try." He called the researchers. "Hey, Jeff, can you find out where Mary Chilton was buried? Sure, I'll hold."

It didn't take long before he said, "Fantastic!" He smiled at me. "She's here all right, at the oldest cemetery in the city. It's a place called King's Chapel Burying Ground over on Tremont Street."

"Riley, that's really smart."

"Thanks."

His smile faded and he reached out to take my hand. I slid my fingers into his, and he gave them a consoling squeeze. "You'll make it through this, Avery."

We called a taxi and a while later climbed out in front of a very old gray marble building. The church sat on the corner of two busy streets, and crowding in from every direction were tall, modern buildings.

"This way," he said, pointing. There was a tree-filled cemetery behind a black wrought-iron fence. Like the chapel, it was hedged in by much newer buildings. We were halfway to the gate when we saw Daisy and Chase inside the fence, facing away from us.

We hurried back to the corner of the building where it blocked us from their view. "Since when did those two start working together? They can't be in the same room five minutes without arguing."

Riley leaned his shoulder against the wall. "And they beat us here."

I heard his disappointment that someone else had the same idea. "No problem. Let's wait until they leave."

I peeked around the corner at my cousins. They didn't really look like siblings. Dark-haired Daisy dressed in black, golden-haired Chase with his California tan. "That diamond-stealing jerk," I said. They started down the path, and I pulled back. "They're coming this way."

A few seconds later we heard Chase. "I still think you should take a picture of me by that marker, too."

"No," Daisy answered in a tone of strained patience. "I've already explained. I'm the one researching Mary Chilton. You're doing Francis Cooke and his son John."

They walked through the open gate, turned in our direction, and stopped when they saw us. Daisy opened her mouth to say something, but Riley startled us all when he grabbed Chase's wrist. In one very fast move he spun my cousin around, slammed his chest against the building, and twisted his arm behind his back. Chase struggled, then let out a yelp as Riley twisted harder.

"Stop it!" Daisy shouted.

Riley leaned in closer to Chase. "Where's the diamond?"

Chase grimaced in pain. "Are you crazy?"

"How about a deal? You give Avery back the diamond you stole, and I let you keep the use of your arm."

Chase's face turned red beneath his pale blond hair. "You're gonna get it!" He winced as Riley pressed harder.

Daisy dug out her phone and started dialing 911. I snatched it from her and threw it over the fence into the cemetery. She swore and ran after it, more concerned about her phone than her brother.

"The diamond, Chase," Riley said. "Where is it?"

"In my wallet, you freak!"

"Get it now."

Chase used his free hand to reach in his pocket. A few fumbling seconds later he dug out the wallet and dropped it on the ground. Daisy rushed back through the gate; she held her cell phone, checking it over. Riley said to her, "Your brother's wallet. Open it and find Avery's diamond."

She hesitated until Chase looked sideways at her. "Do it."

Daisy picked up the wallet, and after a quick search withdrew a small plastic bag. She tossed it to me. I squeezed it in my fingers as Riley let Chase go. My cousin spun around and swung with his other arm but Riley dodged it. With both hands, he shoved Chase, who bumped into Daisy.

She grabbed her brother's arm. "Stop! Chase, did you steal Avery's diamond?"

He rubbed his sore shoulder. "What do you care?"

She handed him his wallet. "I don't; I'm just impressed. But who cares about a diamond? Our inheritance can buy you a million diamonds. We need to get going. Besides, if you win, you can fire his law firm and kick Avery out of the mansion."

Over the top of her head, Chase glared at us and stuffed the wallet back in his pocket. "Yeah. That's exactly what I'll do. You're gonna regret this, Tate." He called Riley a couple of crude names, then turned and marched off.

Daisy gave us an amused look, then hurried to catch up with

her brother. I watched them disappear around the side of the building as Riley came over to me. I opened my fist and stared down at the diamond in the crumpled bag. "You didn't need to do that."

He moved beside me and studied it, too. "Yes I did. Chase threatened our lives to get that diamond. And I just stood there, helpless to stop him. When I watched you hand it over, I made a promise. First chance I had, I was going to get it back."

Riley pointed at it. "You know, that's probably worth a few thousand dollars. And since we're the ones who dug it out of the mine, Chase shouldn't get to keep it."

"You're right."

"When you get home, you can get it appraised."

I shoved it in my pocket. "By the way, did you hear what they said before they saw us? Daisy is researching Mary Chilton, but Chase is looking for Francis Cooke. That must be the other ancestor. I remember seeing his name on the passenger list."

"That's good backup info, and I'll text it to the research team so they can do a second chart. But for now, let's go find Mary Chilton's grave."

We stepped through the open gate and followed a winding path between the rows. The headstones were weathered with age and leaned in different directions, some almost ready to fall over. There were also rectangular tombs with flat tops.

Squinting against the bright sunlight, I scanned the area. "Where do we start?"

"By looking at grave markers, I guess. Let's head over to where Daisy and Chase were."

We began at the end of a row on the far side of the cemetery, reading the names and dates as quickly as we could. Since most of the etchings were faded, it took a while.

Riley peered down the long row. "She's got to be here somewhere."

His phone buzzed and he took another call. Disconnecting, he turned to me. "Jeff from the research team says Mary Chilton is in a tomb."

"Wish he'd told us that before."

We checked several tombs, and then, near a strange obelisk, I saw a stone marker with her name on it. "Here it is."

Together, we read the inscription:

JOHN WINSLOW
PASSENGER ON THE FORTUNE

MARY CHILTON
PASSENGER ON THE MAYFLOWER

He brushed it with his fingertips. "I read about her marriage in the facts list that Jeff sent. She and John Winslow had something like nine or ten kids. Give me your camera and stand here. I'll make sure I get the marker in the photo."

In a stiff pose, I waited for him to take the picture. He didn't. Instead, he lowered the camera. "You know, it's kind of cool that this is your ancestor from something like four hundred years ago."

I rested my hand on the top of the tomb. "She's Grandmother's ancestor."

"But still yours, too."

"Just take the picture."

After clicking three or four shots, he came over and showed them to me.

"I look like I belong in a graveyard."

Riley chuckled as he handed me the camera. "Let's go. We've got three more things to find."

Jeff called back with other ideas. There was supposed to be an iron tablet marking the house where Mary Chilton lived. From what he found, the house was torn down but the plaque remained.

Riley checked an online map on his phone. "It's only a few blocks from here. Spring Lane runs between Washington and Devonshire."

We found the narrow street with towering brick buildings on either side, most of them shops that looked old but sold modern items. We couldn't find the marker, and Riley looked anxious. "We're wasting time."

He contacted the research team and I checked the clock on my phone, surprised to see it was already two thirty. We called another taxi, but this one took a lot longer to show up. Riley gave the driver the name of a car rental.

The traffic was sluggish and Riley kept checking the time on his phone. I couldn't really concentrate, since my mind kept going over the letter from my mother. Finally I asked, "Are we renting a car?"

"Yep. The firm is setting it up for us to drive to Plymouth."

"Where's that?"

"About forty miles from here, on the coast. According to Jeff, there's a place called Pilgrim Hall Museum where there's this painting, *The Landing of the Pilgrims*. It shows Mary Chilton stepping onto Plymouth Rock. He thinks they also have a copy of the will she left and a handwritten inventory of all her goods. The museum has them posted online, but we should be able to see the real things, and that'll give us enough."

It was after three thirty by the time he took care of all the paperwork at the rental place. We inched our way through the heavy traffic to the interstate. Once we made it out of Boston, we were finally able to go faster.

I picked up my cell phone and stared at it, trying to decide what to do. The hospital-room scene from Marija's letter kept replaying in my head, and the mental images became more detailed. The young mother holding her baby, sobbing and begging for mercy, would touch the hardest heart. Yet it hadn't touched Justine VanDemere. Added to that was the huge and ugly lie she'd told me my entire life—that my mother died when I was born.

I scrolled through the contacts list on my phone. Riley watched. "Are you calling the research team?"

"No. Grandmother."

"Avery, are you sure you want to do that?"

I pushed the call button, knowing it would probably get routed to Henry's voice mail. If he did answer, I needed to think of a way to get past him. But then what would I say to her if I did? All I could come up with was, *How could you do that to my mother? And to me?*

"Hello, Avery." It was Henry.

"I need to talk to Grandmother."

"I'm sorry." He had that same stuffy tone I couldn't stand. "Mrs. VanDemere is not available."

"It's important."

"She's not talking to the family right now. It's her wish to avoid anyone trying to influence the outcome, such as playing on her sympathies."

"Oh, I'd never do that." Sarcasm filled my voice. "It would be a waste of time."

He didn't answer. Were his eyebrows raised in disapproval? I could see him sitting the way he always did, both feet flat on the floor. He was probably either adjusting his tie or straightening his cuffs.

"Henry, why'd you even bother to answer instead of letting my call go to voice mail?"

He cleared his throat. "Unlike the rest of your relatives, you've not yet tried to contact Mrs. VanDemere. I was concerned that perhaps you are in some difficulty unrelated to the competition."

"That's right. This is an emergency, so let me talk to her."

"No, Avery. Whatever concerns you have, share them with me, and I'll take care of them."

The self-important little snob! As if I would ever tell him why I was calling. "You can't take care of this." I spoke with so much ice in my voice I hoped his ear got frostbit.

"Young lady, there is no reason for rude behavior—"

I hung up on him. "Looks like Henry finally got what he always wanted, having Grandmother all to himself."

"Why would anyone want that?" Riley muttered, and a bitter laugh escaped me.

We finally arrived in Plymouth, and the car's navigation system led us to the center of the little town. It looked the way I thought it would, and I wondered if I'd seen pictures of it in my grandmother's travel albums. We found a parking spot on Court

Street in front of the museum. To me it seemed like just one more New England building with tall columns. We went up the steps but the door was locked.

Riley pointed to the sign. "Damn! They closed at four thirty."

"Maybe somebody's still inside." I knocked on one of the double doors.

When that didn't work, he hammered it with his fist.

"Never mind," I said.

Riley shook his head as if not wanting to give up. "Let's look around back."

"Why?"

"Maybe there's another way in."

I folded my arms. "We can come back in the morning when they open."

Riley stood there a few seconds, thumbs shoved in the pockets of his jeans. "Are you giving up?"

"No." I dragged the word out; it sounded annoyed.

"I'm checking around back."

"Go ahead."

"I will."

We both walked down the steps, ignoring each other and moving in opposite directions. I went to a shady spot under a tree. For some reason, his question about giving up really bugged me. Right now, the competition wasn't the most important thing in my life. But maybe it was to him. What if that was all he really cared about?

I rubbed my arms and after a while checked the time on my phone. I didn't like waiting but refused to go looking for him. Finally he came around the corner, and I leaned my shoulder against the tree and stared across the street. He jogged over to me.

"It's all locked up and they've got an alarm system."

"Because it's a museum."

"You don't need to say it like that."

"Like what?"

"With *duh!* in your voice."

I just looked at him. His expression mirrored my attitude as he seemed to hold back a comment.

"Why are you even here, Riley?" I finally asked.

He didn't answer right away. "What do you mean?"

"Here. With me. Climbing in caves and running all over Boston, looking for my family junk."

His eyebrows drew in. "I'm here because you asked."

"But why? Why say yes? And why hold hands with me?"

Riley just studied my face with a confused expression until I shrugged and turned away. He said, "You don't want me to hold your hand." Not a question; a statement.

"That's not what I mean."

An embarrassed flush made my face warm. He moved into my line of sight, unwilling to let me ignore him. "The night before we left for the first challenge, my dad gave me this big lecture about being with you. For something like an hour, he kept harping about how you're not eighteen yet, and I'm a whole year older and in college. How he promised your grandmother I could be trusted."

I remembered us dancing together in Venezuela, and how Riley suddenly broke away. He said, "Guess I should've listened to him."

I stared down at the grass and blinked a couple of times, determined not to get teary again. His tone softened. "Is that what you want?"

I shook my head. Maybe it was the last thing in the world I wanted.

He lifted one hand but didn't reach for me. Instead, he squeezed his fingers around his car keys. "Come on," he said at last. "Let's get out of here."

Riley paid for two rooms at a fancy hotel on the Plymouth Harbor. Even though one room with two beds would have been more practical, after what I'd said to him, he didn't even ask. I went to my room, and he went shopping for a new tablet and a portable printer.

I lay on the bed for a while, just thinking. No matter where my thoughts drifted, they made me unhappy. Sometimes I focused on my mother's letter, sometimes on my grandmother's betrayal. Sometimes I thought about what I'd said to Riley and how my trust in him felt shaky. Then I remembered the way I'd sobbed in his arms, the woman asking if I needed help and him saying, *"No, I've got her."*

Finally I picked up my phone and called Megan. She answered, sounding groggy. I'd forgotten the time difference. "Did I wake you? I can call later."

"That's okay. What's up?"

It took me a couple of seconds. "I read the first letter my mother wrote." I wanted to say more but had to stop, trying hard to hold back a sudden sob. I bit down on my lip until it hurt.

"Avery?" Megan sounded more awake.

I tried to steady my voice. "She didn't want to give me up.

Grandmother made her!" Another jagged breath. "And then she deported her."

"No! How could she?"

Megan's outrage helped me keep talking. I told her every detail I could remember and wished I still had the letter, though I wouldn't have been able to read it to her without crying. Finally she asked, "What are you going to do?"

"Find Marija as soon as I can."

"And your grandmother?"

"Face up to her and say that what she did was hideous."

"Cruel," Megan added. "And evil."

I was grateful for our combined anger and how it helped push away the tears.

We talked awhile longer, until her phone started to die. "I'll call you tomorrow," she promised before it cut out.

I took a shower and put on some of my new clothes—tan shorts and a top with a coppery design on the front. After brushing my hair, I clipped it back on one side with one of my favorite barrettes.

For a couple of minutes I stood in front of the mirror. I took out the close-up photo of my mother and studied it against my reflection, then copied her thoughtful, mysterious smile. We looked so alike, both in our facial features and with the same dark brown hair and ivory skin. In ways I could hardly understand, this truth gave me more confidence.

Around six thirty there was a knock on my door. I opened it to see Riley standing there. I'd almost expected him to avoid me, but instead he gave a hesitant smile. "Want to get something to eat?"

"Sure."

We found a small café that served delicious pizza. Afterward, he took me for a walk on the harbor shoreline. Along the beach, large boulders lined a high retaining wall, and far in the distance, at the water's edge, was a launch area full of boats. His shoulder was next to mine, and I reached over, taking his hand.

Riley glanced at me as if to say, are you sure? I slid my fingers between his, and he gave a slight squeeze.

We climbed across the boulders, and I leaned my back against the stone wall to stare out at the glassy water. It was cooler here; quiet and serene.

He said, "You seem better now. Not so down."

The talk with Megan had helped a lot, along with my new perspective. Pulling out the laminated picture of my mother from my pocket, I studied it again. I told him about seeing her in the mirror.

"It's hard to explain, but this strange feeling hit me. It was like finally having permission to be who I am and look the way I do. Except for Daisy, with that whole girl-in-black thing she loves, I was the only one not like them. Now suddenly it feels just fine that I'm not a blond, blue-eyed VanDemere. That's a first for me. My entire life I felt like I needed to apologize for not being one of them. But now, at last, I get it. I was never supposed to be."

I put the photo back in my pocket, wondering why I'd just shared that with him. Riley leaned against the wall, facing me. "Want to know what I see when I look at you?" He moved closer and brushed my bangs to the side. "Amazing eyes. I've never really seen eyes your color."

His fingertip moved to my eyebrow and he traced its arch. He ran a line along my jaw and under my lower lip. My skin tingled. He leaned in. "Avery, have you ever been kissed?"

I swallowed. My lips parted to answer, but no words came out. Less than an inch away, I felt his breath like a whisper. Then he tilted his head, and his mouth pressed against mine, soft and fierce at the same time. I closed my eyes and let Riley pull me against him. My arms slid around his neck, and I lost myself in his slow kiss. My pulse quickened and a new understanding awakened. This was nothing like Kyle's shy, awkward kiss. Instead, it was warm, intense, and passionate enough to leave me breathless.

When he finally pulled away, the movement was reluctant. In the fading light that turned everything a hazy blue-gray, Riley smiled down at me. I finally found my voice and murmured, "Not like that."

His smile faded to puzzlement. "You didn't like it?" For the first time he looked unsure.

I shook my head, then stopped and nodded. "Of course." It was a bare exhale. "I just meant yes, I've been kissed. But not like that."

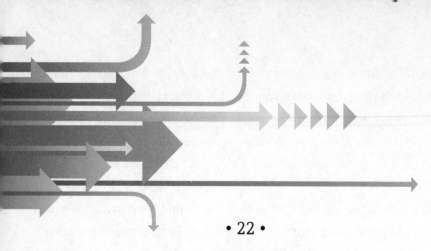

22

CUTTING IT CLOSE

The next morning it was Megan's turn to wake me. "We're waiting for the train to Germany, so I've only got a minute, but I keep wondering if you're okay."

I stretched. "It still hurts, but at least I've stopped crying." Thoughts of last night flooded back. "And know what? Riley kissed me."

She spoke over the background noise. "Is that the lawyer's son?"

"Yes."

A typical Megan squeal was followed by, "How was it?"

"Really great." I smiled up at the ceiling.

Her next comments got broken up, but I could still hear the excitement in her voice. Then she said something that sounded like, "getting on the train," and we were disconnected.

I turned over and closed my eyes, drifting off.

During breakfast at the hotel, I got a text from Mr. Benjamin that made me laugh.

"What is it?" Riley asked.

"Know how we're supposed to meet with everyone at eleven? You'll never guess where." I turned my phone to show him. "It's here in Plymouth."

"Ha! That's perfect. Makes sense, too, since this is where the *Mayflower* landed."

At nine thirty we stood on the steps of the Pilgrim Hall Museum until the doors opened. We paid our admission fee and grabbed several brochures. It didn't take long to find the room with the history paintings, and soon Riley pointed. "Here it is."

We studied *The Landing of the Pilgrims* by Henry A. Bacon, painted in 1877. I frowned. "That's it? Kind of disappointing." The artist showed a young woman in a shawl and cap being helped out of a crowded rowboat by a Pilgrim. "I mean, the artist painted her all prim and dainty. In the story Grandmother told, Mary jumped in the water and waded to shore."

"This is just Henry Bacon's idea of how it happened, and he didn't paint it until around two hundred years later. Besides, who cares? Turn around and I'll take your picture."

As we left the art chamber, we ran into Warren and his wife. They both looked a little startled, but Stasia said hi to me as they passed. For a couple of seconds it seemed she wanted to say something else, but after I said hi back, she just smiled and followed Warren inside.

We found one of the museum guides, a woman with gray hair and glasses on a chain around her neck. Riley said, "Can you help us? We're looking for Mary Chilton's will and also her inventory."

She looked a little surprised. "Since yesterday, you're the third person to ask that."

Riley and I glanced at each other. "What can you tell us?"

"The same thing I told the others. A copy of her will and inventory are found in a genealogy book. Volume fifteen of what we call the Silver Books."

"A book? You don't have her actual will here?"

"No. We only have reproductions of it in the book, which is currently out of print. There's a planned reprinting of the Silver Books, but I can't tell you when."

We thanked her and turned away. Riley blew out a frustrated sigh. "What'll we do now? We've still got to come up with two more things."

He called Jeff on the research team. I flipped through the brochures and was surprised to actually see Mary Chilton's name. I read several sentences, then tugged his sleeve. "Found something."

"What is it?"

"You're not going to believe this. There's an exhibit of under-clothes from colonial times. Listen to what it says: 'The display includes several shoes, stockings, and a lace stomacher. Plus there are two rare surviving corsets, including one from the seventeenth century whose ownership is attributed to *Mayflower* passenger Mary Chilton Winslow.' What do you think?"

"You mean like a Pilgrim Victoria's Secret?"

We laughed and he finished his call with Jeff. I asked a passing museum guide where we could find the exhibit and he told us. It took a few minutes of looking through the glass display cases, but finally we saw it. Brown with age, it seemed more like a torture device than something a girl or woman would want to wear. Still, it gave us one more item. I stood beside the case and Riley took a photo; then he snapped a close-up of the card about Mary Chilton's corset.

While Riley called the research team, I spent the next half hour scanning the brochures, asking questions of the museum staff, and running into more VanDemere relatives. Soon I saw that finding Mary's corset was a fluke. There didn't seem to be anything else belonging to her in the museum.

It was nearly ten thirty when we paused at a drinking fountain. Discouragement showed in the slump of Riley's shoulders. "This is insane! We're so close. There's got to be one more thing here. Or maybe somewhere else in Plymouth?"

Sorting through files on his new tablet, he stopped at the inventory of goods that were part of Mary Chilton's will. "There's so much stuff about her on the Internet, and her name is in dozens of books. But your pig-headed grandma won't let us use any of that."

Riley's phone buzzed and he talked to Jeff again. "Sure. I guess there's nothing else we can do."

He disconnected. "They think there are some locals who might own items from the *Mayflower*. Jeff is trying to get ahold of them to see what they've got." He checked his cell phone. "Twenty minutes until we need to meet Mr. Benjamin. That's not enough time to find a private collector."

A new idea came to me and I grabbed my camera. "I'm brainless! We've probably had it all this time . . ."

I scrolled through the pictures from the upstairs office. He leaned over my shoulder to watch. "What are you doing?"

"My grandmother is a private collector, right? That's what all her display cases are for! Riley, look through the inventory list again and start reading it to me."

He grabbed his tablet and I could hear the excitement in his voice as he began naming off everything from a silk petticoat to pewter dishes and a trunk. Nothing sounded like what I saw. "Hurry, Avery! We're running out of time."

I stopped at a photograph of a very old lace handkerchief. Behind it was an engraved silver cup with looped handles. "Is there a cup on the list?"

Riley moved between screens. "Yes. A silver caudle cup with two ears, at the time worth two pounds, eighteen shillings."

"This is it." I showed him the picture.

"That's great!"

"And the best part? Look, I'm reflected in the glass at the back of the display case. That's me behind the camera. Proof I was there. My grandmother won't be happy when she finds out I snuck into her office, but that's too bad."

Riley laughed. "Avery, you did it!"

He hooked up the portable printer to my camera and right there in the foyer printed copies of the pictures. I stuffed them into a large envelope while Riley checked a map online for the address Mr. Benjamin sent us. "It's nearby, but we've got to move fast."

We hustled out of the museum and jumped in our rental car. It took only a couple of minutes to get to Frazier Memorial State Pier, where there were signs posted for the *Mayflower II*. In the distance we saw an old sailing ship next to the wharf. As we ran, Ms. Franklin came into view. She wore a brown Pilgrim dress with a muslin cap and apron. She didn't look very happy.

"Hurry," she called, pointing at a walkway that led up to the ship.

Breathing hard as we passed, I managed to say, "Hope Grand-mother's giving you a big bonus to wear that."

We reached the top of the gangplank and stepped onto the replica of the *Mayflower*. Ahead of us, some of my relatives lined up to turn in items to Mr. Benjamin. Others had already finished and wandered around the deck. There were several people dressed in Pilgrim clothes who worked on the ship.

Riley showed me the time on his cell phone: 10:57. "Three minutes is cutting it close."

Our turn came, and I studied Mr. Benjamin's costume. He wore a wide-brimmed hat, a fitted brown jacket with a white ruffle at the neck, and short pants with hose and boots. He looked like a real Pilgrim, but those clothes had to be hot. I wondered if he was starting to regret hiring on for this job.

Ms. Franklin joined him. "Well done, everyone! Each of you made it here on time. As already explained, this challenge is different from the last two, and is a pass/fail test. There won't be a winner and no one will be eliminated, if all the right items are turned in."

"However," Mr. Benjamin added, "it will take a few hours to verify your documents. In the meantime, Mrs. VanDemere has arranged a special reward for you. If you don't know this already, you're standing on the *Mayflower II*, a replica of the original. It was built in England, and in 1957 re-created the voyage across the Atlantic. Although most of the time this ship stays docked at the pier, it does—on rare occasions—actually sail. Mrs. VanDemere has made special arrangements for it to do so today."

Muttering sounded from my family members, but Riley said, "Cool! This'll be fun."

Ms. Franklin motioned us to be silent. "Also, there's an

additional reward Chase earned for winning the fortitude challenge and bringing in the biggest diamond. He'll get to act as second mate and learn all about captaining the *Mayflower*."

My cousin did not look delighted and I smiled, until she added, "He'll also receive the VanDemere blue diamond necklace your ancestor Otis commissioned for his wife, Letitia."

Chase turned to his father, and I heard him say, "How much is it worth?"

Uncle Marshall shushed him before leaning in to tell the answer. Chase listened and then pulled back with a big grin on his face. He looked in my direction, and the grin got wider.

I thought about the necklace in a velvet-lined case kept inside the office safe. The single gigantic teardrop shimmered palest blue in a magnificent white-gold setting. Grandmother had worn it on her wedding day. I turned away from Chase's smug look.

Riley said, "That really stinks."

"Know what? I'm glad you made him give back my diamond."

"Me, too. Except it looks like he just stole another one from you that's worth a whole lot more."

I shrugged, tossing off my irritation. "It's just VanDemere stuff. The vault is full of jewelry, but the diamond we mined means something to me."

A salty breeze swept across the deck, and Mr. Benjamin grabbed the brim of his hat. "Better get going. You have less than an hour to grab your things and be back here by noon, when lunch is served. Don't be late, because if the ship sails without you, you'll be eliminated. The *Mayflower II* is taking you to your next destination in the competition."

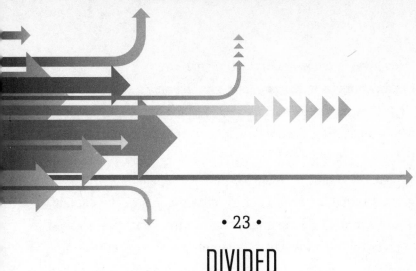

DIVIDED

After we came back to the *Mayflower II* with our stuff, a man in Pilgrim clothes introduced himself as the captain. He started telling us about the ship. I found the facts a little boring until the sails dropped and the crew began grabbing ropes. Riley shielded his eyes and stared up at the tall masts. "I've always wanted to go sailing on this kind of vessel. Except I wish it was a pirate ship."

Soon lunch was served, authentic Pilgrim food that didn't taste good. Riley took our dishes over to a wooden bucket while I stood at the rail. Farther out on the ocean now, the ship rocked on swells of water.

After a couple of minutes, I turned back and saw Thisby talking to Riley. She stared up at him with an expression that said he was fascinating. Her flirting ability always had a way of making guys' brains melt, and even for a regular girl it was a hard thing to watch. But for me, growing up in Thisby's shadow, seeing her hit on Riley was extra hard.

"Hey, Avery," Chase said, startling me.

I hadn't noticed him come to the railing only a few feet away. Silently I chewed myself out. Years of keeping him on my radar so that when he entered a room I could exit, failed because I got distracted.

"Chase," I replied.

A shadow fell between us; I looked up and saw the captain. He reached into a small leather pouch. "Mrs. VanDemere asked me to give you this so you can remember today's experience."

He dropped a coin into each of our open palms. I examined mine. The *Mayflower* was embossed on one side and around the outer edge was written: *1620—Ratification of the Mayflower Compact.* I flipped it over. On the back was: *Commemorative Coin* and *$20.* Beneath were the Latin words: *Dido Dididi Didtum.*

Chase held his between two fingers. "This worth anything?"

"Just the face value," the captain answered, moving on.

I put mine in my pocket as Chase leaned forward at the railing and flipped his in the air. He barely caught it. "Figures she'd give us something stupid like this."

He tossed it higher. On the third try he missed, and the coin fell into the ocean. I thought about how twenty dollars wasn't much, but still enough to pay for a movie and a drink or to buy my favorite brand of eye shadow.

"What?" he asked.

"Nothing."

He shook his head. "It's never just 'nothing' with you. I've seen that look of yours a hundred times. Always judging me."

That's what he thought? I turned away and watched the

ocean. The afternoon sun glimmered on distant jade swells and made small islands of light.

"You're kind of the surprise of this whole thing, aren't you?" His voice was less annoyed but still prying. "Who would've thought you'd get the highest score on the test? Even higher than my dad's. How'd you know all those answers?"

"Lucky guesses."

"I doubt it. The rest of us can't stand the way Grandmother always tries to force-feed us her history crap. But you just drink it up. Kind of like her lapdog, aren't you?"

"Better than a pathetic bully." I felt surprised that I was actually standing up to him. "Though picking on others is probably all you know how to do."

He grabbed my arm and I winced as his fingers bit into my flesh. For a few seconds I was twelve years old again, helpless and scared of him. It didn't last; not when bottled-up resentment exploded inside me.

As fast and hard as I could, I brought my foot down. The side of my new hiking shoe scraped his bare shin before smashing the top of his foot. With a startled yelp Chase let go and stepped back. He grimaced in pain and bent over; when he looked up, he glared at me and spewed several filthy words.

Riley suddenly stepped between us. I hadn't even seen him come over, but now he stood facing my cousin. "You're done."

Chase grew even more furious. "I'll say whatever I want to the little slut."

Riley's fist flew with surprising speed. His punch caught Chase on the jaw and snapped his head back. He hit the deck but jumped to his feet and lunged forward. He headbutted Riley in the chest, and they went down, rolling around and slugging each other. Shocked, I stood there staring at them, not knowing what to do.

From the beginning, Chase was outmatched. He was three inches shorter and not nearly as muscular, and despite his rage he only landed half the punches Riley did. Uncle Logan and Mr. Benjamin ran over and pulled them apart.

Uncle Logan stood between them. "What're you doing?"

"Riley hit me," Chase called in a loud voice. "He threw the first punch!"

Uncle Marshall strode over with an accusing glare. "This true?"

Riley raised his chin. "Yes."

There were a few scattered comments by those who gathered in a lopsided circle, but I could only focus on Riley. A small cut marred his perfect mouth. For just a few seconds, a memory overlaid itself on the scene, from when I was twelve and a young boy fought my rotten cousin. Something tender welled inside my heart, and I went to Riley.

"He was only defending me." I slipped my hand in his and saw there were scrapes on his knuckles. "If Chase hadn't been bullying me, Riley wouldn't have hit him."

Chase glared at me, his face even redder, but Uncle Marshall ignored me. He turned to Mr. Benjamin. "We want that Tate kid out of here! When this ship lands, he's gone."

Mr. Benjamin shook his head. "We don't decide any of that. We only moderate the rules of the game, and there's no rule against fighting. Besides, since Avery is underage, she's got to have someone from Mrs. VanDemere's law firm watching over her."

"I'm calling the police." Uncle Marshall made a show of using his cell phone, but it fell flat when he couldn't get reception. He pointed an accusing finger at Riley. "We get to wherever we're going, and I'm having you arrested for assault."

"Yeah!" Chase snarled, dabbing at a trickle of blood beneath his nose. Then he swore at Riley until his father grabbed his shoulder and led him away.

Mr. Benjamin turned to us. "Better go cool off."

Riley and I walked away. At a spot near two barrels and a large coil of rope, I started to say something, but he shook his head. "Not here," he whispered, motioning to a small box mounted on a mast.

"Camera?" I asked in a hushed tone.

He nodded. "I've seen two others."

We walked to the far end of the ship, both of us scanning the area. Riley leaned against the railing. "I think we're clear."

"Are you okay?"

"Yeah." He pointed to a narrow bench and we sat. "I'm sorry, Avery."

"Why are you apologizing? You took on our family's biggest nutcase to defend my honor. Do you know how that makes me feel?"

He shook his head.

"Amazed. That a guy like you would fight for me is . . . I don't know. Something I've never known before." I glanced across the deck at the rolling water on the other side.

Riley studied his bruised knuckles. "The guy is a total creep.

I've despised him since the day I saw him trying to shove that worm in your mouth. And I'll run interference as long as I can. But I might not be able to finish this competition with you."

"Why not?"

"Didn't you hear your uncle? He's going to press assault charges."

"That's just talk, isn't it? And you were both fighting. I don't think the police will do anything, do you?"

"I'm not sure. I shouldn't have done it, but when I saw him grab your arm, I got to you as fast as I could. When he called you . . ." He let out a slow breath. "I just hope I haven't made things worse."

I rubbed the sore spot left by Chase's grip. "Maybe now he'll stay away from us."

"I hope so." Riley's face looked even more worried. "As soon as we get in cell phone range, I need to call my dad."

"Will he be mad?"

"Worse. He'll be disappointed. I'd rather get punched than hear him say, 'I expected more of you, son.' Especially after all the promises I made about being your chaperone during the competition. That I'd be levelheaded and always remember I represent Tate, Bingham, and Brown." He leaned against the railing.

I studied his eyes, a reflection of the seawater sky. "It'll work out."

He returned my gaze but didn't say anything.

The trip grew long and boring and I secretly admitted that two months on the *Mayflower* would've been miserable. "Point made, Grandmother," I said under my breath as I got two granola bars out of my backpack.

I looked up and noticed Stasia walking along the rail in our direction. Her expression was serious, and I wondered if she was coming to see us. Then something caught her attention and she looked back. Wind ruffled strands of her red hair, and she brushed them away from her face. My brother hurried over and they began talking. We couldn't hear what they were saying because of the wind whipping the sails, but it seemed tense.

Riley studied them. "Newlywed troubles?"

"Looks like they're arguing, doesn't it?"

Stasia seemed to give in, and they walked away, my brother's hand at the small of her back. The ship rose across a large swell, which made my stomach drop as it sent up misty spray. Riley leaned forward and wiped a few damp flecks from his arm. "By the way, what did the captain give your family? I saw him handing out something."

"Oh, that." I took the coin from my pocket. "Here. It's a souvenir of the trip. Grandmother wanted us to have it."

He looked at both sides and started to give it back but paused and studied it more closely. "That's weird. Look at this."

He showed me the engraved banner with the Latin writing. I read the words aloud. "*Dido Dididi Didtum*. I don't know what it says. Do you?"

"I think so. I took a semester of Latin in high school, and I'm sure it means to divide. Once we're back on land I can check the Internet."

"But why would it say that? The Mayflower Compact was supposed to unite the Pilgrims."

He held the coin between his thumb and index finger, turning it back and forth in a slow, thoughtful way. "You said the captain made a point of saying your grandmother wanted you to have this, right? Maybe it's not so much about the *Mayflower* but the competition."

Riley laid the coin on his palm, Latin side up, and I stared at it. "If you're right, why wouldn't it be the Latin word for *resourcefulness* since that's what this challenge is about?"

Both of us fell silent, analyzing. Finally I said, "And if this really is a message to the VanDemere heirs, why give it to us now, during the competition? She didn't do that before."

"How do you know?"

We looked at each other. "Because she didn't give us a keepsake from the last competition, unless you count the diamond. And it's not like there's a Latin message engraved on that." I got my wallet out and found the small plastic bag that held the diamond Riley had taken back from Chase.

He said, "Not on the diamond, but what about the bag? What's all the writing?"

Small letters in black fine-tipped marker showed Chase's name. Beneath that was El Abismo de Diamante and then the carat weight of the diamond. Near the bottom of the bag were seven letters in tiny print: *TS NIA GA.*

"What's that?" Riley asked.

"Probably something the jeweler wrote. Maybe his initials."

"I don't think so. His last name was Juarez. Where's the other diamond? The one you turned in?"

I got it out and we looked at the bag with my name on it. There were similar markings, including the little letters at the bottom. Riley took the bag from me and studied it. After a few seconds he flipped it over and looked at it in reverse from the other side. "Hold on, I think I see what it is. If you push all those letters together and read them backward, it makes the word *against.*"

I stared at both bags. "I don't know, Riley. If they formed *fortitude*, then we'd know it's a message."

His expression showed he didn't want to give up the idea. "After the next challenge, we need to watch for something with a hidden meaning."

"What about the first challenge? You know, the test at your law office? Nothing came with that."

"True."

We were both quiet for a few seconds and then he said, "What about the test itself? Was there anything in the directions that stood out?"

"Not really. And your dad never heard anything about a code?"

He shook his head. "He would've told me. But I still think this might be a message. Look at these two words: *against division.*" He peered at the coin again. "It might mean something."

The whole idea was too vague, but I didn't want to knock down his theory. "It might not mean anything. But if there really is a secret message, then there'll be another piece of it at the next challenge."

"We'll check it out. That might give us an edge, unless someone else in your family figures it out."

I smiled. "Know what Chase did with his coin? Tossed it overboard."

Riley laughed. "Talk about brainless."

I put the little diamond bags back in my wallet and added the *Mayflower* coin.

A while later we saw land. By the time the sun dipped low above the cliffs, Riley got cell phone reception. He had a long conversation with his dad, and I think he must've said "I'm sorry" a dozen times. After he disconnected, he looked relieved.

"It's not as bad as I thought, because the ship left the jurisdiction of Massachusetts. Since I punched Chase in their waters, the police in whatever state we land won't get involved. That means your uncle can't do anything."

"How'd your dad take it?" I asked, already guessing the answer.

"Not good. I swear, no matter how satisfying it might be to punch a jerk like Chase, it's not worth having to tell my dad."

The ship pulled into a bay, and in the distance we saw a weathered lighthouse. We also learned that Mr. Tate was right when we overheard Uncle Marshall blustering into his cell phone. He got huffy with the local police, who hung up.

"Can we have your attention?" Ms. Franklin called, adjusting the apron of her Pilgrim dress.

Everyone gathered around, but Riley and I hung back a bit. Chase glared at us. He had a swollen spot above one eye, and his hair hung across his forehead.

Mr. Benjamin stepped forward, the modern glasses he wore looking out of place with his costume. "Welcome to Virginia. The *Mayflower II* has just dropped anchor, and we'll soon enter the lifeboats. Before we do, Ms. Franklin and I have talked with Mrs. VanDemere about the documents you submitted."

He held up several pages stapled together. "According to the information your grandmother spent many years gathering, there are two *Mayflower* Pilgrims you're descended from. The first was a young girl, Mary Chilton, daughter of James and Susanna Chilton. They were with the Leiden congregation and came to the New World seeking religious freedom. Mary's parents died during the first winter."

Riley and I smiled at each other as Mr. Benjamin flipped a page. "The second Pilgrim you're descended from was a child of a family recruited by London merchants to work as planters. Stephen and Elizabeth Hopkins's son was the only baby born on the *Mayflower*. They named him Oceanus Hopkins."

I glanced at Riley; we both turned to look at Chase. Outside the King's Chapel Burying Ground, we'd heard him and Daisy talking about the Cooke family, not the Hopkinses.

Chase waved a hand as concern clouded his face. "Wait a minute! What about Francis and John Cooke?"

As if he hadn't heard him, Mr. Benjamin focused on the bottom of the page. "Remember that this challenge doesn't have a winner. If you turned in the required items of a correct pedigree chart and proof of four objects you found, then you'll move on to the next challenge."

He motioned to Ms. Franklin who stepped forward. "Mrs. VanDemere asked us to tell you that everyone passed this challenge, except for one."

She turned to my cousin, whose lips clamped together in a worried line. "I'm sorry, Chase, but you didn't hand in items for the correct *Mayflower* ancestor. You've been eliminated from the competition and will be going back to Santa Rosa. At that time you may pick up your inheritance check from the law firm."

Riley and I glanced at each other again, hardly able to believe our good luck.

Chase shook his head, unwilling to accept it. "But my pedigree chart . . ."

"Was incorrect. The original line you followed at first led to Mary Chilton, but for some reason you diverted and created a false line to Francis Cooke."

Daisy had a sly look on her face. She knew! There wasn't any surprise in her eyes, though a mask of innocence slid in place when Chase turned to her. "But Daisy, you told me we had proof. You typed up the pedigree chart for me."

Riley leaned near and said, "She set him up."

His voice must have carried because Chase reacted to those words, a scarlet flush spreading beneath his tan. He ran a hand across his eyes, then turned back to her with a hurt expression I'd never expected to see.

Uncle Marshall tromped over to Daisy and shook his fist at her, his voice a growl. "You dirty little whelp!"

Suddenly Chase was on his feet and heading for her. He swung at Daisy. She ducked and his knuckles only grazed the side of her jaw. She staggered back and gaped at him, sputtering a few words as Chase dived for her. They slammed against the railing and she screamed. Uncle Logan started forward, but Mr. Benjamin got there first. Chase's arm was pulled back to strike, but he grabbed it. Spinning him around, Mr. Benjamin blocked the blow with his forearm. "Enough!"

Chase lashed out but Mr. Benjamin quickly caught his wrist and bent it back until my cousin yelped. "Calm down, Chase. Get it under control."

He stopped struggling, though he was breathing hard and swearing. "Let go!" he finally said.

Mr. Benjamin released him but moved to stand in front of Daisy. Chase pointed at her over Mr. Benjamin's shoulder. "I'm gonna get you for this, Daisy!"

Mr. Benjamin gave him a little shove. "Go cool off. Move it!"

Chase called him a couple of names, then stormed away. We watched him leave until Uncle Marshall turned on Daisy, outraged. "Damn you, Daisy! Why'd you do it?"

A puff of wind fluffed her bangs, and she struggled to keep up her aloof act. After several seconds she straightened her spine. "Because there can be only one winner."

For a few seconds all we heard were the flapping sails and the slosh of water against the ship. When he spoke, my uncle's voice came out a strangled croak. "But he's your brother!"

Daisy raised a defiant chin. "Would you be this upset if it was the other way around? No, you wouldn't. Do you have any idea how sick I am of you always playing favorites? Chase and Jordan are the ones you do everything with. They're the ones you're always pulling for. You tell Chase about the business but won't let me in on anything. Why?"

She put her hands on her hips. "I'm smarter than the boys. I've always gotten better grades. This year a four-point-oh, but you never said one thing about it. Why don't you treat me like them? Because I'm a girl?"

"No. Because you're not mine!"

Daisy's head jerked back as if he'd slapped her, and the color drained from her cheeks. Several seconds passed. Her mouth moved but she didn't say anything, until finally she asked in a half croak, "Did Mom tell you that?"

It was like her question was kindling tossed on a fire, and his face got even angrier. "We've fought about it for years! Your mother won't admit it. But why else did she come crawling back after we were separated?" His eyes narrowed, full of venom. "How could you be? If I had a daughter, she'd look like Thisby."

I stared at Uncle Marshall, hardly able to believe he could say such a terrible thing. Daisy lowered her head and studied the deck. Red blotches began creeping up her neck.

Uncle Logan stepped close and whispered to his brother. Uncle Marshall's shoulders hunched forward. "But look what she did! She ruined his chance . . ."

Riley leaned over to me. "That was low."

I nodded. It seemed strange to feel sorry for Daisy, but I did. I noticed Ms. Franklin had moved back and stood on the other side of Riley. Her arms were folded. She looked like a stern Pilgrim.

Our eyes met. "Isn't our family a mess?"

Her voice was very quiet when she answered. "Yes."

The *Mayflower*'s captain called out to the crew to lower the lifeboats, and then everything happened fast. We grabbed our backpacks, and Mr. Benjamin herded us to the rope ladder. Riley went first and I waited my turn. Uncle Marshall stood nearby at the railing, staring at the distant cliffs. I tapped his shoulder. "Know what, Uncle Marshall?"

He glanced over at me, and I sent him a withering look. "If you're not her father, she's lucky."

Before he could answer, I scurried down the ladder.

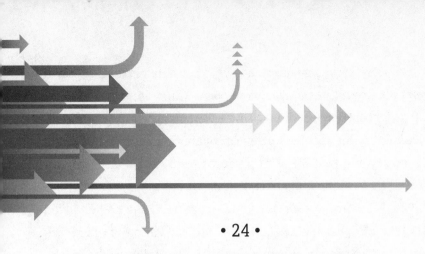

THIRTY PIECES OF SILVER

After the rowboats moored in a wide cove, we crossed the beach and climbed up a path to the cliff top. The Benjamin–Franklin team led us through a wooded area, and we walked for a while until coming to a lodge surrounded by log cabins.

Inside the main building a man met us. "Welcome. You have a few minutes to wash up before dinner is ready."

Soon everyone but Chase gathered in the large dining room. He was on his way to the nearest airport, where the company jet waited for him. It was excellent revenge that after all his bullying and cheating, he was out of the competition because he'd been too lazy to do his own pedigree chart.

Now there were five heirs left in the game: me, Warren, Thisby, Daisy, and Uncle Marshall. I wondered what new test Grand-mother would come up with next, and in a strange way looked forward to it since I'd started to see I had as good a chance at winning as anybody.

We were served salad, steaks with a maple glaze, and grilled sweet potatoes. The family spread out at different tables in groups of two, except for Daisy and Uncle Marshall, who sat by themselves. Everyone seemed on edge, probably because Daisy proved that you had to be careful who you trusted. And Uncle Marshall showed the real meaning of ruthless.

Ms. Franklin and Mr. Benjamin came in. They had changed out of their Pilgrim clothes and back into the white shirt and black suit from the first time we met them. Ms. Franklin waited for the talking to die down. "Here's a message about tomorrow's challenge."

The soft music stopped playing and we heard Grandmother's voice come out of the speakers.

"Did you know that the Civil War was the deadliest conflict in US history? The loss of human lives was well over a half million. You might be interested to know we can trace our family line back to both sides of the conflict. In the Union was the Stuart family from Ohio, who were abolitionists. They lost two sons at the Battle of Chickamauga."

I glanced around the room and saw another small camera mounted up high. She was probably watching us react to her speech, so even though she kept droning on, I made sure to look interested and didn't yawn like Thisby was.

Grandmother said, "And then there was the Markham family. They risked their lives as blockade runners, bringing medicine to thousands of Confederate soldiers dying of swamp malaria."

Riley pulled out his phone. Keeping it below the edge of the table, he sent a text to both the research team and his father: Civil War. Battle of Chickamauga & Confederate blockade runners.

"Our country learned from tragic lessons on both sides," Grandmother said. "But we remained a unified nation. In comparison, it makes me very sad to look at the conflict within our own family. Hopefully, after the next challenge, that will change. Tomorrow you'll learn about both the Civil War and the character trait *unity*."

Mr. Benjamin clicked the remote and the room fell silent.

I whispered to Riley, "If she wants all the VanDemeres to get along, then why is she making us compete against each other?"

"Good question."

The man who ran the lodge came into the dining room. He began calling our names and handing out cabin keys. When I took mine he said, "By the way, an envelope came for you today. You can pick it up at the front desk."

Riley was talking to Mr. Benjamin, so I walked over to the counter and checked with the clerk. She handed me a small padded envelope with no return address. I checked the postmark: *Oakland, CA.* Inside was a pocketknife with a brown handle and a tiny silver label that said *Rough Rider.* It was old, but the blade slid out easily and looked like it had been recently sharpened. I wondered if it was from Mr. Tate, but there wasn't a note and I couldn't see him sending me an anonymous gift—especially this.

After tossing the package, I put the knife in my pocket and went to find Riley. Maybe he'd have an idea about who sent it. I saw him standing with Thisby, his head bent slightly as if to better hear her. He wore the serious expression that made him so handsome, but as she smiled up at him he said something and she laughed. Then he smiled, too. Thisby put a hand on her hip, shaking her head, and his smile stayed.

I left the lodge, telling myself it didn't matter if they talked. I wasn't with Riley except in this dumb competition, which would be done in a few days. One kiss didn't mean anything, so why should I care if she flirted with him and he flirted back? I stomped down the forested path, looking for my cabin in the nighttime shadows.

"Wait up," Riley called.

I didn't look back.

He reached my side. "What a crazy day!" He threw an arm across my shoulder.

I wondered if he was going to tell me what he and Thisby were talking about. He didn't, which meant it was all about flirting and nothing to do with me. I walked faster.

Riley's hand slid down to my wrist, his fingers encircling it. "Slow down, will you?"

I slowed, thinking he was going to say something. Instead, he paused and cocked his head, listening. Warren and Stasia were coming our way. *Lousy timing.*

She called my name, and they hurried forward.

"Hi," she said in a friendly way that seemed a little out of place. "How's it going?"

I glanced at Riley, then back at them. "Fine."

"Avery, we have something to tell you."

"What's that?"

Both paused for a few seconds until Warren dug in his backpack and pulled out two tablets. "Here." He held them out to us.

I took mine and Riley grabbed his. "You're the ones who stole them?"

Stasia smoothed her perfect red hair, which didn't need it. "We both did."

My brother shook his head. "No. It was me. Stasia tried to talk me out of it."

"Only at first," she cut in. "Once we had them, I went along with it and looked at your files." She moved a little closer. "It's just we were desperate. We didn't have a clue about who the *Mayflower* ancestors were. Both your uncles were helping their kids. And Avery, you won the first test, so you had to know where to look. But we were stuck. Then we happened to be walking down a street in Boston and saw you run away from that little park . . ."

Riley held up his tablet. "And you took them."

Warren nodded. "We read about Mary Chilton."

Stasia added, "We're really sorry."

I hardly heard her. Instead, I studied Warren, who looked ashamed—the guy who had always ignored me and didn't seem to care whether or not I was alive. "I don't get it. Why tell us now? And why give them back?"

Warren glanced at his wife and gave a slight shake of his head. Stasia hadn't been expecting my question. "We shouldn't have taken them. That's all."

My brother turned around and reached for her hand. They started walking off and I heard him say, "Happy now?"

She muttered a reply.

"Wait!" I called, hurrying after them. "Hang on a sec, will you?"

When they turned back I had to force out the words. "My tablet was open to a letter. Did you read it?"

Warren kept his face blank, but Stasia didn't do so well at hiding the truth. I felt an inward drop and took a few steps back. She lifted her hands in a helpless gesture.

"It's my fault, Avery! At first I thought it was some kind of foreign document, since the beginning was written in a different language. I scrolled down but didn't understand what it was until I started reading it to Warren." She lowered her voice. "Then I couldn't stop."

My fingers tightened around the tablet. "You didn't have the right."

"No, and I'm really sorry."

"Don't you dare say anything to the others! I don't need Thisby to have more reasons to insult my mother."

Stasia's eyes widened. "We won't! Of course we won't."

Warren shifted his stance. "You know, we didn't have to give back the tablets. Or admit we read the letter. But we're trying to put this right."

Riley came up beside me. "Why?"

"The letter," Stasia answered, still looking at me. "What happened to your mother was horrible! How could your grandmother do that?"

Everything came back to me again, and I felt the same painful tightening inside. She said, "You must've just read it, right? I mean, the way you ran off . . . we could see you were upset. At first we thought you two had a fight, until I started reading." Her voice was full of sympathy, something I'd never seen from any of the VanDemeres, in-laws or otherwise. "I have a friend who was adopted and wants to look for her birth mother. I understand why you're doing this."

Her face was so sincere, my anger softened. I lifted the tablet. "Okay."

"Guess we better take off."

They walked away, but she called over her shoulder, "See you later."

We watched them and Riley slid his arms around me, making me forget about being upset at him. I leaned my head back against his shoulder; we stood that way for a while, the strength of his arms comforting.

His breath brushed against my cheek, a light caress. "What do you think about that?"

"I'm not sure. It's definitely a surprise. I mean, Warren almost never talks to me. Not that he hangs around with any of my cousins, either. Being six years older, to him we were all a bunch of kids."

"So you don't really know him."

I shook my head. "He was right that they didn't have to give back our tablets. None of my other family members would have."

"That had to be Stasia's idea."

"Yes, but he agreed to it."

My cell phone hummed and he let go. I answered and Mr. Tate spoke in an upbeat voice. "Hello, Avery. Riley told me how you were able to come up with the last item on the Mary Chilton list. Well done."

"It almost didn't happen."

"True, but the important thing is that it did, and you're still in the competition. By the way, I'm ready to leave the office and can send you another letter before I go. Do you have a specific one you want?"

I'd already thought about this while we were on the ship. At twelve there was that ugly incident with Chase and the worm. I wanted the letter from that year. "Can you send me the one she wrote for my twelfth birthday?"

"Sure. Also, do you want me to resend this morning's e-mail, since your tablets were stolen?"

"No, we just got them back. Here, Riley can tell you."

I handed him my phone and he explained. Then I heard him tell about Warren and Stasia reading the letter. "No, I don't think they know you sent it to Avery, but I wasn't about to ask."

I pointed to my tablet. "The letter was saved. They wouldn't know unless they opened my e-mail."

"Did you hear that?" Riley asked his dad.

They talked a while longer, and I thought about the letters and the way Mr. Tate handed them out as individual rewards. It reminded me of how I gave treats to Max and Caesar. To him it was all about what happened to his firm when the competition ended. For a minute I stood there, dealing with the same nagging thoughts about Riley's motives.

Once he disconnected, we walked along, both of us quiet. I fixed my eyes on the path, where watery moonlight whitened a scattering of pebbles.

"Are you okay, Avery?" There was concern in his voice.

"I'm fine." *Most useless word in the English language.*

We found my cabin and stood on the narrow porch. I unlocked the door and he pulled me close, his thumb slowly tracing the line of my jaw, then lifting my face to his. He pressed his lips against mine, his strong arms sliding around me. His hands pressed on my back, my own fingers splayed on his chest, heartbeat throbbing like crazy under my touch, and I didn't know if it was his or mine. I began falling into a dizzy place where everything became a blur.

He pulled back slowly—nothing but a breath between us, a kiss that didn't want to die. I opened my eyes to see him gazing down at me. In the thin moonlight, his eyes seemed restless. Anxious, maybe.

"What is it?" I whispered.

His hands slid from my back, though I still felt the warmth of their imprint. He shook his head, his voice husky. "We haven't known each other long enough for me to feel this way."

Riley opened the door to my cabin, turned on the light, gently pushed me inside, and shut it—all in a series of skillful moves. I leaned against the door and tried to understand what he meant. Why this confusing dance of pulling me to him, then pushing me away? I had a nagging feeling that Thisby had something to do with it.

Finally I walked into the room, a rustic cabin with no television. I sat at a small table and opened the attachment from Mr. Tate. Marija's now-familiar writing appeared, a shorter letter than the last two.

My dearest daughter,

Today, since your birthday fell on the Sabbath, I went to Mass at St. Catherine's. I knelt in prayer and asked God to forgive me. Often, I ask him this. And yet how can he, when you are the one I wronged? You are the one I should ask.

Do you get my letters, Tatjana? Is it even allowed? I wish so much to know this. Does your silence come from anger or sorrow?

Or perhaps you never read them at all because they are not given to you.

After I left the old church I walked back through the city. Zagreb is changing. It is not the dangerous place of my girlhood. Life is so much better here now that the long war for independence is over. If only I could have known it would be safe to bring you back here. Or known what I do now, from my friend in the government. They would not have taken you away from me when I came back across the border. I was tricked by a lie that cost me everything. And because of that, I know nothing about you or the life you live.

There are so many questions I have. What favorite things give you pleasure? What do you look like? Do you enjoy school? Do you enjoy to read? I do. For the past twelve years I have spent all my time learning. It became my only way to not think about what I left behind.

At the University of Zagreb I accomplished degrees in both history and English. It is an irony that now I have excelled at your language in my own country, when I struggled with it years ago in America. And just one month past I was offered a very good work position, which I started last week.

Although this opportunity is a happy one, I keep the dark secret about it hidden inside me. The money that paid for my education came from Mrs. VanDemere when I agreed to let her and your father take you. So today, as I knelt at Mass and asked Christ to forgive my burden of guilt, I thought about that. I took their money, just the same as Judas took thirty pieces of silver to betray his Lord. That is what I did to you, Tatjana.

Can you forgive me? Can you ever forgive me?

The letter was unsigned.

I carried the tablet with me over to the bed and lay down. With my hands, I pressed on my chest to try and stop the aching inside. It didn't help. Tears trickled along my temples and into my hair. I pressed harder.

After a while I picked up the tablet and reread her letter. Then I found the birth letter from yesterday and went through it, too. The suffering in those lines cut into me nearly as much as the first time I read them.

Looking closer, I noticed something. Beneath the closing words "Your Mother," there were a few black flecks. It seemed to me that whatever was written underneath had been removed. I wondered if it was her name, and if Mr. Tate had used Wite-Out before scanning it.

I squeezed my eyes shut. I was tired of being used in this forced game. Except there wasn't a choice, and I had to keep going. The only thing left to do was hope I could somehow get Marija's full name and find her Croatian phone number. Then I would call her, and I knew what I would say.

Hello. This is Tatjana, your daughter. We haven't met, but I know who you are. I know you love me. And I love you back.

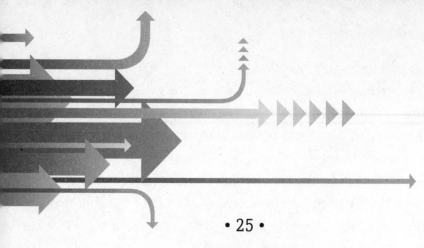

• 25 •

SMUGGLERS

The early wake-up knock on my door meant it was time for showers before class started. I dreaded getting up. Dreaded breakfast in the cafeteria and avoiding Gavin and the obnoxious guys he hung out with. What day was it, anyway?

More pounding, this time louder. I opened my eyes and it slowly came to me that I wasn't at school. Not at home, either. I sat up and looked around the dimly lit cabin, remembering last night. I swung my feet over the edge of the bed and wondered if Riley was the one knocking, and if there was a problem. I finally made it to the door.

"Who is it?" My voice sounded thick.

"Ms. Franklin. Open up."

Rubbing a bleary eye, I opened the door partway. "What's wrong?"

"Get dressed. You've got ten minutes or you'll get left behind. And don't bring your cell phone or anything else electronic."

All I could think to say was, "What time is it?"

She started walking away but glanced over her shoulder. "Nine minutes. Don't get eliminated."

I dug clothes out of my backpack and glanced at an alarm clock on the nightstand. It was four thirty. I pulled on a shirt, shorts, and hiking shoes. A couple of the laminated photos of Marija fell out of my pack. I picked them up, hesitated a second, and shoved them in my pocket. Maybe it seemed silly, but after last night I wanted to have her with me.

I grabbed my brush and put my hair into a ponytail. A few seconds later I sprinted out the door and headed for a dim light across the clearing. Ms. Franklin held a tin lantern with tiny holes punched in it. Just enough light seeped out to see what was close by. Half my family members were already there, and the rest came soon after. Each looked as rumpled and groggy as I felt. Warren was the last to make it over, coming up beside me, and he seemed upset. I glanced around, then turned to Ms. Franklin. "Where's Riley?"

She didn't answer, and I looked in the direction of his cabin. No lights on. I reached for my phone but then remembered it was still in the room. Why wasn't he here? This was no time for him to decide to sleep in. I took a few steps in his direction, when Warren's voice stopped me.

"He isn't coming."

I glanced back. "Why not?"

"They didn't let Stasia, either."

"You've got to be kidding."

Mr. Benjamin joined us. "Keep your voices down and listen." He looked at our faces, which reflected the amber light from the lantern. "There's not much time, and there's some specific info to go over. First of all, only the five remaining VanDemere family members are allowed to join this challenge."

I stifled a groan. With Riley by my side, it could be an adventure. Without him, it would be miserable.

Thisby frowned and waved her hand. Her hair stuck out, and she looked different without makeup. "Why are we starting so early?"

Mr. Benjamin adjusted his hat. "Low tide."

Ms. Franklin added, "From now until noon, you'll re-create one of your ancestor's heroic adventures. Last night Mrs. VanDemere told you about the Markham family of Virginia. She assumes you know the details of the story about Francine Markham and her brother Joshua, whose uncle was a blockade runner for the Confederacy. He brought shipments of quinine and morphine here from England, at great personal risk. Their father, Peter Markham, then smuggled the medicines to the camps."

I had an advantage, since this was a story I knew all about. It was in a book Grandmother gave us for Christmas, and I'd used it for a history assignment back in early January. If only Riley were here, so I could share it with him.

Warren said, "But they smuggled for the South, right? Why would Grandmother want us to learn about the Confederacy?"

"Courage can happen anyplace. Because of the Union blockade, which kept supplies and medicines from getting through, thousands of Confederate soldiers died. In fact, on both sides more casualties happened from diseases like malaria than in battle."

Daisy yawned. "What does that have to do with us?"

Mr. Benjamin said, "In a few minutes you'll begin to reenact the Markham family's story. When Peter broke his leg in a fall from a horse, his teenage children—Francine and Joshua—went to get the goods their uncle left in a secret cache on the beach. You'll need to hurry. Low tide will end soon, and you won't be able to reach the hidden cargo."

Ms. Franklin held out the lantern to Uncle Marshall, who grabbed it. She also gave him a folded piece of heavy paper. "Follow the directions and do exactly what it says." She started handing out other items. As we stood there, she spoke to us like we were a bunch of stupid kids. "Put them on. Hurry up!"

I took one of the belts. It had a metal canteen attached and a pouch holding granola bars and trail mix. Water sloshed in the canteen as I strapped it on.

Mr. Benjamin stepped around her. "One more thing. You've got to stay together. *Unity* is the character trait of this challenge, and it's also the key to making it through. Don't let anyone fall behind. Go now!"

Uncle Marshall opened the paper and held up the lantern. We moved closer, trying to see, but he snatched it away. "Stop crowding. I'll read it out loud. 'During low tide, travel together to the cove. Search the largest stone formation.' That's all there is."

Thisby hurried to the path that led down the face of the cliff. "Come on!"

She didn't make it far without the lantern and nagged at our uncle. We formed a single line and started down the trail. I stayed at the rear, with Daisy just ahead of me. In the distance I heard the sound of waves. On the shore, everything glimmered under the moonlight in varying shades of gray, from sand to looming stone islands on the far end of the cove.

Once we finally touched down on the beach, Thisby and Warren took off running. The rest of us hurried to stay with them. It turned out my hiking shoes weren't meant for sand. Farther on, where the shore was damp and packed by waves, it got easier to run.

"Wait up, Thisby!" Daisy called.

Thisby didn't answer or even look back.

I passed my uncle, who made grunting huffs as the lantern swung in his hand and sent odd flashes of light across the beach.

Even though we moved fast, the giant rock formations seemed to stay in the distance. The low tide exposed barnacle-covered rocks and shallow pools. We finally passed the first rock formation and after ten minutes more neared the second one. I squinted, trying to see the details of the gigantic stone mound that looked like the silhouette of a sleeping dinosaur. The waves had drawn back from the shore, the base circled in wet sand that made a sunken mote.

Reaching it, we stood there for a minute, gulping in air and staring at barnacles and starfish that crusted the lower edge. Higher up were jutting layers of stone, and beyond that plants grew on the top. Uncle Marshall joined us, so winded he could hardly talk, the light from the lantern glistening off the wet scenery.

"We're supposed to stay together," he managed.

"We all got here, didn't we?" Thisby asked, not nearly as breathless as some of us. I remembered that she ran on her school's track team. She started walking around the huge rock, heading to the ocean side. "Come on, Uncle Marshall," she called over her shoulder. "We need that lantern."

When we caught up with them, Thisby was standing on the side of the mound nearest the ocean. The waves were closer, and they hit into small rock formations and sprayed us with foam.

"Find anything?" Daisy asked.

Uncle Marshall lifted the lantern, and we saw a large hole. "Looks like another cave," Warren said.

Thisby grabbed the lantern from our uncle's hand. "Let me see that."

"Hey!"

"I'll give it back in a minute."

A large wave rolled in, and to keep from getting wet we scurried to some of the higher rocks near the base. Water splashed into the opening, and Thisby waited for it to pull back before stepping inside. She held up the light, and we saw it wasn't a cave but just a round hole. Waves crashing into the rock had carved out a small grotto.

"In here," she called.

We began to file inside but had to duck our heads to get through. Uncle Marshall stumbled and then braced himself against the wall.

On a small rise was a wooden crate half buried in a mound of sand.

"There it is," Thisby said.

"What's that smell?" Daisy made a sour face. "It's gross in here."

Warren walked around the far side of the sand pile, then took a step back. "Careful if you come over this way. The ground drops off into a sinkhole, and it looks deep."

I moved closer and peered over the box at a misshapen hole

filled with black water. Daisy pointed at the crate. "Somebody grab that thing and let's go."

"Wait a second," Uncle Marshall said, leaning over it. "There are directions written on the top. It says, 'Each of you must take an item from the crate and be responsible for it. Also, choose one person to take charge of the leather packet. Leave the crate.' We should do what it says."

Thisby put down the lantern. "Fine."

She and Warren pried off the lid as the rest of us gathered close. Inside were dark amber bottles packed in straw, and Daisy picked one up. "Guess this is supposed to be medicine."

Everyone hurried to take a bottle, and I examined mine. It was small and looked antique. The label said *Quinine*, and beneath that, in faded print, was the number *325*. I shoved the bottle into the pocket of my shorts, and it clanked against something. I did a quick check and found the small pocketknife I'd forgotten was there.

"Let's get out of here." I picked up the packet tied with thin strips of leather.

Thisby put her hands on her hips. "Who says you can carry that? We're supposed to vote who gets it, remember?"

"I should have it," Uncle Marshall said, his voice loud inside the grotto. He walked over to me and held out his hand. "The Benjamin–Franklin team put me in charge."

"They just gave you the lantern," Daisy said. "That doesn't mean anything."

He lowered a stare at me. "One thing's for sure. You're not keeping it."

As he reached for the packet, I moved away from him, to the far side of the crate.

Water splashed in through the opening and filled the trough that ringed the base of the sand mound. "Decide later," Warren called. "Tide's coming in."

He headed for the opening but stopped when a wave flooded through the hole and knocked over the lantern. We were plunged into darkness, and I gasped as icy water hit my shins.

Uncle Marshall's hand brushed against my arm and then fumbled for the packet. I tried to pull away, but not before he got hold of it. I clung to the leather straps. "Let go!"

He jerked so hard that it pulled from my fingers and I staggered back. I lost my footing and plunged into the sinkhole.

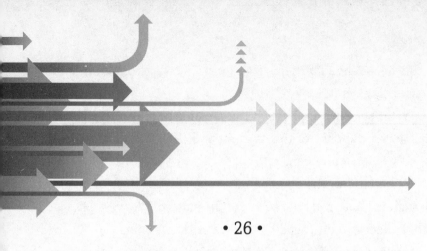

TRAVELING WITH MISFITS

Floundering in the frigid salt water, I panicked until getting my feet under me. Able to finally stand, I realized it wasn't deeper than my waist. The stagnant sinkhole smelled awful but wasn't dangerous. Still, I cursed my uncle for being so pigheaded.

Inside the dark grotto I heard voices, though before I could call for help, something slid against my bare calf. I cried out and jerked up my leg. My hands hit the slippery edge of the sinkhole and a shudder passed through me as I half choked on the rotting odor. Then, by some miracle, there was a little bit of light. A tiny beam flashed around the walls and I turned in that direction. I tried to call out but was so cold it was only a squeak, though at least I could see the dim outline of the crate buried in wet sand. I grabbed the edge with both hands and began to pull myself out.

I was making progress when something slid across my leg again. One knee slammed against the rough stone. I pulled on the crate that shifted in the sand, afraid it would tumble into the sinkhole on top of me. I was crawling out when a hand grabbed my arm. Warren stood over me, holding a small penlight. He helped me up. "You okay?"

I nodded, deciding not to say out loud what I thought about our uncle.

"Come on, then."

The trench was twice as full as before, and we splashed through it. Compared to the dark grotto, the nighttime beach glowed. The moon shimmered between clouds, and I stood there for a few seconds as Warren walked over to the others. Glancing down, I noticed some twisted, slimy thing clinging to my leg. I grabbed it and threw it down the beach before realizing it was only seaweed—not an eel.

I walked around the stone mound, back up the beach, to where Uncle Marshall sat on the ground a few feet away. Thisby crouched low and studied the top of his head as Daisy stood nearby.

Warren focused his penlight on our uncle. "What happened?"

"He tripped leaving the grotto and hit his head."

Considering how I'd ended up in the sinkhole because of him, I didn't feel any sympathy.

Thisby reached for the light. "Let me see that." She moved it closer. "This is bad, Uncle Marshall. You probably need stitches. Maybe you should go back to the lodge."

"And what, just drop out? You'd like that."

He got to his feet, trying to hide how shaky he felt. "Who has the packet?"

Daisy held it up. "It's mine now."

"Give that back." Uncle Marshall stomped over to her, and they started to argue.

"This is a waste of time," Warren called. "Remember what the writing on the crate said? We need to pick someone to be in charge of the packet. That means a vote."

"Oh sure," Thisby said. "Like that'll work. Everyone will just vote for themselves."

"Not if we make a rule you can't."

Warren took back the tiny light. Ms. Franklin said no electronic stuff, but I doubted any of us would snitch on him. With the lantern gone, it was all we had until the sun came up. A breeze wafted in off the ocean and I shivered.

Thisby tugged at the hem of her shirt. "I agree with Warren. Let's vote."

Uncle Marshall stared at us. He was soaked and a little bit of blood trickled down the side of his face. "They put me in charge before we left."

"Which is why we don't have the lantern," Daisy pointed out.

"Thisby did that. She shouldn't have taken it from me and then set it down where the water could get it."

"No more campaigning, okay?" I said.

A couple of them glanced at me but didn't say anything. We voted and Warren won. Daisy tossed him the packet. He knelt on the beach and opened it. Inside was a piece of suede that he unfolded and shone the light on. "It's a map."

Drawings and words were burned into the soft leather, and Warren pointed to the bottom edge. "Look, here's the cove and there's the rock where we got the quinine. This arrow leads in a northwest direction."

He pulled an old compass from his pocket, and Uncle Marshall asked, "Where'd you get that?"

"Thought it might be useful."

It seemed Warren had come to this challenge more prepared than the rest of us. He took off and everyone followed; I fell into place at the end of the line. We headed to the far side of the cove, and as we walked I thought about Riley and last night's kiss. What would he think when he woke up in a few hours and found I'd left without him?

After about fifteen minutes, Warren pointed to a path on the face of the cliff. "I think we're supposed to go up there."

Leaving the wet part of the shore, we trudged through loose sand until reaching the lower edge of a trail that climbed the cliff. It was much rougher than the one we came down, and we were all winded by the time we reached the top. Stopping to rest, I copied the others and took a drink from my canteen, grateful for the water even though it tasted metallic. Warren checked the map and compass again and pointed to a narrow hiking trail across the road. It led through tall grass. "We go this way."

I hoped he knew what he was doing. We hadn't been in this challenge very long, and already I was tired. I was also soaked. My wet shorts chaffed against my skin, and my hiking shoes were soggy and covered with sand. Added to that, I kept noticing a bad smell. I figured that the rotting seaweed and stagnant water from the sinkhole must have saturated my clothes.

The five of us trudged single file along the path, the waist-high grass scratching my bare legs. We passed a marshy place with thin, misshapen trees growing out of a swamp, and ahead of us loomed the edge of the woods.

"Were there trees on the map?" Daisy asked.

"Yes," Warren answered.

The trail led into a swampy forest where the ground was spongy. A breeze moved through the overhead limbs and shivered the leaves, making strange whispers.

When Warren's little light flickered, he turned it off. "Better save the battery."

It was so dark we had to go slower, but once our eyes adjusted, the moonlight guided us. As we followed the twisting path, I let my body go on autopilot, thinking about Marija's letters until interrupted by Uncle Marshall.

"What's that disgusting smell?"

I slowed my steps and hoped he wouldn't ask again, until Thisby said, "I'm pretty sure it's Avery."

He looked back. "Are you the stinkbug?"

"Yes, because you knocked me in the sinkhole when you grabbed the bag."

After that, he didn't say anything.

The forest opened into a meadow and the trail forked. We stopped walking. "Which way?" Daisy asked.

Warren dug out the leather map and focused his small light on it. For the first time I got a good look at the drawings and how the path split. One went farther inland, the other to a river. I also glimpsed a place labeled Sarsoga Swamp and smiled. This proved it was the story I knew.

Warren straightened. "I think we should take the path to the right. There's a dock, and that might mean a boat so we wouldn't have to walk."

Thisby nodded. "Sounds good."

As Warren started to roll up the map, I turned to him. "Won't a river this close to the ocean lead downstream, back to the shore? We don't want to paddle against the current."

Uncle Marshall pointed at the river trail. "The cabin on the map looks a lot closer than the house and barn on the other path. We might find supplies there."

I folded my arms, annoyed. "But we're supposed to follow the trail Francine and Joshua took."

Everyone started heading off and I stamped my foot. "You stupid idiots, you're going the wrong way!"

This got their attention. Maybe because until now, I'd never yelled or called them names. Warren turned around and came over to me. "Avery, do you know something about this challenge?"

"Yes."

The group lumbered back. "*Unity*," I said with a scornful laugh. "What a crock! If I didn't have to stick with you, I'd just love to take off and make it to the barn by myself."

"What is it you know about the story?"

I rubbed my upper arms, trying to get warm, but it didn't help. "Remember last Christmas and it'll come to you."

"What are you talking about?"

"Grandmother gave us all copies of that book." I studied their blank stares. "*Union and Confederate Heroes of the Civil War.* Remember getting it?"

"That piece of crap?" Thisby said.

Daisy studied me. "You actually read it?"

"No, but I did use the story of the Markham family for a history assignment."

Uncle Marshall's mouth got a funny, tight look. "So that's why Ms. Franklin told us we should already know the story."

"Why didn't you say something before now?" Warren asked.

Thisby struck that peeved model pose of hers. "Because Avery doesn't want us to know what a threat she is in the competition."

Under my breath I said, "*Ding, ding!* Give Barbie a tiara."

Daisy laughed but Thisby hissed something nasty. "Shut up, both of you!" Warren cut in. "Let Avery tell what she knows so we can get going."

The breeze picked up and I shivered again. "Francine, and her kid brother Joshua, carried the quinine jars in saddlebags across their shoulders, since the family horse threw a shoe. It was really hard for them, so I guess we're getting off easy. At least Grandmother didn't make us carry twenty pounds of quinine."

"Go on."

"After a long walk they reached a barn where they were supposed to meet two Confederate scouts. They hid there until sunup. When the scouts finally came for the medicine bottles, they asked Francine and Joshua to deliver a message across enemy lines to a place called Sarsoga Swamp. Even though it was dangerous, they agreed."

Warren peered at me through the moonlight. "Guess that means we take the other trail. Let's go."

We fell in line, but this time Warren asked me to stay near the front, in case I thought of anything else. As we walked, I felt the eyes of my relatives drilling into my spine.

The woods began to change. The trees were tall and straight, reaching leafy limbs to the sky. Every so often we had to step over gnarled roots, and one time Thisby tripped and sprawled on the ground. Uncle Marshall helped her up. "You all right?"

She bit back a sob and brushed dirt from her hands and knees. Daisy marched around them, chin up and face forward like she didn't notice how nice her father was to Thisby.

"How much longer, do you think?" he asked.

No one answered, though I'd been silently asking the same thing. My shorts no longer dripped water, but they were still soaked and painfully chafing my inner thighs with each step I took.

Finally Warren slowed. He pointed out a house and barn in the distance, just beyond a grove of trees. The buildings were dark silhouettes outlined by a chalky touch of moonlight. "Just the way they're drawn on the map."

The trail entered the back acreage, and we walked through an overgrown orchard. On the far side of the buildings was a graveled lane. The house and barn were old and abandoned, with an outhouse to the side. We passed a pump and Warren tested it. Water came spilling out.

Inside the barn, it was so dark that Warren had to use his little light. I looked around and saw a ladder leading to the loft.

"What do we do now?" Uncle Marshall asked, exhausted.

Walking over to the ladder, I grabbed one of the rungs. "We wait until sunrise."

With that, I started climbing.

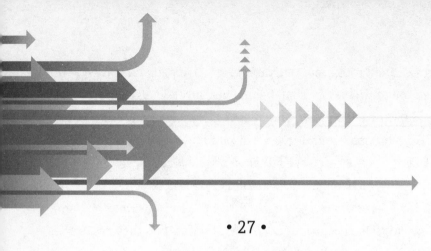

27

RELIVING HISTORY

We'd been in the barn about an hour when the sun finally rose and sent a few bright rays between the slits in the wall. I was the first to head outside and walked around to stretch my stiff muscles. I also filled my canteen at the pump and ate some of the trail mix, until my thoughts were interrupted by clomping hooves. Two men riding mules were just coming around a bend in the road. Dressed in authentic-looking Confederate gray uniforms, they had three more mules in tow.

I met them as they dismounted and tipped their hats to me. "Miss," one said with a Southern accent. "Do you have something for us?"

I worked the quinine bottle out of my pocket and gave it to him. He stuck it in a saddle bag. "Very good. You can ride my mule to the next destination."

"Thanks."

He handed me the reins. Acting like I knew what I was doing, when I'd never been on either a horse or a mule before, I stuck my foot in the stirrup and hauled myself up. The mule looked back at me with what seemed to be a lot of doubt.

My relatives hurried up to the Confederate scouts and handed over their bottles. Thisby wrinkled her nose. "Mules? Really?"

I scanned her washed-out face in the morning light. "Just be happy there's five. Francine and Joshua had to share one." I didn't add that while sitting in the barn, I felt nervous about being forced to ride with one of the VanDemeres.

Everyone mounted, and Uncle Marshall sat in the saddle like he was experienced, though the others looked unsure. The lead scout handed me a folded piece of paper. At first I was a little surprised until I remembered that in the story, Francine was the one who took the message.

He pointed down the lane. "Follow the road inland until you see a sign that says Sarsoga Swamp. Leave the mules there, but make sure you tie them up, and then take the foot trail. Look for a piece of cloth left as a marker and you'll find new directions. Put this note in its place. Any questions?"

"Why does she get the message?" Uncle Marshall asked.

I didn't bother to look back at him as I shoved the paper in my pocket. "All part of the story."

Traveling by mule ended up being slow, boring, and uncomfortable. My mule was extra stubborn and didn't want to be guided with the reins. Every time I tried, he jerked his head. I shifted my position in the saddle and thought about Riley. He'd probably be excited to ride a mule.

Warren came up next to me. "Avery, I thought you said this was dangerous."

"No, only that Francine and Joshua agreed to take the message across enemy lines though they knew it might be dangerous. Instead, it ended up being easy. They never ran into the Union soldiers on their way to the swamp. The trouble happened later. A couple of scouts tracked them down and Joshua was shot. Francine helped him get home but he died."

Warren thought this over. "What about that paper they gave you? What's written on it?"

"I don't know."

Moving the reins to one hand, I got the note from my pocket and studied the calligraphy printing: **T CANON.**

Warren looked at it, too. "Some sort of big Civil War gun, I'm guessing. Like the soldiers used in battle?"

I started to correct him but stopped myself. Though I'd have to look it up, I felt sure the gun he meant was spelled differently. Uncle Marshall called out to us. He wanted to read the note, too. When we told him what was written on it, he wasn't satisfied and insisted on seeing the paper.

A couple of minutes later we stopped near a small stream and let the mules drink. Warren held up the note for everyone to see. He gave them his theory of a battle gun, and I waited for someone to say he was wrong about the spelling of the word "cannon." No one did. He also had me retell the story about Francine and Joshua.

"Is that what was on the real message?" Daisy asked.

I shrugged. "No way to know. Francine never looked at it, though she guessed it might be about Union troop movements."

Warren gave me back the paper and guided his mule to the lane that had narrowed to little more than a trail. The others fell in line, but my mule didn't want to leave the grass along the stream. By the time I got him moving, we were at the end.

Since I didn't have a watch or cell phone, it was hard to know how long we rode. The sun inched up the morning sky and cast shadows across the trail. I was grateful for the warmth and hoped it would help get the dampness out of my clothes.

The scenery began to change, and we passed trees with white bark surrounded by fern fronds. Wild ivy grew everywhere and spiraled up tree trunks. Finally we saw a rough sign: SARSOGA SWAMP.

I was the first to get off my mule, happy to be on the ground again. We tied the reins to nearby trees and paused to drink from our canteens as Warren got out his compass. He led the way into the swamp, Uncle Marshall behind him. Tall tree limbs blocked most of the sunlight, and Spanish moss dripped from branches. There were rustling sounds in the brush, and a couple of times I heard a twig snap. Though I looked back and thought I saw movement behind a fallen log, I couldn't be sure. I told myself that if someone was following us, it was all part of the game.

As we walked, Thisby said to Daisy, "Sorry to hear you and Kyson broke up. What happened?"

"We had this big fight after a gig. He took his keyboard and left."

"Think you'll get back with him?"

Daisy shook her head. "He joined another band. I could handle his flirting with the girls in the crowd, but not that."

"The ultimate betrayal."

There was a little mocking in Thisby's tone, but Daisy didn't seem to notice. She asked, "You still with Sterling?"

Thisby brushed back her hair. "Nope. He was getting too serious and started talking about moving in together after I graduate." She glanced back at me. "What about you, Avery? You have a boyfriend?"

I hesitated, then shook my head.

She smiled. "*Ever* had a boyfriend?"

Daisy slowed and fell in line with me, her eyes curious. "I thought you might, after you finally got out of that all-girls academy and into a regular school."

"St. Frederick's isn't a regular school."

Thisby waited until we were even with her and started walking on my other side. "But there are guys there, right?"

"Not any I'm interested in."

"Or maybe," Thisby commented with a sly smile, "none of those boys are interested in you."

Daisy sent her a sideways look. "Come on, give Avery a break."

This surprised me, especially when she asked in a nice way, "Some of the guys there must've noticed you."

"A few. But the boy who likes me most is a complete Neanderthal. He makes it clear the other guys should stay away."

She snorted her disgust. "A real charmer."

"He is."

Thisby said, "I hate those possessive types. I run into them all the time."

Daisy ignored her comment. "Are you going back there in the fall?"

"I hope not."

Thisby pushed aside a small branch. "So what's your situation with Riley? You two dating?"

I hesitated. One date wasn't dating. "He's my chaperone for the competition."

"And that's all?"

Knowing her skill for taking a little bit of truth and turning it into a weapon, I had no intention of admitting we'd kissed. "He's not my boyfriend, if that's what you're asking."

Thisby smiled. "Well, that's good news."

Warren called back to us, saying we needed to keep up. I hadn't even noticed we'd fallen behind. We hurried forward, moving into a single line, and I stared at the back of Thisby's head. How stupid could I be? I'd practically attached a gift card to Riley and handed him over.

We kept walking until Uncle Marshall leaned against a tree and wiped his forehead on his sleeve. "What is it we're looking for?"

"That," Thisby said, pointing.

In the distance a piece of faded red cloth was tied to a tree stump. We hurried over and searched all around but didn't find anything until Warren spotted an animal burrow under the gnarled roots. He shoved his hand inside and felt around, then pulled out an old jar with a rubber seal. "This must be it."

I figured he was right but didn't remember anything like that in the story. Warren took off the lid and pulled out a rolled-up piece of yellowed paper. "It says, 'Travel north to the river. Take the boat downstream until you see another red marker.' That means we leave the trail."

I took the message from my pocket and put it in the jar, which I slid back into the hole. Warren looked at the compass again and started walking. We followed him as he picked his way across the springy ground, and after a while we heard the sound of moving water. Warren said, "Spread out. See if you can spot the river."

We separated and I moved past trees and thick undergrowth. I walked for a while but didn't find it. After stepping over a fallen log, I pushed my way through a dense patch of ferns and looked around. None of my relatives were in sight, and I hurried in the direction of where I thought they might be. After a couple of minutes I stopped and turned in a half circle, worried I was going the wrong way because I couldn't hear the river at all. I started to feel anxious. The last thing I needed was to get lost in the swamp.

"Hey, Avery," someone called.

I spun around and saw Daisy. She motioned to me. "It's this way."

I sprinted over and we started walking in the opposite direction from where I'd been going. I looked at her. "Why are you helping me?"

She didn't answer right away but finally gave an uncertain glance. "Because of what you said to my . . ." She paused and shook her head. "What you said to Marshall when you left the *Mayflower II*."

"Oh. I didn't know you heard."

We walked for a while, until Daisy stooped to tie her shoe. "By the way, it was smart of you to lie to Thisby. About you and Riley, I mean. I know you like each other."

I started to protest—to protect myself the way I always did—but she smiled shrewdly. "It's obvious. The way he made Chase give back your diamond and later punched him on the ship. He's definitely into you."

I scratched a bug bite on my elbow. "Thisby hasn't noticed."

Daisy stood. "She doesn't want to notice. And if you'd made the mistake of saying you like him, that'd really set her off. He'd suddenly be the most desirable guy in the universe."

I folded my arms. "Why does she hate me so much?"

I hadn't meant to ask that, but Daisy didn't hesitate to answer. "Jealous."

It took a few seconds to find my voice. "Of me?"

"And how you're Grandmother's favorite."

"I'm not her favorite."

"You live with her."

"Because my dad doesn't want me!"

The minute I said it, I wanted to take it back. Daisy didn't smirk though. Instead, she studied me with her dark gray eyes. "Guess that's something I know about, too."

We stood there until she said, "Back when we were kids, it always seemed like you got this great deal. Living in the mansion, playing in any room you wanted to. Having special brunches with Grandmother on Sundays. And, of course, we kept hearing how she showed you off at those meetings of hers, like you were a special princess or something."

"I never felt like a princess." I looked for the river, wanting to get away but in a strange way also wanting to stay. We finally started walking.

"She never let my friends from school come over. And I wasn't allowed to go to their houses, either." A sarcastic note crept into my voice. "Instead, she made sure you and Thisby came to play."

"Oh . . ."

When I glanced at her, she wore an expression I'd never seen on her before. Not wanting it to get to me, I turned away and pointed. "There's the river."

A minute later we broke through the foliage and reached the bank.

"This way," Warren called, heading to a beat-up rowboat. Uncle Marshall already sat inside, trying to undo the rope. Moving around trees with roots that trailed in the river, we finally reached it. Our uncle didn't bother to look up but kept working.

We climbed in the boat, which rocked on the water, joined by Thisby, who had shoved her way through the swamp brush. My brother grabbed the oars, slid them into place, and pushed us out to the center of the small river. The boat was crowded, too small to hold this many people, and it sat low in the water. As it gathered speed I was a little nervous, even though I felt grateful for a chance to rest.

For maybe another half hour we traveled downriver until Uncle Marshall pointed to the bank. "Over there."

Another strip of red cloth hung from a tree. Warren used the oars to push us to a sandy spot and jumped out. The rest of us followed, and we tromped back along the bank.

"There's nothing here," Daisy said, circling the trunk and looking at the ground.

"You're wrong." Thisby smiled and reached up to grab a pouch stuck in a crook between two branches. After opening it, she dumped a bunch of old coins into her palm, along with a piece of paper.

"That money is to pay for another shipment of quinine," I explained.

Uncle Marshall snatched the paper from Thisby and ignored her protest. He read it, then showed us.

Bring this money to the cabin on the river before noon. Avoid the Union army. If they catch you, you'll be eliminated.

Thisby put the coins back in the pouch and looked at her watch. "It's already ten forty."

Uncle Marshall pulled a handkerchief from his pocket and wiped his face. "We better get going. If we follow the river, we'll meet up with the other trail."

"Let's take the boat," Warren said.

Daisy shielded her eyes and looked across the river. "Uh, kinda think we can't. Who didn't tie it up?"

The line of her pointing finger showed the rowboat a long way downstream, snagged on the far side. There were groans and a couple of accusing comments, until Warren raised his voice and said we needed to get it together and figure out what to do.

We never got the chance. The sound of gunshots shattered the air, and a flock of startled blackbirds flew into the sky.

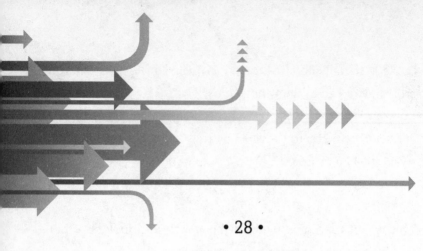

28

UNEXPECTED

We ran through the forest in a headlong rush away from the gun-fire. Thisby sprinted ahead. The shots faded and the only sound was of us crashing through the brush. Between ragged breaths I explained how Francine and Joshua were stopped by Union scouts. Joshua got shot and though Francine managed to get her brother home, he died four days later.

"But I don't get it," I said. "They didn't run into the soldiers in the swamp. It was right before they reached their farm."

No one seemed to listen as we hurried through the woods, the swamp now behind us. Wild underbrush snagged my clothes and scratched my bare legs. Thisby ducked beneath some low pine branches, but Uncle Marshall just shoved his way through. As I followed him, a limb flew in my face and slapped my eye. Wincing, I staggered backward. Pain shot clear up into my head, and my face throbbed. Daisy passed me.

"Go!" Warren said from behind, and I started running again but had to keep my eye shut. I could've punched my uncle.

On we raced, a lopsided line zigzagging through the woods. I followed the others around a grove of slender trees growing close together. Behind me, I heard a sudden cry. I glanced back and saw Warren sprawled on the ground. He lurched to his feet but went down again.

"Wait!" I called to the others.

They didn't slow, and only Daisy looked back. I wanted to run after them but hesitated, then ran back to Warren as panic warned me not to stop. His foot twisted partway behind him and he jerked it frantically. "I can't get loose!"

His shoelace was wedged in the wood of a fallen tree. I grabbed it and yanked but couldn't get it free; then I remembered my pocketknife. Working quickly, I sliced through the lace as my mind screamed at me to get out of there. He got his leg around and stood as I took off. I leaped across a stream and Warren followed. Over my shoulder I caught a glimpse of movement.

We skirted trees and undergrowth that blocked our way, and I ran like crazy as dread pounded at my temples.

A marshy spot slowed us down. Mud sucked at our feet, and I fell forward onto my knees, but Warren grabbed my arm and jerked me up. We slogged to the other side. Behind us was shouting and a blast from a gun. Several seconds later someone tackled me, and we went down. I struggled to breathe, and a rushing noise filled my ears until I finally managed to gulp in air.

The man who'd hit me was dressed in a faded blue soldier's

jacket with a wide leather belt. He had a scruffy beard and wore an odd hat with a square bill. It made him look like he'd stepped out of a Civil War movie. He pulled me to my feet but I jerked free. With his large fists he shoved me in the direction of a tree stump that Warren knelt beside.

I stood there, gasping, my limbs trembling. A second soldier walked up to us. About Warren's age, he had deep-set eyes and a small scar at the side of his mouth. "Look what we got us here. A pair of smugglers."

He moved closer and I backed up a step but decided that was silly. None of this was real. "Get away from me." My voice sounded tougher than I felt.

He shoved me against a tree and pinned me there. "This is a lively one, Zeb."

Warren got to his feet. "Stop it."

I sent him a surprised look as Zeb withdrew an old-fashioned pistol from his belt. He pointed it at Warren, only inches away. "Got no use for smugglers."

With that, he pulled the trigger. There was a loud blast. Warren doubled over and sank to his knees. I cried out as the man holding me let go and spun around. I hurried over, and for a few horrified seconds thought he'd actually been shot.

"What'd you do that for?" the younger guy yelled.

"It's just a blank, Tom. That's what you said, right?"

Tom swore at him. "It's still gunfire! That's why I told you not to shoot any closer than five or six feet."

It was strange seeing the younger guy chewing out the older one like he was a kid. Zeb looked panicked. "But the boy in the story got shot, right? We're supposed to act it out."

Tom came over to Warren and crouched down. "Sorry about that. Just catch your breath and you'll be all right."

Warren rose up and swung his fist, which caught Tom on the jaw. His head snapped back and he plopped down in a bunch of ferns. I knelt beside my brother and studied his pale, sweaty face. "Warren, are you hurt?"

Lifting the hem of his shirt, he stared at an ugly red welt on his stomach. "I feel like I've been slugged, only ten times worse."

Tom glared at Warren, his face flushed. "I'm not the one who shot you." He rubbed his jaw, got to his feet, and stomped off. "You're on your own."

Zeb hurried after Tom and we heard him say, "But aren't we supposed to take them to the cabin if they're out of the game?"

Tom hissed an answer as they left.

After resting for a couple of minutes, Warren got out the map and compass. I helped him stand. "Sure you're okay?"

"Yeah." He looked thoughtful. "Why'd you come back and help me, Avery?"

I put on a calm act but knew my flushed face was probably giving me away. Finally, I shrugged.

He said, "Can't believe you did that."

I managed a weak smile. "Me, either."

His fingers fiddled with the compass. "Thanks."

"Not like it did any good. We're both out of the game." I picked up a rock and threw it as hard as I could. It missed the tree I was aiming for. I threw another one.

He folded his arms and watched. "It might help if you envision Uncle Marshall."

The next one hit dead center and I smiled.

Warren picked up a rock. "The idiot who shot me." His smacked the tree.

I grabbed two more. "Thisby outrunning us." Near miss. *And flirting with Riley.* Direct hit.

"Grandmother." His rock struck with so much force it tore off a chunk of bark.

I laughed, the sound bitter as I stooped to get another.

He lifted a huge stone with both hands. "Dad." It didn't reach the trunk but landed on the roots.

Both of us stood looking at the tree so that we didn't have to look at each other. I dropped the rock I was holding and rubbed my shoulder. "What now?"

"If we head southeast, I think we'll reach the trail to the cabin. We can meet up with the others there."

For twenty minutes we worked our way through the forest until it started to thin out. As Warren predicted, we found the trail. Neither of us said anything, caught up in our own worries. The longer we walked, the more sick I felt about losing. Knowing all the details of the story, I'd been riding high, so sure I had the best chance of winning—or at least of making it through the challenge. All of that turned around in a minute.

During the last few days, my fear of getting sent back to St. Frederick's had faded. Now it loomed over me again. If I ran away, could I still collect the big inheritance check on my birthday? I seriously doubted Grandmother would let me. And without that money, it would be a lot harder to find Marija. There was only one option. I'd have to be the obedient granddaughter and serve the rest of my time at the boarding school.

I thought about the way Gavin Waylenz once cornered me in the stairwell, backing me against the wall with an arm on either side. I also remembered what he said when I left—that he'd be waiting.

"There it is." Warren walked faster and I hurried to keep up.

The small cabin sat among rough bark trees. It looked really old, the wood shingles faded to a silvery gray and layered with pine needles and dead leaves.

We went up the steps and inside. Warren looked around. "They aren't here yet."

"I wonder what time it is."

"Don't know. Wish I had my phone."

The cabin's front room was small and without much furniture, except for a pine table and a couple of chairs that had sagging wicker seats. I unbuckled my belt and let the empty canteen drop to the floor. Warren did the same as I wandered through the cabin. I found two odd little bedrooms with nothing but cots. When I came back to the main room, Warren was seated, feet out in front of him, eating a granola bar.

I sat down, realizing how hungry I was, and took one out.

He studied me with a curious look in his eyes. "You never answered my question. Why'd you come back and help me, especially after I stole your tablets?"

"Trust me, I've been asking myself the same thing." I took a bite and chewed for a few seconds. "Maybe because Mr. Benjamin said we should stay together and not leave anyone behind. Uncle Marshall, though? My whole life I've wanted to leave him and his kids behind. Especially Chase."

Warren nodded, even smiling a little like he got it. I brushed stringy hair out of my face. "Anyway, not like I'll see any of you again."

"Unless we come to the mansion."

I looked at him like he was crazy. "You think I'm still going to live there? I've been planning for years to move out on my eighteenth birthday."

I stood and went to the window. Sunlight rested in bright patches on the trees and ground, showing it was midday. "If the others will just get here, we can go back to the lodge." I didn't look forward to telling Riley the bad news.

Warren pushed back his chair; it made a soft scraping sound. "Not that it matters now, since we're both out of the game, but Stasia said if we didn't win, she hoped you would."

I turned back. "You're kidding. Why?"

"She thinks Grandmother owes you more than the rest of us. That even if she left you her whole fortune, it doesn't make up for what she did."

"The letter."

He nodded.

I walked back and sat down. "Do you remember her?" All on its own, my voice dropped to a whisper. "My mother?"

He hesitated. "Barely."

"I have a picture of you."

I dug the two laminated photos out of my pocket, sad to notice they were a little bent. The one of Marija with Warren was on top, and I held it up for him to see. He reached for it and I paused just a second before handing it over. Warren studied it a long time, and I watched his face. He hid his feelings well but still gave a glimpse of something wistful. I said, "My nanny was Jean. When I went to school, they sent her away. I cried every night for a long time."

His eyes stayed on the picture. "All this time they told everyone she died."

I nodded. "A big, fat lie."

His gaze drifted from the picture. "I bet everything would've been different for me if she hadn't gotten involved with my dad."

Even though his tone wasn't harsh, I felt immediately defensive. "I'm sure she's regretted it her whole life."

"I'm just saying. Anyway, no matter what Preston and she did, you didn't deserve to be punished for it by the rest of our family."

For the first time since I could remember, it felt like the weight of family disapproval I'd carried for years lifted a little. "Thanks, Warren."

He handed the picture back. "After my parents got divorced, Dad would sometimes come around. It always upset my mom, and I was angry with him, too. When I was fourteen, I told him I didn't want to see him again. After that, he stopped coming. The stupid thing is, I always thought that if he still cared about me, he would've come anyway. When I have kids, I'm going to be there for them. Even if they say they don't want me to."

"Our dad is broken." I realized the truth as I said it. "How could he give us what we need when he doesn't have it himself?" I slid the photos back into my pocket.

"Listen," Warren said. "Someone's coming."

The door opened and Mr. Benjamin came in. His hiking clothes were rumpled, his face flushed and sweaty. I thought about how more than once on the swamp trail, I sensed someone behind us. Had he been following our group? He looked at Warren. "I heard what happened with the pistol shot. You all right?"

"The guy was an idiot, but I'll live."

"Glad to hear it."

He turned away, pulled something small from his pocket, and aimed it. A remote. My eyes searched the room and found a tiny box mounted in the corner. I was so focused on talking with Warren I'd forgotten to look for a camera. My heart dropped. Had Grandmother eavesdropped on us? I shoved Marija's pictures in my pocket and tried to remember all the stuff I'd just said. But then I saw a slight pulse of light from the camera; it looked like Mr. Benjamin had just turned it on.

There was the sound of feet running up the steps, and the door banged open. Thisby stumbled inside. She was sunburned, bug bitten, and filthy. She was also elated.

"Made it!" She rested her hands on her knees and gasped for breath. Then she held out the pouch of coins to Mr. Benjamin, who took it. Glancing in our direction, she smiled. "Heard you two were already here. The Union soldiers get you?"

Warren rested his fists on his thighs. "Don't be so freaking happy about it."

Thisby burst out laughing like this was really funny.

Nearly five minutes later, Daisy and Uncle Marshall dragged in. They were followed by Ms. Franklin, who also looked rumpled and worn out. She and Mr. Benjamin must have both shadowed us.

Daisy's black hair stuck out, and bits of leaves were clinging to it. She walked up to Thisby, her expression hurt. "Why didn't you wait for me? You know I can't run as fast as you."

Thisby tapped her watch. "Eleven fifty-five."

"But we agreed to stick together."

"You didn't keep up. That's not my fault."

Daisy's brows drew in. "Guess you don't really get the idea of being partners."

"We had to bring the coins here before noon, remember?" Thisby put her hands on her hips. "We'd all be in trouble if I didn't. So instead of being so touchy, maybe you could show a little appreciation."

Daisy wiped a trickle of sweat from her temple. "Sure, Thisby. I'm real grateful to you for ditching me, the way you always do." She went to a wall and slid down to sit cross-legged on the floor.

Uncle Marshall, still out of breath, shook his head at Thisby. She folded her arms. "Hey, I can't help it if you're out of shape and had to keep stopping."

Ms. Franklin pulled a thick piece of ivory paper from her pocket and unfolded it. "This is a quote Mrs. VanDemere asked me to read. It's from the writings of your ancestor Francine Markham. 'Every day I grieve for the loss of my brother. His young life was sacrificed to save the suffering troops, and many soldiers survived because of the quinine we brought across enemy lines. Yet it is the memory of guiding Joshua home in his wounded state that haunts me still, even after all these years. I do not believe the sadness of it will ever depart.' "

I remembered using that same quote in my history project.

Ms. Franklin refolded the paper. "We know you're all tired and it's been a long ordeal, so let's make this quick."

I braced myself for the bad news and for the smirks that would follow. But at least I wouldn't be alone. Warren glanced my way and gave a friendly shrug as if to say, *Who cares?*

Mr. Benjamin stepped forward. "The VanDemere who failed to achieve the character trait of unity is Thisby." He went over to her. "I'm sorry to inform you, but you're eliminated from the competition."

We all stared at her. *Thisby?*

She stood still for a few seconds, her face turning red as she sputtered in protest. Finally she pointed at me. "But Avery got caught by those soldiers! So did Warren!"

Mr. Benjamin shook his head. "This test was about learning to be unified. I told you not to leave anyone behind. You ran ahead of all the others."

"To get here before noon, so I could give you the coins!"

Ms. Franklin said, "Doesn't matter. You see, Avery was captured by the enemy because she turned back to help Warren, just the way your ancestor Francine did with her brother. If you had read the story, you'd have known that. This is why, instead of being eliminated, Avery is the winner of the challenge."

I let out a choked breath, my head buzzing. I was still in the game, and Thisby wasn't. *And I'd won!* It was all I could do to keep from jumping up and doing a victory dance.

Warren gave me a wide grin. "Terrific, Avery!"

"It's crazy," I said in a shocked voice.

He held up a high five and I slapped his palm.

The disbelief on Thisby's face was replaced with devastation, and I could almost see what she was thinking: both she and her dad were now out of an inheritance. Turning in my direction, she channeled it into anger. "You did that on purpose, didn't you?"

My smile faded. "I don't know what you mean."

"The story! You kept the details to yourself so you could win."

"No I didn't. I told you everything I knew."

Her eyes were wild. "You're a lying whore, exactly like that Russian mother of yours!"

I flew at her. My fingers clenched into fists and I raised them. It took the last bit of my control to keep from striking her. "Shut up, Thisby."

Her eyes flicked away for just a second, and I sensed her uncertainty. When I spoke, my voice sounded murderous. "You ever say that again, I'll take you out."

There must have been something in the tight lines of my face that unnerved her, because she took a step back. Facing the others, she let out a phony laugh. "Watch your back, everyone. Avery's out to win this game, and she'll take it from you just like she did from me."

With that she spun around and left the cabin.

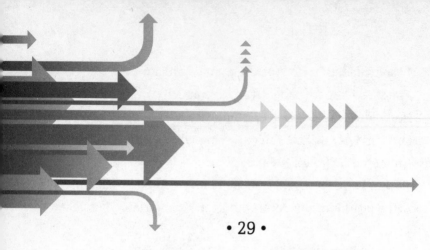

29

DAUGHTER AND MOTHER

After I showered, I examined my injuries in the mirror. With the dirt gone, there were a ton of scratches on my arms and legs that I hadn't seen before. A few bruises were starting to form; sunburn and bug bites rounded out the new Avery body art. Worst of all was my black eye. It was ugly, with scratches around it from the sharp pine needles.

Did it matter? I'd heal. My thoughts kept going back and forth between the excitement of beating out everyone in the challenge and my fight with Thisby. I'd never stood up to her like that, and in its own way it felt as good as winning.

I dressed in comfy clothes and a few minutes later heard a knock. Riley called, "Room service."

I let him in. He carried a tray to the table and set it down as I walked over. "What's that amazing smell?"

"Pot roast with homemade corn bread."

He turned around and for the first time got a good look at

me. "What happened? You fight the whole Civil War by your-self?"

I laughed and he asked, "Are you still in the competition?"

"Yes. And guess what? I won the challenge!"

He let out an excited yell and scooped me up in a hug. "Terrific!"

I hugged back.

He set me down and asked, "So, who got eliminated?"

"Thisby."

Riley brought down a triumphant fist. *"Yes!"*

He looked so elated that I stared at him. "You're really happy."

"Of course. Why wouldn't I be?"

I shrugged. He leaned in and studied my face. "Avery?"

I tried to think of the best way to explain and finally decided to just say it. "Thisby's been flirting with you."

"So what's new? She's done that since she was fourteen." His face grew thoughtful. "You don't really think I like her, do you?"

I brushed a damp tendril of hair from my cheek. "Whenever you and she talk, you smile."

"I'm the lawyer's son. It's my job to smile at the VanDe-meres." He reached up and lightly touched the bruise on my cheek. "To be really clear, I don't like Thisby. It doesn't matter how much she throws herself at me, I could never be interested."

Riley looked down for a few seconds. "See, a long time ago there was this little girl with dark brown hair and a bloody lip." His hands went to my arms. "She'd just been picked on and was trying to hold it together when Thisby said horrible stuff to her. I watched her run away. Thisby stood there and looked all smug about it."

One thumb slowly stroked the skin on my arm, sending tingles. "Avery, how could you think I'd ever like that kind of girl?"

I didn't answer. My heart was beating too fast.

He guided me over to the table. While we ate, my mind kept going back to his words and the fact that he didn't like Thisby—that he'd never liked her.

Riley asked about the challenge and I told details, including my fight with Thisby. He said, "You stood up to her. How'd that feel?"

"Like I should've done it years ago."

He lowered his fork. "I still can't get over how far you've made it. And now there's only four of you left. Half are gone."

His enthusiasm was catching. I'd come a long way from the girl in the conference room who was afraid she'd be the first one eliminated.

I told him about my conversation with Warren, and he nodded. "I'm not surprised after what I found out today. I went for a walk and ran into Stasia, who's a real talker. She told me some things about your brother, including the reason he's going into psychology. It's helped him handle some of his own problems. We both agreed your grandmother left more than money as a heritage."

"You mean like screwed-up kids and grandkids?" I tilted my head to give him a goofy look.

He chuckled. "Yep."

We talked more about the challenge, and Riley said, "Wish I could've been there."

"Me too! It was way harder without you."

"Happy to be of service. You know, I asked Mr. Benjamin if I'm going to be cut out of the next challenge, and he said unlikely."

The relief I felt must have showed. "Great news."

"By the way, what about a hidden clue? Was there anything that might've been a message?"

"Only a couple of things, but I'm not sure. Remember the quinine bottle? The number three hundred twenty-five was on the label."

"Hmm. That mean anything to you?"

"No. And the other one might be nothing, either."

I picked up my tablet and did an Internet search for *T Canon* while I explained about the paper from the Confederate scout. The main item to come up on the screen was a camera. "Does this make sense to you?"

Riley shook his head. "Add the Civil War to your search."

I did, and then we were looking at old-fashioned artillery labeled *cannon*. He said, "That's more of a match, but why would your grandmother misspell it?"

"She wouldn't. And here's another funny thing, nobody else noticed it was spelled wrong. Warren said he thought it was a big gun, and Uncle Marshall agreed."

"Maybe he was just being sneaky and not letting on."

"Or maybe he didn't think it's important. It might not be."

Once we finished eating and my storytelling wound down, Riley started putting the dishes back on the tray. "You had a tough day. Want to crash for a while?"

I nodded and stood. He came over and put his arms around me; it felt hugely comforting. He kissed my forehead, then stayed that way, just letting his lips rest there. Finally he murmured, "You're amazing. You know that, don't you?"

Unable to answer, I lifted my face and gazed at him with my

pitiful black eye. He kissed me, and the warmth of his mouth on mine spread a delightful buzz through my limbs. He pulled back and I studied his face. There was a direct way he had of looking at me with those eyes of his. On the surface he made it seem like life was casual and nothing to worry about, but just behind that was something a lot more intense and probing—something that made me want to connect with him.

"Next to finding out my mother is still alive, you're the best thing that's happened to me during all this," I said.

He reached out and stroked my hair in one slow movement. Then he grabbed the tray and headed out the door. "Get some rest. I'll see you later."

I called Mr. Tate and asked for another letter. He said, "You're doing great, Avery. I'm really proud of you for making it through another challenge. Just fantastic."

I could hear the encouraging dad he was to Riley—no wonder they were so close. It made a sad comparison to my father.

"Which letter do you want?"

I thought for several seconds. "The fourteenth one."

That was a rough year—before I figured out how to sneak off the estate.

"I'll send it right away."

While I waited, I read several texts from Megan, who was still in Germany. She also included two pictures of a gorgeous castle with a name I couldn't pronounce. I texted her back, then took my tablet and flopped onto the bed. My whole body seemed to sigh with relief, as if I could sleep for hours. First though, I needed to read my mother's letter.

Today, my daughter, you are fourteen.

During this past week, as the day of your birth neared, I kept recalling the newborn feel of you in my arms. Even though you are a young woman now, I have not quite been able to envision this. Always, to me, you are the tiny infant, as if time is frozen. But then something happened.

Last night I had a dream, and it was about you. At first you stood looking in a mirror at your reflection, and I was surprised to see you were very much like me as a girl. I talked to you but you didn't hear or see me. In the dream, I was a ghost just watching you. I followed where you walked, sat with you when you read a book. In the dream there was no remarkable thing, just a quiet hope. After I woke, my heart was not heavy. Fear and anger, which oppress me when I think of you, were not there this time.

And now I must confess something that you will not like to know. I do not think of you every day. Nor many days in a row. I have learned not to allow myself this because of the guilt. It weighs me down, a stone on my heart, and so I set it aside that I may function. In its own way it brings more guilt, as if I only abandon you in a different way.

Yet always will you be there in my heart, even on the days I do not think of you. And always will I grieve for each year that goes by. One more year I have lost.

Wishing you a good life,

Marija

I read the letter through a second time. There was still so much suffering in those words. How heartbreaking were the other letters I hadn't read yet? The familiar angry thought kept coming back. Marija and I were just two people who longed for the same thing; she wanted me as her daughter, and I wanted her as my mother. Why couldn't my self-centered grandmother have left us alone? And how could I ever forgive her for separating us?

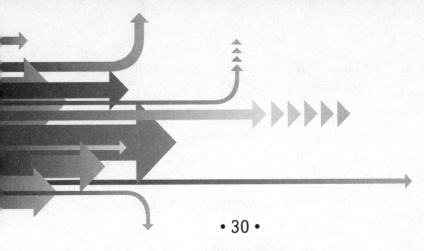

30

CONFINED

By nine the next morning we'd boarded the VanDemere jet and left the Richmond Airport. The good news? Thisby and Uncle Logan weren't there. According to Mr. Benjamin, they'd already left for California.

Riley grinned. "Kind of gives you that warm, fuzzy feeling, doesn't it?"

I laughed, happy in the freedom of having them out of my life. Permanently, I hoped.

The flight staff started serving breakfast, and Uncle Marshall walked past us to sit beside Daisy in the section behind our seats. We couldn't help but overhear her calling him Marshall.

"Stop saying that, will you?" he said.

"And what, call you Dad? Like I'll ever do that again."

"How many times do I have to apologize? I was furious about what you did to your brother. Chase trusted you, and so did I."

"You think that makes it all right to tell our entire family you think I'm a bastard? By the way, I had a long phone call with Mom, who says you're the bastard, not me. We decided as soon as I get back to California, I'm getting a DNA test."

His voice turned surprisingly sincere. "All right, Daisy, so I was wrong! Especially to say what I did in front of everyone. I reacted emotionally."

"And because it's what you've secretly believed my whole life."

He shifted in his seat. "I don't know what else to do but keep saying I'm sorry."

She let out a sigh. "What do you want, Marshall?"

He lowered his voice, but we could still hear. "I want us to work together as a team. Warren has his wife. Avery has that Tate boy. Together, we've got a better chance."

Daisy mumbled something I couldn't make out. I grabbed my stuff and motioned to Riley. We moved up a few rows and ate our breakfast away from them.

A little while later, as I headed to the restroom, I passed Stasia. She stopped me. "Your poor eye!"

"Looks bad, doesn't it?"

"It does," she admitted. "Hey, I've got an idea! See you in a minute."

When I came back she was waiting for me in Riley's seat, a large floral makeup bag in her lap. He'd moved next to the window and gazed at me over her shoulder with an amused expression. Stasia told me to sit down as she unzipped the bag. "I've got some really good blemish concealer. Just lean your head back a little."

As she worked on me with a makeup sponge, I filled the silence. "So how did you and Warren meet?"

"My first year of college, our roommates were dating. They dragged us along, and we hit it off. After a few months they broke up, but Warren and I stayed together. You know, when we first met, he was standoffish. I thought it was because he was so handsome and girls were always approaching him. But then I got to know him and saw how shy he was. Kind of vulnerable, even. I had to fight my way past that hard act of his to find the real Warren, but it was worth it."

It was hard not to blink as she worked on my eye. "You're good for him."

"I try to be . . . Now you look better. I'll leave this concealer with you." She dug in her bag. "You have great skin, Avery."

Stasia started adding eye shadow and who knew what else. She said, "Can I ask you something?"

"Sure."

"Did you know going back for Warren would win you the challenge?"

I hesitated, surprised. "No. How could I?"

"Then why'd you do it?"

I shrugged, not having a better answer than when Warren had asked me that. "It seemed like the right thing to do."

Stasia dipped a brush into the eye shadow, then glanced back to where Daisy and my uncle sat. She lowered her voice. "I've been thinking. We could help each other. Maybe the four of us can work as a team."

Was that where this kindness came from? A hidden motive?

Riley leaned forward. "The problem is that in the end only one heir can win. Before this is over, Warren and Avery would have to turn against each other. Is that what you want?"

She busied herself with the makeup bag. "No, it's not. Never mind. Dumb idea." She handed me a mirror. "There, Avery. You look gorgeous."

I had to admit she'd done amazing work in hiding the black eye, even if the rest of the makeup was a bit overdone. "Thanks. It hardly shows."

Stasia put the other items back in her bag and smiled at me. She seemed so much different from my first impression of her in the law firm's waiting room. Which was the real Stasia? We watched her go sit by Warren, who put his arm around her.

Riley moved closer. "Hey, beautiful. The way things are going, you might even end up at their house for Thanksgiving."

I let out a very un-beautiful snort. "I doubt that. Besides, maybe she's only acting friendly to help Warren."

He took my hand. "There's no way to know for sure."

Our flight lasted a long time, and we both wondered more than once where we were headed. Riley said, "Not back to California. We're flying in the opposite direction."

Mr. Benjamin and Ms. Franklin refused to answer questions, and finally she shook her head at us. "Stop asking! We can't tell you until we land."

Riley grabbed his tablet and pulled up the list of character traits Grandmother gave us before we left for the first challenge.

1. Intellect
2. Fortitude

3. Resourcefulness
4. Unity
5. Commitment
6. Courage
7. Integrity

He said, "We're more than halfway through."

"So the next one will be *commitment*. That doesn't sound too bad. Except number six, *courage*, makes me a little nervous."

Riley smiled. "Don't worry. Nothing could be scarier than going down in the diamond mine."

We flew for nearly seven hours, and I was sick of being on the plane. Finally, Riley pointed to the darkened window. Looking at the night landscape below, I saw lights. A city came into view, and Ms. Franklin moved to the head of the aisle. "We'll be landing soon. Set your watches to nine p.m. There's a five-hour time difference between here and Virginia."

Riley checked his cell phone. "With the time zones, that means an eight-hour difference from California. In Santa Rosa, it's only one in the afternoon."

Mr. Benjamin stood, his lean features unreadable as ever. "You are about to begin the next challenge of the competition. Welcome to Edinburgh."

There was a whole lot of muttering, and Riley leaned into me. "What is it? Why's everyone excited?"

"The Scottish kings," I whispered.

I didn't tell him the rest of what I knew. We were in trouble.

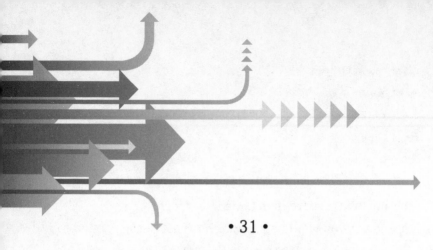

31

A ROYAL PAIN

I only got a glimpse of Edinburgh as they drove us to the George Hotel. We were led to a private dining room, a table laid out with food waiting for us. As we ate, Uncle Marshall searched for info on his laptop while Daisy read over his shoulder.

Riley whispered, "She must've accepted his offer."

"Too bad. They'll be more of a threat as a team."

In their usual way, Ms. Franklin and Mr. Benjamin came and stood in front of us, and everyone immediately focused on them. It was funny how we'd practically trained ourselves to be quiet and listen the minute they took center stage.

Ms. Franklin said, "As in the *Mayflower* challenge, this part of the competition will have no winner. It will be either pass or fail. Turn in the required items, and you'll move on. Fail to do so, you'll be eliminated. Mrs. VanDemere has another message for you."

Mr. Benjamin pressed a remote.

"Welcome, my remaining heirs! Well done to those of you who are still in the competition. As you've certainly guessed by now, this next challenge has to do with the heritage of the Reide line. We can trace our family tree all the way back to Duncan, Lord of Mormaer, born in Atholl, Perthshire, in AD 949. It's quite amazing to realize he lived more than a thousand years ago."

Grandmother started talking about our greatest European legacy and the character trait *commitment*, her one-sided conversation going on and on. I glanced around the room and saw Uncle Marshall trying to hide a smug smile. Warren whispered to Stasia with a lot of enthusiasm. Feeling even more nervous, I didn't make eye contact with Riley, though he was looking at me.

Grandmother said, "In case you think this is all a bit vague, just remember back to a year and a half ago at the Scottish party I threw. Everything I talked about applies to this challenge. And for those of you who paid attention and remember the history lesson, I also discussed the blight of scandal. It takes only one rash action to blacken a heritage."

Mr. Benjamin pressed the remote and scanned our group. "You'll need to find a written message left for you at the legacy site. Bring it back here by tomorrow afternoon at two o'clock, Edinburgh time."

Ms. Franklin added, "A room upstairs is booked for each of you. Your key cards are at the front desk." She walked over to me and held out an envelope. "Avery, since you won the last challenge, here's your reward."

Our suites were impressive, but I hardly had a chance to look around. Riley came through my door, still talking to his father on the phone. From what I overheard, he'd already texted the info to our research team. He disconnected and turned to me. "So who's this Duncan of Mormaer guy?"

"A dead ancestor."

I opened the envelope and pulled out a brochure for Edinburgh Helicopter Charters and a prepurchased reservation. Riley scanned it. "This is great! They'll be able to fly us wherever we need to go." He looked up. "Which is where, exactly?"

"Hard to say." I sat down on the bed. It had a crimson brocade cover that was so slick I nearly slid off.

He started to get that concerned expression I sometimes glimpsed. "You don't know?"

I shook my head.

"But your uncle and brother seem to."

A new thought came to him and he raised his eyebrows—those handsome guy eyebrows that were darker than his blond hair. They slanted up, then made a sharp downward curve, and I traced them with my eyes. He didn't notice. "Weren't you at your grandmother's party that year?"

"I've been to all of them. It's just I wasn't really paying attention."

I moved to a plaid loveseat. "Did you ever come to one of my grandmother's theme parties?"

He sat beside me. "I'm not sure."

"She's thrown a few. Like one Halloween five or six years ago, we had a masked ball." I remembered how Chase stuck his half-eaten caramel apple to the back of my black cat outfit. It left a gooey mark. The memory made me cringe until I remembered: *Eliminated!*

"Go on."

"One of her parties was about the California gold rush. Another the French Revolution. And in December five years ago, she did this whole medieval thing." I was almost thirteen and so happy in my Juliet dress and cap, until Thisby showed up in an even fancier one. And back then, I still didn't have a chest, while she'd just come into full bloom. I felt like a little caterpillar next to a monarch butterfly.

"That's what I mean by theme parties."

Riley's eyes got a pleased glint. "Sure! We were invited to one with mountain men and Native American dancers. It was really cool."

"Right. That was her Rendezvous party. Anyway, the party Grandmother is talking about was for family only and had a Scottish theme. She'd just learned about her Reide family line going back to royalty and was super excited."

"So she talked about the Scottish kings?"

"Yes." I tried to remember some of the details of that night. "But before she did, this Shakespearian troupe performed *Macbeth*. At dinner we had real haggis—and I can tell you right now, I'm never eating that again, even if I am in Scotland. Next came bagpipes and Highland dancers. And when it was all over, Grandmother made this big presentation about the kings and queens we're descended from."

"Did she talk about Duncan, the first king?"

"Probably."

He lowered his chin to peer out from beneath his eyebrows.

"Stop looking at me like that, will you? Do you know how mind-numbing it was? Especially after what we'd already sat through? So I was in the back reading the book I hid under my purse."

"You didn't listen to any of it?"

"Not really. I was upset because my dad hadn't shown up. When he visited me on my birthday a few months before, he promised he would. I even wore the stupid necklace he gave me, this silver heart that's not my style."

"A locket?"

"No. I thought it was at first, but the heart didn't open. Fitting on so many levels."

I slouched and put my feet on the coffee table. He took my hand and studied my fingers. A bruise crossed my knuckles, left over from yesterday's challenge.

"Guess I can't blame you. But Avery, what about other times? Brunches or dinners with your grandma? She must've wanted to talk about the Scottish kings."

"I didn't see her as often this last year. She went on a lot of research trips. We talked a little, but I got to where I didn't care about the history stuff."

"Some of it must've sunk in."

"No, since mostly I was making plans to sneak out." I did my imitation of a puppetlike bobblehead. "Uh-huh, Grandmother. Very interesting! Scottish royalty? Really?"

He laughed, then glanced at his phone when a text came in. Grabbing his tablet, he opened several attachments from the research team. "Uh-oh. There are lots of names here. All of them descendants of Duncan."

Looking at the long list, I felt even more discouraged.

Riley stretched, then focused on the tablet. "Let's see if any of these rings a bell. What about Crinan Mormaer Dunkeld."

I shook my head.

"King David the first? Or Malcolm the third?"

"I'm not sure."

"Isabel, princess of Scotland?"

"Sorry, Riley. They all sound familiar. I just don't know anything about them. Especially the one who left us what Grandmother kept calling our 'greatest European legacy.'"

"I wonder what it is. A castle, maybe?"

"Could be. But there are lots of castles in Scotland. Or it might be something else. What about artwork like statues or tapestries? Maybe everything the ancestor left is in a museum somewhere."

"And until we find out who he or she is, we're stuck." He pulled up the lists from my grandmother's notebook, and we read through them. It took a while to check each name, but after an hour we realized none tied into the Reide line.

I rubbed my stiff neck. "It was such a waste to even try and use her stupid notes!"

Knowing I needed to focus, I picked up my tablet and read through pages of documents sent by the research team. Even though some of the names seemed familiar, I couldn't figure out which of the Scottish kings was important to Grandmother. I began my own search on the Internet and followed strands of thought that ended nowhere. After that I got my camera and scrolled through the pictures from her office. The only things related to Great Britain were a sword, an illuminated manuscript page in a fancy frame, and several antique watches. Discouragement settled in as the shadows of failure seemed to inch closer.

Near midnight, Edinburgh time, I went to the window and

looked down at the street. There was almost no traffic and lamplight reflected off damp pavement. Was it raining? Suddenly I longed for the smell of a summer storm. "Let's go for a walk."

Riley looked up from his tablet. "Now?"

I grabbed the key card and shoved it in my pocket.

"Avery, there's not much time left to find the right ancestor. And I don't want to cut it close again like we did with the *Mayflower*."

Couldn't he give it a rest for five minutes? I headed into the hall as he called my name and half expected him to come after me, but he didn't.

Downstairs, I crossed the elegant lobby and stepped outside. A light rain was just drizzling to a stop, and I took a deep breath. Nothing smelled as wonderful to me as city streets after a storm. I started walking away from the hotel and an odd little taxi whizzed by. It looked so funny I almost laughed, except for the knot of despair inside.

It was late enough that the sidewalks were empty and all the buildings closed. I reached a corner and turned onto a street that wasn't as well lit, much of the walkway masked with shadows. It helped to be outside, the stress easing just a little as I stepped across a puddle and took in several slow breaths. I tried to clear my mind, to think of anything except the challenge. Maybe I should just go back to the hotel and tell Riley how much trouble we were in. Or maybe he already knew.

The air was damp with mist. A shiver passed through me and I wished I'd grabbed a sweatshirt. After walking for almost a block, I heard the sound of footsteps behind me. I stopped and looked back, thinking it had to be Riley, but he wasn't there. I didn't see anyone else, either, and peered into the dark recesses of shops facing the street. Instinct told me someone was watching from the shadows, though after several seconds of waiting I still hadn't seen any movement. I finally started walking, this time faster, and also listened. By the time I reached the end of the block, I'd decided it was nothing. But then, just as I turned the corner, I heard the footsteps again—fainter but also moving more quickly.

I started jogging, running the full length of the block. I raced around the next corner and hands grabbed me. With a startled gasp, I took a step back.

I stared up into Riley's face. He did not look happy. "Why'd you take off like that?"

I was relieved to see him but didn't appreciate his tone. Especially when he added, "I'm responsible for you, remember?"

I'd been half listening for footsteps, but his comment drew my full attention. I pulled free. "Guess I did forget that's why you're here. Stupid me."

I stomped past him. Two seconds later he was marching by my side. "Slow down."

I didn't.

He took hold of my arm and spun me around. I had a bunch of angry words ready when he pulled me to him, his mouth coming down on mine. His lips were forceful, urgent. His palms pressed my back, crushing me to him, their warmth seeping through my shirt. My hands moved beneath his open jacket. My heart beat twice as fast as when I'd been running.

The kiss ended almost the way it started, so abruptly I could hardly catch my breath. He let go of me, and in the nighttime shadows his features were more angular, a crease between his eyebrows giving him a harsh look. He took a step back and shoved his fingers through his hair.

"You make me crazy, know that?"

I just stared at him.

"Don't disappear like that again, understand?"

His bossy attitude should've bothered me, but the heat of his kiss still lingered on my lips. "I needed a break, that's all."

"I didn't like not being able to find you. Worrying that you'd wandered off, and us in a foreign city . . ."

"Not that big a deal."

He looked away, his voice turning quiet. "It is to me."

The rain started again, and he pulled me under a window awning. I listened to the sound of water plopping on the sidewalk. Though hardly able to see him, I could hear his breathing. His hands moved to my chilled arms. "You're cold."

He took off his jacket and helped me put it on; the warmth of it felt like a hug, even though it was too big. I pushed the cuffs up to my wrists and forced myself to say what I should have back in the hotel room. "It's no use, Riley. The challenge, I mean. I can't figure it out."

Just saying the truth made me feel hollow. How could I have come this far to end up losing now?

He moved closer, pulling me in. "Even with all the other stuff you know, you've really got no idea who the Scottish heir is, do you?"

"No."

My head tipped forward, my forehead resting at his throat. I inhaled the scent of him, comforted by his arms around me. "I know I'm letting you down. I'm such a failure."

Riley let out a slow breath. "No such thing."

I raised my face to him and he kissed me again. This time it was softer, sweeter. And it seemed like I was falling, sinking into him. I slid my hands to his ribs and felt him smile against my lips. Ticklish. Just like that first night in the darkroom. How could I forget?

Riley pulled back but just a few inches. "What now?"

"You need to call your dad. Tell him we're at a dead end."

"Maybe if you look at the names again . . ."

My stubborn head forced my body to pull back, even if it didn't want to leave his arms. "And what, Riley? The answer will magically appear? I'm not a genius. I've only gotten this far because of a whole lot of luck and the mistakes of others. But the dough-head relatives are gone now. Warren and Uncle Marshall both know what they're doing."

"Okay," he said at last. "I'll call my dad and tell him. But in the meantime, you still need to try. I don't care what you say, Avery. I know you've got more inside that smart head of yours than you believe."

In the darkness he reached for my hand.

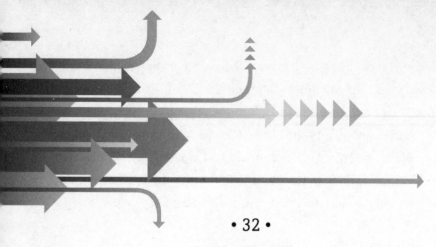

32

PRANKED

Back in my suite, I studied the list of Scottish kings while Riley had a downhearted conversation with his dad. He disconnected and sat beside me on the loveseat. We read through more bios of long-dead people, and it seemed hard to relate to the fact I was descended from them.

About an hour later I checked the time on my phone and had a voice mail from an unavailable number. I listened to it, shocked to hear a guy's voice calling me a bunch of filthy names. I jerked it away from my ear, and Riley looked at me.

"What's wrong?"

"Somebody left me this." I replayed it and handed him the phone.

His eyes narrowed like he was ready to strangle the caller. "Blocked. Avery, who was that?"

I shrugged. Though the message upset me, I put on a calm

act. "I don't recognize the voice, it's kind of muffled. It's probably just a prank."

"A threatening prank. From Chase, maybe?"

I took the phone back. "But why pick on me? Don't you think he'd go after Daisy right now?"

"Yes, unless he wants to help his dad by shaking you up before the next challenge."

I thought it over. "Doesn't sound like Chase, though."

"Think he got someone else to do it?"

I remembered the kid from all those years ago who handed Chase the worm. "Could be. He's got this friend named Devin. They've hung out forever and he's a big jerk, too."

Riley laced his fingers together, processing this. "Anyone else you suspect?"

"What about Thisby? She was fuming after she lost the last challenge, and she blamed me. There are all sorts of boys hanging around her. One of them might've agreed to pull a sick joke."

He nodded. "I could see her doing that."

"But how would they get this number? I haven't given it to any of the VanDemeres."

Riley started to say something, but my phone beeped to let me know I had a text. Before I even clicked on it, more texts showed up. I opened one as Riley watched, then the second and third. He grabbed the phone from me and checked each of them. There were ten, and they all said the same thing: U r dead

Suddenly, it wasn't just a simple prank.

Even though Riley tried not to show how much it bothered

him, I could still see it. And during the next hour, he talked to his dad twice and Mr. Benjamin once. He even got up and paced. At that point, I decided not to mention hearing the suspicious footsteps, though it was hard to imagine somebody like Uncle Marshall following me. And the mental image of him hunched over his cell phone, texting threats, was so ridiculous I had to bite back a nervous giggle.

No matter who was playing this vicious joke, I figured it wouldn't be smart to take off on my own again until the challenge was over.

Finally I said, "Know what, Riley? I think those texts are getting the results the caller wanted."

He came back and sat beside me. "What do you mean?"

"It's distracting us from working on the challenge."

"Oh." He leaned against the back of the loveseat. "You're probably right."

I picked up my tablet. "Let's just keep working."

For another couple of hours we researched the Reide line, until sometime in the early-morning hours when jet lag finally hit. My head hurt and I closed my eyes for just a few minutes. The next thing I knew, Riley was muttering in his sleep and I woke up. My eyes felt gritty from fatigue, and I blinked at the pale light coming in through the window sheers. The clock on the mantel said it was nearly seven.

I sat up and stretched, then winced. My neck was stiff from sleeping on Riley's shoulder, and I had a headache behind my eyes, probably from so much reading. Walking quietly, I grabbed my backpack and went into the bathroom. After painkillers, a quick shower, and clean clothes, I felt better but still anxious.

Time was slipping away. I came back to the main room and saw Riley just starting to wake. He checked the time on his cell phone, then bolted up. "Not good."

Walking over to him, I headed past the door and stopped. There was a folded piece of paper stuck underneath, and I picked it up.

"What's that?" he asked.

"A note." The words looked a little blurry and I pulled the paper closer. "This can't be right."

"What is it?"

"You're not going to believe it! This is signed by Duncan Mormaer. And I'm pretty sure that's impossible since he's been dead for something like ten centuries."

Riley was off the loveseat and beside me so fast it made me blink. He looked at the paper and we both read the printed words: *King not barbarous of a barbarous nation.*

He turned the paper over but we didn't see anything else. "What's it mean?"

"Must be another joke. Someone's trying to trick us."

Riley reached for his tablet. "Probably, but let's check it out anyway."

He did an Internet search. "Top of the list for that quote is David the first, king of Scotland. Some famous guy said it about him. David was the great-great-grandson of Duncan Mormaer. The last son of Malcolm Canmore and Queen Margaret, he inherited the throne when his brother died."

I read over his shoulder. "Look. It says he set up a feudal system in Scotland. Maybe that's what Grandmother meant."

"But you can't visit that." Riley pointed to a different paragraph.

"David the first also founded fifteen religious houses and monasteries."

It suddenly came to me and my eyes widened. I bounced the heels of my palms against my head. "Oh, I'm an idiot! Abbey!"

"Who?"

"Not who. What. It's the abbey guy. Of course!" I grabbed my tablet and typed in a search for Scottish abbeys and monasteries. "I'm pretty sure that on one of her trips, Grandmother came to see some abbeys, but I forgot all about it. They must've been built by King David. Look, here's a list. Or the ruins of what's left. It's got to be the legacy she talked about."

"You did know! All this time, Avery!" He pointed at me in mock criticism tempered with elation. "So which abbey do we go to? And what's the message we're looking for once we get there?"

"I'm not sure." I stared down the list of a dozen abbeys.

"One of them has to be your grandma's favorite, right? Or the most famous?"

A scrap of memory came to me from a drive with her to the museum in San Francisco. "The king had a dream. Something about a sword and a bird, I think."

Riley pulled up info on each of the abbeys and skimmed their histories as I started searching, too.

"Avery, I think I've found it! Listen to this. While he was hunting, King David got lost in the woods. He prayed and a dove guided him to shepherds, who gave him food and shelter." Riley skimmed several sentences, then added, "During the night, he had a dream telling him he should build a chapel on that exact spot. The next morning he used his sword to mark the ground where the walls would go. This has to be the same place."

I looked at the Web site. "Kinloss Abbey?"

"Yes."

"But what's the message we're supposed to find? I don't know that part."

"We'll have to figure it out when we get there. At least we've gotten this far."

Riley snatched the helicopter charter brochure off the coffee table and scheduled a flight. "Thanks!" he said into the phone. "We'll be there in forty-five minutes."

He disconnected and turned to me with a smile that made my heart flutter. Literally. I felt girly and silly but didn't care. However, his enthusiasm faded a bit as he picked up the message from the coffee table and reread it. "This wasn't a hoax."

I stared at it, too. "No."

"Who sent us this note?"

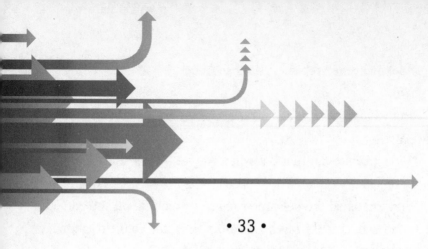

33

THE MESSAGE

Of all the experiences so far, zooming over Scotland in a helicopter to reach Kinloss Abbey was definitely the most fun. Neither of us had been in a helicopter before, and it was a whole lot of amazing with a little bit of scary thrown in. During the hour's flight north, we soared above the Cairngorm Mountains. I looked over Riley's shoulder at the wild country with a vast green swell sliced apart by barren outcroppings of rock. Near the end of the flight, we passed over farmlands that formed a patchwork quilt, and I tried to take pictures of everything.

The pilot landed in an unplanted field, and soon Riley and I headed down a narrow road to Kinloss Abbey. When we got there we saw that except for one crumbling central building, the abbey was mostly stone ruins. Lawns and garden bushes surrounded ancient freestanding walls, pillars, and a few decorative archways. What looked like very old monuments and headstones cropped up here or there, along with low benches. In an odd way it was really beautiful.

Riley looked across the scene. "Imagine what this was like when it was still standing. Not much left now, though."

"Well, it is a thousand years old."

The grounds were busy with summer visitors and tour groups. I turned in a slow circle, taking everything in. "There's a message for us hidden somewhere around here, right? That's what Mr. Benjamin told us."

"Yes. Any idea where we should start looking?"

I shook my head. "I wish whoever left us the note at the hotel had included that, too."

"Maybe a monument around here talks about King David, since he was the founder."

We headed over to the main building. Another tour was just starting, and he asked the guide about it. She handed him a bro-chure and told us to join the group—something neither of us wanted to do.

I shaded my eyes to better see Riley's face. "We might have to go on the tour, though I'm not thrilled about the idea of another history lesson."

He hardly seemed to hear as he stared across the grounds. Suddenly he caught my wrist and led me behind the group of waiting tourists. "See over there?"

Peering around the shoulder of a large woman in a floppy hat, I glimpsed Daisy and Uncle Marshall as they hurried past a row of columns. Riley said, "Uh-oh. They're coming this way."

We took off to the far side of the central building. Riley

glanced in the direction we just came from. "Maybe your uncle knows where to look. Let's watch what they do."

I followed him around another corner, then past a crumbling wall. We hunched low, moved to an arched window, and paused there when we heard voices inside. I recognized my uncle's low grumble. At first it was hard to make out what they said, but the sound of footsteps let us know they were coming in our direction. Riley and I sat down under the window, our backs pressed against the rough wall and our heads below the sill.

They stopped walking, neither of them saying anything, and I wondered if they knew we were listening. I scrunched even lower, practically holding my breath.

"So what's this place?" Daisy finally asked.

"The sacristy."

"Huh?"

Uncle Marshall's voice became impatient. "Didn't you read the attachment I sent you? It's the room where they kept holy objects and ceremonial clothes. Your grandmother also believed this was the spot where King David first marked the ground with the tip of his sword."

"You're starting to sound like her."

"Just go stand in front of that altar while I get your picture, will you? Then you can take mine."

"Why the altar?"

"This is where your grandmother had a photo taken of her from the Scotland trip last year. It's in a small frame on one of the shelves in her office."

Riley raised his eyebrows at me. I shrugged but got out my camera and scrolled through all the pictures. I'd missed it, even though it should have caught my attention. Grandmother almost never let anyone take snapshots of her, and all her pictures were done by professional portrait photographers who came to the estate.

For a few minutes we listened to their shuffling until Daisy asked, "What now?"

"Look for the messages, of course. They've got to be hidden here somewhere."

"Would you stop talking to me like I'm six?"

He said something in a low voice but I didn't catch his words. When I turned my head to look at Riley, he smiled and winked, and I knew what he was thinking. It was funny how we were letting Marshall and Daisy do the work for us. But as more time slipped by they didn't find anything and started to argue. My uncle said, "Just turn over those stones beside that wall. I'll check the arches."

"It'd help if we knew what the thing looked like. And what if you're wrong about searching here? We only have another hour before we need to catch the train back to Inverness."

Riley and I crouched lower as one of them passed the window, and I began to worry that Daisy was right. If Uncle Marshall made a mistake about where to look, we were wasting our time, too.

A couple of minutes later Daisy hollered, "Found it!" We heard my uncle hurry over to her, and then the rustling of paper.

They were both silent for a full minute until she said, "But what does it mean?"

"I'm not sure. I think it's something from the history of the abbey, though it probably doesn't matter. All we have to do is bring this note back, along with pictures of us."

"Hold on, Marshall. Just because we're working together doesn't mean we're a team. This one is mine. You're going to have to find your own."

I was surprised when he didn't say anything, though it was easy to imagine his red face. Soon we heard the clunk of rocks being moved, and a while later his excited voice. "Got it!"

"Good. Let's get out of here."

"No. We need to keep looking. If we can find the other hidden messages, then Warren and Avery will be out of the game."

"Unless they've already been here."

Riley and I looked at each other. He motioned to me, and I followed him as he crawled past scraggly bushes. Once away from the window, we stood and hurried around the corner to the other side of the building, then back along the wall of the sacristy. "Go," he whispered, sending me through a doorway just ahead of him.

We entered the narrow hall formed by a series of stone arches. Inside it was dim and smelled dank. The ancient walls, a hodgepodge of weathered brown and gray, had dark green moss growing in shadowy places. Loose rocks of every size were shoved against the walls and piled in corners. At the far end of the sacristy a carved stone altar stood in front of an arched window.

My uncle spun around, a big rock still in his hands.

"Care if we join you?" Riley said in a friendly voice.

"Tate," Uncle Marshall replied with so much dislike his nostrils flared.

I walked over to the corner near the altar where rocks lay in a jumble and started lifting them. Riley joined me. I half expected them to leave, but as Daisy stood there looking uncertain, Uncle Marshall kept searching.

"Jerk," I said under my breath, suddenly frantic to find the piece of paper that would keep me in the game.

We started sorting through the rubble even faster. Riley headed to a different spot not far from my uncle, quickly flipping over rocks and debris. We searched for a few minutes, and I glanced over my shoulder to see how he was doing just as Uncle Marshall lifted a giant piece of sandstone. Riley dived in his direction and grabbed something two seconds before my uncle's fingers touched it. He sat back on his heels, a thick square of folded paper in his fist.

"Give me that!" Marshall shouted.

Riley stood. "Don't think so."

I couldn't see my uncle's face, but his posture was tense with fury. "It's mine."

I hurried over to them, Daisy right behind me.

"No, it's not," Riley said. "The rock you picked up belongs to the abbey, not you."

My uncle held out his hand. "I'm telling you again, Tate, give it to me."

Riley shook his head. "Nope. This one is Avery's. You already got yours."

"What? Oh, I see! You've been spying on us. Followed us here, didn't you?" He jabbed his finger against Riley's chest, the same way he did to Mr. Tate at the law office. "You're nothing but a damned cheater!"

Moving fast, Riley grabbed Marshall's finger and squeezed hard. My uncle had to yank twice to pull free. He took a step back and shook his hand. "You'll pay for this! And so will your father."

Riley leaned forward and stared at him like he was a worm. "Your threats don't work on me, Mr. VanDemere."

Daisy tugged her father's sleeve. "Come on. Let's get out of here."

Marshall spun away, his chin jutting out in a way that reminded me of my grandfather's photo on the mantel in the library. "Fine." He walked past me without a glance. "This isn't over! You just remember that."

They left. "At least I didn't hit him," Riley joked, though I could tell he was more upset than he let on.

I handed him my camera and went to the altar. A dusty beam of light filtered through the window and rested on the pitted stone, and I placed a hand there. He clicked the camera several times and checked to see how the photos turned out. Then he held out the thick piece of folded paper. "Want to look at this?"

"I'm still blind from the flash. We can read it better outside."

"Or we can stay in here a while and keep looking."

I paused for a couple of seconds. "And find the last hidden message? The one meant for Warren?"

Riley nodded. "It's underhanded, I know. But this is a competition. If your uncle found the other papers and kept them, you and Warren would be out of the game. Or at least you, since we don't know if Warren and Stasia have already been here."

I thought it over. "You know, I really want to win. But I don't want to be like Uncle Marshall."

Riley studied me. "Good call."

I turned and headed out of the sacristy. He followed.

"Here you go." Riley handed me the parchment. I unfolded it and we saw a message written in calligraphy.

Wrath owns no place in the Cistercian way,
yet wrath it was that the abbot's butler showed.
Crimson stained the robes of the white monk,
for 'twas his blow that slew the apostolic boy:

He straightened. "Looks like some kind of riddle. Your grandmother is getting tricky."

"I don't think she wrote this. It's got to be copied from something she found in her research, or maybe at a museum. I remember after she came back, she told me about the really old illuminated manuscripts. In fact, she bought a framed page from an auction house."

I took my camera from Riley and sorted through the pictures. "Look at this."

He studied the Medieval Latin writing with scrollwork in gold leaf around the edges, the background a faded purple. A plaque at the base of the frame said: *Sacramentary from the Gospel of Luke, 11th Century.*

"I see what you mean. Smile." Riley snapped a picture of me. "But do you know what the message is about?"

"Some of it. While you were signing papers at the helicopter charter, I read through documents the research team sent about the history of Kinloss."

We sat down on a low rock wall, and I grabbed my tablet and started searching. "Here it is. The Cistercians were a sect of really strict monks who ran the abbey. The locals called them the White Monks because they wore white or gray habits."

"So what's an abbot's butler?"

I scrolled through more pages to find the article. "William Butler was a monk who lived in the late 1400s. Look what it says here. He flew into a fit of rage and struck a young boy, murdering him."

"That explains the part about crimson staining the robes. Do you know what happened to him?"

"This says the abbey sent him to the pope, along with another monk. And though Kinloss eventually got letters of absolution, neither man returned. It looks like the killing caused a huge scandal for the abbey."

Riley gazed across the ruins as if trying to put the pieces together. "Your grandmother talked about scandal in her last message. She said to remember the history lesson or something like that."

"She's always saying no matter how strong our family is, it takes just one big mistake to blacken our name. Me. The product of the family scandal."

Riley turned his head to study my face; I watched the way the breeze ruffled his wheat-gold hair. "I don't think so, Avery. If your grandma really thought that, then why did she insist on raising you? It would've been easier to let you disappear with your mother. I think she wanted you. Even though what she did to you and your mom sucks, it was probably because she felt desperate to keep you."

A tiny ache welled inside me. Riley added, "Besides, that scandal was a long time ago. What about all the other stuff your family's done that she's not happy about? Like your Uncle Logan's two divorces? Then there's Thisby's DUI and Chase almost flunking out his senior year."

"Not really scandals."

"No, but they're things that upset her. She said so in the PowerPoint."

"Maybe you're right. A couple of times during the past year she's lectured the family about their choices. She's always so obsessed that our dumb family name doesn't get tarnished."

He read through the message again. "So what're we supposed to do with this? Just take it back to Mr. Benjamin, along with a picture of you by the altar?"

"Probably. That's what Uncle Marshall seemed to think."

Turning the paper over, he studied it before flipping back to the printed side. "I was hoping we'd find another clue, but it's tough to tell. Anything jump out at you?"

"No, except the colon. Why's that the end mark? Doesn't it seem like the message is supposed to go on, maybe tell us something more?"

He didn't answer, just kept staring down at the writing. Finally he asked, "When you read about the abbey's history, did it tell you where the boy was killed?"

"I think so." I searched my tablet. "It happened in the cloister."

"Which is here."

I looked across the large grassy area with scattered stone pillars. Two rough walls met at one corner, and through a huge archway I glimpsed more crumbling stone. "If there's another message hidden out here somewhere, we'll never find it."

Riley pointed to a couple of words on the paper. "Why is the abbot mentioned? Why not just say 'William Butler'?"

Without waiting for an answer, he pushed off the wall and gave me the camera. I stuffed everything in my backpack as Riley got the abbey brochure from his pocket. He slapped it against his palm and started walking. "Come on."

I hurried to catch up. "Where are we going?"

He took my hand and pointed across the narrow road that ran alongside the abbey grounds. "Over there, to the abbot's house."

The ruins of ancient yellow sandstone were overgrown with weeds, and wild ivy climbed up the stair tower. It was all surrounded by a fence, and a sign warned that until the restoration was finished, this area was unsafe. That didn't stop Riley, and I hesitated only a second before following him. He climbed across a few large stones and I did, too. The breeze billowed, whipping my hair until we stepped through the narrow opening into the tower. Even with the high windows and no ceiling, it was dim inside and I felt closed in by the circular walls.

"I hope it's safe in here."

He looked at me with a teasing smile. "It hasn't toppled over in ten centuries, so we're probably okay."

I smoothed my hair with my fingers and twisted it into a hank across one shoulder as he started to search. I scanned the rock wall while he turned over stones on the floor. We worked for another ten minutes until I checked the time on my cell phone. "Maybe we should head back. We've got the message and picture. That's all we need."

"Don't give up yet." His eyes strayed to me and held.

I studied a series of broken stones beneath a high window until he came over and stood behind me. His hands moved to my waist. He bent his head and grazed his lips over my neck, sending shivers. "Riley?" I murmured.

"Yes, Avery?" he answered between kisses.

The words I meant to say evaporated into a haze that consumed my thoughts. I tipped my head slightly to the side and let him place a trail of slow kisses across my tingling skin. His hands slid farther around until his arms encircled me. His lips reached my ear and he whispered, "You're beautiful."

My head gave a slight shake—denial, uncertainty; disbelief he would think it. He turned me within his embrace until I faced him. One of his hands moved to the back of my head, and he pulled me closer, capturing my lips with his. Intensity coursed through my body until, with a last touch, Riley ended the kiss.

He pulled back, reluctant. I opened my eyes. His were still closed. I memorized each feature—the curve of his lids above a dark gold fringe of lashes, the straight line of his nose, the angled arch of his eyebrows; most of all, the softness of his mouth now tinged by uncertainty. His eyes opened and he studied me. Both hands slid to my back and rested there. He bent his head beside mine until our temples touched. His voice was low. "What am I doing?"

I felt my throat tighten. "Don't doubt us," I whispered. The words were also meant for me. My entire life, trusting others had been hard, but I sensed having this with Riley was worth any risk.

He didn't answer, though his arms gave a slight squeeze. Looking past him, I gazed at the wall. In the dim light, the sandstone squares were the color of honey; between two of them was a lighter smudge. "Riley?"

He pulled back and gave me an unsteady smile. "Yes, Avery?"

The feel of his mouth on mine still lingered. "The clue is behind your head," I managed.

"Huh?"

One hand moved away from my back as he turned, but the other stayed. I leaned into it just a little, unwilling to break loose. He tugged the wedged paper from between two stones until it came free. We stared at it. Much smaller than the other message, it was folded to a square inch.

"You found it." Riley sounded impressed. "Want to open this one?"

"No, you do it."

His other hand slid from my waist, but we stood close together. The strip of paper had a single sentence and we both read. Then I pulled the first message from my pocket and held it above his paper, looking at the five sentences together.

Wrath owns no place in the Cistercian way,
yet wrath it was that the abbot's butler showed.
Crimson stained the robes of the white monk,
for 'twas his blow that slew the apostolic boy:

Hence it was noised abroad: Mark is left

"It matches," Riley said. "But still doesn't make sense."

A rustling noise startled us as a bird flapped upward from a nest high on the wall. We laughed and I glanced at the doorway. "Let's get out of here."

We stepped through into the light and headed away from the tower. Riley took my hand again, our linked fingers together between us. I stopped for one last look at the abbey and took a few more pictures. "This really is an amazing place."

"And your ancestor built it more than a thousand years ago. I've never been crazy about all the VanDemere bragging, but this is impressive."

We started down the road and were partway to the helicopter when I looked back and saw Warren and Stasia climb out of a car. My brother held a cell phone to his ear, and I wondered if he had a research team, too.

Riley followed my gaze and we watched them hurry to the abbey. "So now we know for sure they weren't already here."

"Think it was a mistake not to look for the last message and knock Warren out of the competition?"

Riley threw an arm around my shoulder. "No. You had a point that it's better to win because you're smart, not because you're a cheater like your uncle."

"Sure, unless I lose this stupid thing."

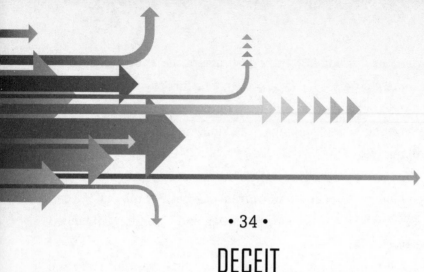

• 34 •

DECEIT

We flew the hundred and fifty miles back to Edinburgh, an even more awesome trip than the first time because I wasn't worrying about finding the message. And with the memory of our latest kiss, a quiet happiness stayed with me.

Riley and I both acted casual, each focusing on small actions. He got the portable battery-powered printer out of his backpack and printed a photo of me standing by the altar. I watched him work, the way his fingers slid the picture and messages into an envelope. How he handed it to me. His knee pressed against mine as I put everything in my backpack. I looked at his hand resting on his thigh, the muscles and veins of his forearm, the way sunlight turned the hairs a pale bronze.

I noticed he was studying my face. It gave me a flush of pleasure I couldn't hide. During the entire time we sat beside each other, and the helicopter skimmed across the Highland moors, my mind kept going back to the circular tower and the way his lips had pressed against mine. The memory was powerful, consuming—as if I wore the invisible locket of his kiss.

By noon, Scotland time, we landed in Edinburgh. It was hard to believe that after last night, when we had no hope of winning, suddenly we were back in the game.

We ate lunch at a tiny café called the Bakehouse Company, and Riley sent a text to both his father and the research team, telling them of our success. I checked my phone and saw Megan had sent a text and three photos from Amsterdam. One picture was of her brother on a river barge. I studied Kyle's attractive half smile and waited for the usual feeling of hurt. It didn't come. Riley studied me with serious eyes, looking more handsome than ever. I snapped a picture of him and sent it to Megan along with a text.

As we ate roast beef and Swiss cheese sandwiches, he said, "I've been trying to figure out who gave us that message from Duncan Mormaer, but I am coming up with nothing. You have any ideas?"

"Maybe one, but I'm not sure. I wonder if it's Ms. Franklin. She can't stand Uncle Marshall. Not that she says anything, but I notice the way she looks at him when he gets demanding and talks down to her. And she seemed happy for me when I won the last challenge."

Riley shook his head. "Sorry, but I can't see her risking her job. Besides, how'd she even know we needed help? You didn't tell anyone about not knowing who Duncan's heir was."

The waitress brought us each a serving of crumb cake. Riley cut into his with the edge of his fork. "My guess is that it's your new best friend Stasia."

"Really? I mean, she's nice and everything, but helping me

win means helping her husband lose. Besides, same situation. She didn't know we were stuck."

After we left the eatery, we still had time to do some shopping. Since I now had Grandmother's credit card, going on a buying spree became my new favorite hobby. It was great fun wandering down Edinburgh's Victoria Street. I took pictures of the odd little shops crammed beneath tall buildings. Flower baskets hung outside storefronts painted white, gray, bright blue, and Barbie pink.

We spent some time inside a tartan shop where everything was plaid. I left Riley at the ties and went to the front window where there was a display of cashmere scarves. I was trying to decide which one to buy Connie, when I glanced up. Through the glass panes I saw a bunch of pedestrians across the street, waiting for the light. One caught my attention—a tall blond man who looked like Uncle Logan. He was too far away to tell for sure, and I leaned forward to get a better view. The light changed and the people started walking. I kept watching, waiting for a reason to prove it wasn't him. But even from this distance, the way he moved seemed familiar. What was Uncle Logan doing here?

I hurried through the shop, around a couple of white-haired ladies blocking the aisle, and reached the door. Once outside, I looked around. The pedestrians were all heading off in different directions except for the man. I couldn't see him anywhere.

I stood there for several seconds, thinking. Logic told me it couldn't be him, since he'd gone back to California with Thisby and was thousands of miles away. Besides, there wasn't any reason for him to come here because nothing he could do would change the outcome of his lost inheritance. Finally, I shrugged and went back through the door. Maybe it was just me being jumpy and seeing VanDemeres even where there weren't any.

Back at the window display, I picked out a scarf and Riley came to find me. As we left the store, I got a text from Megan that made me smile: That's the lawyer's son?!!!!!

We made our way back to the George Hotel with a half hour to spare. In the waiting room, I gave my envelope to Mr. Benjamin, who took out the message and the picture of me by the altar. Then he pulled out the strip of paper we found in the abbot's house and looked up with surprise. "Well done."

I said, "You didn't think we'd find the last part of the clue, did you?"

"Actually, I didn't think anyone would."

"Is that piece required to stay in the game?" Riley asked in a hopeful voice.

"No, and don't ask anything else because I really don't know what it's for."

We watched him fax everything to Grandmother. Sitting together on a floral chaise, Riley and I checked our phones, and I sent Megan another text. Ms. Franklin came in, and about fifteen minutes later, Warren and Stasia showed up. Their clothes were rumpled and they looked tired, but my sister-in-law was also smiling. Riley and I glanced at each other, and I thought about the last hidden message at the abbey. Stasia opened her purse and pulled out a photograph plus the folded parchment. She handed them to Warren, who turned them in.

Stasia plopped down on a chair next to me, her excitement obvious. As if in need of a distraction, she pointed to my shopping bags. "What'd you buy?"

I showed her everything, including my new purple leather purse, a silver Celtic bracelet, and a Scottish tam. I took the bracelet out of the box and put it on.

"I love that." She glanced up at Warren. "Think we'll get a chance to go shopping?"

He didn't answer, just leaned against a wall and studied us with an amused smile. I wondered if Riley was right. Was Stasia the one to slip us the hint? If so, I felt good about not taking their message from the abbey.

After Stasia helped me put everything back in the bags, Riley whispered in my ear, "What'd I tell you? Thanksgiving dinner."

I just smiled at him.

Warren pointed to a fancy clock. "Six minutes left."

Daisy and Uncle Marshall weren't back yet. All of us started watching the time. I glanced at the others and knew we were thinking the same thing: *What if they both get eliminated?*

My hopefulness at the idea kept growing, until they came hustling through the door with only three minutes left. Uncle Marshall dug in a black case and pulled out two envelopes. One had his name on it, the other Daisy's. He handed them to Ms. Franklin. She opened his first and gave the items to Mr. Benjamin at the scanner.

Next she opened Daisy's. Puzzled, she turned over a white piece of photo paper and unfolded a blank sheet of cardstock. "There's nothing here."

Daisy flew forward so fast her backpack slid from her shoulder. She grabbed the envelope and ripped it open. "They were in here!"

She snatched the papers from Ms. Franklin's hands and stared at them. Then she opened her fingers and they fluttered down to the marble floor. She stood frozen as we all stared at her. The small amount of color in her face drained away, and Daisy looked chalky beneath her black bangs. She walked over to her father. "Where's my stuff?"

"I don't know." His practiced attitude couldn't hide the lie.

"Oh. Of course. On the train. You switched them out when I went to the restroom." Two spots of red showed on her ashen cheeks though her voice stayed surprisingly calm. "Well, how idiotic could I be? The only reason you asked me to team with you in the first place was to take me down. Perfect revenge for what I did to Chase."

"No, that's not it! I have to be the one to win this. And after you agreed to partner with me, remember what you said? If you're the winner, you'll cut me out of everything. I can't let that happen, Daisy. But you're my heir, and you'll inherit from me. When I win, so will you."

There was a glimmer of wetness in his eyes, like he was ready to cry, and it gave me the creeps.

Finally reacting to what he'd done, Daisy screamed and swung her backpack. He ducked but it still grazed the top of his head. She swung it again, and this time it hit his chest. He grabbed the pack, jerked it from her hands, and took a step back.

"Calm down! I'm still your father, Daisy. And I promise what I inherit will pass on to my kids." He tossed the backpack on the floor. "You'll be taken care of."

"You're not my father," she hissed at him. "You've never *been* my father!"

She scooped up the backpack and turned to go. Seeing me, she paused. "Beat him, Avery! And after you do, fire him."

She ran off. Uncle Marshall called her name but didn't follow her. Instead he stood there, trying to hold on to his superiority. She disappeared through a doorway and I heard Stasia whisper, "How could he do that?"

"Just finishing what Daisy started," Warren answered.

Mr. Benjamin made a call and had a short conversation. After he disconnected, he turned to us. "Warren, Avery, and Marshall, you have all successfully completed the fifth challenge. There's a hotel shuttle waiting to take us to the airport. Get your things from upstairs and meet back here in twenty minutes."

Uncle Marshall tried to call Daisy. We heard him leave a message saying the plane was taking off. Warren walked past him. "Don't be ridiculous. She's never going to talk to you again. And it's pretty sad, Uncle Marshall. She's more your child than either of your sons."

I studied my brother, who was usually so quiet. I liked that he was starting to say what he really thought and sent him a look that said so.

I hurried to my room, stuffed things into my backpack, and condensed my shopping bags. Then I went to find Riley. The door to his room was half open, and he was talking on his phone, facing away from me. I hesitated, not wanting to interrupt.

"But what about Avery? Don't you think she has a right to know?"

Was he on the phone with his dad? What did I have a right to know?

"Of course I realize you want her to stay focused . . ." His voice trailed off and he kept listening.

Finally he shoved his tablet in his pack. "Okay. I'll call you when the plane lands."

Suddenly uncomfortable, I stepped away from the door and hurried back to my room. Should I admit I'd overheard his conversation and ask what was going on, or should I trust him to tell me on his own?

"Hi," Riley said half a minute later, leaning through the doorway.

I looked up at him. He only smiled at me—that sweet, friendly smile I'd been falling for. My cell phone blipped and I read the text. "Mr. Benjamin says it's time to go."

We went downstairs and crossed the lobby. Outside, a shuttle waited for us. Once everyone buckled in, the driver pulled onto the road. Uncle Marshall left Daisy another message. The shuttle followed a series of winding roads back to the airport, and it felt weird to be driving on the opposite side of the street. My eyes drank in the sights of Edinburgh and its castle high on the hill. I wished we could stay longer.

After we boarded the VanDemere jet, Uncle Marshall started throwing a fit. "We can't leave Daisy behind!"

Mr. Benjamin shrugged. "She's eighteen and can legally decide what she wants to do."

"That's not old enough to be roaming around all alone in a foreign country! You have to wait for her."

"Sorry, but Ms. Franklin already left two messages telling her our departure time. If Daisy doesn't call back, or show up in the next half hour, she'll have to make her own way home."

Personally, I thought it'd be smart of her to get away. Maybe she'd find a Scottish rock band to join or just tour the local sites for a while. Anything was better than hanging around her father.

Ms. Franklin said, "Before the plane takes off, we need you to make a decision about the next challenge. Each heir can invite a partner to help them. Warren, I'm assuming Stasia will go with you?"

My brother gave a single nod.

She turned to me. "Riley will stay with you?"

I looked at him and he smiled. "Definitely."

Everyone focused on Uncle Marshall, who seemed to be thinking. Finally he raised his chin. "Chase will be my partner."

Stasia murmured, "Sure, because no one else wants to."

Mr. Benjamin got out his phone. "We'll make arrangements for him to meet us at the next challenge."

"Just great," I whispered to Riley, hating the idea of Chase getting back in the game.

While we sat there waiting, I got an e-mail from Mr. Tate.

Avery, again you've done outstanding. Each time, I'm even more impressed by what you are able to accomplish. So instead of just sending another letter, I have a special reward for you. Open the enclosed attachment. And good luck in the next challenge!

I opened it and saw the photographs of my mother, the same ones Riley secretly copied. I was disappointed, but what could I do? Mr. Tate had no idea I'd already seen these pictures and obviously thought he was sending me a big reward. Besides, what I really wanted to know about was that phone call. I looked over at Riley.

He leaned in and said, "By the way, my dad's contacted Mrs. VanDemere's security team. They're looking into that threatening call and texts."

"Oh. Think they'll find out anything?"

"I hope so."

He glanced out the window, distracted, and I wondered if they'd already learned something. Was that what Riley meant about not telling me so I'd stay focused? Maybe he was just being protective, trying not to worry me, but I wished he wouldn't. I wanted to think of a way to explain it but remembered late last night when I'd gone for a walk in the rain. Riley took this whole being-responsible-for-me stuff way too seriously.

We were told to buckle up and started taxiing down the runway. In spite of my uncle's loud demands that we wait for Daisy, the plane took off without her.

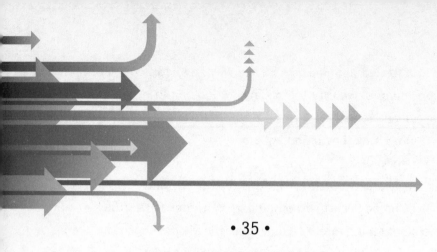

35

FUN AND GAMES

We'd been flying for hours when I made the decision to stop checking the time. After crossing the international date line and so many time zones, the only thing that made sense was whether the sun was up or down.

Riley was working with a program on his tablet and typing a list. I leaned over to look at his screen. "What's that?"

He glanced around to make sure no one was listening. "Remember my idea that there's a clue at the end of each challenge? Back at the hotel I downloaded an anagram decoder. I just plugged in the Civil War message, *t canon*, and the most common anagram that comes up is *cannot*. I also tried it with the last two words from the Scotland note we found at the abbot's house. Looks like *is left* might be *itself*."

"That's smart, Riley."

"Thanks." He switched to the list. "I've put the words in the order we got them. Take a look."

1. _____
2. against
3. divide
4. cannot
5. itself

I read through them, and he pointed to the first one. "I left that blank. Maybe there wasn't a clue, but I don't see why there'd be one for each of the other challenges and not the first. Are you sure something wasn't hidden in the test? Either in the directions or a question that stood out?"

I started to shrug but paused. "Now that I think about it, the bonus question at the end was a little weird. It was a fill-in-the-blank that didn't ask anything about our ancestors. And it was super easy."

"What was it?"

"'The Battle of Little Bighorn was also known as Custer's Last . . .'"

"Stand," he finished, then smiled at me.

"Yes."

He added it to the top of the list and read, *"Stand, against, divide, cannot, itself."*

We looked at each other. "Does that sound familiar?" he asked.

"Maybe, but I don't know why."

He closed the program. "I'll do a search for it when we land."

After that we didn't talk much, mostly sat and held hands or shared earbuds to listen to music. I dozed off, but not for long. When I woke, I looked out the window. We were flying above thick white clouds that reminded me of Connie's meringue frosting.

Riley was playing a game on his tablet, but he closed it and leaned into me. "We've been heading west ever since we left, which probably means we're going back to the US. If the next challenge is based on the character trait courage, what do you think we'll be doing?"

I stretched and tried to focus. "Well, we've already done the *Mayflower* and the Civil War. Grandmother's other favorite historical time in America was the Revolutionary War."

"That sounds like a good guess."

"You're the one who keeps telling me I've got everything I need inside my head."

He pulled up the list of ancestors from Grandmother's notebook and looked for any who lived during that time. I pointed to the name Abel Spalding, a private in the Vermont Militia. "See this guy? She was excited about him. He was the very first name she found going back to the war, and that let her join the DAR."

"What's that?"

"Daughters of the American Revolution. It's an organization for women descended from Revolutionary War soldiers. Three or four years ago, she was a state regent."

A memory surfaced of Grandmother hosting a luncheon at the mansion. I could still see her in an embroidered gray suit and her sapphire necklace. She wore a blue-and-white sash across her chest, and it had several fancy pins on it that represented each of our family patriots. She introduced me to the other ladies, proud of how well behaved I was. At least I thought so. Maybe I just imagined it, always so eager for her approval.

Riley shifted in his seat to look at me. "So what do you know about that war?"

"Let's see . . . they used muskets, didn't they? And then there was George Washington. He led his men across the Delaware River in the freezing cold on Christmas Day to surprise the British. She used to tell stories about that, sometimes during Christmas dinner."

"And the British were called redcoats. You know, if you're right about this challenge, it might be fun." He had the same enthusiasm he'd shown through the whole competition.

I lowered my chin a bit and lifted my eyes as if he had to be joking. "Fun?"

He grinned. "Hey, it's all fun and games until someone gets hurt."

I pointed to my black eye and squinted. "Or loses an eye."

"Falls to their death."

We both snickered.

"Gets rabies."

I rubbed my side. "Or bitten by a centipede."

He touched the corner of his mouth. "Slugged in the face."

"Bucked off a mule."

"Arrested for assault."

"Death threats."

Our smiles faded. We stared at each other. Three seconds later we started roaring with laughter.

After several more hours, the lights of another city sparkled across a nighttime landscape. Mr. Benjamin called out, "In a few minutes we'll be landing in Charlotte, North Carolina."

Disappointed, I looked at Riley. "Looks like I guessed wrong."

"Another Civil War challenge, maybe?"

"I hope not. Or if it is, maybe at least this time you'll get to come with me."

It was still dark when we arrived at a bed-and-breakfast. "Grab some rest," Ms. Franklin said. "We'll call you for brunch."

I felt so wiped out that when I got to my room, it was all I could do to pull off my shoes and socks before flopping into bed.

The next morning, the ten-thirty wake-up call came too soon, and I stayed under the covers for another fifteen minutes before finally dragging myself out of bed. I was still brushing my hair when there was knocking and I opened the door. Riley stood in a relaxed stance. He smiled, ready to compete, and I shook my head.

"What?"

"You're one of those happy morning people, aren't you?"

"You haven't figured that out by now?" He reached up and touched my cheek. "Your black eye looks better."

"Stasia's concealer helps. Come inside."

He followed me into the room, where I slipped my feet into sandals.

"Hey, I've got something to show you." He stood close and I caught a clean soapy scent that made me want to touch his hair.

Riley held out his tablet. "I did a search for those code words this morning. Look at this."

**"A house divided against itself
cannot stand." —Abraham Lincoln**

"Except for 'house,' it's got our five other words," he said. "And my guess is that'll show up at the end of today's challenge. Then we'll know for sure."

"Wow, Riley. There really was a hidden message, and you found it. Awesome!"

He looked happy but didn't answer, because we both got texts at the same time telling us to head down to the dining area right away. When we got there, everyone was seated. That included Chase, next to Uncle Marshall. He stared at me with that I'm-so-cool expression I'd seen a hundred times, but I ignored him. I hoped he figured out what my body language said: *You're less than nothing to me.*

I'd only eaten half my blueberry pancakes when Ms. Franklin checked her watch and stood. "Here's another message from Mrs. VanDemere."

Grandmother's voice filled the room. "In 1780, the Battle of Kings Mountain was a decisive victory for the Patriots. Thomas Jefferson referred to it as the turn of the tide in the Revolutionary War."

Riley reached over and squeezed my hand. He mouthed, "You were right!"

I smiled at him.

"The Overmountain Men were Americans living west of the Appalachians, on the frontier. Even though they had no military training or uniforms, they were skilled at shooting moving targets since they hunted game with rifles instead of British muskets. Relying on both their courage and knowledge of the land, they ousted Cornwallis and his men!"

I leaned over to Riley and whispered, "She's kind of overdo-ing it."

He gave me a playful wink.

"Of all our ancestors, we can certainly be the most proud of those who served in the Revolutionary War. We owe them a debt of gratitude for the freedoms we enjoy today. For this reason, I've brought you here to learn more about your ancestor Lieutenant Isaac Lane. You will be given a special mission, just as he was. Get ready to participate in a reenactment of the Battle of Kings Mountain."

Mr. Benjamin pressed the remote and the room fell silent. No murmuring and no complaints. Just the realization that we had to accept whatever Grandmother told us to do.

Ms. Franklin said, "Ten minutes to get your things and meet us out front."

Riley and I headed upstairs and he followed me to my room. "Quick. You need to change."

I glanced down at my patterned purple-and-pink top above shorts. "Why?"

"Don't you get it? We're going to be running through the for-est with redcoats chasing us. Your shirt will make a perfect tar-get. And remember all the branches scraping your legs during the Civil War challenge? You might be hot in jeans, but they'll protect your skin. Do you have a brown shirt?"

He seemed so serious that I started to feel that way, too. "No, but I've got one that's kind of olive green with black designs." I dug through my backpack and pulled it out.

"That'll work. Meet me in the hall."

I was just zipping up my jeans when I got a text from a blocked number. I opened it and saw a list of dirty names followed by another U r dead.

Chase. It had to be. I thought of how he'd looked at me in the dining room, as if trying to hide his sneer. What an obnoxious freak! And how'd he get my number?

Deciding I'd have to worry about it later, I grabbed my bag and went to meet Riley. He'd swapped out his white shirt for a black one. Outside, I glared at Chase but he didn't even look in my direction. Everyone filed into two waiting limos. The Benjamin–Franklin team rode with us, and I was happy I didn't have to be in the same car with Chase.

After a forty-minute drive, we turned onto a narrow lane that entered a forest of leafy trees and green brush. The car pulled over near an open area, and as we got out, they made us leave our cell phones and other electronic devices with the limo drivers. In the distance, we saw a large group dressed in Revolutionary War costumes. Men wore red coats, white leggings, and black tricorn hats. They aimed muskets at the forest. Three cannons sat beside them, and soon a fife and drum corps came into view. As if on cue, they started playing. The soldiers raised muskets high and fired into the air, and Mr. Benjamin came to stand in front of us.

"Each year in October, on the anniversary of the Battle of Kings Mountain, there's a reenactment. Mrs. VanDemere has gone to a great deal of expense for an early production."

The cannons boomed, smoke rising from them. I glanced at Riley, who grinned. His enthusiasm was infectious.

Mr. Benjamin raised his voice. "As you might already know, the battle happened when the Patriot militia charged up Kings

Mountain. The Loyalists were driven back to the top of the hill and forced to surrender."

Ms. Franklin handed each of the three remaining heirs a small parchment envelope closed with a wax seal. On the front, in black calligraphy, it said, *Colonel William Campbell.*

"In just a minute the battle will start. You need to join the American Patriots and fight your way to the top of the hill, where there's a large stone marker. The Centennial Monument was erected in 1880 to commemorate the hundredth anniversary of the battle. That's where you'll find Colonel Campbell. Give him this unopened letter."

I took mine and shoved it in a pocket. Muskets sent up a round of loud shots and the cannons fired again; this time I smelled smoke. Mr. Benjamin pointed at the wooded hill. "You'll need to make your way past three different British lines: the yellow, orange, and red. Elimination will be based on who makes it the least distance."

"But how will you know how far we get?" I asked.

"This reenactment is authentic except for one thing. Instead of muskets, the Loyalists trying to stop you will have paintball guns."

A grin lit Riley's face. "Awesome!"

Uncle Marshall scowled.

The limo drivers brought over large equipment bags and put them on the ground in front of Ms. Franklin. "Those hit with a yellow paint pellet will have made it the least far, orange the second, and so on. Hopefully, you'll avoid getting shot. Remember, once you're hit it symbolizes being wounded or dead, and you have to stop playing. Riley, Stasia, and Chase, if you get shot, do not continue helping your partner."

Mr. Benjamin unzipped the bags and began handing out protective vests of dark gray. We pulled them on over our heads and connected the straps under our arms with Velcro tabs. Next were the fitted goggles. Riley examined his. "It'd be safer to have full face masks. But at least the lenses are thermal so they won't fog up."

I put mine on and he helped me adjust the straps. There were more shots and a lot of shouting. Looking up we saw Patriot frontiersmen coming from the trees. Dressed in brown, many of them had dark rags covering their heads and satchels across their chests. They carried rifles and dodged behind trees, shooting at the Loyalists. Some of the redcoats began to fall.

"Go now!" shouted Mr. Benjamin.

Riley and I took off, heading into the forest.

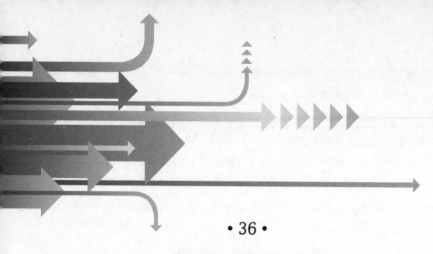

36

REVOLUTIONARY

We soon found ourselves in the middle of a huge battle. Some soldiers had muskets and others were armed with paintball guns. Some of them fought hand to hand. Riley shouted, "This way."

"But those are redcoats over there!"

"They've only got muskets. It's the ones with paintball guns we've got to worry about."

As I followed him through the forest, I realized how smart he was to think of that. We ran past more fighting troops and zig-zagged between trees. Thornbushes clawed at my jeans, and I was glad Riley warned me to change out of my shorts. We kept going until the bang of muskets faded.

"Stop here." He pulled me down beside a thick pine.

We were both breathing hard in the muggy air. The reenact-ment would be a lot more enjoyable in October, when it was cool, and I wondered how much Grandmother paid to set this up in the summer heat.

"Now it's going to get harder," he whispered. "We'll be coming up on the guys with the paintball guns, and they'll be looking for us. Stay low, move fast."

"You've done paintball before?"

"I love it. Haven't you ever tried it?"

I cocked my head at him, peering through the goggles.

"Sorry, forgot. Girl stuck in a mansion. When this is over, I'll take you to my favorite paintball warehouse."

"Sounds fun."

"One more thing, Avery. If I get taken out, you've got to keep going."

After a couple of seconds, I said, "You're planning to act as my shield, aren't you?"

"Yes, except I'm hoping we get far before that happens. If I get shot, keep going to the top of the hill. Don't run in a straight line and stay away from any paths. Take hard routes and ways that are blocked with brush or fallen trees. Remember, this isn't about speed and who gets there first. It's about getting there untagged."

I hated the idea of being separated but nodded. "Got it. Let's go."

Moving from tree to tree, we worked our way through the forest. At one point we had to sprint across a paved trail in the open. Back inside the woods, we stayed silent and tried to listen. It paid off when I heard footsteps, grabbed Riley's arm, and pulled him down. From behind a thick bush we saw two soldiers. They were about our age and carried paintball guns.

Riley pointed to a direction away from them and I nodded. He started moving in stealth mode, and I thought he'd have made a natural mountain man. A twig made a loud snap under my shoe, and after that I tried to watch where I stepped.

We walked past a muddy spot and suddenly I heard a series of pops. Yellow paint splattered on a tree next to my head. I scooted behind the trunk, dropped down, and glimpsed a red jacket. We were trapped! I looked at Riley with questioning eyes as he motioned me to stay still, and I crouched lower. He moved off, his back to the tree as he peeked around the edge. Why was he leaving me? I considered following but told myself to trust him.

There was the sound of footsteps and a guy said, "I know you're there, Miss," in the absolute worst fake English accent I'd ever heard.

Then there was a loud "Oof!" and some scrabbling sounds. I looked around the tree and saw that Riley had tackled him. He jerked the paintball gun out of the kid's hands and pointed it at him. "Take off!"

"Hey!"

"Now, or I shoot. And this close, it'll smart."

The boy muttered something in a very non-English accent and stomped off. Riley turned to me. "Let's go."

I looked at the gun. "Is that allowed?"

"Mr. Benjamin didn't give us a rule about it."

Walking again, this time faster, we heard the sounds of musket fire. I realized we had doubled back. The climb grew steeper and we were breathing fast as we worked our way through dense brush that stabbed our legs.

A series of loud pops sounded, and Riley pushed me down. I scampered behind some thick foliage as he turned and fired several shots. Through the branches I saw three redcoats who now all had yellow splatters of paint on them. They looked irritated but turned and marched off. I stood and gazed at Riley with admiration. "You're really good at this!"

"Not that good."

He turned and showed me the back of his shoulder. There was a large orange stain on his vest. "I'm out of the challenge, Avery."

"Oh no . . ."

"One good thing, this is orange paint. It means we made it past the first line."

I glanced away, sure he could see my disappointment. "Guess I better get going."

"Hey." Riley moved closer. He had a smudge of dirt on his jaw. "I need to tell you something."

I waited. He seemed to be searching for the right words as he pushed up his goggles. "Avery, I just want to say . . . I mean, this is probably the worst possible place and time to admit it, but . . . I'm falling for you."

I pulled off my goggles. "Actually, it's perfect." I lifted my mouth to his. He kissed me quickly but with passion and then looked into my eyes. "Whatever happens, we'll have time after this to talk. Now take off."

I touched his jaw, wanting to stay and forget the whole stupid game. But he took my goggles and put them back over my eyes, then brushed my hair out of the way. His fingertips lingered on my face. A few seconds more and he reached for the gun, quickly checking it. "Out of ammo." He put his free hand on my shoulder, turned me around, and whispered in my ear. "Go now."

Heart hammering, I headed into the densest brush on the hill.

It scratched and as I bumped against a tree, sticky sap clung to my arm. I struggled for air through my mouth, but it kept me from hearing anything, so I clamped my lips together and breathed through my nose. After a few minutes I heard voices and dropped behind a mossy log.

I held still and thought of the confession Riley made about falling for me. And I had already fallen hard for him. It caused a happy little glow inside me. My whole life all I ever wanted was someone to care about. To love me and like me and want to be together. And now, the most gorgeous guy I'd ever met was willing to do and be all that.

There was the sound of running footsteps, and I scrunched lower. A few seconds later I peeked over the log and saw several men in brown Patriot costumes pass by. If they were going up the hill, then maybe I could follow them at a distance. I started walking, more hopeful with each step, until startled by a flash of movement.

Someone flew through the air and slammed into me. We hit the ground and rolled. The blow when my back hit the hard ground knocked the wind from my lungs. Before I had a chance to recover, a fist smashed into my jaw and my head snapped back. A haze of darkness passed across my eyes.

When I gained consciousness, I was disoriented and couldn't move. Everything hurt and nothing made sense. Finally my eyes focused on plant stems in front of my face. I was on the ground. The smell of damp earth was strong, and dead leaves stuck to my cheek. My goggles were down around my neck and dug into the side of my throat, and my hands were tied behind my back.

I tried to call for help but my voice came out as a weak croak. My dry throat begged for a drink of water. Then a pair of boots came into view. The toe of one pushed hard against my shoulder, and I rolled onto my back, crushing my already aching hands. I bit back a cry and looked up at Chase. He stood over me with a wide grin, revolting in its smugness.

"You're awake. Good. It took a while to find this." He showed me a paintball gun. "Had to get yellow."

On his chest I saw two orange splatters. "But you're out of the game." It came out pathetic and he chuckled.

"How will you prove that, brat? Especially when you're tagged with yellow?"

Chase pointed the gun at my chest but seemed to rethink it. A malicious glint came into his eyes as he moved the nose of the air rifle to my forehead. "How about in the face? This close, it'll leave a nasty wound. Think Riley Tate will like that?"

Panicked, I turned my head to the side. "Your choice," he said. "On your temple, then."

Terrified, my whole body tensed.

From the corner of my eye I saw a blur of black boots running, followed by a smacking sound and a grunt from Chase as he hit the ground. Someone grappled with him, and they rolled around. Had Riley come to save me? But it wasn't him. A man in frontier clothes, with a dark brown cloth covering his head, sat on my cousin's chest. He slugged Chase in the face with so much anger it scared me.

Chase yelped in pain. Finally he shoved the man off and scrambled to his feet. Staggering back, clutching a bleeding nose, he tore off into the trees. The man stood and walked over to me.

I gazed up at him from an odd angle. There was something familiar about his build and the line of his jaw. "Uncle Logan?" I murmured.

He got out a pocketknife, one similar to the gift I'd been sent, and crouched down. I stared at his boots until he pushed me on my side, away from him. A couple of sharp tugs on the zip tie, and my hands were free. He moved to my feet and cut them loose, too. Pushing myself to a sitting position, I stared at the man who crouched down in front of me.

"Avery," he said in a stern voice. "Why didn't you listen? I warned you to drop out of this competition before you got hurt."

I gaped up at him. "Dad?"

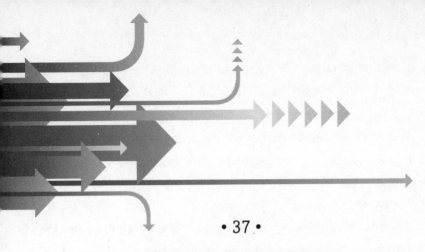

SURPRISING EVENTS

My father helped me to my feet. I brushed the dirt from my jeans, trying to hide how unsteady I felt. Even though Chase didn't shoot me, the idea of what almost happened left me shaky. So did the scene of my dad beating him up. And now here he was, standing in front of me.

"Are you all right?"

It sounded just like the father who used to visit me—the nice stranger who asked about school, books, and the weather. But he wasn't that man to me now. He was the loser who deserted my mother and me. Almost before I knew what I was doing, I slapped him.

My palm stung. It felt hot, but my voice was cold. "How dare you ask how I'm doing, like you're a father who really cares? You don't care! You abandoned me, just like you did Marija."

Until I said her name, he looked surprised. But then color drained from his face. My anger softened a little, replaced by anguish. Tears stung my eyes, but bitterness rose again and I blinked. I walked over to where Chase left the paintball rifle, picked it up, and marched off.

It didn't take long to realize he was following me. I could hear his footsteps and I almost laughed at how idiotic this whole competition had become.

He caught up with me. "I'm sorry."

My breath came in agonized gasps. "My whole life you and Grandmother lied and told me my mother was dead. But she's not."

His shoulders sagged and shame etched the lines of his face. "It was supposed to be easier that way."

I stopped and turned to face him. "Easier!" I practically choked on the word.

He raised a hand in protest. "I know, I know! Ridiculous. Your grandmother didn't want to talk about her because she was embarrassed by what I'd done. And if you knew your mother was alive, you'd ask more questions. She said it was best to just bury the whole thing."

My voice sharpened to a razor's edge. "That was her decision. What's your excuse?"

"Talking about your mother . . . thinking of her. It was too painful. So I went along with it."

"That's cowardly."

He gave a meek nod. "Yes, you're right."

His submission only made me angrier. "Do you know Marija writes me a letter every year on my birthday? After nearly eighteen years, she still feels terrible grief and guilt. Even though she had no choice, since Grandmother was getting her deported. And

342

the immigration agent told Marija they'd take me away from her at the border."

He grabbed my shoulder. "What?"

The sudden fury in his eyes made me hesitate. I still managed to scowl at him. "Don't tell me you didn't know."

"Marija didn't care about either of us!" he stammered. "Mother paid her to go home to Croatia. She took money, and she was happy to go back home."

"You're so stupid! Of course she took money, but just to survive because she was being forced back to a war-torn country. She didn't want to leave. And she begged Grandmother to let her keep me."

Studying his face, I saw slapping him didn't compare to this. He shook his head but couldn't talk.

I said, "Exactly."

He moved to a log and sat. I heard running feet and saw two redcoats coming my way. I lifted the paintball rifle and shot them with so much skill it would have shocked me if I wasn't too upset to care. "Back off!" I shouted, and they did.

I walked over to my dad and tossed down the gun. "Even if you didn't know what happened to Marija, it doesn't explain why you left me alone in that big mansion with no one who really cared about me but the servants."

He looked up with damp eyes, and for the first time I saw deep lines in his face. He'd always been the handsome but distant father. Now he looked more real.

"Your grandmother said I'd only ruin your life. I was an alcoholic. I mean, I am an alcoholic. But I've been sober for almost a year now. She insisted it would be better if she raised you. Said if

I tried to take you, she'd cut me off from everything and get you through the courts."

"You didn't fight for me."

"No."

"Because I'm nothing to you."

He shook his head. "How can I explain? After Marija left, and you were so tiny, I fell apart. I drank until I was worthless. I'd tell myself to quit, and I'd promise to do better and be there for you. But it was a cycle I couldn't break."

"You could've at least spent more time with me."

He glanced away, looking guilty. "Yes, but even as a little girl you reminded me so much of your mother." His eyes returned to my face. "As you got older, it was harder. Whenever I saw you, I'd think of her and what I lost—the only little bit of happiness in my life. It always hurt too much. I'm sorry, Avery. Sorry I was never there for you. Sorry that I let the alcohol and my mother keep controlling my choices. I was weak. It's taken your whole life for me to get sober."

My hot anger began to seep away. "At least you're finally being honest. Why are you here?"

We heard some distant musket fire, and he guided me inside a cluster of brush beneath a giant pine. "I told you not to do this competition. I left a note that you could get hurt. Why didn't you listen?"

"You're the one who threatened me?"

He raised his eyebrows as if surprised. "Not a threat. A warning to get you to understand that competing against the family is too dangerous."

Now everything started to make sense. "So you came in my bedroom and left the note. And you took the Christmas picture of us together."

"Yes. I didn't remember seeing it before, and I liked it. I'll give it back after I make a copy."

"If you were standing right there, why leave a note but not talk to me?"

Sadness crossed his face, and I wondered how he could seem even unhappier. "Seeing you sleeping at your desk, your head on your arms, you looked just like your mother. I thought about waking you but was too emotional. What would you think if I started crying?"

"I'd finally think my dad was human." I paused. "But how'd you get inside the mansion?"

"There's a small door in the south wall under the ivy. All of us boys knew about it. I used an old key I still have and gave the dogs some bits of steak."

A door in the wall? If only I'd known!

"Listen Avery, there's not much time left. Maybe in the beginning I didn't want you to compete, but you've gotten this far and you might as well finish. That's why I'm doing everything I can to help you. It's why I slipped the message under your door at the hotel in Scotland."

"That was from you?"

There were so many surprises unfolding in front of me that I started to feel dizzy. "But how did you know what we needed? How'd you even know I was here?"

"Matilda Brown."

It took me a second to react. "Mr. Tate's law associate?"

He nodded. "We were in college together. She got the job with the firm because I recommended her to Mr. Tate."

"You're friends with Ms. Brown?" It seemed impossible.

My dad smiled and shook his head. "Not friends, really. She's not a friendly person. But years ago we were in a study group together, and she helped me get through college. When she contacted me and explained the competition, I refused to show up. I wasn't going to do anything my mother wanted, so I asked Matilda to say she couldn't find me. After you went ahead and agreed to compete, she secretly kept me posted on what was happening. I've kind of been trailing you."

"In Scotland?" Stunned, I stared at him as it all started to make sense. "I saw you! But I thought that was Uncle Logan."

"I tried to be discreet."

"Why? If you were there, you should have told me. We could've teamed together."

"And let your grandmother know where I was? No way. Besides, you've been doing great on your own. So has Warren. I'm really proud of you both for making it this far. And I've been helping in my own way. Like that night I saw you leave the hotel in Edinburgh, I followed you. I knew you were upset about something, and then I heard you and Riley Tate talking about not knowing who the Scottish heir was. But I did know, because when I was still in touch with your grandmother, she sent me postcards from her trip to Kinloss Abbey."

My dad was the one following me that night? He said, "But I wanted to be fair about helping both my kids, so I slipped the same message under Warren's door."

"And now you're here."

"I heard about those threatening texts and decided I'd better come. Matilda signed me up with the reenactment group."

"Thanks for saving me from Chase." I shoved my hand in my pocket and pulled out the knife. "You mailed me this, too, didn't you?"

He nodded. "That was mine, back when I was a kid. I also sent Warren my old Boy Scout compass. I knew you two were going into the Civil War challenge and thought they might come in handy."

We heard footsteps and crouched down. Uncle Marshall hurried past, still very much in the game. My father's eyes narrowed with dislike until his brother disappeared behind a line of trees. He turned to me. "Avery, you've got to hurry. See if you can make it to the end. I'll follow you at a distance and meet you afterward." He hesitated. "If that's all right."

I studied him for a few seconds and nodded. He reached up as if to touch my face but stopped himself. "You look just like her. So beautiful."

I didn't want to let him see how his words affected me and pulled on my goggles. Then I moved from behind the bushes and headed up the hill. My mind whirred until I told myself to keep it together. I began to run, every sense focused on picking up movements and sound. I darted around trees, crouched behind cover, and dodged redcoats; it felt like I was a real Patriot messenger.

After fifteen more minutes, my legs ached from the workout. Beneath the stiff vest, sweat stuck my shirt to my back, and my head ached from Chase's hit. Still, I kept pushing forward. Going uphill and around a line of trees, I stepped into a clearing. A redcoat was waiting there, his gun pointed at me. He was mid-twenties with an excited smile beneath a hawkish nose.

"Hey!" someone shouted, and the soldier turned a little, still firing but missing me.

Warren slammed into the redcoat. I noticed he had a yellow paintball stain on his back. Stasia pushed through some bushes. "Run, Avery!"

As I raced off, I saw Warren take a shot of orange paint in the chest. I ran up the hill, and my heart hammered like crazy. Chase had attacked me. My dad showed up out of nowhere to save me. Warren jumped in to save me, too, which blew my mind. And Riley confessed he was in love with me. I didn't think I could handle much more.

I burst through a grove of small trees and saw a smooth, grassy area with paved paths and a tall stone marker in the center. The monument! The lack of cover made me nervous, but standing at the side of the pillar was a man dressed as a Patriot and wearing a hat with a feather in the band. He had to be the actor playing Colonel Campbell. I sprinted forward and then heard several pops. Paintballs hit my back, and despite the vest, it knocked the breath out of me. My heart sank. So close! I staggered over to the colonel, dug in my pocket, and pulled out the small envelope. It was bent and not in the best shape, but the seal was still in one piece.

I held it up to him. Gasping for breath, sweat trickling down my temples, I waited until he took it from my shaky fingers. He gave a nod of approval. "Well done, soldier."

I yanked off the goggles and dropped them on the ground. Ms. Franklin came around the monument and handed me a bottle of water. I drank half of it and when I could talk, asked, "What color is the paint on my back?"

"Red."

Warren, I knew, had taken a yellow hit. I undid the Velcro tabs on the uncomfortable vest and pulled it off, the air cool on my sweat-soaked body. "Have you seen my uncle?"

"Yes. He gave the colonel his message about five minutes ago. And he didn't get tagged."

Others began pouring into the clearing; it seemed the reenactment was over. That's when I saw Riley running in my direction, a big grin on his face. He grabbed me in his arms. "I can't wait to hear everything."

I pushed up on my toes to whisper in his ear. "You are not going to believe what's happened."

Before he could ask, we were distracted by Warren and Stasia walking out of the forest. They were holding hands, and she smiled up at him like he was the greatest guy who ever lived. Warren handed the colonel his envelope just as Mr. Benjamin came over.

I took Riley's hand, and we went to my brother. "Why did you do that, Warren? Why did you save me?"

He pointed an accusing finger at Uncle Marshall, who'd just come around the side of the monument. "See that jerk?" His voice was loud enough for everyone to hear. "He shot me with a yellow paintball to get me out early, even though I was already past the orange line. So Stasia and I decided to help you. We wanted you to beat him."

Riley and I stared at Uncle Marshall, who raised his chin. "Warren is lying."

"Of course he isn't," I said. "Mr. Benjamin, are you going to allow that?"

He shrugged. "There's nothing I can do. No rule against the players themselves taking each other out."

Ms. Franklin stepped up to us. "Congratulations to everyone for completing this challenge. The winner is Marshall, who made it back without getting shot. Second place is Avery. Warren, I'm sorry, but you've been eliminated."

"Yeah, yeah."

Stasia slid her arms around his waist and gazed at him with a glowing sort of love that was almost embarrassing to watch. "Warren, I've never been more proud of you than I am right now. I'm so glad I married you."

And then, for the first time that I could remember, my brother looked happy. As if he'd waited his whole life to hear that.

I hugged him, too. He stood stiffly for two seconds before giving a hug in return. I stepped back. "Thanks for helping me, Warren. I'm sorry you're out of the competition."

Stasia smiled and I wondered how someone streaked with dirt and sweat, and with her red hair all in a tangle, could look prettier than Thisby in full makeup. And how could she be so different from my first impression of her?

"Don't worry, Avery. It'll work out. Warren is going to have a great career as a psychiatrist. We don't need his grandmother's money." She came over and gave me a hug. "And I'm really sorry we didn't invite you to our wedding. I'll always feel bad about that."

When she let go, Riley said, "You could make it up to Avery by asking her to Thanksgiving dinner."

I raised my eyebrows at him, but she didn't see, since she'd just turned back to my brother with a whole lot of enthusiasm. "That's a wonderful idea!"

I smiled. No way not to like that girl.

Ms. Franklin called my name. I saw her and Mr. Benjamin standing with Uncle Marshall. Riley and I walked over.

Mr. Benjamin said, "Marshall and Avery, well done. You've made it through a lot of difficulties to end up as the final two heirs."

"Yes," Ms. Franklin added. "And now our responsibilities come to an end. The limousines will leave in fifteen minutes to return you to the Charlotte Airport, and we won't be going with you. From this point, you'll be on your own. That includes finding your way to the final challenge. We wish both of you good luck." Her eyes were on me when she said it, and I wanted to believe she was secretly rooting for me.

I shook their hands. "Thank you."

Uncle Marshall didn't say anything to them, and he definitely didn't offer his hand. Instead, he looked around. "Has anyone seen Chase?"

I laughed. "Oh yeah. Last time I saw him, the coward was running away and holding his broken nose."

"What?"

Mr. Benjamin handed back the sealed letters we'd given to the colonel. "This message holds your final piece of information."

Then he and Ms. Franklin walked away, two people whose real names I didn't know. My uncle also hurried off. I broke the seal and opened the note that read:

HOUSE
@
MIDNIGHT

"There it is!" Riley said. "'House' is the last word we needed for the Lincoln quote."

A mental image of the mansion came to mind and I blew out a tired breath. "I know. But it also means we better get going."

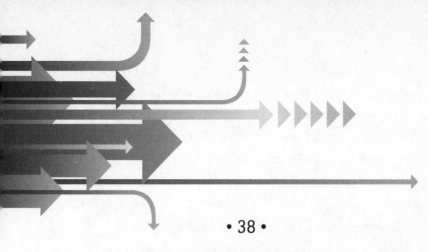

• 38 •

THE TAKEOVER

While Riley and I waited by the limousine, I told him everything. "You're kidding," he said when I explained about my dad and that Ms. Brown was his sort-of friend.

Mostly, though, he was furious at Chase. "How dare he attack you? And if he'd shot you in the temple, it could've killed you! Did the idiot even know that?"

"Maybe he wanted to kill me. He's got to be the one who sent those texts."

"What was I thinking to let you go on by yourself, Avery? I should've stayed with you no matter what." Riley looked serious and more handsome to me than ever.

"You were playing by the rules."

"But the VanDemeres never think the rules apply to them! And I already knew that. I'm a total idiot."

"It's okay. I'm fine. I need a shower in the worst way, and I have a headache, but that's all."

He slid his hand to the small of my back and pulled me close. "Come here, you. I'm never letting you out of my sight again."

"Sounds good to me."

Riley bent his head and we kissed. It was wonderful, comforting, and exciting at the same time. I lost myself in it until a concerned voice interrupted. "Riley Tate, what are you doing?"

I opened my eyes and we both turned to see my dad walking over. He wore a teasing smile and had changed out of his Patriot costume into tan slacks and a dress shirt. "Avery's not even eighteen yet. She's still in high school, you know."

I put my hands on my hips. "Don't even think about trying to play father. You're seventeen and three-quarter years too late."

He smiled again and shrugged. "I know, just decided to try it on for size." He held out his hand to Riley. "How are you?"

After a slight hesitation, Riley shook his hand. My dad asked if he could travel back to California with us, and we agreed. Inside the limo, I got out my tablet and let him read Marija's letters. It was a hard thing to watch. He couldn't hide his grief and anger. The letter written when I was born was the worst, and at one point he broke down. Covering his eyes with his hand, he whispered, "I'm sorry. I'm so sorry!"

I didn't know if he was talking to me or Marija. He took out a handkerchief and wiped his face. After he'd read through everything, he handed me the tablet.

"Are you all right?" I asked.

"How can I be? How can I ever be all right again? Why did I listen to Mother's lies and let her ruin our lives?"

"That's a very good question."

My dad studied me. "Marija was kind. That's why I fell in love

354

with her, not because she was beautiful. I'd been around a lot of beautiful women. In fact, I was married to one. But your mother was different from them all. She had this sweetness in her, surprising since she grew up during a terrible war. I'd watch her play with Warren or how she rocked him to sleep. Her hands were gentle."

The expression in his eyes softened, as if talking about my mother changed him. "We didn't mean to fall in love. But in a house full of people, sometimes you can still feel so lonely. When we were together, Marija and I weren't lonely."

He turned his head to look out the window. "My whole life I'd felt like I was slowly dying of thirst, until her. But then it all went wrong."

My anger at my dad evaporated. It was hard to stay mad at someone who couldn't forgive himself for the mistakes he'd made.

"Where did you get these?" he asked.

I hesitated for a couple of seconds. "Marija sends them to Mr. Tate's office. Grandmother doesn't know he's been keeping them."

"Are there more?"

"Yes, but I don't have them yet. Or a way to contact her. I've been desperate to call her ever since I read the first letter. But I don't even know her last name."

"Klanak," he said immediately. "Marija Klanak."

"Finally!" I did a search for her name, along with Zagreb, Croatia. There were no matches, only names that looked similar. Disappointed but not willing to give up, I clicked on one. It was an ad for a male dentist, and the text was in a foreign language. I checked others, but there was nothing even close to someone who might be my mother.

At the airport, it took a while to book our flights, and we learned the plane wouldn't leave for several hours. Riley studied his boarding pass. "With the time zone difference, we'll be fine. We should get to Santa Rosa around ten thirty. That gives us an hour and a half."

In the lady's room, I washed up the best I could and mainly got the dirt off my face and arms. I slipped inside a stall and changed into clean clothes. Back at the mirror I combed my hair and put on a little makeup, then took out the photograph of Marija and compared it to my reflection again. Dad was right; we really did look a lot alike, and I saw it more each time I studied her picture. Of course, there was a little bit of him in me too, and after watching him more closely today, I caught a glimpse of that in the mirror. I thought about their story and what he'd said, how it was her kindness he fell in love with. Maybe he'd been as alone and isolated as I'd always felt. But now I at least knew there was a mother who loved me and a father who cared enough to secretly watch over me in this crazy competition.

With time to kill, we got something to eat at an airport restaurant. My dad asked a couple of questions about Warren. I took the pickles off my hamburger before taking a bite. "Did you see him at Kings Mountain?"

He looked disappointed. "Yes. I wanted to talk to him. But when I headed his way, he walked off."

I remembered what my brother and I talked about while we were alone in the cabin. "Can you blame him? When was the last time you even saw Warren? At one of Grandmother's parties?"

He didn't answer right away. "I don't remember. And no, I

don't blame him. Besides, a few years ago he made it clear he didn't want me around."

"But he was a kid back then. Kids say stuff when they're hurt and angry." I took another bite, thinking about Warren and Stasia. "Maybe you should try to get in contact with him again."

"What if he won't see me?"

"Then at least you know you tried. And he'll know it, too. Let him give you some grief, and then apologize. Tell him what you told me about getting clean. The thing is, Warren and I were talking a couple of days ago, and he let it slip that he's upset you walked out of his life."

"Really?"

I nodded. We were both quiet for a minute. "And if that doesn't work, you could always talk to his wife, Stasia. That girl won't give up on anything she thinks needs fixing."

Riley smiled in agreement. "True."

A more relaxed look settled on my dad's face. "I'll give it a try. Thanks, Avery."

The conversation turned to a different topic, and soon he and Riley were discussing sports. I watched them. It all looked so normal, a father talking to his daughter's boyfriend, like what might happen in a real family. But there was nothing normal about my relationship with my dad, and him being here still felt strange.

We were nearly done eating when he said to me, "By the way, I'm sorry about what a rotten experience you had at that boarding school. Your grandmother never should've sent you there."

"No kidding! It was horrible. But how'd you know about St. Frederick's?"

He hesitated. "Well, I've been following your blog for a while."

I stared at him. He added, "Bet you're relieved you don't have to go back there."

I dropped the french fry I was holding. "What?"

"You didn't know?"

I shook my head and he smiled as if excited to share the news. "Your grandmother read that blog you wrote. Henry showed it to her. She did not like finding out how the school was run and what it was really like for you."

I almost stopped breathing. "I *never* have to go back?" It came out as a half-choked gasp.

Dad smiled. "No, Avery, you don't. At least from what I've heard. And not only that, but there's going to be big changes to St. Frederick's because she set up a twenty-four-hour takeover."

"Huh?"

"That means she gave their board of directors an offer they couldn't pass up. If they agreed to an immediate hand-over of the school, she was willing to pay them three times its value. The final paperwork won't be done for a couple of months, but it basically belongs to VanDemere Enterprises now."

"You're joking." I could see from his face he wasn't.

"And for now, she's closed the place. Students were sent home with a notice to parents that it will reopen sometime in the future, though who knows when. That'll only happen after a complete restructuring of the staff, which started with sacking Mr. Hatlierre."

"She got rid of him?" I remembered the way Gavin Waylenz had practically worshipped the guy and felt like laughing.

"During a phone call with her, Hatlierre made the mistake of saying it wasn't surprising you had problems, considering you didn't grow up in a regular family environment."

I tried to hide the discomfort I felt because it was true. I could see in my dad's eyes he was doing the same.

"Bet she didn't like that."

He shook his head. "Definitely not. That's why he was the first to go. I'm surprised you don't know any of this." He glanced at Riley. "The law firm handled the takeover."

I looked at Riley, too. Right away I knew, probably because he didn't even try to hide it. "Why didn't you tell me?"

I could see he was struggling to come up with an answer, and I stopped him. "Never mind. I know why. Just before we left Scotland, I overheard you tell your dad that I had a right to know something. This is what it was."

I hated that my voice sounded hurt but couldn't help it. "As long as I thought losing would send me back to St. Frederick's, then I'd try harder."

For the first time since I'd met him, Riley looked ashamed. He touched a fist to the edge of the table. "I wanted to tell you."

"But what your dad said was more important to you than what I needed to hear."

He didn't deny it.

I scooted out of the booth. All I could think about was getting away from him. Outside the restaurant, I headed down the airport walkway. I tried to mask my unhappiness with anger and not feel so vulnerable. I hurried past dozens of people going in different directions with their luggage. I walked faster, trying to get by, until a hand grabbed my arm and spun me around.

"Avery, wait." Riley's fingers slid down to my wrist. "Hang on a minute, will you?"

I pulled free and kept going. He easily matched my stride, which only annoyed me more. He said, "Will you please talk to me?"

Finally I stopped and faced him with arms folded in a way that said, *Don't even think about touching me.*

"I'm sorry." He looked it.

For some reason, that made me even madder. "I thought I could trust you!"

Maybe it was my turn to do the hurting, because a miserable expression came into his eyes. He took a step closer. "I should've told you."

That was so obvious I didn't bother answering. Riley leaned in a little, though not reaching for me. "You were really driven to win, and staying out of the boarding school was a big part of that."

"Which makes it okay to hide the truth? For you and your dad to manipulate me?"

"It's not that simple."

"Yes it is, Riley. It's so simple that all it means is you trust me to keep trying no matter what. But you didn't do that."

"Because your grandmother didn't want us to tell you!"

I took a step back, almost bumping into a lady dragging a wheeled suitcase. He followed. "Listen, Avery. For one thing, she wanted to be the one to tell you about taking over the school. And she also knew the threat of going back there would make you keep trying your best at the challenges."

"So what, then? Is everyone against me?"

Riley moved closer. "No, *for* you, Avery." Another step, too close this time, but I didn't back away. I let out an annoyed sigh that didn't discourage him. His hands went to my sides. "I'm for you. Always for you."

I wanted to pull away, but he was looking down at me with intense eyes, desperate to make things right. "Don't be mad, okay?"

I lowered my gaze, not wanting to be persuaded. But I also didn't protest when his arms pulled me closer. His mouth was near my temple. "It'll all be over soon, you know. And no matter if you win or not, I'm happy I came with you. I hope you feel the same."

"I'm still mad, Riley." I stepped back and he let his hands slide away. "I can't get over it in two seconds."

He nodded. "I understand."

"I need time to think."

"Okay."

My dad walked up to us, carrying my backpack. He checked his watch. "We need to catch our flight."

I didn't say anything else to Riley. The whole time we were boarding the plane and finding our seats, my thoughts were a confused mess. The fear of being sent back to St. Frederick's was finally gone, but at a price. I thought about how driven I'd been to make it through each challenge. Maybe Riley was right. It had made me try harder. But I should've been the one to make that decision.

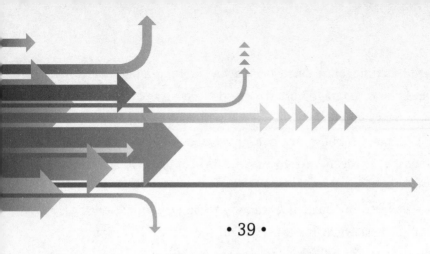

THE FINISH LINE

We sat on the runway for nearly an hour, and Riley kept checking the time on his cell phone. Once we were finally in the air, he leaned back. "No problem. We've still got enough time." He sounded nervous for someone who was so sure.

I rested my head against the seat and closed my eyes. Not that long ago, flying in an airplane to Venezuela was the most exciting experience of my life. Right now jet lag was starting to take on personal meaning. I fell asleep but woke about an hour later to see Riley snoozing.

My father sat on my other side, reading. I stretched and looked over at him. "Dad, it's still hard for me to believe you're here, know that? I mean, I haven't seen you in forever."

He closed his book. "I know. But even though we haven't been together, I've spent a lot of time thinking about you."

"You have?"

"Yes. While I was getting sober, I searched for you online and found your blog. I've read every post, but then four months ago there was nothing. Of course now I know it's because you were sent to that rotten boarding school."

He frowned, his eyes turning angry. "When I read your post about it, I got really mad. Mad at my mother for sending you there, but even madder at myself for being so out of your life. I decided the only way to help was to make sure your grandmother learned the truth."

"*You* told her about my blog?"

"In a roundabout way, yes. I got Matilda Brown to contact Henry, who of course forwards everything on to her."

It took a few seconds to process what he'd done for me. "Thanks, Dad."

"It's just that I've tried to think of a way to come back into your life. To close the gap I allowed by not being there for you all these years."

He shifted in his seat to better look at me. "Avery, I know I can't fix the past or even make up for it. But I'd like to create a future with you."

I glanced down at my hands, trying to think what to say. I couldn't come up with anything. He added, "I know the road will be bumpy as we deal with everything we've lost. But I'm willing to take that road if you'll come with me."

I blew out an emotional breath. "It's just I've been hurt for so long. I don't want to be hurt any more."

He accepted this, though I could see the sadness he felt. I said, "But I've spent a lot of time being unhappy that I didn't have a dad. So I'll give you a second chance, as long as we take it slow."

There was hope in his eyes and he nodded. "Sure."

Neither of us said anything for a while, and then he added, "I have an apartment over in Sonoma. Would you like to come to dinner sometime?"

I thought it over. "Sounds good."

"Why don't I give you my cell number? Then you can text me when you're ready."

I added his number to my contact list.

A couple of hours later, we landed at the Santa Rosa airport, and Mr. Tate had a car waiting for us. Soon we were traveling through the nighttime streets, and when the mansion came into sight, I told the driver to take us around to the delivery gate. "I can get us in the back way faster."

We left the car and walked up the drive to the gate. Standing beneath the glare of a floodlight, I grabbed my wallet and got out the key card. Riley checked the time on his phone again. "Hurry, will you? There's only ten minutes left."

"I've got it." I swiped the card and the gate latch popped open. Just as I started to push it back, there was a deafening gunshot. A bullet hit into the pillar near my head and stone chips rained down. With a startled cry I spun around.

An angry voice called out, "Stop right there!"

Dad and Riley were a few steps away, and when they inched toward me, the guy said, "I mean it! Stay there or I'll kill you."

"Don't move," I whispered to them. We stared at the spot of darkness as someone limped forward. It was Gavin Waylenz from St. Frederick's. And he was pointing a gun at me.

"What are you doing here, Gavin?"

And how did he even know where I lived? A quick memory

came to mind of him helping in the school office. I could almost see him searching my file for my address and cell phone number.

"You're the one who sent me those texts."

His eyes narrowed. "This is all your fault! Getting your rich family to buy the school and shut it down!"

I took a step back and bumped into the bars of the gate. It moved a little. "I didn't do that."

"She's telling the truth," my dad said.

"Shut up!" Gavin screamed at him, waving the gun.

I heard a familiar snuffling sound behind me that brought a tiny bit of hope.

"Your grandmother told Mr. Hatlierre about that blog you wrote. I read it. All that stupid crap you came up with! 'A motivational speaker whose real motive is getting money. A man who brainwashes students into becoming his little robots.' How could you write that garbage?"

Gavin's eyes showed fury and a little insanity, and though I tried to think what to say, I also knew nothing would stop him.

He raised the gun. "You are dead."

"No!" Dad shouted.

I pushed back on the gate and Max and Caesar were around it in a flash, just as Riley leaped at Gavin. The gun went off with another loud blast, but it missed me. The snarling dogs attacked, and then Dad rammed into Gavin; he grabbed the gun. The guard dogs were all over Gavin, who rolled on the ground. He covered his head with his arms, screaming. The limo driver ran up, a cell phone to his ear.

I gave a short whistle to call off the dogs. Both of them turned and trotted over to me, tongues lolling. With shaky hands I patted their heads and put them inside the gate.

"Avery," Dad shouted. "Get over here."

I hurried forward. The driver had Gavin's chest pinned beneath his knee, and the stupid kid was moaning. I turned to Riley, who sat on the ground. His fingers pressed against the side of his neck as blood seeped through them.

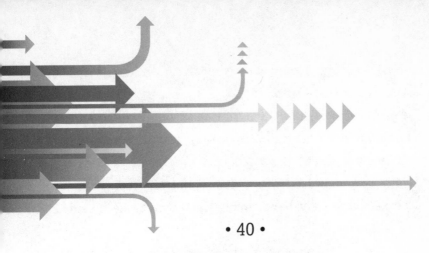

• 40 •

A HOUSE DIVIDED

"No!" I dropped down beside him.

"I'm all right."

He didn't look it. His face was white and blood was everywhere.

Dad knelt next to him and pressed his handkerchief against the wound. "You're going to be fine," he told Riley. "The bullet just grazed the side of your neck." His voice sounded sure, and I desperately wanted to believe him. But there was so much blood. Wasn't a major artery there?

We heard sirens in the distance. Riley grabbed my wrist. "Look at me, Avery. In my eyes."

I did. Beneath the yellow floodlights, their usual blue was the gray of a nighttime ocean. "This looks worse than it is. In about two seconds there's going to be a ton of cops and EMTs here. I'll be okay. But you have only a few minutes to make it upstairs."

I shook my head, barely able to speak. "I can't leave you." It came out a crushed whisper.

He gave a short laugh, then grimaced. "Girl, I'm crazy about you. But if you don't get into that mansion right this minute, I'm never taking you on another date again."

I felt a wash of relief. Nobody dying would say that.

Dad sat back. "My handkerchief has slowed the bleeding. This isn't life threatening."

The sirens grew piercing as the glare of emergency strobes flashed across the driveway. I leaned in and kissed Riley. The touch of his lips felt warm and alive.

His hand squeezed my wrist. "Promise me you'll finish the challenge. You deserve to win."

"Okay," I said in a half sob.

Dad shouted over the sirens. "I'll stay with him. Just go!"

I jumped to my feet, ran to the fence, and squeezed through. Max and Caesar were at my heels, all excited like this was a game. I told them to stop and ran in through the kitchen door, half expecting to see Connie, but no one was there. Flying across the sunroom and then down a hall, I slipped on a small rug. My elbow smacked into a large painting and knocked it off center. I ran for the stairs and took them in leaps. My heart was pounding by the time I reached the third floor. I raced down the long hallway leading to Grandmother's office and saw Henry waiting there. He tapped his watch. I ran faster as he opened the door, which I bolted through.

I stumbled inside, panting so hard I couldn't speak. My limbs felt weak but I managed to walk forward calmly. Uncle Marshall was already in one of the two chairs facing the large desk. Grandmother sat behind it.

"Ha!" My uncle pointed to the antique German wall clock. "She's late by two minutes!"

I looked at the second hand. It was just past midnight. But then Grandmother said, "Oh Marshall, loosen up. That clock runs a few minutes fast. Avery, come in and sit down."

Still breathing hard, I dropped into the other chair and stared at my grandmother, hardly recognizing her. It had been more than four months since I'd seen her. She looked ten years older. Her face was thinner, more wrinkled, and her cheeks were sunken. Her skin, always fair and clear, looked sickly. Her hair was thinner, too, although still curled the way she liked it.

"I know, I know. I look terrible," she said. "I was ill and almost died, or didn't you believe me?"

Uncle Marshall used his most tender voice. "You still look like my mother."

She pierced him with her gaze. "Stop sucking up."

A small laugh escaped me because she never talked like that. Then I thought of Riley and felt a wash of fear. Were the EMTs taking care of him? Had the bleeding stopped? The desk phone rang and she answered. She listened for a few seconds before speaking. "It was gunfire, then?" Another pause. "I see."

Her eyes turned in my direction, and she studied me with a concerned expression while someone on the other end gave her details about the shooting. I assumed it was the security firm. Finally she said, "And Riley Tate is going to be all right?"

I held my breath until she nodded. "Good."

She hung up and looked at me. "The EMTs are taking care of Riley, and he's going to be fine. They'll be heading to the hospital in a few minutes. Also, the police arrested the boy who shot at you."

"Gavin Waylenz, from St. Frederick's."

"Who?"

I gave an explanation of what happened outside, and how close I'd come to being killed. Grandmother shook her head as if hardly able to believe it. I'd never seen her look so upset.

"Avery, I owe you an apology. It was wrong to enroll you at that boarding school. I didn't know, until I read your blog, what a mistake I made. And what just happened proves everything you wrote about that school is true. Which is why I've taken over St. Frederick's. We own it now, and it will stay closed until it is completely reorganized and has new policies. By the time that happens, you'll have graduated from Greenleaf."

"Thank you," I said, and I meant it. "But Grandmother, why did you send me without even talking to me?"

She paused, as if thinking how best to explain, and finally let out a tired sigh. "I didn't know what else to do. At first, when I heard you were sneaking off the estate, I didn't believe it. Until I saw proof. You really were going out and doing who-knew-what with those friends of yours—including kissing boys! And I couldn't properly take care of you since I was still recuperating, not well enough to come home. My plan was for you to stay someplace safe, and that school came highly recommended. Don't you see? There just was no other choice after Marshall mailed me those photos."

Stunned, I turned to him. "You?"

He ignored me, instead staring at her in surprise. "Why do you say it was me?"

"Come now. There's nothing I can't find out, and you know it. I have proof you hired a private investigator to follow Avery."

Finally he shrugged. "All right, so I did. But only because you needed to know what she was doing. I'd just visited you here and was driving downtown when I saw her coming out of a movie with two other girls. You thought she was still at home that night."

"Why'd you care what I was doing?" I asked him. "I'm nothing to you! Your kids have always hated me—I get that. But I thought you never even noticed I was alive."

My uncle studied the Tiffany lamp on her desk as if he hadn't heard me. Grandmother said, "That's a good question. Give Avery an answer."

"Fine!" He sent a sideways glance at me. "Mother kept talking about you. Every time I was here, it was always about how good you were. How smart and well behaved. How your cousins should follow your example because you were the only one willing to really learn about our ancestors. And she'd go on about what high grades you got at that fancy academy. She even showed me one of your English essays."

I looked back at Grandmother. "Really? I mean, you were proud of me?"

"Of course." She frowned. "Marshall, I never imagined you'd feel so threatened by a teenager. What did you think? That I'd disinherit the rest of the family and give everything to Avery?"

His face flushed and I realized that's exactly what he thought.

"Enough of this." She picked up a small notepad and looked at a list of several items. "It's late and we still have a lot to do. Let's move on to the competition. I want to start with a question. Do either of you have a message for me?"

Uncle Marshall's forehead puckered, creating a weird line between his eyebrows. "What do you mean?"

She studied him for a few seconds, then turned to me. "Avery?"

I took a deep breath and hoped Riley was right. "Abraham Lincoln said, 'A house divided against itself cannot stand.'"

She leaned forward slightly, studying me for several long seconds. "Well done! I would not have thought . . ." Her voice faded and she glanced past my head, then back at me. "Go on, child."

There was more? I felt a flutter of panic. Did the quote have a deeper meaning? And if so, what was it?

Uncle Marshall looked confused. "What's that supposed to mean? Why's she quoting Lincoln?"

"Hush! Avery is explaining how a secret message ties in to our family."

That meant the answer had to be somewhere in her office. I stood. My mind raced as I scanned the walls, including behind me to where Grandmother had glanced. I walked in that direction and noticed the faded brown sampler stitched by Genoa Stuart, the girl whose brothers fought in the Civil War. A Bible verse was at the bottom, stitched in tiny letters. I leaned near and examined it.

"Mark three: twenty-five." I thought about two of the clues. *Mark* had been on the abbot's paper, and the number 325 on the quinine bottle. "This is it right here. 'If a house be divided against itself, that house cannot stand.' Lincoln was quoting the Bible."

A slow smile came to my lips, and I felt like laughing at myself. A picture of this sampler was on my camera the whole time! I'd scrolled past it but never bothered to read the words. I looked back at Grandmother, who returned my smile.

"Excellent, Avery! Henry said none of my heirs would figure it out, but you proved him wrong."

I came back and sat down. She picked up a square black box from her desk and held it out to me. Inside were six rows of very old coins. She said, "Your grandfather's Revolutionary War coin collection."

My uncle's eyes practically bugged out of his head. I closed the lid. "Thank you."

She checked the list on her desk, then looked up. "Now, it's time for a quick explanation of what happens next. This is the last challenge, and the character trait is *integrity*. It's about being honest."

She pointed to the far wall where there was a large, beautiful painting of George Washington beside his horse. It was the same painting that covered her safe. "As you probably know, I've always had deep admiration for the father of our country. George Washington's honesty has been passed down to us through history, and he should be a great example to you. It's now time for me to decide who will take control of VanDemere Enterprises. I am going to give you an opportunity to tell me the truth about what you learned from these challenges. This is your chance to persuade me that you should be named the last standing heir."

Inwardly, I groaned. This was worse than doing a class project. She added, "Marshall, since you won the Revolutionary War challenge, your reward has two parts. First, you may choose any item from the estate for your personal collection, either a family heirloom or one of the art pieces. Do you need time to think about what you'd like?"

He gave a brief shake of his head. "The Cézanne." It came out as a strangled wheeze, though his face looked elated.

I thought about the still life that hung in a gilded frame

beneath special art lighting in the formal salon. It wasn't the most beautiful painting in the mansion, but it was definitely the most valuable.

Grandmother added a brief note to her list. "I'll have Henry arrange for its delivery to your home." She put down the pen. "The next part of your reward is that in this challenge, you get to go first. Is there anything you'd like to tell me about your experiences in the competition?"

Uncle Marshall sat up even straighter in his chair. "Yes, Mother. There definitely is."

He began saying a lot of stuff about our ancestors. He discussed what they had accomplished, the contributions they made to society, and why their lives were an important part of history. He had dates and places memorized, almost like a university professor.

I realized that while I'd been busy shopping, kissing Riley, and reading my mother's letters, my uncle was prepping. He readied himself for the biggest test of his life. Most impressive of all was how he kept referring to the character traits. He talked about the way Otis VanDemere showed fortitude, and how the Overmountain Men were really courageous. He covered each quality and made it sound so moving and patriotic that I wondered if he'd hired a speech writer. He also added a big spiel about how the challenges had personally influenced him to be a better person. Did Grandmother know how he'd treated Daisy or how he shot Warren with a yellow paintball?

Uncle Marshall wrapped it up by saying, "I want to thank you for this amazing opportunity. What I've learned through these challenges will stay with me for the rest of my life."

I muttered, "Along with the money."

"Avery, don't be coarse." Grandmother again focused on my uncle and gave him an approving nod. "Well done, Marshall. I must admit I'm pleasantly surprised and impressed."

A self-satisfied glow bloomed beneath his phony sober expression; she didn't seem to notice it, though. "Your turn, Avery."

I took a deep breath. "It kind of surprises me to admit the challenges were great. At first I was just really happy to be out of St. Frederick's and willing to do anything to keep from going back. But along the way, I learned a whole lot about my own life."

"Interesting. Can you explain?"

"Absolutely. I really do want to know my history, but I don't care what ancestor came over on the *Mayflower* or who went mining for diamonds. Wait, I'm supposed to focus on integrity, right Grandmother?"

"Yes," she said, though her face looked a little tense.

"Well, then, let's talk about your integrity. The most important history in my whole life was taken from me. And you're the one who stole it."

Her face flushed with anger, but I pressed forward, unwilling to stop. "You see, I could've had a mother who loved me. Marija and I should have been together. She desperately wanted to raise me, but you separated us. And what you did was meaner and more dishonest than any tragic story you could ever tell about your ancestors. You forced my mother to give me up."

Grandmother pulled back as if I'd struck her. "Who told you this?"

"It doesn't matter. What matters is that while you've always demanded I be truthful, you were the one telling the biggest lie of all. Marija is not dead! And she has spent her life grieving for the daughter who was ripped from her arms."

It took her a few silent seconds to compose herself. "Avery, you don't understand how it was. What Preston and Marija did devastated us all. It destroyed his marriage and became a huge scandal. Your grandfather and I were humiliated. We could hardly hold up our heads. In fact, I believe the stress of it led to the heart attack that caused his death."

I thought this over. "And so you punished them."

She raised her chin. "What they were doing couldn't go on. I absolutely could not allow her to stay here. Do you have any idea what it would have meant if they were together? Preston marrying the nanny!"

I wondered how someone could spout about character traits and still be so cruel. "I get it. You've always been about family pride. What other people think is more important than what we feel for each other. But what about me? Why ruin my life by taking me away from my mother?"

"You were my granddaughter! And a VanDemere. It was my responsibility to keep you in our family."

"Family?" I scoffed. "Your family has made my life miserable! Chase found sneaky ways to pick on me. Thisby was just as bad, with the spiteful stuff she and Daisy said. And look what Uncle Marshall's done. If that's what family is, and what it means to be a VanDemere, then I don't want anything to do with it!"

She lifted a hand in protest. "Until I saw what Thisby said to you in the cabin, and Chase on the ship, I didn't know!"

I pushed to the edge of my seat. It felt like an electric charge was going through me. "And another thing. After you took me away from my mother, why didn't you let Dad raise me?"

Grandmother lifted her chin slightly, as if to justify her position. "You and I both know Preston is not a fit parent. He has a drinking problem."

"Call it what it is. He's an alcoholic."

"Yes," she admitted. "And that's why it seemed best for you to stay here."

"Hidden away because I was the daughter of a scandal? You were ashamed of me."

"No, Avery. You proved to be so much more than I ever believed you could. Better than the other children. As you grew, I was pleased with how intelligent you were, how well behaved. You had a difficult start, it's true. But I tried to make it up to you by being sure you went to the finest schools. I provided you with a good life."

"By keeping me locked away in this big mansion!"

"I was keeping you safe! Making sure you didn't turn out like the others. And from what I've seen, it worked. How can you be ungrateful for that, when I gave you the best of everything?"

"Don't you get it, Grandmother? I don't care about money!" I swung my arm in a wide arc, indicating her priceless collections. "All I ever wanted was real parents. I could have had a mother who loved me. Or at the very least, a father who's more than a stranger. You say you tried to protect me, but all you did was lock me in a prison. You've isolated me from having real relationships with anyone, except Connie and Peter. Even yourself. What I needed was to be loved!"

I ran a hand across my eyes, trying to hide my raw emotions. After several seconds I added, "You're never going to understand."

She studied me with a sorrowful expression. For so much of my life I'd cared about what she thought of me. Now I didn't care at all.

Uncle Marshall shifted his position in the chair. "Are you done?"

I nodded.

He turned to her. "Mother, I hope you can finally see Avery is not what you believed her to be."

Grandmother splayed her fingers on the desktop. "No," she answered in a quiet voice. "She's a lot more. And a better person than you, Marshall. Or any of the other kids."

My eyes widened. Uncle Marshall's face flushed, and his fists pressed against the tops of his legs as if forcing himself to stay seated.

Grandmother looked at each of us with one last assessing stare. "All that aside, I've finally come to a decision."

I half expected a drumroll as she squared her shoulders. "Marshall, I am turning VanDemere Enterprises over to you."

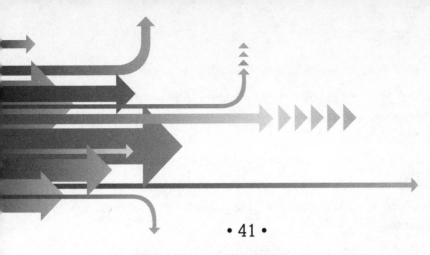

41

GRANDMOTHER'S CHOICE

A few silent moments passed, the German clock ticking like a bomb, and I told myself not to be surprised. With all the stuff I'd just said, this was bound to happen. Maybe if I'd pretended it was a high school presentation, I could've made a fancy speech to compete with Uncle Marshall. Stupid me. I thought the character trait of *integrity* actually meant I could be honest.

My uncle finally found his voice. "Yes!"

He threw a fist in the air like he'd just scored the touchdown of a lifetime. He grinned so wide the top of his gums showed; not an attractive look on him.

Grandmother's head gave a slight shake. "Try to be gracious, Marshall." She turned to me. "I know you must be disappointed. Truly, I had no choice in this, Avery. You are the best heir and should win this challenge, but it is clear you don't care about Van-Demere Enterprises. If I left you the company, you'd probably sell it off and donate the proceeds. Marshall will never do that."

He folded his arms in a very justified way as she added, "He cares about the company his father built. That's why he has to be the winning heir and inherit, even if he is a selfish money-grubber."

"Hey!" he cried.

"Marshall, be quiet. I'm trying to help Avery understand." Grandmother leaned across her desk as if to get a closer look at my reaction. "His focus is on doing what's best for VanDemere Enterprises."

I tried not to care. After all, at the beginning of the competition I'd explained to Mr. Tate that running the family business was the last thing I wanted. "You're right. I don't know anything about the company."

Uncle Marshall gave a sharp nod. "I'm assuming we'll sign papers on this soon?"

She just looked at him for a few seconds. "So eager. Perhaps now is a good time to also let you know of something else I've set in motion. After I saw what happened in the law firm's conference room, I've arranged for Jim Tate to receive a permanent assignation on our board of directors. Though he doesn't know it yet, he'll have full veto rights."

My uncle half rose out of his seat. "What?"

"Well, I can't just let you take off with my company in any direction you want to go. I have to establish a safeguard. Tate, Bingham, and Brown have contributed greatly to our success, and I'm not going to let you fire them just because you don't like Jim Tate."

Marshall slumped in his chair. I felt secretly pleased for Riley and his dad. This also meant I could get my mother's letters.

I stood. "So everything's decided, then. If you don't mind, I want to go check on Riley."

"I'm not done," Grandmother said. "Sit back down, young lady."

I sat.

"That's better. Now, Avery, even though I'm giving Marshall the company, you're also to receive an inheritance. After all, you made it through the challenges just as he did. And equally important, you were smart enough to solve the hidden clues that Henry and I devised. Considering this, I've decided to leave you everything else I own. The mansion, my collections, and all my personal and worldly goods, which are extensive. The net worth actually surpasses what I'm giving my son."

This time Uncle Marshall did jump out of his chair. "But I'm the winning heir!"

"No, you're the heir who'll run the family business. Avery will run the family assets. There's a difference."

I sat there feeling a bit numb until she said, "Just so you both know, the family is gathered in the first-floor library. They've been watching this."

Uncle Marshall looked around. "What? How?"

She pointed to a small piece of electronics on the bookcase behind her. "That's a camera with a live feed to the library."

I wasn't sure how I felt about that. "They all agreed to come? How'd you manage it?"

"I offered each of them an additional hundred thousand dollars to attend. Marshall, go downstairs and talk to Daisy." She handed him a folder. "Here are the results of a DNA test I ordered long ago. She really is your daughter."

His mouth formed a surprised O but no sound came out. Grandmother added, "Regardless of what she did to Chase, and what you've always secretly believed about her parentage, you acted abominably. See if you can settle the problems between you, and those with your wife. Not only that, but from now on, include Daisy in the family business. Let her earn back some of her inheritance. Until you get that worked out, I'm not giving you the company."

He stood and tromped out of the room.

More silence. More listening to the ticking clock. Finally I touched the achy spot between my eyes. "I'm not the right choice."

"Well, it has to go to someone. And you're the only one money hasn't ruined. My fortune would be the downfall of someone like Thisby or Chase. Taking it away from my heirs is about the best gift I can give them." She turned to the camera. "Did all of you hear that?"

Then she looked at me again. "What about you, Avery? Can you handle the money?"

"I don't know, Grandmother. I'll probably do stuff with it you won't like. For one thing, I'm going to Croatia to meet my mother just as soon as I can."

She mulled this over. "You're almost eighteen. I suppose that's all right. What else?"

"Buy Connie and Peter a house of their own with a beautiful garden. Share some of the money with Warren and Stasia."

"But what will you do for yourself?"

"Oh. Get my own apartment. Buy a car. Take driving lessons and then drive down to Disneyland with my friends."

I could see her ticking off a mental list. "Fine. I can live with that." She motioned to the display cases, books, and her collections that covered the walls. "And when I'm gone, what will you do with this? Sell or give away everything . . . donate it to a museum? No matter what you said earlier, I hope there's a chance you value your heritage."

It took me a few seconds to answer. "After going down inside the diamond mine and seeing what Otis VanDemere went through, I realized our family legacy actually meant something. He left us more than just a lot of money to become a bunch of rich brats."

"Well said." She rose to her feet but looked a little shaky.

I stood, too. "Grandmother, do you still want me to be honest?"

"Yes."

"Well, I know the polite thing would be to say thank you. But I'm just not there yet and maybe never will be. Mostly I'm furious with how you treated my mother. Aren't you even a little sorry?"

She seemed to shrink back and turn within herself. "I can't talk about that now." There was a weak tremble in her voice and she sounded old.

I waited, not willing to make it easier for her. "Yes," she said at last, her shoulders hunching inward as if trying to protect herself. "I shouldn't have done what I did."

I let out a slow breath, as if exhaling years of pain. From someone like Justine VanDemere, that was probably all I'd ever get. I said, "So, you know, it's going to take time for me to get over being hurt and angry. I can't just wipe it away, even if I want to."

"I understand that." A downcast look crossed her wrinkled face. "Except I may not have a lot of time left. Will you come visit me anyway?"

Seeing her standing there, looking so frail, I couldn't help but feel sorry for her. It was as if she finally understood that all her family pride and possessions were like gold turning to ash.

"What about Sunday brunch?" I suggested.

"That would be lovely."

She picked up a stack of envelopes from her desk and held them out to me. "Now, head downstairs and meet with the family. You can distribute their checks. It will give them a chance to tell you they're sorry for how they treated you. I'm sure they're eager to apologize."

She looked back at the camera. "Aren't you?" she added in a stony voice.

"Sorry, Grandmother, but I'm going to the hospital. I need to see Riley." I turned and headed for the door.

"Avery!"

"Disinherit me if you want," I called over my shoulder, unable to hold back a light laugh. "But I'm done taking orders."

I heard her let out a tolerant sigh. "All right; go then! If you see Henry, tell him to get in here."

As I left her office and hurried down the hallway, I smiled. Freedom felt great.

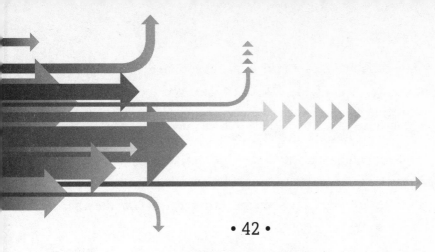

42

MORNING LIGHT

I rushed through the hospital and found the room number Mr. Tate gave me when I called from the estate's car. The door was open; he and my dad stood at the foot of a bed. I knocked on the door frame and they motioned me inside. Riley was propped up with pillows. There was a large piece of gauze taped to his neck and an IV in his arm. His hair was mussed and his face was too pale, but he had a big grin for me.

He held out his hand and I went to him. Riley wrapped his fingers around mine and gave them a squeeze. I squeezed back. "Are you going to be all right?"

"Yes. This is ridiculous. There's nothing wrong with me that a shower and a big breakfast won't fix. I keep trying to tell them that, but they're making me stay here for at least two more hours."

Mr. Tate said, "He lost a little too much blood. The doctors want to keep an eye on him before we go home, that's all."

I studied Riley's face and longed to lean in and kiss him, to tell him how much he meant to me, and how scared I'd felt for him. But having both our fathers standing there was too awkward. He seemed to sense this and gave me a barely perceptible wink.

"So, Avery, how did the last challenge go?" Mr. Tate asked.

Still holding hands with Riley, I turned to him. "I guess you could say I lost the battle but won the war." Then I laughed a little because that sounded like something from one of Grandmother's history lessons.

Riley looked confused. "Does that mean you won the competition?"

I shook my head and told them how Grandmother split the inheritance. "So you see, Uncle Marshall gets the company but I get everything else."

Mr. Tate's smile disappeared. "That's it, then. The first thing Marshall will do is get rid of my firm."

"No he won't. After what she overheard at the family meeting, Grandmother is giving you a permanent seat on the board of directors."

I explained in more detail and watched his disbelief change to delight. Riley looked happy, too. "By the way," I added. "I probably wasn't supposed to say anything. When Grandmother tells you, act surprised."

My father had an amused expression. "How did Marshall take the news of her decision to split the inheritance?"

"Kind of like getting a chicken bone stuck in his throat."

They all laughed, and Dad folded his arms. "I can just imagine."

As he studied me, Riley's face grew concerned. "One problem, though. After everything I've seen, I don't trust your uncles.

And Chase is even more dangerous. I want you to let our law firm set up a restraining order against them."

My father nodded. "I agree."

I thought back to the forest when Chase pointed the paintball gun at my head. "Fine, but let's not talk about them right now, okay?"

Mr. Tate picked up a gray folder with a latched flap. "Then how about this instead? You've done super in all the challenges. I'm very proud of you. And Riley, too. I had this sent up from my office. Here are your mother's letters and the original photographs. I decided that win or lose, you earned them."

"Thanks, Mr. Tate."

"And there's something else. After our phone conversation when you were in Boston, I had the research team look for your mother. Her phone number is in here, too."

He held the folder out to me and I took it, squeezing it between my fingers. "This means a lot," I said in a voice that was too emotional.

Riley studied my face. "We know."

I turned to him, thinking about how upset I'd been at the airport. But then he'd fought to save me from Gavin and none of the rest even mattered now. "You know, without your help I never would have made it."

Though it sounded a little lame, he didn't seem to notice. "Dad and Preston? Can I have a few minutes alone with Avery?"

My father nodded. "Sure." They headed out into the hallway.

Riley patted the side of the bed and I sat down. With our dads out of the room, it felt like a curtain was pulled back. Now I was comfortable and happy just being this close to him. He reached up and ran the backs of his fingers down my jaw, his face so serious.

"When that big creep Gavin tried to kill you, my heart about stopped. It was like time stood still, and in a tiny second I held everything about you inside me. All our experiences together, and all the stuff I knew about you. Which I also saw wasn't enough. I'd barely gotten to know you and was terrified he'd take away your life. And my chance to be with you. In the last couple of years I've done a lot of reacting because I was angry. But last night, all I felt was cold determination. No matter what, I had to stop him."

"Oh, Riley," I whispered, reaching up to barely touch the bandage on his neck. "You risked your life for me."

"It was worth it." His serious tone changed. "Think you can love a guy with a scar?"

I started to nod, then said, "Love?"

He let the joke fade, his beautiful blue eyes deeper than well water. "I think so. It's crazy. We've only known each other a couple of weeks."

"Actually, I've known you a lot longer than that. When I was twelve, you fought for me. Guess I've just been waiting for you to come back into my life."

"I'm happy I did."

I leaned closer until our lips were only a breath apart. "I love you, Riley Tate."

He kissed me, that amazing mouth of his pressing against mine; soft and pleading and affectionate all at the same time. He pulled back just enough to say, "I love you too, Avery."

A few minutes later our fathers came in. They found me

sitting on Riley's bed, our foreheads together and him whispering something that made me giggle.

"Riley!" Mr. Tate sounded flustered.

My dad put a hand on his shoulder. "You know, Jim, your son's a brave young man. He took a bullet for Avery. I don't think there's anything you can do to keep them apart now."

Mr. Tate looked at my dad, who said, "I wish I'd had Riley's courage when I was his age."

A lab technician wheeled a cart into the room, and Riley brushed a strand of hair from my cheek. "Why don't you go home and crash? I'll call you this afternoon."

I gave him another quick kiss and said good-bye. Dad walked me outside, where the estate car waited. We crossed the lawn, and in the distance I saw a faint shimmer of predawn light.

He pointed to the folder. "Can I ask a big favor?"

"You want to read the rest of Marija's letters."

"Yes. Once you're finished with them. Would you mind?"

"Of course not."

"And after you talk to her, when everything is straightened out between you? Maybe she'll let me call her. Can you find out?"

I thought about it. "I don't know, Dad. She's suffered so much. Maybe you think it's like some sort of romantic story, where you come back into her life and everything's forgiven. But I'm just learning about love, and I don't think it works that way."

"How did you get so wise when you're still just a girl?" He gave me a sad smile. "But I need to at least tell her how sorry I am."

"That'd be a good place to start."

Mateo got out of the car to open my door. Dad held out his hand and I gave his fingers a squeeze. We'd never hugged, and I wasn't sure if we would, but that was okay. Knowing he cared about me was what counted. I climbed into the limo and watched him walk away.

Once I got home, and in my own room, I took a quick shower and changed into comfortable clothes. It felt great to be clean, even if my head pounded and my eyes burned. I sat on my bed and opened the file. Picking up the priceless letters from my mother, I began to read them in order, even the ones I'd already seen.

Tears trickled down my face, but I just kept brushing them away, like wiping off sorrow. The words she'd written helped me know her. I was finally catching up on a lifetime of feeling desperate to understand who my mother really was. By the time I reread the very last letter, written just one year ago, I felt emotionally drained but also calm.

Then, at the back of the file, I saw a sheet of paper folded in half. On it were my mother's name and a Croatian phone number. I glanced at the clock on the nightstand. It was eight a.m. in California, so that meant in Zagreb the time was five o'clock in the evening. Pressing the buttons on the house phone, I waited for several long seconds until I made the international connection and it finally began to ring.

A bunch of anxious thoughts went through my mind. Was she home from work yet? Would she answer? Did she live alone?

"*Dobra večer,*" a soft voice said.

It took a couple of breaths for me to get the words out. "Hi. My name is Avery VanDemere. Is this Marija Klanak?"

I heard a slight gasp. "Yes," she said in English.

"Then I think you're my mother. And I've been waiting my whole life to talk to you."

ACKNOWLEDGMENTS

There is a popular quote: *It takes a village to raise a child.* I've recently come to learn that this also applies to a manuscript's process of evolving into a finished novel, and I am extremely fortunate to have my own small but very involved village.

My super-savvy agent, Jessica Regel, met this project with dedication, encouragement, and some excellent ideas for improving the first draft. From the very first reading, my editor Caroline Abbey embraced this story and brought keen insights for ways to strengthen not only the characters but also my writing; plus, her exceptional eye for details has taught me a great deal. Also, my thanks to the enthusiastic and creative Bloomsbury team: Hali Baumstein and Cindy Loh in editorial, Cristina Gilbert and the marketing/publicity team, Melissa Kavonic and Kerry Johnson in managing ed., and Donna Mark and Nicole Gastonguay in design. You truly are the support system that completes this village.

In my personal arena, there are three people who have had a

major impact on this work. Rachel Bruner, my media specialist, webmaster, proofreader, brainstorming partner, and daughter. Rachel, you have continually cleared the path for me to keep writing; more than that, you've understood my dream and offered unending support. Writer and friend Deserét Baker, your initial line editing consistently makes me look more competent than I am. And, of course, to my husband, Kelly, who has always been my *true north star.*

Last of all, thank you to the rest of my terrific family for understanding why—when it comes to the writing process—I am such a hermit. You are my heroes and inspire me every day.